"It's fine, Danny—he didn't touch me."

"I saw him shove you." His grip tightens. "You'd better watch yourself."

His tone grates against my nerves and reminds me why I don't like cops.

"He didn't shove me," Charlotte says.

"Watch myself?" I say to him. "It's my mother's funeral."

He gives a little laugh, and he lets go of my hand, somehow making it feel like a shove. "Yeah, you look really broken up about it, taking the time to rough up a girl."

My hands are in fists again, anger weaving its way through the less aggressive emotions. This narrow stretch of shade has turned too hot, almost stifling. I can smell my own sweat.

I hate this suit.

Danny's watching me, his eyes almost predatory. I've gotten in my share of scrapes, and I can read the signs. Dangerous potential rides the air. He wants to hit me.

My mother's voice is like a whisper in my head. *Behave yourself, Tommy.*

I force my hands to loosen. Danny's right, in a way. I did shove her. I shouldn't have put my hands on her. Someone spends five minutes being kind, and I act like a caged animal.

It takes a lot of effort to back down. "Sorry," I say, turning away from them. "I didn't mean to cause a problem."

"Yeah, well, I don't want to find my sister dead in her bed. Get me?"

Something snaps inside of me. Anger splits into fury. My fist swings.

THICKER THAN WATER

BRIGID KEMMERER

KENSINGTON PUBLISHING CORP.
www.kensingtonbooks.com

KENSINGTON BOOKS are published by

Kensington Publishing Corp.
119 West 40th Street
New York, NY 10018

ISBN-13: 978-0-7582-9441-8
ISBN-10: 0-7582-9441-7

First Kensington trade paperback printing: January 2016

10 9 8 7 6 5 4 3 2 1

Printed in the United States of America

First electronic edition: January 2016

ISBN-13: 978-0-7582-9442-5
ISBN-10: 0-7582-9442-5

For Sarah Fine, the bravest woman I know.
I'm so glad I forced you to be my friend.

THICKER THAN WATER

ACKNOWLEDGMENTS

These are going to be rambling acknowledgments, but I'm better at telling stories than making lists, so here goes.

I started this book while lying in bed. Thomas leapt into my head, fully formed, and I had to start his story immediately. I didn't even waste time grabbing my laptop—I just started writing his book on my e-reader. On a touch-screen keyboard, people. I still remember my husband rolling over and saying, "Who are you writing an email to, this late at night?"

I said, "I'm not writing an email. I'm starting a new book."

And in his usual way, he laughed a little, rolled over, and said, "Okay, honey. I'm going to sleep."

So in *my* usual way, I'm going to say thank you to my amazing husband, Michael Kemmerer, for being my best friend and the man I'm lucky enough to spend my life with. I couldn't do this without him.

As always, love and gratitude to my mother, who is an inspiration to me, and could not be more supportive. As a registered nurse, she's also my quick go-to for medical questions. I just have to be careful to let her know it's for book research. I still remember the night I texted her to ask what would happen when someone got to the ER with a bullet wound. Her response? "WHO GOT SHOT?"

I'm lucky enough to have critique partners who are also my closest friends. Bobbie Goettler, Sarah Fine, and Alison Kemper, you help me more than you'll ever know, and you inspire me as women, mothers, and writers. I couldn't do this without you guys.

My agent, Mandy Hubbard, is beyond compare. I once

wrote an email to Mandy while sobbing so hard I could barely see the screen, and her uplifting response is still one I trot out when I tell aspiring authors, "*This.* This is what you want your agent to do for you."

Alicia Condon and the entire team at Kensington, especially Alex Nicolajsen and Michelle Forde, have been in my corner since day one, and I'm so glad to be working with you all. Thank you so much for allowing me to bring new characters to my readers. I'm so glad you loved Thomas and Charlotte as much as I did.

Jodie Webster and Eva Mills and everyone at Allen & Unwin are delightful people, and I'm so lucky to have gotten the chance to work with you all. Thank you so much for all you've done for the Merrick brothers, and now for Thomas and Charlotte.

Huge, huge, HUGE thanks to Officer James Kalinosky of the Baltimore County Police Department, along with his wife Nicole Kalinosky, for all the advice, insight, and anecdotes about the world of police work and the impact it can have on a family.

Much gratitude to the friends who read some (or all) of my early drafts and offered words of advice to help make the story better: Nicole Mooney, Nicole Choiniere-Kroeker, Tracy Houghton, Brenda Freeman, and Amy Laura Jackson.

(Looks like I can make a list after all.)

Huge thanks to Dr. Darin Kennedy for providing medical knowledge when my mom wasn't around, especially for helping me with some tricky situations. Any errors are mine.

I owe a great deal of thanks to the Kemmerer boys, Jonathan, Nick, Sam, and Baby Zach, for allowing me time to follow my dreams.

Finally, extra special thanks to Jim Hilderbrandt for reading an early draft and telling me where I was going wrong. You saved this book, friend. Your day is coming soon.

CHAPTER ONE

THOMAS

I hate this suit.

Mom bought it two weeks ago, and I hated it then. But she started with the whole *please* and *for me* and *just this once* and I gave in. Because she knows my buttons.

Knew. She *knew* my buttons.

I hate the past tense.

I'm definitely not a suit guy. She *knows* that.

Damn it.

She *knew* that, like she knew how I liked my oatmeal and the reason my hair got too long and how I still don't like to sleep with my door closed even though eighteen is way too old to be afraid of the dark. If she'd walked into a store to buy me clothes on a random day, she'd walk out with the right things: T-shirts and hoodies and jeans and dark socks. She knew the right kind of charcoal pencils and the right brand of sketchpad and the right time to leave me alone.

The last time she bought me a suit was for Homecoming sophomore year. I wasn't a suit guy then either, but I'd worked up the nerve to ask Anne Marie Lassiter and she'd said *yes,* so a suit it was.

I outgrew the girl before I outgrew the suit.

Just this once.

Of all the things Mom said to me, that's the one that keeps echoing. Because it wasn't once.

I'm on my third try with this stupid tie, and I'm getting to the point where I just want to hang myself with it. It's yellow and navy, the colors of the ribbons on her wedding bouquet.

The colors of the bars on Stan's police uniform.

Ironically, they're the colors of the bruises on your neck when you die of strangulation.

Trust me. I got a firsthand view.

Just this once.

My hands are shaking now, and I yank the tie free and fling it on my dresser.

Stan knocks on the door and sticks his head in without waiting.

He does that. I hate that.

I don't hate him, though. Not yet, anyway. I barely know the guy.

Stan probably figured he was hitting the jackpot, marrying a single mom with an eighteen-year-old kid. Get the stepdad brownie points without the work. At first I was worried that he'd be a pain in the ass, being a cop and all. That whole gotta-be-the-bigger-man crap. But I stayed out of his way, he stayed out of mine. He treated her well and made her happy. Good enough for me.

He's still standing there, looking at me in the mirror.

"What?" I say.

"You about ready?"

I think about telling him I can't get the tie knotted, but then he'd offer to help me and this would be all kinds of awkward.

This is already all kinds of awkward.

"Yeah," I say.

He disappears from the doorway.

I ball up the tie and put it in my pocket.

Stan doesn't say anything during the drive to the church. I don't either. When he makes a turn, the click of the signal makes my head pound.

It's weird sitting in the front seat with him. I should be in the back. Mom should be up front, providing a buffer of conversation, asking me about school and graduation while simultaneously asking Stan about cases he's working on.

Stan is a detective.

I wonder if it's a blow to his ego, a cop's wife murdered in his own bed ten days after their wedding. Poor ol' Stan, the subject of police gossip.

God, I'm such a dick sometimes. Maybe I do hate him. Words are trapped in my mouth, and I'm afraid to say any of them, because they'll explode out of me with enough force to wreck the car.

Why haven't you done something?

Why couldn't you protect her?

HOW COULD YOU LET THIS HAPPEN?!

Stan was at work when she died. I was in my own bed.

I don't know which is worse.

I didn't hear anything. I found her when I woke to use the bathroom.

Maybe I hate myself. Maybe I hate everyone.

"You all right?"

I glance at Stan. His eyes are on the road ahead, and his voice is quiet. I don't know why he's even asking. Of course I'm not all right. "Fine," I say.

He doesn't ask anything else.

Mom would pry. She'd dig the secrets out of me with the dexterity of an archaeologist, leaving my feelings intact while letting the truth rise to the surface. Like I said, she knew my buttons.

Then again, Stan is a detective, so he can probably do the same thing. Maybe he doesn't want to pry.

The dead heat of summer gives me a big wet kiss when I climb out of the car, reminding me why I don't wear suits. Reminding me that I probably should have gotten a haircut when she asked me. My neck already feels damp, and I'm glad I didn't mess with the tie.

I've never been to this church, a long, squat brick building with a steeple at one end and an aluminum roof. Stained glass windows glitter with the Stations of the Cross. Nice. Colorful depictions of suffering and torture. Great place.

I don't know why we're having the funeral in a church anyway. Mom dragged me to church all the time when I was a kid, but we haven't gone in years. Maybe she and Stan went. I don't know.

Cops are everywhere. Clustered in groups clinging to the shade along the side of the building, off by the parking lot grabbing a quick smoke, slapping Stan on the shoulder.

They ignore me. Good. Sort of.

The atmosphere is wrong here. There's no sense of loss, no anguish and grief. I feel like I'm trapped in a glass box with my own twisting emotions, watching everyone else at a social event.

It's infuriating.

I don't know anyone except Stan. I'm sure I met a few of these people at the wedding, but it was a small ceremony at the courthouse, and no one stands out. Mom's two friends from back home called to tell me they couldn't get time off again, couldn't make the drive out for the second time in two weeks. I said fine, whatever. The only thing worse than being here alone would be mom's friends treating me like a six-year-old who can't get a straw into a juice box.

Everyone is standing in groups. Only one other guy is across the parking lot, standing under a tree. He's not in uniform, but that doesn't mean he's not a cop. He's built like one. He looks like he's texting. Must really be feeling the loss.

He feels me watching him, because his eyes lift from his phone.

I look away before he can catch my gaze, then pull into the shade myself. It doesn't help. Part of me wants to put a fist through this brick wall. Another part wants to run from here, to pretend none of this is happening.

Suspicious glances keep flicking my way, as if I'm the odd-ball here, instead of all the people who don't even know the woman they're supposed to be mourning.

Maybe it's just me. Cops make me nervous. Always have. Maybe it's a teenager thing, the way they always look at you like you're on the cusp of doing something wrong. Maybe it's the year Mom and I spent avoiding the law because Daddy was a very bad man, and we couldn't risk any kind of trouble.

Maybe it's the interrogation I had to sit through after finding Mom's body.

I don't know what I'm doing here. When we moved in with Stan, I left my friends three hours away. Now we're way on the south side of Salisbury, in the middle of nowhere, at this frigging church with death scenes embedded in the walls and a bazillion cops who are all here for *him*, not her.

I yank at the collar of my shirt and feel someone watching me.

At first I think of the guy with the cell phone, but when I glance across the parking lot, he's gone. It's a girl in a purple dress. She stands with an older woman, and by *older* I mean that there's a chance her wrinkled skin might give up the fight and slide the rest of the way down her body. Ol' Wrinkly is wearing an honest-to-god navy blue hat with a veil. She looks emotional while she talks to Stan, dabbing at her eyes with a tissue.

What a joke. If she knew my mother, she didn't know her well. I've never seen her before.

I've never seen the girl before either, but since she's looking at me, I look back at her. She's got to be about my age. Thick, curly caramel hair, skin too pale for summertime, dark framed glasses, curves in all the right places. She'd be a challenge to sketch, because the tiny waist and the curves would make her look like a superhero comic, especially with that rack.

I jerk my eyes away. I shouldn't be checking out a girl at my mother's *funeral*. Mom would cuff me on the neck and tell me to behave myself.

But the girl peels away from the overwrought woman and heads my way. She's wearing high-heeled sandals, and she stumbles a bit on the crooked pavement. The movement makes her hair sway, and she brushes it out of her eyes.

I'm staring.

Then she's in front of me, holding out a hand. "I don't think we've met."

I shake her hand, and it feels too formal, like I'm meeting a college recruiter. But I can play this game because it's better than thinking about my mother rotting inside a wooden box. "We haven't."

"I'm Charlotte."

"I'm Thomas."

She doesn't let go of my hand. "Tom?"

She could call me Princess Sparklepants if she wants. I couldn't care less about my name at this point. "Whatever."

She finally releases my hand. Her expression says she's picked up on some of my tension. "Thomas, then. How do you know Stan? Is one of your parents on the force?"

Of course she thinks I'm here for him. No one in this place knows Mom.

I have to clear my throat, because my answer will embarrass this girl, but it's not like I can lie about it. "He married my mother."

Her face goes more pale, if that's possible. I don't like that. It reminds me of another pale face, which makes me start thinking about bruised necks again.

"It's fine," I say, even though it's not. I try to keep the anger out of my voice, because she doesn't deserve it. I don't even know what good it's doing me. My voice comes out all gravelly. "I've only lived here a few weeks. I don't know anyone."

"I'm so sorry," she says softly.

What am I supposed to say to that? I don't even know this girl.

I find myself shrugging before realizing that makes me look indifferent. People are watching me again. The attention weighs on my shoulders. Do they know who I am, or are they wondering like Charlotte? Which would be better?

I've been quiet too long. My jaw feels tight. She reaches for my hand again. Her fingers are small and gentle and soft against my palm, such a contrast to the businesslike formality of her handshake. "You don't need to stand here by yourself. Come meet my family—"

"I'm fine." I hold fast, jerking my hand away from her. I can keep it together here, alone, by the wall, but I can't take a dozen strangers talking at me.

"Okay," she says softly.

I take a long breath, then blow it out through my teeth. "Sorry," I grit out.

We stand there in silence for a moment.

"Do you want me to get Stan?" she finally asks quietly. "You don't seem . . ."

Her voice trails off, and I frown. "I don't seem what?"

Again, my tone is rougher than she deserves, and she licks her lips, recalculating. Her spine straightens, but she doesn't move away. "You don't seem like you should be alone right now."

Stan is thirty feet away, talking to two other guys in uniform. They're doing the guy version of sympathy, clapping him on the shoulder.

I knew her longer, I want to shout.

Mom would shush me and tell me to be more respectful.

I don't miss her yet. It doesn't even feel like she's dead. It feels like she's on vacation or something. I keep thinking I need to store all these thoughts and memories for later, when she gets back.

I look back at Charlotte. "No. Leave him."

"Is anyone else here for you?"

I laugh humorlessly. "None of this is for me. I feel like I'm crashing a stranger's funeral." I sound like an angry freak, and I rub my hands down my face. "I don't know anyone."

Now I just sound pathetic.

"Is that your tie?" she says suddenly, and I realize she's looking at my pocket. "Too hot?"

"I couldn't tie it," I admit without thinking, and then I feel like a real moron. What kind of guy can't tie a tie? And then brings it with him, like he's waiting for someone to get around to helping? I glance away, embarrassed. "She bought me the suit. Made a big deal about matching it—"

I have to stop talking. Pathetic has reached a new level. I want the anger back. Anger was better than this tight, choking feeling in my throat.

Charlotte tugs it out of my pocket and threads it between her fingers. "May I?"

It takes me a moment to figure out what she's talking about. She's too short to get the tie around my neck without my cooperation. I could refuse. I could grab the tie and shove it back in my pocket and send her scurrying back to her people.

But it's a needed distraction, and I find myself ducking down, letting her loop it over my head, enjoying the soft feel of her fingers as she tucks it below the collar of my shirt. She's close, and I catch her scent, something clean and citrusy.

"People are staring," I murmur.

"Let them stare."

"Is this a service you provide?" I say, intending to tease, but my voice is too broken for that.

But she's kind, so she takes the bait and runs with it. Her eyes are on the knot as she threads the fabric. "Absolutely. Tying ties, buttoning jackets . . . you should see me pin on a flower."

I almost smile, but then her hands make the final loop. Satin slides against cotton, and then the knot hits my neck. Quick and sudden and tight. I can't breathe.

I jerk the fabric out of her hand without thinking.

My movement is too sudden. She stumbles back, catching herself against the wall.

I gasp, pulling at the knot of fabric. It's barely tight, but I can't stop myself.

"I'm sorry," she whispers. "I'm sorry."

"No, it's fine," I choke out. This is insane. I need to get it together. The knot finally gives an inch. Air can't seem to make it into my lungs. "It's not even tight."

I suck in a breath and sound like an asthmatic. I run a hand down my face. This is not getting it together.

"You all right, Char?"

It's another cop in dress uniform, talking to Charlotte but looking at me like I'm a purse snatcher or something.

No, looking at me like I'm a murderer.

This guy's young, not much older than I am. His hair is military short, almost blond, and his eyes are just looking for trouble. I swear to god he's holding his hand near his gun, and I'm tempted to fake him out, just to see if he'd pull it.

Knowing my luck, he'd shoot me.

Right this instant, I'd welcome it.

"I'm fine, Danny," Charlotte says. "This is Thomas. Stan's new—"

"I know who he is." Of course he does. Everyone in uniform probably does. I'm sure some of them still think I did it. But Danny takes the edge off by putting a hand out. "I'm sorry about your mother."

I shake his hand. "Thanks."

His grip is solid, almost too tight. He doesn't let go, and I can tell he'd hold fast if I tried to pull free. "You want to tell me why you put your hands on my little sister?"

Oh. Now I get it.

Charlotte is looking worriedly between the two of us. "It's fine, Danny—he didn't touch me."

"I saw him shove you." His grip tightens. "You'd better watch yourself."

His tone grates against my nerves and reminds me why I don't like cops.

"He didn't shove me," Charlotte says.

"Watch myself?" I say to him. "It's my mother's funeral."

He gives a little laugh, and he lets go of my hand, somehow making it feel like a shove. "Yeah, you look really broken up about it, taking the time to rough up a girl."

My hands are in fists again, anger weaving its way through the less aggressive emotions. This narrow stretch of shade has turned too hot, almost stifling. I can smell my own sweat.

I hate this suit.

Danny's watching me, his eyes almost predatory. I've gotten in my share of scrapes, and I can read the signs. Dangerous potential rides the air. He wants to hit me.

My mother's voice is like a whisper in my head. *Behave yourself, Tommy.*

I force my hands to loosen. Danny's right, in a way. I did shove her. I shouldn't have put my hands on her. Someone spends five minutes being kind, and I act like a caged animal.

It takes a lot of effort to back down. "Sorry," I say, turning away from them. "I didn't mean to cause a problem."

"Yeah, well, I don't want to find my sister dead in her bed. Get me?"

Something snaps inside of me. Anger splits into fury. My fist swings.

I'm strong, and years of being the new kid taught me how to throw a punch. It's stupid, and reckless, and my mother's voice is screaming in the back of my skull.

Tommy! He is a police officer!

It sucks that he's a cop, too, because he knows how to deflect a punch. He catches my arm and slams me into the wall of the church. My hand is pinned behind my back and I inhale brick dust. The tie drags on the bricks, too, pulling tight against my neck.

I am such an idiot.

He's enjoying this. We're the center of attention now. He's

probably hoping I'll fight him so he can continue playing the badass.

I don't want to fight him. This is her funeral. Her *funeral*. My throat is tight and my eyes are hot. Reason catches up with action and I'm swimming in a special blend of humiliation and shame.

I will not start crying right now. I *will not*.

Charlotte is smacking her brother, it sounds like. "Danny! Danny, stop it! What is *wrong* with you?"

Hot breath finds my neck, followed by a little shove. The bricks scrape at my skin. I expect him to hold me here, to suffer the judgmental stares of the crowd that I can hear gathering. Or maybe he'll tell Stan to keep me in line, or something equally demeaning.

Instead, he speaks low, just to me. "Did you get off on it? Think about it in the shower this morning? All hot and bothered for killing your mother?"

Rage flares, hot and painful, blinding me with fury. I jerk back, trying to break his hold, knowing it's futile.

But suddenly I'm free. My head is buzzing, and he's on the ground, yelling. Clutching his head. Charlotte is standing back, glancing between me and him, her breath quick.

Did I hit him? What just happened?

Before I can get it together, a hand falls on my shoulder, pushing me back against the wall. I feel metal against my wrist.

I freeze. Another one of these jerkoffs is cuffing me and talking about assault on a police officer.

Now Danny's on his feet, talking about resisting arrest. He grabs my arm and drags me away from the wall. The crowd grows.

We're heading for a police car.

I'm going to miss the funeral.

CHAPTER TWO

CHARLOTTE

I still can't believe Danny arrested him.

It's his mother's *funeral*.

Ben leans down and whispers. "Easy, Char. You're going to break a nail if you keep clutching the pew like that."

"I want to break Danny's neck."

"He's just looking out for you."

Ben is my favorite brother, and his tone is sincere, so I don't glare at him. "He doesn't need to look out for me. Thomas wasn't doing anything wrong. He just lost his mother, and instead of standing here grieving, he's getting fingerprinted at central booking."

"Shh!" Grandma leans around my mother to give me the evil eye. "Charlotte, have some respect."

She doesn't glance at Ben, despite the fact that he started the conversation. Shocker.

It's not like our discussion matters anyway. The most depressing thing about this funeral is that there's not much mourning going on. No one knew Marie well enough, and Stan is at the front, away from the crowd. It's like we're all going through the motions.

Ben shifts closer and drops his voice. "He started the fight, Char."

"No, Danny started the fight."

Ben sighs, but I can tell he agrees with me. "The kid made it physical. First with you, then with Danny."

The kid. Ben is five years older than I am, but you'd think he was sixty-three instead of twenty-three. He never would have arrested Thomas. He never would have let it get to that point. He would have shaken the guy's hand and offered him a kind word. He probably would have invited him to stand with our family. Ben is the kind of cop who carries pepper-mints in his pockets for scared kids and remembers the name of everyone he meets. He's the brother I run to when I need a shoulder to cry on.

Danny is the brother I avoid, and he's the last person I would have wanted witnessing that moment beside the church. He takes everything a little too personally. He just graduated from the police academy. Ben says he'll calm down once he realizes that the Eastern Shore of the Chesapeake Bay isn't exactly a hotbed of police activity. More than once, Ben has defused a situation after Danny lit the spark.

"Danny provoked him," I say.

"How?"

"I don't know. I couldn't hear what he said." I can imag-ine it was horrible. Almost everything that comes out of Danny's mouth *is*. "But I know he provoked him."

Ben shakes his head. "I don't care what he said. It's not an excuse to hit someone."

"I didn't see Thomas hit him." I've run it through my head a dozen times in the last hour. Danny shoved Thomas into the wall, leaned in to speak, and then he was suddenly on the ground. Thomas didn't throw a punch—unless he's the Flash or something. I didn't see a hand swing.

Maybe he threw his head back? Cracked Danny in the forehead? Would that be enough to throw someone to the ground?

"Why were you talking to him, anyway?" says Ben.

It's a good question, and I don't have a ready answer. I keep my eyes forward. The priest is giving a blessing and the scent of incense is thick in the air.

I think of Thomas standing outside the church. He was

unfamiliar, with thick, dark hair that fell somewhere between edgy and hipster. When I got close, I noticed the high cheekbones. The strong jaw. The lean frame.

The eyes clouded by distress.

If I say any of that, Ben will accuse me of being a romantic. "I was being polite. I didn't know who he was."

"You should stay away from him until this is all sorted out."

"He didn't look guilty, Ben. He looked like he wanted to punch the wall to keep himself from crying."

"I'm not kidding, Char. Don't let your hormones cloud your judgment."

Now I do glare at him. I might actually be gaping. I fight to keep my voice at a whisper. "Did you seriously just mention my *hormones*?"

"Save the attitude." Ben's face is stone serious. "I'm looking out for you, too."

It's not like Ben to play the heavy. I frown and try to reevaluate the interaction with Thomas. No matter how I replay it, Danny comes off as a real prick.

Ben leans closer, until I catch a hint of his aftershave. "I know that breaking into a detective's house when he's working the night shift, killing his wife, and then leaving without taking anything, all while her son sleeps down the hall, sounds pretty unlikely."

His tone catches me by surprise. "You think he did it?"

"A *lot* of people think he did it, Char."

When I pulled the tie tight, Thomas reacted like I'd tried to strangle him. Grief? Or guilt?

Grief. Had to be. "You all think he killed his own mother?"

"It wouldn't be the first time someone did something horrible." Ben shrugs a little. "Besides, would you rather think there's a murderer sneaking in bedrooms and strangling people?"

"It wouldn't be the first time for that either."

He doesn't say anything, but his lips flatten into a line, and I wish I could take the words back. He's remembering Lilly Mauta.

Well, he's remembering her murder. He never laid eyes on Lilly until her mother called nine-one-one three years ago. It was Ben's first call as a police officer. His first dead body. He didn't sleep for days. It takes a lot to rattle him—but that did it.

I had laid eyes on Lilly lots of times. She lived half an hour north of here, but her parents drove her down for ballet lessons. We weren't friends, but we were ballet classmates.

Her murder is still unsolved.

I already know from my brothers that the murders were dissimilar. We don't get a lot of violent crime around here, so the two cases drew a comparison immediately. Two killers, no question. Lilly's death was slow and sloppy. A night of teen passion gone too far was the leading theory.

This one was clean and precise and deliberate.

Well. From what I've heard. No one is discussing the details of the case with *me*.

"I don't think he did it," I say to Ben.

His eyes flick skyward. "That clears him, then. I'll get the Sergeant on the radio right now."

"Hey. What are you two whispering about?" Matthew leans between us.

At twenty-eight, he's my oldest brother. He's sitting in the row behind us because his kids tend to sprawl. Jenna and Lexi are eating goldfish crackers and scribbling in Disney Princess coloring books while Matt's wife tries to keep them quiet. The youngest, Madalyn, is nine months old and heavy-lidded, her head crashed on Matt's shoulder. Her chubby fingers are fiddling with the bars on his uniform.

He's a cop, too. He doesn't work with Ben and Danny on the county force—Matt is a state trooper. Mom says it was his way of rebelling against Dad, who pushed so hard for him to follow in his footsteps and join the local precinct. If so, it's a stupid rebellion. Becoming a state trooper is about sixteen times more difficult than joining the local force. Besides, he's still a cop, even if his uniform is tan instead of blue.

Then again, that's very Matthew. He'll do what he's told, but he'll do it his way.

"How I can't wait to smack Danny," I whisper back.

The baby starts to fuss, and he bounces her a little, shifting her to his other shoulder. "He's just looking out for you."

My mouth forms a line. They must have a big brother script.

My father is on duty this afternoon, or I'd be getting it from him too.

The baby fusses again, and Alison, Matt's wife, starts moving coloring books off her lap.

I reach out, hoping to save her the trouble. "I'll hold her. I need some baby snuggles."

Madalyn protests when Matt hands her over, but I've been babysitting these girls since they were born, and I can usually get her settled better than my brother can. She's quiet and warm against my shoulder in a heartbeat. Her fingers tangle in my hair, and her pacifier makes a *suck-suck-suck* sound near my neck.

"You're so lucky you don't have brothers," I whisper to her.

"What was that?" says Ben. He bumps me with his hip, so I know he heard me.

I ignore him.

The service is shorter than I expect. Stan is the only person to get up and say something about his dead wife. That makes sense, I guess—she and Thomas only just moved here. Still, it seems like *someone* else should make a speech. Didn't she have any friends who would come to town for the funeral? Is everyone here for Stan?

It seems like it. The church is full of uniforms, and I know almost everyone. Stan is well-liked and well-known. He and my father play poker once a month at the VFW hall. We're a close-knit community, and we band together in times of suffering. The turnout here isn't surprising.

I wonder if Thomas had planned to say something. Now he won't get a chance.

My grandmother pinches my arm. "Charlotte!" she hisses. "For heaven's sake, girl, stop looking so pained."

Grandma thinks girls should wear dresses and smile sweetly and take care of the menfolk. If you ask her age, she'll tell you she's on the bad side of eighty, but she acts like she was born in the eighteen hundreds. My grandfather, her husband, was a police officer, too. With that kind of legacy, you'd think they'd be encouraging me to join the force after graduation. No way. Not in my family. According to my grandmother, *feminist* is a dirty word invented to placate women who aren't pretty enough to find a husband. She used to be tolerable when she lived in the independent living facility on the other side of the county, but she moved in with us last year. I thought she was going to write Ben out of the will when she found out he was taking me to the shooting range once a month.

I keep the targets—full of bull's-eyes—on my wall just to mock her.

I can rebel in my own way, too.

After the burial, there's a reception in the church hall. My mother made four of the casseroles, and I know she expects me to help serve, so I take my place behind the table beside her. People haven't lined up yet, but she's setting out serving spoons and napkins.

"Have you eaten anything yet?" she says.

I roll my eyes. This is part B of the overprotectiveness of my family: my diabetes. I've been monitoring my own blood sugar for years, but to hear my mother tell it, she should still be feeding me spoonfuls of pureed meats. "I'm fine."

"Have you?" she presses.

"Maybe you didn't notice that we were at a funeral, and you're literally unpacking the food while we speak."

"I want to see you eat something."

I'm not even hungry, but I pick up a roll and tear off a hunk with my teeth, just to shut her up.

"That was nice of you to help with little Madalyn," she says.

"I have to be on my toes or I'll lose my 'favorite aunt' status."

She smiles at me. I'm their only aunt.

"Set out those tongs for the vegetables," she says.

While I do, she adds, "I saw what happened with Stan's new stepson. Daniel shouldn't have started something."

Finally! Someone on my side!

"Right?" I exclaim. "I can't believe Danny had to be such a jerk!"

"Don't misunderstand me." My mother levels me with a sharp look in her eye and a jab with a salad spoon. "I don't want you speaking to him again until this crime is solved."

It didn't hurt, but I rub my arm anyway. "Over thirty cops showed up for the funeral. I felt pretty safe."

"I don't care if a hundred cops showed up for the funeral. There is something unusual about that boy."

I scowl and start slicing into the chicken noodle bake. I made the crust on top, and it's perfect, slightly brown and crispy. "All of you are treating me like I'm four years old. He wasn't trying to lure me into the woods with a lollipop. I was being *polite*."

"Polite girls don't offer to tie a stranger's tie."

Now my cheeks flare with heat. It's no secret that my grandmother passed on her views on how young ladies should be raised. It doesn't help that Mom says it like I was helping Thomas adjust his boxer shorts. "It wasn't like that."

"I was young once. I know what it's like to see a strange boy, full of drama and mystery."

"Mom!" I have to restrain myself from stomping a foot. "This is not a romance novel. I was being polite. That's all. I know what he's been accused of."

"Do you?"

"I'm sorry, are we executing people immediately after the crime now? Maybe Danny should have just shot him. Would that make you happy?"

"Charlotte." She gives me a dangerous look.

People are beginning to file into the church hall, milling around and talking in hushed voices. I know a lot of people here, but not everyone. The younger officers rotate through weekend flings like they have a police version of OKCupid, and I can never keep the girlfriends and boyfriends straight. There's a man standing alone near the corner, but he looks as though he's waiting for someone—he keeps glancing at the doorway. He's young, very clean cut. No wedding ring. He looks like a cop, the way he's surveying the premises.

No one has approached the line of food yet, but that's because no one wants to seem insensitive—like they're only here for cornbread and sweet potato pie and not because a woman died. I don't see Stan anywhere, which makes it more awkward.

Then again, maybe his absence will make it *less* awkward. It will definitely make it less like a funeral. That's a little sad.

"Stan's not here," I whisper to my mother.

"I know," she says, her voice equally low. She tears open a bag of cutlery. "He left to go down to the station."

"No one could bring Thomas back up here?"

"He's being held. I called your father to tell him what was going on. He said Danny was insisting on pressing charges."

My head almost explodes. "Are you *kidding* me?"

"Calm down, Charlotte. You're causing a scene."

A scene. Maybe four people are looking at me.

Mom gives them a kind smile.

My grandmother makes her way over to the table. I can't take another lecture about how I'm not smiling widely enough or how nice young ladies never raise their voice above a whisper. I say I need to make a visit to the ladies' room and I bolt.

"Walk, dear!" my grandmother calls behind me.

"You'd better come back and get some food!" my mom calls.

Honestly.

The late summer air is heavier than it was before the funeral. Clouds are thickening south of here, and the slightest breeze lifts my curls. A storm is coming.

Matthew's voice catches me before I get far. "Hiding from Grandma?"

He's standing by the church wall. Jenna is leaning against the bricks, doing something with his phone. He downloads any games they ask for, but they usually watch My Little Pony videos on YouTube.

"You don't know me," I say.

He snorts. He and I aren't as close as Ben and I are, but there's not much that escapes Matt's attention. He's a good cop. Of my brothers, he's probably the best.

"What's she after today? Your bare legs or the fact that you're not wearing lipstick?"

I blink. "I don't know if I should be impressed or creeped out that you noticed either of those things."

"It's my job to notice things." He hesitates. "You doing okay, Char?"

"Sure. Just pissed at Danny."

"Hmm."

I frown. "*Hmm* what?"

Jenna leans back against his leg, and he teasingly shakes her by the shoulders until she giggles and squeals, "Daddy!"

He hasn't answered my question, and now he's not looking at me. "*Hmm* what?" I ask again. "Why are you all treating me like I sat down to dinner with a serial killer?"

His eyes flash up. "Because you're not too far off the mark."

"What's a cereal killer?" says Jenna. "Why would someone kill cereal?"

Her voice is so earnest it makes me laugh, but Matt is still stony faced. "I saw the pictures, Charlotte. Someone who could do that—I don't want you near him."

"If you all think he did it, why isn't he locked up?"

He doesn't say anything.

"What?"

He fidgets.

"You don't have enough," I say. "Do you? You don't have enough to hold him?"

"It's not my case," he says. "Local police are handling it."

"But I'm right, aren't I?" Another thought occurs to me. "Did Danny pick a fight on purpose?"

"I didn't see Danny pick a fight."

But now I can put the puzzle together. The cops might not have enough to hold Thomas for murder, but hitting a cop, in full view of a bunch of other police officers—that would stick.

I storm away. "You guys are ridiculous. He's a teenager. He just lost his mother."

"He's eighteen years old," Matt calls after me. "And you're the one acting like a teenager."

I want to give him the finger, but Jenna is still standing there, and I would *definitely* lose the favorite aunt status if I taught her how to flip someone off.

I head across the field, into the cemetery. There's no one there. Stan is at the police station, and everyone else is in the church hall, at the reception. The new graves are in the back corner, and there are a few trees for shade.

No one is paying respects, and my brothers are responsible for her son's absence. I think of my closeness with my mother, and something about that tugs at me.

I stride across the field, looking for the mound of fresh turned earth.

CHAPTER THREE

THOMAS

This is my first time in a jail cell.

It sucks.

I don't have many memories of my father, but one of the few clear ones involves a policeman. I was sitting in a car, an old sedan, staring at my father's back while he talked to someone in the alley between two brownstones. Sunlight beamed down, turning the car too hot in about fifteen seconds. I wanted to get out, but he'd told me to stay put and we'd get ice cream.

I don't remember the ice cream. I don't even remember his face.

But I remember a police officer coming to the car, grabbing my arm, and trying to drag me out.

And then I remember the cop collapsed on the pavement.

I had to have been about five. I always used to think I was remembering it wrong, that maybe my father had hit him, or maybe someone had shot him. There was a lot of yelling.

And then there was my father, his hand on the back of my neck, his voice low. "Don't tell your mother."

I can't remember if I ever did or not. I was five years old—I must have, right? It's not something we ever discussed later. We ran out on him after that. Mom never kept any pictures, so while I remember the rasp of his voice, I can't put together the image of his face. I've tried to sketch the memory, but it never comes together on paper. I'll end up with half-drawn images: the door of a car, the bricks of a wall, the shadow of strange men standing at a distance. All penciled shadows and half-profiles. Sometimes a stray reminder will thread its way through my thoughts, but it's never anything solid enough to catch or identify. Dark hair like mine, maybe. The smell of some spicy cologne.

I don't remember being afraid of him. Mom was, though, especially after we left. She home schooled me for years, the kind of helicopter parent who'd have a Band-Aid out before she saw blood. Other moms would be buried in a book at the playground while their kids fell off the slide or busted their noses, but my mother would be standing there, always within arm's reach.

She made me crazy.

She knew it, too. I made sure she knew it. You know how with a cat, if you squeeze it too tight, it'll claw the hell out of you? Imagine being ten, wanting to play a pickup game of basketball, and your mommy's standing right there, looking at the other kids like they're potential felons.

I ran away. Twice.

The first time, it took her forty-five minutes to find me. I know it was exactly that long because she kept screaming it at me.

"Forty-five minutes, Tommy! Forty-five minutes! How could you *do* that to me?"

She smacked me good, too. She might have been crying, but I was too pissed to care. Told me that she couldn't lose me, that she'd already given up everything *for* me, and how could I do that to her?

Like I was supposed to care. I didn't *have* anything to lose.

The second time, I made damn good and sure it was longer than forty-five minutes.

Eleven years old, forty stolen dollars in my pocket, and I ran like hell. Spent half my money on a cab into the city.

Spent the other half on two pizzas and a bottle of soda. I slept curled into a doorway. Some cops picked me up around four in the morning.

I gave them my phone number, and they asked my mom why she hadn't reported me missing.

I don't remember her answer. I just remember her kneeling in front of me in that gritty city police station, holding my hands with her shaking fingers, asking me if they'd taken my picture.

They hadn't.

She took me home, and I thought she'd beat the hell out of me. She didn't.

"What do I have to do?" she asked. "We can't keep doing this, Tommy. What do I have to do? What do you want?"

"I don't want *you!*"

I screamed it at her. I might have thrown something. God, I was such a shitty kid.

But she was a good mom. She saw through the rage. She gripped my arms and forced me still. "No. I mean it. Tell me what you want. Tell me."

I was crying, then. "I want to go to school. I want friends. I don't want to be alone."

She nodded. "Okay."

Two days later we moved. I got what I wanted: a new town, a new life, a new start.

I have no idea what she wanted. I have no idea if she got it.

And now it's too late to ask her.

After I found Mom's body, after my hysterical nine-one-one call, they put me in a police car and drove me to the station to ask me some questions. They could have taken me to the middle of the desert and put a gun to my head and I wouldn't have known the difference. That night, when I was sitting in front of a little steel table with a cup of cooling coffee sitting in front of me, my brain was locked on repeat, playing the same twenty seconds over and over again.

Me sitting up in bed. Checking the time. Two eighteen a.m.

Walking down the hall to use the bathroom.

Seeing her door open. She never slept with her door open.

Calling her name.

Hitting the light switch.

The bruises. The bulging eyes. The scent of urine.

Tripping over my feet to get to her side. Fumbling the phone until I could get my fingers to dial.

They made me repeat the chain of events, asking questions for an hour before I realized I was sitting in an interrogation room, that I was a *suspect*.

Until this afternoon, when Officer Danny threw me up against the wall of the church, I hadn't realized I still *was*.

I keep replaying the way he fell. Like when I was a child, I'm missing a moment of time.

My hand doesn't hurt. Maybe I didn't hit him hard.

I definitely didn't hit him hard *enough*.

I've got some rage saved for Stan, too. He stood there and watched that prick shove me into the backseat of a cop car.

At least I'm the only one here. Not a lot of crime in this craphole town. They took my belt and my tie, like I'm a threat to myself. I think about counting the bricks, but that sounds like such a cliché. Before you know it, I'll be singing "Nobody Knows the Troubles I've Seen." Instead, I lie on the little cot and inhale bleach and disinfectant and whatever else goes into cleaning this place.

After an hour or so, I wonder if Stan is going to bother coming to get me.

I wonder if I want him to. There's a part of me that would rather sleep here than down the hall from the room where Mom—where she—

Suddenly my throat closes up, and I make the most embarrassing sounds. There's a guy at a desk down at the end of this hallway, and I don't think he can hear me, but maybe he can.

I press my fingers into my eyes, and they're wet. I can't believe I missed her funeral.

This is terrible. I'm a terrible son.

I'm shaking. I can't stop crying. I scrape at my eyes and suck in air.

During the interrogation they kept asking if I knew anyone who held a grudge against her. Like I'd have a clue. We just moved here, and Mom and I aren't exactly Bunco Buddies. We haven't heard from Dad in years, and once we got away from him, Mom never seemed to worry about him coming after her—not like this. I don't know anyone, much less someone who'd break in and press a cord to her neck until her eyeballs almost fell out of their sockets and she pissed the bed.

I have a thousand memories of her face. Every expression you can imagine.

The one memory, the worst one, is the one that keeps coming to the forefront.

She'd never let me get away with sitting in this jail cell while her funeral was going on.

The irony strikes me, and I almost laugh. But it's not enough to chase away the tears.

I swipe at my eyes again. I need to think of something else.

Voices echo down the hallway. Someone is talking to that desk clerk. They talk for a while, until I grow bored with trying to piece together the words. My tears dry up. I've got it together now.

Counting the bricks is looking better every minute.

Shoes march down the linoleum and come to a stop in front of my cell.

I glance over, then sit up. I'm glad I had time to get myself together. "Hi, Stan."

I can't read his expression, but he doesn't look happy.

Then again, he just buried his wife. It's not like I expected him to skip down the hall, whistling.

"Tom." His hands are in his pockets, and he just stands there looking at me.

It's been days since it happened, and this is the first time I consider whether Stan thinks I did it, too. We stare at each other.

Mom used to tell me he was a good detective. I have no idea whether that's true. He hasn't solved her murder, but when I asked him about it, he said he wasn't allowed to be on the case.

And that was the end of that conversation.

I'm probably not revealing state secrets by saying Stan and I don't talk much.

He clears his throat. "You know it's a felony to strike a police officer?"

"Too bad it's not a felony to be an asshole at someone's funeral."

Mom's chiding voice bounces around the inside of my head. *Thomas! Language.*

Now I can swear all I want. I don't want to.

Stan is still staring at me. The weight of it presses down on me, until I start to sweat under my collar again. That idiot didn't have to mess with me at the church, but I didn't have to provoke him. Guilt won't let me meet Stan's eyes.

Even without looking at him, I can almost hear him thinking.

I'm eighteen. He's not my father. He owes me nothing. He could wash his hands of me right this second and there is absolutely nothing I could do about it.

He jingles keys in his pocket. "I talked to Danny Rooker. He isn't going to press charges."

He says it like I should be throwing confetti. "Does that mean I can leave?"

"It means you can leave." He hesitates. "Are you coming home with me?"

He knows I don't have anywhere else to go. Now I have to clear my throat. I pass a hand through the damp hair on my neck and look at the walls. "You tell me."

His voice turns a little rough, a little surprised. "I'm not going to turn you out on the street, kid. You're Marie's—" His voice breaks and he takes a second to get himself together. "You're her son."

If he loses it, I'm going to lose it, too.

I haven't thought about Stan hurting. Maybe that's selfish of me, but he didn't have the history with her that I did, like my time with her bought me more of a right to this kind of grief. But I've been reading his silent pain as a kind of judgmental distance. Maybe Stan is hurting as much as I am.

I used to have this friend back home, Brendan Pembleton. He caught his girlfriend cheating on him the same day his dad got laid off and told them the bank was probably going to foreclose on their house. I knew what it felt like when life grabbed the ground right out from under you, so I paid this guy I knew to get us a case of beer, and Brendan and I stayed out all night getting shitfaced in the woods.

I don't think Stan would be up for that.

But maybe some of this awkwardness is my fault.

"Thanks," I say. My voice sounds thick, too.

He pulls the ring of keys from his pocket and unlocks the door. As I'm stepping past him, he puts a hand on my shoulder, and I freeze. Stan has never touched me beyond a handshake, and that was the first time we met. His touch feels foreign, and I realize *no one* has touched me with any sort of kindness since she died.

Except that pretty girl from the church. Charlotte. I remember her gentle fingers sliding the tie against my neck. I like the memory, but it's wrapped up in guilt, as if I shouldn't like anything ever again.

My head is a mess.

Stan clears his throat. "I shouldn't have let Danny take you away from the funeral. I'm sorry."

He should be, but I don't say that. "I shouldn't have let him get to me."

"I was pretty angry at you, causing a scene . . ."

I turn and shrug his hand off. I try to keep the heat from my voice. There's no way I'll repeat what Danny whispered into my ear, but the rage is still fresh. "I didn't cause a scene. He did."

"I know." Stan pauses. "That's why I'm sorry."

I don't say anything. I don't know what to say. This is such a backward apology, and I don't know if I deserve it. I don't even know if Stan is on my side.

He runs a hand through his hair. His dress uniform is pressed to the nines, but somehow he still looks rumpled. "I'll take you out to the gravesite, if you want to pay your respects."

He's not looking at me, but I can tell he expects me to refuse.

That fills me with that same mix of shame and anger, again, and I want to push past him and storm out of here.

But I don't. I don't want to admit it, but I need Stan.

I swallow my emotion. "Thanks," I say, my voice rough. "I'd like that."

CHAPTER FOUR

CHARLOTTE

I thought for sure my mother would send one of my brothers to come fetch me. Casseroles to serve and cookies to arrange and paper plates to clean up. I know my duties. There's no reason for me to be sitting at the edge of the cemetery, drowning in the late summer heat, waiting for a storm to arrive.

I didn't know Marie Bellweather. Visiting her grave should be awkward.

It's not. I've been out here for an hour, and there's a nice oak tree just beyond her gravesite, so I can sit in the shade. The air here is peaceful. Quiet and heavy, promising rain, but not quite yet. My grandmother would have a hissy fit about grass stains and unladylike behavior, but I'm alone, and I really don't care what she'd think. My earbuds are plugged into my phone, music pouring into my skull. I inhale, and my brain is overtaken by honeysuckle, cut grass, and fresh-turned earth.

I'm hungry, but I ignore it. If I go running back to the church for food now, Mom will scowl and watch me even more closely. I should still have plenty of time, anyway. Besides, there's a tube of frosting in my purse for sugar emergencies. *Suck it, Mom.*

Almost immediately, my phone chimes with a text.

Mom: Lunch?

I ignore her. Honestly. I'm almost eighteen years old.
A hand brushes my shoulder. "Hey."

I jump and scramble and scrape my knees. The earbuds pull free and my phone goes skittering across the grass.

Thomas is standing there, his hands up. He looks as startled as I feel, but in a defeated way, like his body just can't generate any more emotion. "I didn't mean to scare you," he says, his eyes dark and troubled. "I didn't know you had headphones in."

"Hey. Hi." My heartbeat chokes me. I'm wavering a little, and I don't know if it's the heels, the heat, or the lack of food, but it takes me a second to steady myself.

Thomas's tie is gone, but he's still wearing the suit he had on earlier. It's rumpled, like the rest of him. His hair is a little mussed, and his eyes shine dark and heavy. His shoulders slump like he's gone a few rounds with life, and now he's down for the count.

My head spins with my brothers' warnings versus the obviously broken boy in front of me. "I thought—I thought they were keeping you."

He shrugs and looks out across the graveyard. His eyes go everywhere except the mound of dirt directly in front of us. "They let me out on good behavior."

Is that a joke? I don't know what to say to that. I feel like I should apologize to him, but I think of how Danny hit the ground. I'm not sure what to offer. *I'm sorry you got arrested.*

Not quite appropriate.

His eyes return to mine. "I missed the whole thing, huh?"

I can't exactly say that there wasn't much of a *thing* to miss. I nod and tuck a piece of hair behind the arm of my glasses. "The reception is still going on. If you're hungry."

"Yeah." He gives a bitter laugh. "I heard there's a party."

His tone makes me flinch, and I remember my brothers' warnings.

But then he winces. "I'm sorry. That was a shitty thing to say." He doesn't sound like he fully means it. Thomas glances in the direction of the church, still avoiding the square of ground in front of us. "Stan went in. He tried to get me to join him, but I don't want to go in there."

I want to tell him that no one would bother him, but that's probably not true, even if he went with Stan. Not after the little show with Danny. If he walked into the church hall right now, half the cops would put a hand on their sidearm.

"I'm sorry," I say softly.

"You don't have to be sorry for anything."

His voice is sharp, and the words sound more like an accusation than a reprieve. Part of me feels like I deserve it. Another part wants to remind him that *I* didn't try to punch Danny, and maybe he can accept some of the blame.

The smartest part of me remembers that this guy could be a murderer. I clamp my mouth shut, since nothing right has come out of it.

Thunder rolls in the distance, but Thomas doesn't move. He squints at me a little. "I don't want to be insensitive, but . . . what are you doing here?"

"You and Stan weren't here." I frown at him. "I thought someone should be." My voice is carrying a shred of accusation. I didn't mean for it to, but it's hot and I'm tired, and the emotions of the day keep ricocheting around, never settling where I expect.

Thomas is on edge, so I am, too.

He takes a long breath and stares out across the graveyard again. His face twists and his breath shakes for a second, but he holds himself together.

God, I am *such a bitch*.

For an instant, he looks like such a little boy, trying not to cry. I want to take his hand. Hug him. Something.

"I'm sorry," I say quickly. "I didn't mean it like that."

"You did."

"No. I didn't. You should have been here. Danny shouldn't have—"

"Shouldn't have what? Shouldn't have dragged someone

away from a funeral?" His anger pushes any sorrow off his face. He points at the gravesite. "My mom just died. Your brother is an *asshole*."

Thunder booms, accenting his words. I jump and take a step back. The sky is dark in the south, but no drops have fallen yet. The humidity is so stifling that I feel a bit woozy.

"God." He runs his hands down his face. He's shaking. "This is so fucked up."

I'm so used to knowing what to say and how to act during times of stress—thanks, Mom and Grandma—but he's all over the map. I'm not sure if anything I say now will come across as sincere. "Do you want me to leave you alone?"

"No."

His voice is so frank, but he doesn't sound needy. I hesitate. "Okay."

He glances at me. "That's not what I mean. I don't want to be *here*. I don't want *her* to be here." He has to clear his throat, and thunder rolls in the sky. Light flashes behind the gathering clouds.

A storm is coming, but still we stand here.

"I saw her," he says. His voice is hollow. "That night. I saw what happened to her."

"I know," I whisper.

He looks at me. "Yeah. I guess you would."

I don't know what to say to that.

He looks up at the sky, and I wonder if the sheer force of his fury and sorrow are holding off the rain. His intensity is a force to be reckoned with. Just standing beside him, I feel cold and hot all at once, and I'm beginning to feel like we've stepped out of reality.

"I'm such a coward," he says.

"Why?"

He winces, keeping his eyes on the sky. "I don't want to remember her that way. I don't want to remember her *this* way. I didn't . . . I didn't want to see the box. I couldn't sleep all night. I've been dreading it. And now it's in the ground. No one is here." His breath catches. "It's like, for everyone else, it never happened. But for me—"

His voice breaks and he stops. Anguish is thick in the air, battling the humidity. If Ben heard the grief in his voice now, he wouldn't suspect Thomas for a second.

Or maybe he'd suspect him more. My dad always says that grief and guilt often go hand in hand.

"You were close?" I say quietly.

He shakes his head. "No."

It's not the answer I was expecting, and it must be written all over my face. He takes one look at me and his eyes droop. "We didn't go on lunch dates or see movies. I didn't tell her all my secrets. We weren't close like that. We were . . . *us*." He swallows. "Does that make any sense? She was my mother. It was just me and her, for so long."

And now it's just him.

I think of my own mother, playfully poking me with the salad fork. She'd beat me upside the head with it if she saw me right now.

I try to imagine her funeral, and my mind doesn't want to go there. She and I *are* close. I can't even picture it. "I wouldn't want to see it either."

"But you're here."

"Like I said, I really thought someone should be."

His face closes down, and he begins to turn away. "Thanks."

"No!" He thinks I'm still jabbing at him. I grab his hand, and he freezes. "I meant—I came because it was partly my fault that you couldn't."

He glances down at my hand on his, but he doesn't pull away. "That wasn't your fault." His eyes find mine, and his fingers curl around my own. "You're the first person who hasn't treated me like they think I did it." He gives a quick, humorless laugh, before his mouth tightens into a flat line. "They should have kept me locked up."

His voice is dark, and a thrill of fear licks up my spine. My father and brothers would lock *me* up if they knew I was out here alone with him, talking about the murder. His hand is warm, a weight in mine. I should be letting go, pushing him away.

I don't want to. I feel connected. Anchored. His hand in mine feels right, not wrong.

Thunder rolls again. Another flash of light fills the sky.

He hasn't let go of my hand. In fact, he's clinging to my fingers. His tension is potent. He's going to rattle himself apart.

My phone chimes again. I fetch it from where it landed in the grass.

Mom: I have a plate waiting for you. Answer me, Charlotte, or I'm sending Ben to get you.

My heart rate triples, and I nearly choke. If my brothers find me here with Thomas, we'll both be locked up. Him in jail and me in a nunnery.

I quickly text back.

CR: I'm fine. Back in 15.

"Your mom is overprotective?" Thomas says.

I snort. "That's the word I use when I'm being kind."

"You need to go back?"

I should say yes. He doesn't need me to stay here. He knows where the reception is. He could walk up to Stan and ask for a ride home. My head is buzzing, and I'm beginning to think maybe my mother had a point about lunch.

Thunder rumbles across the sky. It's probably going to pour any minute.

I've been standing in silence too long. I need to say something.

I look up at him, ready to tell him that *yes,* I need to get back.

Instead, I hear myself saying, "Want to go for a walk?"

His eyes widen. Thunder cracks overhead. He'd be crazy to agree.

But Thomas swallows and nods. "Yeah," he says. "I'd like that."

I leave my purse by her grave. I tell Thomas I don't want to carry it while we walk—but really, I need a break from the onslaught of text messages.

We walk away from the grave, heading toward thick copses of trees. There's a creek beyond the cemetery that widens to form a small lake farther out, before narrowing again to a channel that runs all the way to the bay. The creek is at least thirty feet across, and deep enough to swim. I used to come out here to play with my brothers when I was little. I can still remember trying to keep up, wanting to see frogs and sand crabs before they stirred up the water with sticks and rocks and horseplay.

The heat weighs on me. Sweat pricks the back of my neck.

"You know this place," he says quietly.

"I used to play here."

"It's quiet." A raindrop finds my wrist.

He's right of course, but I don't remember it being quiet. I remember my brothers roughhousing, throwing each other down in the grass with mock aggression. Now, there's no breeze to stir the long grass. The earth is waiting for the storm.

He's calmer here, away from his mother's grave. Maybe he doesn't feel the weight of her death so acutely when he's not presented with the aftereffects. We've reached the edge of the creek, and the water flows so slowly as to seem still. We could walk farther down, to where it really opens up, but Thomas picks up a stone and skims it across the surface. He achieves four skips before the stone disappears.

He does it so effortlessly, it seems magical. "Do that again."

Another rock finds his fingers, and he flings this one more

forcefully. Only three skips, but he gets a lot more distance. Another rock, another throw, another few skips.

After a moment, I realize his movement isn't full of magic. It's full of anger.

Maybe he can hear me thinking, because he says, "Until today, I didn't realize that everyone still thinks I did it."

There's really nothing to say to that. I can't even deny it.

"Including you?" He turns to face me head-on.

I meet his eyes and hold them. Rain drops appear on his cheeks like tears. If he's a killer, he's an attractive one.

"I don't know," I say.

He turns and looks back at the water. The next rock to find his hand is larger, the size of a potato. He weighs it in his hand for a second, his fingers clutching it tightly.

For a flicker of thought, I imagine him slamming it into my skull. The thought comes out of nowhere, and I stop breathing.

Then he draws his arm back and throws it, hard, like a baseball. It completely bypasses the creek to land on the other side.

My breathing sounds so loud that I'm sure he can hear it. I'm sweating. I can't tell if it's from the heat in the air or the fear in my mind.

"You're brave, then," he says.

Brave? I can count on one hand the number of times someone has called me brave.

"I'm not sure anyone in the church would call me *brave* right now."

He finds another large rock and throws a glance my way. "What's your brother's name again?" he says. "Danny?"

"Yes."

Another rock sails across the creek. This one flies farther and cracks into a tree, echoing like a gunshot. "On the way to the police station, he said I should get ready for them to give me the chair."

I wince. "If they really thought you did it, you wouldn't be walking around free."

I'm probably staking my life on that assumption.

Thomas snorts. "That has more to do with Stan than me."

"Stan's a good guy." Then again, maybe Thomas doesn't think he's a good guy at all.

But he nods. "He seems all right. I know my mother was crazy about him. He could have turned me out on the street, but he didn't."

Surprised, I turn wide eyes his way. The horizon tips a little, then settles. I have to blink. "He's going to let you live with him?"

"Yeah." He shrugs. "I'll find a job, get a place of my own. But at first . . . I don't know where else to go."

Find a place of his own. I rake my eyes over him again. He's young, but not too young. "How old are you?"

"Eighteen." He makes a disgusted sound. "Old enough for them to charge me as an adult, too. Make my life hell." He studies me. "Are you all right?"

I lift my hair from my neck and nod. "It's just hot." The grass is longer here, and it tickles my ankles. I shift my feet and almost stumble. Damn heels.

His eyes follow my movement, and he frowns a little. "You're not drunk, are you?"

"No!" But honestly, I feel a little drunk. I have this bizarre moment where I try to remember if I left him alone with my drink, and then I realize I haven't had anything to drink.

He's still watching me. "How old are you?"

"Seventeen." I hesitate. "Did you graduate already?"

"Yeah." I can't tell if he pauses, or if my brain is processing his words more slowly. "Are you still in high school?"

I nod again. "Starting my senior year next month."

He moves closer, his eyes narrowing. "Are you sure you're all right?"

Yes. No. I have no idea. "Can we sit down?"

"Sure. Here." He slides out of his jacket, then spreads it on the grass. "Sit."

Chivalry. It's so unexpected that I just blink at him stupidly. No, wait. That's my vision. Blurring.

I pat at my side, looking for my bag. Where is my purse? I need my purse. Where is it?

Back at the grave. Right?

"I need . . ."

He frowns at me. "You need . . . ?"

I need him to catch me. My world goes dark.

CHAPTER FIVE

THOMAS

I nearly miss her. Charlotte collapses so suddenly that she's almost in the grass before I notice she's falling. I break the fall before she hits her head, then lower her the rest of the way down.

She's completely limp. Her head lolls to the side and her eyes seem to have rolled back.

Fuck.

What is this? Is this a seizure? She's not shaking. For all she's sweating, her skin is cool to the touch. Clammy. She feels like a dead body.

I need to stop that train of thought right there.

From habit, I slap my pockets, looking for my phone. Gone—gone for days. Confiscated by those damn cops.

I get down close to her, putting my cheek beside her mouth. I can't tell if she's breathing. "Charlotte. *Charlotte.*"

Her chest moves, but infinitesimally, so I'm not sure if I'm seeing it only because I want to see it so badly. She's slick with sweat, even more than I'd noticed a few minutes ago. Droplets collect in her cleavage, on her neck, and across her brow.

I give her a little shake. It's like shaking a doll with loose joints.

"Charlotte."

Nothing.

A few more raindrops strike her chest, mixing with her sweat.

Does *she* have a phone? Wasn't she listening to her phone by the grave?

I bolt from her side before the thought is complete in my head. I don't want to look at the site. I don't want to see Mom's name on the headstone.

I can't miss it. Charlotte's things are there in the grass, right beside the newly turned earth. The marble slab looms large, burning itself into my brain to rest alongside other things I don't want to see.

I imagine Mom sitting there, holding out the phone, giving me a look and a heavy sigh. "Honestly, Tommy, the way trouble finds you."

I shove the thought out of my head and scoop the phone off the ground, then sprint back to Charlotte. Rain begins to fall in earnest, rustling as it collects in the grass. She's so sweaty—maybe this is hyperthermia? Dehydration? Is it that hot outside? I have no idea.

A pulse. I didn't check for a pulse. I put fingers to her neck with one hand, then press the button on her phone with the other. My own hands have started sweating, and it takes two tries to swipe and unlock the phone.

The device asks for a passcode.

A frigging passcode!

Wait. There's an emergency button. I dial nine-one-one, then realize I never found a pulse.

The phone beeps at me. No signal. Of course not, because we're in the middle of *nowhere*.

"Damn it," I mutter. I think of the way Danny fell beside the church, and some tiny, dark part of my brain wonders if I somehow did this too.

I still can't find a pulse.

Fuck, I *can't find a pulse.*

A whimper crawls out of my throat. I can't do this again. I can't do this.

Then I spy the twist of silver and turquoise stones on her wrist, which I thought was a strange hipster bracelet. It is—

but it's wrapped around a steel chain with one of those medical alert symbols.

I twist the stones out of the way so I can read what's written on the back.

Type I Diabetes

Diabetes. I know nothing about diabetes, except that you have to give yourself shots. Does she need sugar? Did she have too much sugar?

I put my head against her chest and listen. *There.* A breath. A heartbeat. It's slow, but it's there.

I have her in my arms before I have a clear idea of what to do. I can't leave her here. We're a good distance from the church, but I start running anyway. Her head lolls over my arm, and one hand hangs limply from her side.

Thunder cracks and the sky opens up.

Water soaks her face, her chest, her dress. It's dripping in my eyes already. For a heartbeat, I have this crazy hope it'll wake her up.

Her eyelids flicker, then go still. A reflex, I'm sure.

We're almost through the wall of trees. Maybe someone will see us and come to help.

"Come on," I whisper, my voice tight with the strain of carrying her. "We'll be there soon."

Then we're through the trees and the rain is pelting us full out. I shake water out of my eyes.

Cops are suddenly there in front of me. They look as surprised to see me as I am to see them.

They get it together first. Guns are drawn. Pointing at me.

"Put her down!" one yells. He's blond, late twenties maybe. His voice promises a bullet to the forehead if I don't get her on the ground.

I can't put my hands up, but I lift Charlotte a little, showing them that she needs medical attention. "She's hurt. She needs an ambu—"

"*Put her down.*" This from the other, with darker hair. His voice carries a little touch of panic.

I hate this town. I take a step forward.

They raise their guns. A slight movement, but they might as well have cocked the hammers. A warning bell rings in my head. They'll really shoot me.

"Fine," I say, speaking clearly over the rain. "Fine."

I gently ease her to the ground, then look up. The blond cop holsters his gun and approaches me, though the other keeps his pointed. My jaw is tight, and I emphasize every word. "She. Needs. An—"

His fist comes out of nowhere.

I hit the ground.

Now I might need an ambulance.

An hour later, I am in the same interrogation room. Soon I'll need a mug with my name on it.

I want to get out of this goddamned suit. I didn't like it before, and I like it even less now that it's crumpled and damp. My jaw aches, and I wish I had a bag of ice or a bottle of ibuprofen. I move it gingerly and wince.

I want to claim assault, but I want to get out of here more.

The detective in front of me must not have been at the funeral. He's wearing a polo shirt and jeans instead of a shirt and tie. The polo isn't doing him any favors, especially since he's chosen salmon pink. There's a badge clipped to his belt, and he has a thick, graying mustache.

I can't remember his name. He's leafing through a folder. I want to smack the reading glasses right off his face.

"Tell me again," he drawls. His voice isn't quite southern but close. We're close enough to Virginia down here, I guess. "What did you do to Miss Rooker?"

"I didn't do *anything* to her. We were talking. She collapsed. Would you tell me if she's all right?"

He makes a quick note in his folder, then looks at me over the rim of his glasses. "And why would she be talking to you?"

"You've asked me that six times now. I found her by my mother's grave, and we started talking."

He surveys me for a long moment, then closes the folder and sets it on the table. He leans forward and places the pen on the center of the folder.

For the first time, his voice finds an edge. "Let me make something real clear for you, son."

"I'm not your son."

He snorts, and it's not a friendly noise. "Lucky for you." He lifts the pen and sets it back down. "There aren't many people who care for you around here. You understand me?"

"Trust me, I got the memo."

"When you're under suspicion of murder, it looks pretty shady when you lead a young girl into the woods alone, you hear me? Especially when only one of you has the ability to walk back out."

"I didn't lead her." I grind out the words. "*She* led *me*. I told you that." I pound my handcuffed—yes, *handcuffed*—hands on the table. "Why the hell would I lead *her* into the woods?"

"Well, why don't you tell me about that, son? Why would you?"

I'm about to snap. Pressure is building in my head, and I've never been an aggressive guy, but all of a sudden, I want to slam my hands into this man.

The sad thing is, he wants me to. I can see it in his eyes. He wants me to haul off and deck him. Then they'd have a reason to throw me in jail. He's probably provoking me on purpose.

My mind flashes on Charlotte, on the way her arm hung so limply. I wish someone would tell me what happened to her. Her eyes rolled back in her head just like—

Stop it. I have to stop these thoughts. I don't want to see her death, too.

I sit back in the chair and blow out a breath. All of a sudden, I feel very small. Very trapped. My voice is low, and I all but speak to my hands. "I want to talk to Stan."

"I'm sorry. That's not possible."

"Fine. Then I want a fucking attorney."

"You bring an attorney in here, son, and I can't help you. You understand that?"

"I understand that you need to stop calling me son, or I'm going to—"

He leans forward. "You're going to what?"

I grit my teeth and force my voice to remain level. "Just get me an attorney. I'm done talking to you."

He picks up his folder and leaves, and I expect to wait for a while. When they first put me in here, I sat for an hour before anyone came to talk to me. It's all a tactic of some sort, I'm sure.

There's a little part of my brain that wonders if Mom might find this hilarious, in a character-building kind of way. *See, Thomas? I told you that you shouldn't stare at a girl's rack before a funeral.*

Sorry, Mom. She was hot.

A key rattles the door, and then it swings open. Stan walks in.

He looks a little drained. And a lot pissed off.

"Thomas."

I didn't screw up this time, but I still can't meet his eyes. He's not having a very good day either, and some of that is my fault. "I asked for an attorney."

"I know you did. I want to talk to you."

"Well, you sound like you want to kill me."

"Part of me does."

I set my shoulders and keep my eyes on the plastic tabletop. The room is small, and I can hear him breathing. "I guess you're rethinking the offer to let me stay with you, huh?"

He's quiet for a long time. Long enough that I finally cast a glance up.

His whole frame sags. "What were you thinking, Tom?" he says quietly. "Please. Just tell me what you were thinking."

I don't know what to tell him, but his quiet voice takes

some of the rage out of me. Mom liked that about him, too, I know. Even angry, his presence is settling.

"Can you tell me if she's okay?" I say softly. "No one will tell me."

He nods. "She'll be fine. Insulin shock, but the paramedics were able to bring her around. Might have to spend a few hours in the hospital, but she'll be all right." He sighs. "Thank god."

I don't know if he's thanking God in a general way, or if he thinks I might have done something and he's glad I was interrupted.

"I wasn't . . ." I hesitate. "I wasn't doing anything. She was at the grave when I walked up. She was listening to music. She said—she said she felt bad that no one was paying respects."

He nods slowly, like it's the same thing he's heard from someone else—maybe Charlotte herself.

He clears his throat. "Why did you go into the woods?"

I close my eyes. "I couldn't stay there."

"By her grave, you mean?"

"Yeah."

"So it was your idea to walk."

Was it my idea? Or was it hers? I can't remember. "I don't know. I just know we were walking. She seemed to know the path."

I know she felt peaceful beside me, when everyone else feels like a pressure cooker full of anger, hate, and suspicion.

Yeah, like I can say that. I'd sound like I belonged in the looney bin.

Then again, a psychiatric institution would probably be a step up from prison.

Stan's voice is very low, very quiet. "Do you understand that every cop in this town is looking for a reason to lock you up?"

"No. That has completely escaped my notice."

His eyes flash with sudden anger. "Don't joke about this. I'm not kidding, Tom. They don't want you walking around. So heading off into the woods with Charlotte Rooker was probably the stupidest thing you could have done."

"So what, she has one prick of a brother who wants to give me a hard time? Fine. Whatever. I'll stay out of his way."

"*Three* brothers," Stan snaps. "All cops. And her father, too. And Charlotte is a minor, so it doesn't matter if she wants to press charges or not. It's up to her parents, and right now, they're claiming assault. They're doing a toxicology test in the hospital to make sure you didn't give her something. Someone mentioned a rape kit. Do you understand me? Do you get it, now?"

My blood freezes. "I didn't touch her."

"You were carrying her."

I shake my head fiercely. "I didn't *touch her*. Not like that. I thought she was dying. Her phone wouldn't work." I've told all of this to the cop in the pink shirt, but I knew I didn't have a shot in hell of making him believe me. With Stan, I have a chance.

"So you went for a walk, and she just collapsed."

"Yes!"

"Why was your jacket on the ground?"

I blink. "What?"

"They found your jacket on the bank of the creek. Her hair was on it. Why was she lying on your jacket if she collapsed?"

His tone is level, no judgment. In this moment, I see how Stan could be an effective homicide detective. He could be ordering sliced chicken at the deli counter.

"She asked if she could sit down," I say. *A rape kit.* God. Poor Charlotte. I hope she tells them. I hope she doesn't have to go through that.

I frown and look at Stan. "How did the cops know we were out there?"

Stan blinks. "What?"

"How did they know? They were just there, with guns out. How did they know?"

His eyes flick toward the mirror on the wall. I'm not stupid. I know it's a two-way mirror—I just don't know who's on the other side.

His gaze returns to me, but it's more appraising now. "I don't know."

"Pretty precise timing, don't you think?"

He frowns. "What are you getting at?"

"I'm wondering if this was a setup to get me back in jail."

Stan sighs a little, like he hears this kind of thing from perps all the time. "The police don't work like that."

"Do they randomly stroll through the cemetery?"

"Tom." His tone is a warning.

I point at myself. "Is it police procedure to punch someone in the face?"

I don't know who's on the other side of that mirror, but they don't like me asking these questions. I can almost feel the irritation through the glass.

Maybe Stan can, too. He's looking at the mirror on the wall behind me.

"One of them punched you?" he says evenly.

"No, I did this shaving."

His eyes snap back to mine. "I'm serious. Did one of them hit you?"

"It's not a big deal."

"It is a big deal."

"Is it a big deal to set someone up? Because that's what this feels like."

Stan's voice is tired. "There was no setup, Tom."

"Whatever." I flick my hand. No one believes me. No one cares about me. It doesn't matter. Nothing matters.

"There wasn't a setup." Stan's eyes hold mine. "Those weren't cops patrolling the cemetery. The police officers who found you are Charlotte's other brothers. They were coming to check on her because she hadn't eaten lunch."

Her brothers. Now I understand the punch. "Do you have your gun on you, Stan? Why don't you just shoot me and save them all the trouble?"

He sighs.

I shove out of my chair and turn to face the glass. "Are you in there?" I yell.

No one says anything, but I know they are. "Why didn't you all just shoot me in the woods?" I yell. "I'm such a danger, right? It wasn't enough to drag me out of there once. Can't have the murderer visiting his own mother's grave—"

My voice breaks, and I almost collapse. The grief hits me hard and fast, more painful than a bullet. My hands press into my stomach, as if I've been shot and I need to hold my intestines in.

I don't even realize my eyes are shut until Stan's hand is on my shoulder, and he's guiding me back to the chair.

The room is so silent that the fluorescent lights tick overhead.

It's so silent that when someone shouts from the other side of the mirror, I have little trouble making out the words.

"We didn't shoot because we might have hit Charlotte."

Of course.

My cheeks are wet. I held it together in the jail cell, when I was alone, but here, in this fucking fishbowl, my emotions are on full display. It's humiliating, but maybe they can't tell. I keep my hands down, because wiping my eyes would make it obvious.

"I want an attorney," I say to Stan. The words are thick, but I manage to keep my voice level. "Just leave me alone and bring me someone who can help me."

Stan doesn't respond. The tears are drying on my cheeks, but some made it all the way to my collar. I duck my head to wipe my face on my shoulder, and the chain of the hand-cuffs rattles.

"I can help you," says Stan.

"You don't want to help me."

He acts like I didn't respond. "It might take me an hour," he says. "You need to sit tight."

I don't say anything. I don't even look at him. Stan feels like the enemy now. I don't trust him.

"No more shouting at the window," he says, his voice very quiet. "Get me? Not another word at all."

He sits there for so long that I know he's not going to move until I respond.

I look at him. "Fine. Whatever."

Then he's gone, and I'm left alone with my thoughts.

It doesn't take an hour.

It takes three.

By the time he comes back, I'm irritated and starving and sitting on the floor of the tiny room, leaning into the corner. The lights have given me a migraine. My shoulders ache, and my wrists are sore from being held together for so long. I can barely feel my legs.

"We're out of here," Stan says. He throws a windbreaker on the table. "Get up. Let's go."

I blink up at him. "What?"

"I'll take the cuffs off. Come on. You've got to be hungry. I am."

"Wait. They're letting me leave?"

"Yes." He sounds irritated about it. "Move it before they change their minds."

I move it.

He leaves the handcuffs on the table, then holds up the windbreaker. "Put this on."

I take it from him. It says POLICE across the back in bright yellow letters. "Why? Is it still raining?"

He looks aggrieved. "Just put it on. We've got to run the gauntlet."

I have no idea what that means, but lack of food doesn't leave my brain too sharp. I slide my arms into the sleeves, and Stan takes my arm as if to escort me.

"I can walk, Stan."

"Put the hood up. I want to make sure you keep walking. Don't talk to anyone. Just walk, straight to the car. Ready?"

Every cop in this place probably knows who I am. "What's with the big—?"

"Don't talk. Walk." He jerks the hood up. The entire jacket is too big for me, and the hood hangs over my face a bit.

I feel a little giddy. Maybe I've fallen asleep and this is all a dream. "You're not, like, breaking me out of here, are you?" I whisper.

He gives me a withering look. "Walk, kid."

The police station is busier than it was earlier, but no one really pays attention to us. The hood of the windbreaker cuts down my vision, making me feel like a horse with blinders on. I keep trying to peek around.

"It's change of shift," Stan says, his voice low. "Just keep walking."

"You're not—"

"Shh! Not a word."

His voice is so tense that I wonder if he really *is* breaking me out of here. I clamp my mouth shut and walk.

Before I know it, we're through the first set of double doors, and we're in the little vestibule before pushing through the heavy fire doors into the outside air. Pamphlets about spousal abuse and drug rehabilitation line the walls. There's a flyer for a family day at the local fire department. The small area is blessedly silent and free of people.

I breathe a sigh. "That wasn't worth all the drama. No one even looked at us."

"It's not cops I'm worried about," he says. "You're allowed to leave. I'll give you the details when we get home."

"Then what's with the cloak and dagger?"

"This." He pushes the door open, and my world explodes with light and noise.

CHAPTER SIX

CHARLOTTE

I'm on house arrest. I'd prefer a jail cell. Or even the hospital, for god's sake. At least there they wouldn't be checking on me every fifteen minutes.

My mother actually sent me to bed. It's not even seven o'clock at night, and I'm stuck in my room. You'd think I was twelve years old and got caught sneaking out with the local bad boy.

The thought sticks in my head. Aside from the whole insulin shock, that's a pretty solid description of what happened.

No. It's not. We weren't sneaking. We weren't hiding. We aren't romantically involved.

I was walking beside him pretty closely. I can still smell him, some faint mix of sandalwood and sage. When he took his jacket off, he was more built than I expected. The suit hid some real muscle.

You're brave, then.

His voice was rough and bitter, but there'd been grudging respect under his tone. Remembering it throws a blush on my cheeks.

I was blushing in the hospital, too, and I couldn't get my cheeks to knock it off. Matt wouldn't let me hear the end of it. His voice could have cut ice. "We're trying to convict this kid of murder, and you were out swooning all over him."

I was *not* swooning. I was falling. Distinct difference.

I was ready to fire back at Matt, but then Ben said, "We thought you were dead, Char." He swallowed. "When he carried you out of the woods—we thought he was carrying a body."

The fear in his tone stole the fight from me.

I pace the floor again, wrestling with boredom and agitation. My insulin levels are fine, now. I don't need to be in bed at seven o'clock. Like a *toddler*.

They can't honestly think I'm sleeping up here, but there's nothing else to do. My mother never let me have a television in my room, saying it creates distance in the family. Danny has a television in *his* room, and when I bring it up, she says, "Danny is an adult, earning a living. He bought that with his own money." Then I ask if I can buy a television with *my* own money, and I get a glare. I should tell her he watches porn on it.

Yes. That's exactly what I should do.

My cell phone chimes, and I leap on it. I'd sell a kidney for a smartphone, because at least then I'd have Internet access and some way to entertain myself. A text message is almost as good.

It's Nicole. My best friend.

About time, since I've sent her twenty texts without a response. I told her everything that happened, but I haven't heard anything back. I knew I just had to wait until the dinner hour was past—her parents don't allow any "techno-gadgets" at the table.

NK: Still in the clink?

My fingers fly across the keys.

CR: This is brutal. At least it's giving me time to plot an escape plan.

NK: Does the funeral fiasco have anything to do with why you're on the local news?

What? I'm on the news?

I look around my room like a television has somehow appeared on the corner of my dresser.

My phone vibrates in my hand. Nicole is calling.

I have no idea if my parents will come up here and confiscate it if they hear me on the line, so I answer as quietly as I can.

"Hello?" I whisper.

Nicole's voice is low and ironic. "Oh, sweetie, I told you to take that picture off Facebook. Now your boobs are all over the news."

"What picture? What's going on?"

"The picture from the lake. The one where you're in that purple tankini and a life jacket. You need to turn on the television."

What? I know the picture she's talking about. It's from last summer, and I'm half sunburned. Why is it on the news?

"Are you watching yet?" Nicole says.

"I don't have a television in here!" I hiss.

"I don't care. Find one. Climb out your window and watch your neighbor's."

I open my bedroom door and peek out. The hallway is hushed. Danny's door is closed, but that could mean anything. If it was open, I might have tried to sneak in there to watch, but closed . . . I mean, he really *could* be watching porn.

I hear running water and dishes clinking downstairs. Mom must be cleaning up from dinner. My father always watches television after dinner, so I'm sure it's on, but he usually avoids the news. Thank god.

OMG. If my grandmother sees me in a bikini on television . . .

Nicole is still feeding me the play-by-play. "Now they're showing some guy being dragged out of the police station. What a fox. Is this the guy you texted me about?"

My brain decides to kick into gear. Is there a story about me and Thomas on the news? I need to find a television.

"I don't know," I whisper. "What's going on now?"

"He's being dragged across a parking lot. They're saying his name is Thomas Bellweather. Do you think they're taking him to prison? Maybe you could offer him a conjugal visit."

Only Nicole would think about sex with an accused killer at a time like this. "I can't even leave my bedroom. Pretty sure he's going to be sleeping alone."

"*That's* all that's stopping you? Being grounded? You mean you'd offer him a conjugal visit if you *weren't* in trouble?"

Heat hits my cheeks before I can stop it. "Let's just say I wouldn't kick him out of bed for eating crackers."

Then I stop. What is *wrong* with me?

I ease my door closed and go back into my room again. "What's happening now?"

"He's being shoved into a car. It's a circus. Are you sure something else didn't happen at that funeral?"

My text version wasn't too specific, but I can't imagine anything about our interaction in the woods that would have generated a media circus. "Is it a police car?"

"No. Just a sedan."

That doesn't mean it's not a police car. If I could see it, I could tell. I wonder if he's being moved to a more secure facility. "Is he in handcuffs?"

"No. Doesn't look like it. Is he a cop? He's wearing a POLICE windbreaker."

"No. He's not. Who's with him? Do you recognize them?" We've been friends long enough that she knows most of my brothers' friends and some of their colleagues.

"No," Nicole says. "Whoever it is, he's not in uniform. Older. Forties, maybe. His lawyer?"

If Thomas isn't in handcuffs, that probably means he's not being held. He got out. I thought *for sure* my dad would have him on death row by Saturday.

Okay, not really. But I didn't think Thomas would be walking around town anytime soon.

"He's free," I whisper.

"He's being chased by news vans. Not sure that counts as 'free.'" She stops abruptly, and the line goes silent.

"Nicole?"

Nothing.

"Nic? What's happ—?"

"Shh!"

I shh.

"Sorry," she finally says. "I wanted to listen. Apparently he's not being charged at this time. Oh, and he's filing a harassment complaint."

"Shut. Up." Danny is going to give birth to a large, mooing cow when he hears about this. Right in the middle of our living room. Matt will probably be doing the same thing across town. I can see it coming.

"The police have declined to give a statement," Nicole says.

"Of course."

"Oh, look, your picture again. At least you're fully clothed in this one."

I still don't understand why I'm featured in Thomas's story. "What are they saying?"

"They're totally lifting all of these from the Internet. I don't know why they even bother crediting Facebook, like Mark Zuckerberg took the photo himself—"

"Nicole! Oh my god! *What are they saying?!*"

"Oh. That he . . ." She falls silent.

She. Is. Killing. Me.

"What?" I demand.

Her voice is less animated. "That he lured you to a secluded area and attacked you." She hesitates. "You didn't tell me that, Char. I didn't know he hurt you. I didn't mean to make a joke about a conjugal visit."

Nicole is crazy, but she has the biggest heart of anyone I know. She's probably realigning all her thoughts so nothing involves sex in a prison cell and is now envisioning stroking my hand while I weep into a pillow.

"No. Nicole. That didn't happen. I didn't eat lunch. It was hot, and I didn't pay attention to the signs. My sugar got too low, and I collapsed."

She doesn't say anything. The line is silent.

"Really," I insist. "There was no assault."

"They said he lured you."

Breath leaves my mouth in a heavy sigh. "I'll explain." And I do. It takes a minute or five.

When I'm done, I can tell she's imagining conjugal visits again.

"He *cried*?" she says softly. "He must be so sensitive."

"No. That's not the right word for him. And he was trying *not* to cry."

"What is the right word?"

I don't say anything. How to describe Thomas?

I think of his fist wrapped around the rock, propelling it across the creek to crack into a tree. The indignant fury in his voice when he talked about Danny.

I lick my lips. "He's different."

"In a good way?"

"I don't know."

"Yet," she says.

My mother would kill me if she could hear this conversation. Thank god we're not on the house phone.

But I agree with Nicole.

"Yet," I whisper. "I don't know *yet*."

CHAPTER SEVEN

THOMAS

Stan is a pretty good cook. Better than Mom, though I feel a little traitorous to say that. When he's home, he always cooks. Tonight, we're eating this baked chicken casserole with saffron rice. I don't even know what saffron is, but it's fantastic. It took him less than an hour from the time we got home to have dinner on the table.

Where Mom had him beat, however, was in conversation.

He's cleared his throat twice now, and each time it sounds like a shovelful of gravel is trapped in there. He's barely said more than a handful of sentences since we got through the press mob and into his house.

One of those sentences was, "Why don't you take some time to get yourself together?" So I took the opportunity to ball up the suit on the floor of my closet and take a shower. Now I'm in jeans and a T-shirt.

What's really sad is that this moment—eating chicken, sitting in silence, and wearing my own clothes—is the absolute high point of my day.

We weren't sitting in silence at first. The phone kept ringing, and Stan kept picking up the receiver only to set it back down. He peeked out the window and said three news trucks had followed us from the police station. Eventually, he just unplugged the phone.

He didn't yank the cord out of the wall or anything like

that. Stan's not a "big reaction" kind of guy. Even since Mom died, there haven't been any wracking sobs, no anger, no fury. He's held it together. A little stricken, maybe, but more or less composed. He's a quiet man, and her death didn't do anything to change that.

He's staring at his plate, eating his baked chicken methodically.

For the first time, I sit and watch him.

This is going to sound crazy, but until this moment, I hadn't given too much thought to *who* killed my mother. I've been so fixated on telling people that I *didn't* do it that I haven't had a spare moment to wonder who *did*. Actually— that's not true. I've thought about it, but without close examination. I've assumed some random criminal broke in. Some caricature of a bad guy, someone with a knit cap, a blindfold, and a five o'clock shadow. Some sleazy freak from an episode of *Dateline* crossed with last week's guest star on *Law and Order*. Maybe a rapist who killed her when she fought back. Maybe a thief who killed her when she discovered him. Her wedding and engagement rings were gone, so either would fit.

In all cases, a stranger. Not someone who knew her.

Now I think about it. I try to remember if anyone questioned Stan.

He must feel me looking at him. "What's on your mind, Tom?"

"I was wondering what you were doing that night."

He knows what night I'm talking about, and he doesn't pretend not to. "I was on Patrick Street. Staking out a drug dealer."

He might be quiet, but he's intense. It's hard to hold his eyes, so I push chicken around my plate. "Were you with anyone?"

"You think the cops are investigating the hell out of you, but they've left me alone?"

The profanity lets me know I've gotten to him. Otherwise, his voice doesn't change. "I'm just asking a question, Stan."

He holds my gaze, and for a moment I think he's going to throw me out of here. I don't really suspect him, so I don't know what I'm digging for.

Or maybe I do suspect him. Maybe I'm wondering if I've been living under the same roof as a murderer.

My head is a mess.

"No," he says. "No one was with me. But based on reports and check-ins, I was nowhere near here."

This is the first time we've talked about my mother since she died, and it's completely the wrong kind of conversation. We're not really talking about *her* anyway. We're barely even talking about the crime. We're talking around it.

"Check-ins?" I say. "Like on a radio?"

"Yeah. Just like that."

"What, you can't lie about where you are?"

He puts his fork down. "Do you really want to do this, Tom?"

"I'm not doing anything."

"You're funny." The way he says it implies there's nothing really funny at all.

"Everyone is pointing at me," I say. "I didn't do it."

"Do you suddenly think I committed this crime?" he says evenly.

"You're one of the few people who don't think *I* committed this crime. Maybe that means something."

He frowns. "I don't know what you mean."

My heart beats so hard it hurts. "Everyone thinks I killed my mother," I say, keeping my voice even. "You don't think that, or you wouldn't be letting me stay here. Maybe there's a *reason* you don't think that."

We stare at each other for the longest time. I can hear myself breathing. I can hear *him* breathing.

We're both sharing the same thought. It's so clear, I swear I could read his mind right now.

I don't think he did it. But I can't be sure.

Stan breaks the eye contact first. He slices into another piece of chicken. "Charlotte Rooker doesn't think you did it either," he says. "You want to interrogate her next?"

I wouldn't mind five minutes to ask her a few questions about what happened in the woods. "I'm not interrogating you," I say.

"But you'd like to," he says. "Go ahead."

"What?"

He looks up again. "I said, go ahead. If you need to clear me in your own way, go ahead."

I swallow. I expected a fight. Maybe I *wanted* a fight. He's taken me by surprise again.

People don't usually surprise me. Definitely not twice in one day.

When I don't say anything, he pushes food around his plate again. "I loved your mother, kid." He hesitates, and emotion weighs down his words. "Sometimes I wonder what she saw in me, because I'm almost fifty years old, and I'm pretty set in my ways. When I bought a ring, I wanted to do some big proposal. Go to a ballgame and write it on a scoreboard. Hire a skywriter. I don't know."

I swear he's almost blushing, but at the same time he sounds like his voice might crack and he'll cry. I hold my breath and don't move.

"She was so unassuming," he says. "So simple. In a good way, you know?"

I know. How could I not know?

He looks at me. "Of course you know."

"Of course," I agree. My voice is hollow.

"I had all these plans, but when I had the ring in my pocket, I couldn't wait. She was coming over to cook me dinner. I didn't even let her get in the door."

I laugh, but there's a hitch of a sob in there with it. "She thought you set that up. She thought you let her think she was coming over to cook dinner, but you planned to propose."

"Really?"

I nod. "She thought you were going to propose at the table, but you couldn't wait."

I remember when she told me, the following day. She spent the night, of course. They'd gotten to that point, and I was almost eighteen years old, and more than capable of staying home on my own. I could think more carefully about that, but I don't need my mind to draw any pictures, thank you very much.

Especially not now.

It was more practical anyway. We used to live two hours away from here, so it wasn't worth driving all that way just for an evening. When they first started dating, they used to meet in Annapolis and go to one of the chain restaurants there, followed by a movie. It was all so high school. Mom loved it.

She met Stan online. I knew something was up when she'd stay up late at night, giggling over the ancient desktop we kept in the corner.

Stan's lost in the memory. His eyes look damp.

I clear my throat. "I didn't mean to interrogate you," I say, my voice rough.

"It's all right, Tom. I've got questions, too."

Immediately, my defenses click back into place. "For me?"

"No. For everyone." He waves a hand around. "Like you said, everyone thinks you did it. If you didn't, everyone is on the wrong path."

My eyebrows go up. "Can you do anything?"

"You mean, can I assist with the investigation?"

"Yeah."

"No." He gives a heavy sigh and picks up his fork again. "Conflict of interest. And I'm not going to be investigating much of anything for at least a few days."

"Why not?"

He takes a sip of his beer. "Because I filed a harassment complaint against Charlotte Rooker's brothers, and the commanding officer thinks it would be best if I went on administrative leave until official charges are filed."

Holy crap. There's the third surprise. You could knock me out of this chair with a feather. He's dropped this news so unassumingly, like we've already had a conversation about this.

I cough. "You what?"

"You heard me."

"Is that how you got me out of there?"

He nods and takes another bite of chicken.

I blink at him. "You filed a harassment complaint? Seriously?"

He looks at me, and his eyes show a spark of anger for the first time. "Yes. Seriously. Maybe what happened beside the church was a misunderstanding, but for them to come after you in the woods like that . . . that should never have happened."

My stomach sinks. "So you think it might have been a setup, too."

"Charlotte is a nice girl. I've known her family for years. I don't think *she* set it up." He snorts. "You can't exactly fake insulin shock."

There's more to say. I can hear it. "But?"

He shrugs a little. "I think maybe her brothers thought they'd catch you doing something that would stick. I told them you were out by her grave. I didn't know Charlotte was out there, but *they* did."

I scowl and stab at my chicken. "And I thought Danny was a prick."

"That one wants a moment in the spotlight. It's probably a good thing he wasn't the one to find you with her. You stay away from him, Tom. You hear me?"

I snort. "Gladly."

"I'm not kidding."

"I'm not either. I don't want anything to do with any of them."

His fork goes still on his plate. His voice takes on a knowing tone. "Not even Charlotte?"

I think of the way she felt when her body crashed into mine. All curves and warmth and vanilla and sugar.

When she was unconscious. I'm such a freak.

I take a bite of chicken. "No girl is worth getting shot over."

He laughs. "You might change your mind about that one day, kid."

Then it's like he realizes he laughed, and the comment hangs out there. We fall silent for a while, eating our food. The kitchen clock ticks away the minutes.

"They're not going to solve it, are they?" I finally say.

Stan doesn't say anything, so I glance up. "It's been too long, without any leads," I say. "That's why they're putting all the pressure on me. You've got to lock someone up."

"That's not how investigations work," he says. "We don't lock someone up because it's *convenient*."

My eyes narrow. "So you're saying everyone in prison is one hundred percent guilty? They're not there because the community needed someone to punish, just to prove that the bad guy was off the streets?"

"You're making me out to be a prosecutor, a defense attorney, and a judge," Stan says. "I'm none of those things. All I can tell you is what I do, Tom. Not any of those other people."

"But there's nothing left to investigate. Your house has been cleaned up. The murder is almost a week old. There are no clues. It's me or nothing, isn't it?"

"There has to be something left," he says.

"How do you know? How can you be so sure?"

He leans forward and puts his forearms on the table. "Because you're telling me you didn't do it. I know I didn't do it. There's a clue out there. We just haven't found it yet."

"Maybe you're not looking in the right places."

He points his fork at me. "That's exactly what I'm saying."

"So where do we start?"

He puts his fork down and sighs. "The cops have been over this house. They've been over the video camera of the two convenience stores on this block. They've been over the body. They've looked at you, and they've looked at me. No forced entry. No sign of a struggle. I'd been off for three nights, and then I was on, so whoever did it knew my schedule—or they got lucky."

"So what else is there?"

He sighs. "That's the problem, Tom. There *is* nothing else."

The cops might be pointing their fingers in the wrong direction, but that doesn't mean they're not being thorough.

During interrogation, they've asked me about my father. Several times.

I don't have anything to tell them.

If this had happened when I was young, when every day felt like a game of hide and seek, I might have shared in their suspicion. I didn't keep anything about him a secret—there just wasn't much to share.

I remember nights when I could have sworn that my mother stayed up all night, sitting beside my bed.

I remember days when she'd show up at school to check on me, worry lines permanently creased into her face. She'd ask the teachers if she could volunteer for the afternoon, and she wouldn't leave my side for hours.

This was all years ago. None of it is helpful. I never actually saw my father, not after we left him. My mother never verbalized her worries. She let me live my life, and I let her live hers.

They asked if I knew of a way to contact him. That was almost laughable. I don't even have a picture.

I told them about the memory of the car and the alley and the promise to get ice cream.

I might as well be reading from a paperback for as helpful as that is. It didn't take the police long to tire of that angle. Why chase my father down when they had a prime suspect right in front of them?

I asked what they thought would make me do such a thing.

They said I did it because I resented her for marrying Stan.

They asked over and over again where I hid her rings. They asked in different ways, hoping to trip me up, I guess. *Are we going to find her wedding ring in your room, Tom? What did you do with her rings, Tom? Her rings are somewhere safe, aren't they, Tom?*

For some reason, this bothers me more than the murder accusation. I asked Stan about it, why they'd think I'd rob my own mother of her jewelry, and he pointed to motive. He said it might be personal, removing the rings. It might be something someone would do if they weren't happy with the wedding.

He gave me a pointed look when he said that part.

Here's what doesn't look good for me: I *wasn't* happy with the wedding.

Not for any weird reasons. I don't have mommy issues. I wanted her to be happy.

So even though I wasn't thrilled with the wedding, I wasn't unhappy, either. I thought it was too fast, but she's an adult, and she can make her own decisions. Mom and Stan didn't date long. Just a few months. Then he popped the question, and a month later they signed a marriage license at City Hall.

I had a problem with moving here.

I had just graduated from high school, and I had plans. Nothing big, but *plans*. I had friends. A job. A routine.

I didn't have the means to stay there on my own. Mom dragged me out to the middle of nowhere to tell me we were moving here. She sold it hard. *Think of it, Tom. We're surrounded by water. We're less than an hour from Ocean City. This town is full of charm! You'll love it. I know you'll love it.*

I didn't love it. I pitched a fit.

Not for long. But enough to let her know I wasn't happy.

One of the detectives who first interrogated me, a guy named Eckels, I think, tried to buddy up. He told me about how his mom used to make him do things he didn't want to do all the time, and he always wanted to punch her.

I looked him dead in the eye and said that I've never hurt her. Not for this, not for anything.

He didn't appreciate my suggestion that maybe he should see a therapist if he still feels like punching his mother.

My mind wanders back to my father. Those days of my mother moving through life in fear are long gone. She stopped visiting school and staying up all night when I turned twelve or thirteen. *Years* ago. She was on Facebook and posted regularly. She met Stan online, for god's sake. Not exactly the movements of a woman hiding from a mysterious ex.

I've long since thought he moved on. Or, considering her early fear of him, I occasionally wondered if he was dead.

Even if he was alive and harboring some bizarre desire to have her back, how would he know to find her here? We've only lived in Garretts Mill for a few weeks. Half our boxes are still packed. She and Stan didn't drag out their courtship, but it wasn't *that* quick. If someone felt resentful about their relationship, why take action *now*?

And if it wasn't my father—which is already ridiculously far-fetched—who the hell did it?

CHAPTER EIGHT
CHARLOTTE

There's a news van outside my house in the morning. I don't notice it at first—I'm not of the mind to inspect the front yard when I crawl out of bed.

No, I find out when I'm coming down the stairs and my grandmother gasps.

It takes a lot to tear her attention away from *The View*.

"Pajamas?" she says. "With the local news on the front lawn? Charlotte. Get upstairs and put on something decent."

Let the record show that I'm wearing a T-shirt and cutoff sweatpants that used to belong to Ben. Not exactly a lace nightie.

But I know how a fight will go, so I head upstairs to change. When I come back down, I find Mom making banana bread muffins, and she doesn't seem too concerned that our house is under surveillance. Then again, she's married to a police officer, and she's watched her three sons follow in his footsteps, so maybe a little news van is nothing special.

Still, it's a big deal to me.

"What does the news van want?" I ask.

"To talk to you," she says equably. A muffin pan is on the stove and she's gently pulling the muffins free to cool them on a metal rack. She's not looking at me, and I can't tell if she's still mad about yesterday.

"Why?"

A muffin sticks to the side of the pan, and she all but stabs it to get it free. "To figure out if you're involved with that boy, or if you're collaborating with your brothers to harass him."

So she's still mad.

I pull a jug of orange juice out of the refrigerator. "Why would I be doing either of those things?"

The timer goes off and she yanks the second pan out of the oven, slamming it on the ceramic cooktop.

"I don't know, Charlotte. Why would you go off in the woods with a boy we all warned you to stay away from?"

I don't say anything to that. I take a drink of juice and reach for one of the muffins.

She smacks my hand away. "Did you check your levels this morning?"

"Of course."

"Your insulin?"

"*Of course.*" Maybe next she'll ask if I need a bottle and a diaper change. I reach for a muffin again, and she smacks my hand a second time. It's hard enough to sting. Hard enough to make me realize that she's still *really* mad.

"Do you have any idea," she starts, "what it felt like to hear that no one knew where you were—but then to hear that that boy was carrying you out of the woods? *Unconscious*, Charlotte. With a murderer. What were you thinking? What? Tell me."

"He hasn't been convicted yet, so maybe we can stop calling him a murderer."

"That's all you have to say to me? There are lots of people who haven't been convicted yet, and I don't want you associating with them either."

"I'm almost eighteen," I say. "I'm not going to apologize for having a conversation with someone who missed his mother's funeral because my brother has a stick up his—"

"*Charlotte.*"

"No, Ma, let her finish." Danny enters the kitchen. He must be on duty soon because he's in full uniform.

I want to throw my glass of orange juice at him.

"Go ahead," he says, his eyes full of malicious taunting, and for a second I think he's egging me on to soak him in Tropicana.

But no, he's asking me to finish my sentence. I smile sweetly. "I'm sure you can fill in the blank."

He gets a glass and pours his own glass of orange juice. "What's with the news van?" he says. "Can't wait to get a look at our Hester Prynne here?"

"What are you even talking about?" I snap. "I didn't sleep with anyone."

"Never said you did."

"That's what *The Scarlet Letter* is about!"

He shrugs and leans over to give our mother a kiss on the cheek, then grabs a muffin. She holds out a second one. "Take two if that's all you're eating."

Danny grins at me. "I didn't really read it."

This is how he gets away with so much. He acts like a complete jerk, but then he flashes a charming smile, throws around some wicked humor, and people give him a pass.

I glare at him. "The A is for Adultery, you jackass."

"Charlotte!" my mother gasps.

Danny makes a tsking noise, grabs a third muffin, and heads out of the kitchen. "I'll get the news van to leave," he calls as he goes.

Like he's the chief of police or something. He's lucky he doesn't get a fourth muffin to the temporal lobe.

I'm starving and I want one for myself, but my knuckles still sting from the first time I tried to take one. I wish Ben still lived at home. He'd be sneaking some up to my room, taking some of the edge out of my temper before I had to deal with my mother or my other brothers.

I suppose I should be glad that my father isn't home. He was fit to be tied last night.

My mother is at the sink, washing dishes with a vengeance.

I don't want to apologize. I didn't do anything wrong. They're all overreacting. Especially the news van sitting outside.

But she really *was* worried.

I reach out for the sponge and the glass bowl. "Here. I can do that."

For an instant, I don't think she's going to relinquish anything. Mom is a total rage-cleaner. But she hands me the sponge.

"Thanks," she says grudgingly.

The water is just this side of too hot, but I scrub away. "Why would they think I'm collaborating to harass Thomas?"

She slams a cabinet door. "I don't want to talk about this, Charlotte."

Well. Fine, then.

I scrub in silence for a bit, while she lays out ceramic ramekins and various other cooking instruments. The tension begins to leach out of the room, so I try again.

"What are you making?"

"Chicken pot pies. Your father is working a double shift. I'll take him one at lunchtime."

"I can take it."

"No, I'd like you to stay right here where your grandmother and I can keep an eye on you."

I scowl and scrub harder. I can rage-clean, too.

But half an hour later, she runs out of flour, and she tosses me her car keys.

"No comment!" she yells at me as I'm pulling my thong sandals onto my feet.

"I know," I yell back. But maybe Danny worked some sorcery, because the news van *is* gone.

The grocery store is packed. Mom likes to do her regular shopping at the Super Giant closer to the main part of town, but I don't feel like driving twenty-five minutes for flour. Lauder's pretends to be a full-sized store, but it's really a mom-and pop type deal. Their bakery is to die for. Sunday morning, after-church shoppers crowd the aisles. More than one baby is fussing in a cart, ready to go home for a nap.

Even though I only have one item and can go through the express lane, three other people are still ahead of me. I put the flour under my arm and pull out my phone to check for texts, but Nicole is working at the library this morning, and Mrs. Kemper gets on her case if she's texting while she's supposed to be shelving books.

Because of the crowd and the noise, I don't recognize the commotion to my left until the guy in front of me makes a comment about it. "You think they caught this kid shoplifting?"

I glance over. The store manager is standing behind the service desk, her arms folded over her chest. One of the bag boys is blocking my view of whoever she's talking to. Another employee is blocking whoever-it-is from the other side.

The manager points at the store entrance. I can't hear her over the general cacophony, but it's pretty clear that she says, "Go."

A hand slaps a piece of paper down on the counter in front of her. A male voice, tight with irritation, carries over the din. "This is the third place I've gone that won't take an application. Haven't any of you heard of due process?"

Then he leans forward, and I see his profile. Thomas.

I stop breathing. He's wearing a baseball cap pulled low over his eyes, but it's definitely him.

The manager doesn't lower her hand. "Go," she says again, her tone loud enough for me to hear her now. "If you're refusing to leave the store, I'll be forced to call the authorities."

"Fine," he snaps. "*Fine.*" He picks up the piece of paper and rips it in half. The aggression in his motion doesn't match the almost preppy outfit he's wearing, a red polo shirt with khaki pants.

The man in line in front of me shuffles forward, but he's

still watching the interaction, too. "That guy looks familiar," he says. "Does he look familiar to you?"

"Yeah," I say absently.

Other people are staring, too. I wonder how many people saw him on the news last night. The murder was big news, but no one knew Marie. Her son's involvement wasn't well known outside law enforcement circles.

Now it is.

Thomas storms past the line of registers and barely waits for the automatic doors to give way. People give him a wide berth.

The entire interaction is somehow infuriating and pathetic and disappointing, all at once.

I look at the gentleman in front of me. He's a typical local: plaid shirt, sagging skin, gray hair. I thrust a five dollar bill at him. "Would you mind paying for my flour? I've gotta go."

"Wait—you can't—"

"Thanks!" I call, already jogging through the electronic doors myself.

I look around, blinking eyes that are blinded in the sudden sunlight.

He's gone. I don't know what kind of car he drives, and everything around looks like a mom-mobile or a late model pickup truck. My lungs are sucking in oxygen like I've run a race.

I don't know what I'd do if I found him. I don't even know what I'm doing out here.

There is absolutely no chance that he wants to see me.

How did he get out of here so fast?

My car has only been sitting in the sun for ten minutes, but it's already baking inside. I fling the flour on the passenger seat and crank up the air conditioning. Sweat blooms on my forehead, and I'm glad I went with the cotton sundress this morning.

I have this crazy urge to apologize. Danny made things bad, my other brothers made it worse, and now the local news has their teeth in it. I'm surprised there's no news van in the store parking lot.

I'll find a job. Get a place of my own.

If he can't do the first, he definitely can't do the second.

I pull out onto the main road, and I almost miss the flash of red in the woods to my right. There he is, walking along just inside the tree line.

What is he *doing?*

Before I think about it too hard, I pull over onto the shoulder. Road grit crunches underfoot, then dried grass. He hasn't noticed me. His steps are full of rage.

I don't want to leave the car. All I need is for someone to report that my car was abandoned on the side of the road.

"Hey!" I call.

He spins, startled, and looks up at me.

Surprise lights his face for a brief moment, but then it shuts down. He turns around and starts walking again. "Go away," he calls back.

"Stop! Wait."

"Your brothers looking for another chance?"

I'm not entirely sure what that means. A car flies by, sending gravel spraying. Some hits my ankles. "My brothers aren't here."

"Good." He pulls a little farther into the woods.

"I'm trying to talk to you!"

"I'm glad you weren't hurt, but you've done enough, Charlotte."

The words aren't a smack in the face. They're a needle of guilt, sliding into my skin, injecting me with pain.

I tried to help, and now his situation is worse.

He's deeper in the woods now. He must know a shortcut to Stan's. All I can see are tiny glimpses of red as he walks.

I glance at the car, then back at the woods. After a moment's hesitation, I lock up the vehicle and jog down the grassy berm, nearly falling on my face.

A sundress and flip flops aren't the best clothes for traversing the woods in summertime, especially woods that don't often have humans plowing through them. My feet keep sinking into ground made soggy from last night's rain. The sun dried out the ground by the road, but here, under the shade of the trees, some mud still remains, mostly covered by underbrush. I've accumulated half a dozen scratches from brambles by the time I catch up to him.

He still doesn't stop. "I'm not looking at you," he says.

"You don't have to look at me." He's walking fast enough that I'm out of breath trying to keep up with him. I'm glad he's not treating me like a fragile flower, but I could do with a little less rage-walking. "I just need to talk to you."

He doesn't say anything.

"I'm sorry," I say. "Would you please stop and let me apologize?"

Still nothing.

"My brothers aren't trying to harass you. Whatever happened—that was my fault, okay? I didn't eat lunch, and then it was so hot . . . They're just protective."

Nothing.

"I'm *sorry*," I say again. I don't know why this is so important to me. I can't believe I'm chasing someone down for an apology. "I didn't mean to—"

The ground gives way. I stumble. Then fall. It's so sudden that I don't register the pain in my ankle as quickly as I feel the mud soak into my dress.

So yeah. This is not good.

Thomas has stopped, and he's looking at me, but he hasn't spoken, and he's breathing fast.

There's also a bruise across the right side of his jaw. That wasn't there yesterday.

I shift and try to right myself. My dress is high on my thighs, and he's getting a good look at my legs. In a second

I'll be full-on flashing him. There must have been a hole under the leaves.

Now the pain hits me. It's my ankle, it's my hip—and it's strong enough that I'm more than a little worried I've really injured myself. I try to move again and a whimper escapes my throat. Nausea hits me even harder, and for a terrifying moment, I'm sure I'm going to throw up.

I seem to have discovered a hidden talent for making a bad situation worse.

And OMG this hurts. I don't know if I can talk without crying.

Thomas swallows and looks around. His eyes are swimming with unease. He starts forward, but then seems to check himself.

"Are you okay?" he says, his voice very low.

He's afraid. He thinks this is another setup.

I feel so horrible I'd be totally all right with the ground swallowing me up right here. It's more than the pain. It's the situation. It's him. It's my role in his problems in the community.

It's the fact that I'll *never* be able to keep this from my parents now. I'll never be allowed to leave the house again.

I'm such an idiot.

Emotion crawls up my throat and finds my eyes. I put a hand to my eyes to stop the tears, but it's full of mud. I'm painting streaks of dirt down my cheeks.

At least the nausea seems to be abating.

"I'm sorry," I say again, my voice breathy and full of hitching almost-sobs. "I'm sorry. I should have left you alone. I just felt—" I choke and try to get it together again. I pull a forearm across my eyes and drag the tears away.

More mud is soaking into my dress. I can feel it. My left ankle throbs, pulsing pain up my leg. Even if I can get back to the car, I don't know if I'll be able to drive. There is no way to explain this. My mother will kill me.

Thomas is still standing there. Silent.

"Go away," I finally say. I bury my face in my hands. Mud is everywhere anyway. "Just go. I won't bother you anymore."

He sighs. Leaves and underbrush crunch under his feet. He's going. Good.

But a hand brushes my ankle, and his voice is very close, still very soft. "Can you stand?"

My hands slip down, enough so I can look at him. He's crouching in the leaves in front of me. I have to sniff. "I don't know."

He takes a breath, then glances around again. "If I help you?"

"No one is here," I say. "I'm alone. I promise."

"I think I've heard that before." But he reaches out, and before I'm ready for it, his hands are under my arms and he's lifting. I'm off-balance, braced against his chest, inhaling his scent.

"Good?" he says.

Very good.

Thank god there's mud on my cheeks, or he'd see me blushing for sure. I realize he's asking me about whether I can stand. I attempt to put some weight on the injured ankle.

Too much. It hurts. A lot. I whimper again and keep a grip on his shoulder.

His eyes flick at the trees around us. "Not good."

Then he sighs, stoops a bit, and before I figure out what he's doing, he's put my arm around his shoulders.

I hobble for a second, torn between falling on my butt again or clutching him more tightly. He doesn't tower over me or anything, but he's too tall for this. Or I'm too short, especially in flip-flops. I'm not going to be able to walk like this.

And I thought this was awkward before.

"This isn't going to work, is it?" he says.

I don't want to cry again, but I might anyway. "Just leave me here. Can I use your phone to call someone?"

He snorts. "One of the disadvantages of being a murder suspect is that they confiscate your phone for evidence."

Somehow I feel like that's my fault, too. "I'm such an idiot."

"You're not an idiot." But his tone suggests otherwise. I'm ready to snap back at him, but his shoulders drop as he stoops again, and suddenly I'm in his arms.

I nearly scream in surprise, but I bite it off. My hands grab his shoulders. "You can't carry me!"

"I'm pretty sure I already have." Only a bare hint of strain hides in his voice. He heads deeper into the woods, away from my car.

Immediately, I remember who he is, and why we're in this bizarre position at all. "Stop. Wait. Take me back to my car."

"Oh, so I can be seen carrying you out of the woods, covered in mud and wearing a torn dress? No, thank you. I've already heard the word 'rape' thrown at me once."

"What? *When?*"

"Yesterday." He pauses, and now he sounds like he wishes he hadn't brought this up. "Someone said something about a rape kit."

I'm speechless.

He glances down at me. "I'm assuming that didn't happen."

"No! I'm just—what exactly did they think happened?"

"They thought I killed you." His tone is flat now. "At least I guess that's why they hit me."

My eyes light on the mark on his face. "Someone *hit* you?"

"Your brother, I think."

"Danny?" I wonder if it was retaliation, for what happened beside the church.

He shakes his head. "Not him. It doesn't matter."

My hand flattens against his shoulder. "It *does* matter!" It wouldn't have been Ben, and Danny is the most likely suspect. Matt? He's not violent. He would have had to be pushed past a limit.

Ben's words echo in my head. *When he carried you out of the woods—we thought he was carrying a dead body.*

Thomas just walks silently, not offering more information. The bruise on his face is a glaring reminder that a few stupid mistakes on my part led him down a more dangerous road than the one he walked yesterday.

I swallow. "Where are you taking me?" I ask quietly.

"Back to Stan's. He can drive you home." The baseball cap keeps Thomas's eyes in shadow, but they glint with light from somewhere. He gives me a wicked smile. "You can make up your own story about how he found you that way."

I wonder if Stan driving me home would be better or worse than me driving myself.

The muddy dress is going to be the tough part.

"I'm sorry I came after you," I say.

He snorts. "I'll bet."

"No. I meant—"

"I know." His expression sobers. "I know what you meant."

"And I really didn't set you up. At the funeral."

"I really didn't think you did." He boosts me higher, adjusting the arm carrying my legs.

"I'm too heavy," I say. "Put me down."

His eyes flick to mine, then away. "You're fine."

There's a light sheen of sweat on his forehead. He's not breathing hard, and he's speaking easily, but I know he won't be able to keep carrying me forever.

Part of me likes it.

Part of me knows this is a bad idea.

If he's strong enough to do this, he's strong enough to do a lot of other things.

Like strangle someone.

Fear is a quiet friend, sneaking up to slip its fingers between mine.

"It's a thousand degrees out," I say.

"I hadn't noticed." His voice is dry.

"Maybe you should put me down." My voice is careful. Like yesterday, no one knows I'm here. Once again, I'm completely vulnerable and at his mercy. "I'll figure something else out."

Just when I'm worried that he's going to refuse, he gently lowers my legs to the ground. He holds onto my arms, though, making sure I'm not going to fall.

"Do you want me to let you go?" he says.

Yes. No. I don't know. I wet my lips and have no idea what to say.

His hands don't move, but he looks up at the sky as if searching for answers. "Everything is upside down," he says.

I wait for him to elaborate, but he doesn't. "I don't know what you mean."

His eyes return to mine. "This," he says, as if that explains everything. "All of *this*."

"Much clearer."

He lets go of me to press the heel of one hand to his forehead. "I've never had an entire town hate me. I've never been so . . . alone." He says it matter-of-factly, not self-pitying at all. The words aren't empty, though. For an instant, the emotion in his gaze is so potent that it feels like it might leach into me and start a round of tears again. His eyes hold mine, and his voice is quiet and low. "I've never given a girl a reason to be afraid of me."

He sounds so earnest, so wounded. All at once, I want to beg him to pick me up again. Nicole would be a melted puddle on the ground.

I'm not afraid of you, I think. And it's almost true.

Whatever I feel, it's definitely not the same automatic revulsion that everyone else in town seems to feel.

Quite the opposite, in fact.

"What do you want, Charlotte?" he says.

He's so close, we could dance. We could kiss. A few inches of motion could turn his grip on my arms into an embrace.

Or an assault.

The thought hits me so suddenly that I almost stumble away from him.

He must read it in my face, because his expression shuts down. "I'll take you back to your car." It sounds like he's biting the words out. "Or you can wait here while I go back to Stan's. Whatever. Just tell me what you want."

I shake my head. "No. Stop. I didn't mean—"

"What?" he says, his tone cruel. "What *didn't you mean* this time?"

Those words are the slap in the face.

I had no idea you could be attracted to, afraid of, and irritated by the same person, all within a three-minute period.

"Go away," I snap. "Just go away. I'm sorry I tried to be kind to you."

He deflates like I've poked him with a straight pin. The fight goes right out of him. He shakes his head and his face twists. "You're right," he says. "I told you I don't have any idea how to do this. You and Stan are the only two people who'll give me the time of day, and I'm wasting time being shitty with you both."

"I'm pretty sure if you got shitty with anyone else, you'd end up in a jail cell again."

"Exactly." He takes a deep breath. He looks aggrieved. "I'm sorry. I didn't mean to drag you into the middle of the woods. If someone sees me, they see me. I'll help you back to your car."

"No." I swallow. I might have played a part in his trips to the police station yesterday, but I'm not playing a role in another one today. "You can take me home with you."

His eyebrows go up, and I wince at the double entendre. "I mean. Um. You can take me back to Stan's."

"Can you walk at all?"

I try to put weight on my ankle. It feels like I'm stepping in fire.

I can't ask him to carry me. It's too awkward. I bite back the pain and try to take another step.

"Don't be a hero," he says.

And then, before I can say another word, I'm in his arms again.

CHAPTER NINE

THOMAS

So here's the irony of this whole situation. I used to think I could read people. Mom always warned me I'd grow up and find myself in messes I couldn't charm myself out of. She said that's what happened to my father—which made me hate the comparison. I've never been a troublemaker, but I'm pretty good at reading people and figuring out what makes them tick.

Or at least I used to be. Forgot to study for a test at school? I could tell the teacher I was so busy working because my mom couldn't afford the electric bill this month, and they'd give me another day. (Even though we always had enough money for the electric bill.) Didn't have lunch money? I could compliment the heavily made-up cafeteria lady on anything about her appearance, and then feign shock when my wallet turned up empty.

It wasn't just school, either. I worked nights at Best Buy, moving stock. If I showed up late, the manager never hassled me. Once I dropped the end of a big screen television, shattering the screen—something I'd seen a guy get fired for. My apology got a smile and a "Don't worry about it, kid."

Here? In this town? I'm a murderer.

No one trusts me.

No one will hire me.

Everyone hates me.

And Charlotte is afraid of me.

I wish I could hold her away from my body somehow. Her sundress isn't skimpy, but it's not Puritanical either, and my bare arm is under her bare legs, and I'm trying really hard not to think about that too much.

Stan's going to flip his frigging lid. I'm glad he's home, though. He can be a witness to the fact that I'm being a perfect gentleman.

I think about her warm body in my arms and almost wish he *wasn't* home.

My mother would be smacking me on the back of the head right about now.

Charlotte clears her throat, and I wonder if she's found the silence as awkward as I have. "My friend said she saw you on the news last night."

I nod. "Yeah. It was great. There was a news van in front of Stan's house this morning, too, but apparently the mayor was caught with his pants down somewhere, and they went chasing a better story."

"There was one in front of my house, too."

"What, your brothers didn't open fire on them?" She looks taken aback, and I sigh. The not-being-shitty thing still needs work. "Sorry."

"No. You're right. I'm not happy with them either."

"I'm sure they think they're being protective."

"More than they should be. Part of it is the diabetes, but I also think it goes along with the cop thing. You spend all day trying to keep citizens safe from stupid people, and it leaks into your personal life."

"Am I the stupid person in this scenario?"

She blushes and looks away. "I didn't mean it that way."

My grip is starting to slip, and I have to readjust her in my arms. She wasn't paying attention, and she catches my shoulders. A quick gasp escapes her lips.

"Sorry," I say.

"I'm too heavy."

"You're not. It's just hot and you're sweating."

The words come out like they're loaded with double-meaning. She's blushing harder now. She doesn't have a response to that.

But she's not shoving at me to put her down.

I can't decide if that's progress or not. She's not a potential girlfriend. I might as well just ask Stan to shoot me if that's what my brain is considering.

"How much farther?" she asks.

"Not much." I'm starting to feel it in my back and shoulders now, and I have to adjust her *again*. She doesn't ask me to put her down this time. I grunt. "Had to be the boonies. Mom couldn't marry some guy who lived in a major metropolis. I almost want to blame her for this."

As soon as the words are out of my mouth, I realize what I've said, and it's like someone punched me in the back. All the wind goes out of me. My feet stop, but I have to keep walking or I'm going to drop Charlotte.

I force my feet to move. My eyes feel hot, and I have to take a long breath to settle my voice. "I didn't mean that the way it sounded."

"I know."

I glance at her. "I just meant we wouldn't have been in the woods."

"It's okay."

It's not okay, but it's nice of her to say so. She *is* kind. I've only known her for a day, but she's probably one of the kindest people I've ever met.

Kinder than I deserve, for sure.

I clear my throat. "A city probably would have made this whole thing *more* likely." I grimace. "Not some little town where no one's ever been killed before."

She inhales quickly, but then doesn't say anything.

It was a loaded breath, though, like she was going to correct me. My eyes zero in on hers. "What?"

"It's nothing."

"You were going to say something."

Her face squinches up like she doesn't want to answer. "I'd like to plead the fifth."

I sigh. "You're one of two people who will speak to me, and now you're crossing yourself off the list."

"I just—" She hesitates, biting her lip. "It's not the first murder in this area."

"I was kidding. I'm sure someone was probably run over by a Model T back in nineteen-ten . . ."

"No, two years ago," she says. "Someone was killed two years ago."

She sounds like she wants to say something else, but she doesn't. Her voice is too hesitant to be referring to some convenience store holdup gone wrong.

"You make it sound like it's significant," I say.

"I'm not a police officer. I'm sure they've considered it."

"Can you stop talking *around* it and just tell me what happened?"

"A girl was strangled in her bed."

I almost drop her. She gasps and holds on.

She looks up at me, and her eyes are full of something like guilt, like maybe she feels bad for telling me this.

Or maybe she feels bad for not telling me earlier. I have no idea.

I don't know what to say. She's right—the cops have probably considered a connection. I don't exactly want to buy any of them a cup of coffee, but I feel fairly sure they're not completely incompetent.

"Is that all you know?" I finally ask.

She hesitates. "Pretty much. I knew the girl. She lived about twenty minutes from here. We took ballet together. But—she was a kid. She had just turned fifteen. Your mom—" Her face twists, and I know she doesn't want to say the wrong thing. "It was different."

"*How* different?"

She pulls away from me a little, and I realize I must sound fierce. I can't help it.

"How different?" I repeat, less harshly this time.

"I don't know," she says. "I don't know all the details. I heard it was a boyfriend or someone who knew her, but . . . it was never solved."

Stan would know. I can't believe he hasn't mentioned this to me. I wonder if it's deliberate. We found some solid ground last night, but maybe it was only solid to me. Maybe he's still playing everything close to the chest. This unravels my feelings about our entire conversation, especially how easily he deflected my questions about what he was doing that night.

I want to put my fist through a tree trunk.

Charlotte watches me, but she doesn't say anything. I can almost feel her pulse pounding through her body, and it's a touch too fast.

She's still afraid of me.

She's not asking me to put her down, so I keep walking.

"Don't tell me," I say. "I should start lining up an alibi for that murder, too."

"I didn't mean to bring it up," she says. "I thought—I thought you knew—"

I shake my head. "I don't know anything anymore, Charlotte. Not a damn thing."

We've come to the tree line behind Stan's house, and before I walk out of the woods, I check the driveway for any sign of a news van. All clear.

Also absent: Stan's car.

"Shit." I ease her feet to the ground and now I do slam my hand into a tree. "*Shit.*"

"What?"

"Stan's gone."

"You don't have a car?"

"If I had a car, you think I'd be walking through the woods to get to the grocery store?"

"Shit," she agrees, and the word doesn't sound right from

her mouth, like profanity is a new thing. Despite everything, that makes me smile. It takes a bite out of my tension.

"What?" she says.

"Nothing. What do you want to do?"

She looks at the house, and then back at the woods. It's taken us about fifteen minutes to walk here from there, and I can see her doing the math in her head.

"My mother doesn't know I was buying the flour at the local store," she says. "We don't usually shop there. But she might assume it. She needed me right back. I was hoping Stan could drive me home and I could make up some story about a flat tire and falling in the mud."

"You didn't have a flat tire."

She makes a face. "That, too."

"I could run back and stab it." I can't believe I'm suggesting this. I imagine the headline. *Local teen suspected of murder caught vandalizing car.*

Her face lights for a second, but then she sobers. "I think that would generate more questions. And I don't want anyone to see you." She heaves a big sigh. "Can we get out of the heat, at least?"

I hesitate. There's a part of me that doesn't want to bring her inside. It's ridiculous, especially when you consider that we've been alone in the woods all this time, and theoretically, there's nothing I could do to her in there that I couldn't do out here. But still. Taking her behind closed doors feels like a risk.

Her eyes light with understanding. "You don't trust me."

"That's not it." That's exactly it.

"It is. You don't trust me. You still think this is some kind of setup."

"Let's just say that I'd rather Stan not come home and find us alone together."

"We're alone together right now!"

I sigh. "We can sit on the porch."

I try to avoid being a complete asshole. I help her into one of Stan's cushioned patio chairs, and bring her a bag of ice and some Advil. Then I go inside to put on a clean shirt. Stan's air conditioning is a welcome reprieve, and I almost reconsider leaving her outside. The heat out there is oppressive, now that I'm out of it.

Then I remember her brothers arresting me at gunpoint, and I take my time.

Just when I'm feeling like an asshole again, I pour us each a glass of iced tea. I return to the porch and sit across the round glass table from her.

A good safe distance.

Charlotte has used the paper towel from around the ice bag to wipe her face clean and her hands as well. We sit there awkwardly for a minute. She doesn't seem afraid of me anymore—but maybe discovering that I don't trust *her* has somehow reassured her. Hard to be afraid of someone when you realize they're a little afraid of *you*.

Her eyes glance up after a moment. She gives me a hesitant smile. "My grandmother would have your head for wearing a hat at the table."

"I'm sure she'd have my head for a lot more than that." I pull the hat off, though, then ruffle my hair with my hand. I've never had a girl chastise my manners, but maybe she's right. "Sorry."

"I didn't mean—" She falters. "Now I feel like your moth—"

She stops. Grimaces. "Sorry."

We fall into silence again. I'm still mulling over the revelation about her ballet classmate. Is it significant? I need more details. I just don't have any idea.

Then I realize I might still be acting like a jerk. I clear my throat. "Can you drink that? It has sugar in it."

She takes a tiny sip. "It'll be okay."

"Do you need something to eat?"

Her eyes flash with anger. "Don't you start, too."

"Start?"

"I hate that, you know. I get enough people telling me how to dress, how to act, and especially when to eat. This is *my life*, okay? You don't need to protect me."

"Protect you? Five minutes ago you were afraid I was going to kill you."

Her eyes go wide, and her cheeks flush. "That's not—it's not—"

"Isn't it?"

She clamps her mouth shut. We sit there and stare at each other for another minute.

Finally, I have to say something. "I'm sorry about your friend."

She looks puzzled for a moment, then pieces it together. "No—she wasn't—we weren't friends. Not really. I just knew her."

"Oh."

"It was one of Ben's first cases. He'd know more."

"Who's Ben?"

"My brother. Another one."

Oh. I frown. I'm pretty sure Ben won't want to grab a soda and talk about the case.

"He's not like Danny, though," she rushes on. "He's my favorite brother. I could ask him."

"How exactly are you going to slip that into conversation?"

My tone is just a bit nasty, but I'm surprised when hers matches. "Maybe I could tell him while we're planning our next attempt to trap you alone with me."

I scowl. She scowls.

Finally, I say, "Do you want me to get the phone so you can call your mom? Or do you want me to call Stan?"

She sets her mouth in a line and shakes her head quickly. "Call Stan."

I get the cordless phone from the kitchen and call him. He picks up after two rings.

"Tom?"

"I need you to come home."

"Are you okay?"

"Sort of." I pause. "Charlotte Rooker is here."

"I'll be right back." He hangs up.

I stare at the phone.

"Did he just hang up on you?" she says.

"Yeah."

"He didn't even ask why I was here." She sounds incredulous.

"I'm pretty sure he didn't care why you were here."

"Are you going to be in trouble?"

It's such a foreign concept that I can't quite wrap my head around it. In trouble? Like, grounded? I'm eighteen. He's not my father. What is he going to do, send me to bed without my saffron rice? Take away the phone that the cops have already confiscated?

Stan is so stoic that I have a hard time imagining him doing anything like that. He'll probably take one look at both of us and tell Charlotte to get in the car. Then he might not mention it again until dinner, when it'll be an offhand, "So what exactly happened with Charlotte Rooker today?"

Then again, maybe I'm not thinking clearly. Stan's car comes flying up the long gravel driveway less than five minutes from when I called, and his police flashers are on. He slams the car door and strides across to the back porch. He takes one look at Charlotte's torn and muddy dress, and looks like he's about to call nine-one-one himself.

His voice, however, is level. "Tell me what happened."

I tell him. I start with the grocery store, and I end with the iced tea.

I leave out what Charlotte told me about the other murder. We'll be talking about that later.

His eyes turn to Charlotte. "Do you realize what kind of position you've put me in? What kind of a position you've put Thomas in?"

She glances between me and him, and her expression is frozen in some combination of contrite and irritated. "I'm sorry."

"Leave her alone," I tell him, even though he's right. "It was my idea to bring her here."

This is the first time I've seen him truly mad. "What do you want me to do, Tom? I'm trying to keep you out of jail, and you seem to want to walk right back in." He pulls his keys out of his pocket. "I'm taking you to the police station, Charlotte. Your father can drive you home."

Her face goes white. "No. Just take me back to my car—"

"No. I'd have him come here if I didn't think that would cause more problems." He looks at me. "You stay put. You hear me?"

"You don't have to be so hard on her—"

"This isn't hard, kid. You have no idea. Charlotte. Walk."

She hesitates. Glances at me.

I sigh. "She can't." I realize that maybe I've left out another detail. "I had to carry her here."

Now his face looks like thunder. "Go in the house, Tom."

"She didn't do anything—"

"Go in the house!"

I don't move. "Why?"

"Because I'm about to call her father, and I don't want you around when he gets here."

CHAPTER TEN

CHARLOTTE

Stan doesn't tell my father anything more than that I've had car trouble, I stumbled in a hole on the side of the road, and I'm sitting on his porch.

That means the story is going to have to come from me.

This sucks.

I don't know if this is a good thing or a bad thing, but my father doesn't roll up Stan's driveway in a police cruiser.

My brother Ben does.

He shakes hands with Stan, then puts his hands on his hips and looks at me with this whole condescending *what-are-we-gonna-do-with-you* look.

It's probably three thousand times kinder than the look my father is going to give me when he sees me, so I don't glare back. I shift to the edge of the chair. Despite the Advil and the ice, my ankle has blown up like a balloon.

Ben looks at it and gives a low whistle. "Dad said you might need to go back to the hospital. I thought he was being ironic."

"Don't just stand there," I snap, trying to keep my voice from descending into surly. "Help me up."

Ben pulls my arm around his shoulders and hauls me to my feet, letting me hop along on my good leg. It's as awkward as it would have been if Thomas had done the same thing, but at least we're on level ground, not navigating our way through underbrush.

As Ben gets me into the front seat, he says, "Dad told me where you left the car. How on earth did you get all the way here?"

I turn my head and look out the passenger side window. "I'm pretty sure you don't want to know."

"I'm pretty sure you need to tell me. Buckle your seatbelt." He starts the ignition, but I know from experience that he won't put the car into gear until I'm buckled in. I heave a sigh and drag the nylon strap across my chest. My ankle is throbbing, and now I'm completely irritated.

Gravel crunches under the car as we pull down the driveway. Ben's police radio chirps updates intermittently. I know most of the codes, just from living with it for so long, but I don't know all of them.

"You're not talking," he says as we pull onto the road. He glances over.

I purse my lips and keep my eyes locked on the window.

His radio squawks at him. "Car eight-one-two, what's your status?"

I glance over, and Ben picks up the microphone to speak into it. "Suspect in custody. En route to Southern Maryland Hospital Center. Over."

"Ha ha," I say. "Just take me to the station."

"Your ankle could double for a wiffle-ball bat. You're getting an X-ray."

"Ben—"

He snaps his fingers and points at me. "Talk. Tell me what happened. Then we can smooth it over for Dad."

I hate being ordered around. I glare at him. "Did one of you punch Thomas? That's a detail you left out yesterday."

"You might remember that he knocked Danny on the ground yesterday."

"That's different. Danny was—he was—"

"Yeah? Danny was what? Trying to keep a murderer away from you?"

"*He is not a murderer!*" I'm seething now. "You shouldn't have hit him."

"No kidding. I think that's the whole reason they were able to get a harassment complaint to stick." His radio squawks again, and he flips a dial to turn the volume down.

Shock steals my voice for a moment. "It was you? You hit him?"

His eyes don't leave the road. "No. It was Matt."

Wow.

Ben glances my way. "I think he wanted to take the kid's head off. He's lucky he doesn't have a broken jaw."

I don't have anything to say to that.

Ben taps me on the back of the head, a total brother move. His voice, however, is gentle. "We care about you, little sis. That was—I don't ever want to see you like that again."

He means it. I can hear the love in his voice.

"Come on," he says, his tone cajoling now. "What happened with the car?"

I study the array of controls on the dashboard. My voice comes out very small. "You'll think I'm an idiot."

"*Talk.*" Ben's photograph could be used in a Wikipedia entry about kindness, but he has a limit. I've hit it.

I sigh. "Thomas was trying to get a job at Lauders. They wouldn't even let him fill out an application. They practically chased him out of the store."

He doesn't say anything to that, and I don't offer more. Trees and houses fly by.

"*And . . .*" he prompts.

"And I felt bad."

"And?"

"And nothing. I felt bad. I followed him."

Ben doesn't explode the way Danny would. He doesn't lecture the way Matt would. He just gets quiet for a mile or two. "That's a little nuts, Char."

"I know. But some of it's my fault. I started it at the funeral—"

"Your *fault*? Are you crazy? None of this is your fault. That guy might have *killed his mother*, Charlotte. Do you have any idea what it sounds like when you tell me you followed him? That you were *alone* with him?" He hits the steering wheel, in a very un-Ben-like show of frustration. "I want to drive you home and put a lock on your bedroom door."

My father might actually do that. "Thomas didn't hurt me."

Ben flinches a little at the use of his name. "It doesn't help your case that I practically had to carry you to the car."

"He *actually* had to carry me through the woods. He had plenty of opportunity, and he didn't hurt me."

Ben draws a tight breath, and he glances over at me again. His eyes take in the mud, the torn dress. He's seeing me with new eyes, and he's drawing the wrong conclusions.

He clinches it when he says, "Forget what I said. There's no way to smooth this over with Dad. I didn't realize you were with that guy in the woods. I didn't know he *touched you*. I don't know what I thought happened—I don't know what you're thinking anymore, Charlotte. I don't know—"

"I don't know why you all think I'm some wispy little thing who needs to be protected! He's never done anything to anyone here!"

"Do you even hear what you're saying?"

"He just lost his mother, Ben."

"Little sister, you are out of your head."

I fold my arms across my chest. The worst part is that I know he's right. Sitting here now, repeating the events in my brain, I know he's right. If Nicole were telling me about how she followed an accused murderer through the woods, I'd go ballistic. I can't even defend myself. What am I going to say? *Come on, Ben, he doesn't* seem *guilty.*

Because, you know, cops have never heard that before.

"Are you sure he didn't slip you something?" Ben says.

"What about yesterday? The tox screen came back negative, but—"

"Of course not!" I snap. "He didn't even give me the glass of iced tea until he was calling Stan to come home."

"You accepted a *drink* from him? I swear to god, Charlotte—"

"Enough! Okay?" I hear the worry through his words, and my voice breaks. I can only imagine what my mother will sound like. "Enough."

You accepted a drink from him.

Ben is right. At the same time, even though my actions were stupid, they don't feel *wrong*. Even when Thomas got angry, I didn't feel like he was going to throw me to the ground and bash my head in with a rock—and he was obviously strong enough for it.

"I'm sorry," Ben eventually says. His voice is hollow. "You're my sister. I can't . . . I don't want you to get hurt. That could have been a very different call we got. Especially after yesterday. You know?"

I swallow. "I know."

"I got a call like that once before. That was bad enough."

Lilly Mauta. The girl who was strangled.

He finally turns onto the highway, and the thrum of road noise fills the car. He doesn't have lights or siren on, but people get out of our way, and he flies in the left lane. Sometimes it's great riding in a police car.

I fidget, picking at a line in the upholstery. "Are you sure there's no connection between that murder and this one?"

He looks at me. "Yeah."

"Yeah?"

"*Yeah.*"

I let that sit there for a while, but I have to pick at it. "How can you be sure? You never caught the guy."

"You don't want details."

"Actually, I think I do."

"Fine. I don't want to *give* you details."

"There are two strangulations within thirty miles of each other, and you don't think there's a *possibility* that it could be the same person?"

"I'm not doing this."

Ben's practically a saint, but he's a stubborn one. I punch him in the shoulder. "Come on."

"Come on, what? I'm not a detective. All I know is what I saw when I found her."

"And you don't remember."

"No. I remember all of it." He sounds haunted, and I wonder if memories invade his dreams. "Too much of it."

I can't needle him now. I won't be cruel to him. I turn my eyes back to the window.

After a while, he clears his throat and speaks into the silence. "With Lilly Mauta . . . it looked like a boyfriend."

His tone is level and even, his cop voice. Detached but not emotionless. The voice he uses to read Miranda rights or deliver bad news.

He glances over, as if to make sure I'm still listening. "Her parents had never seen her with anyone, but there were emails indicating she'd had a secret relationship. We interviewed one guy from the local community college whose name matched the emails, but he didn't even know her, and we couldn't trace the email account as belonging to him. Her house had an alarm system, and she'd disabled it to allow someone inside. There were no defensive wounds. We found a used condom in her trash can. It was done with a belt pressed over her throat. Honestly, Char, it's like she lay there and let someone do that to her. Or maybe it was an accident. Some people do crazy things when they're chasing a thrill. Maybe the guy realized she wasn't breathing anymore, and he panicked and ran."

Part of me wishes he could suck those words back into his mouth. I don't want to know all these details about the shy, innocent girl who used to *plie* next to me at the barre. "She wasn't even sixteen."

"Not like that matters nowadays."

"It matters to *me*."

He gives me that condescending look again. I've seen it from all of my brothers. *We know more about the world than you do, little girl.*

I hate that look.

I hate that it's true.

"I'm assuming Marie Bellweather's murder wasn't anything like that."

"No. She fought like hell." His voice is still dispassionate. "It was done with rope. No evidence of . . . any other activity."

"Did you get anything from under her fingernails?"

"A lot of clothing fibers. No skin."

Aha! "Did they match what Thomas was wearing?"

"No."

I brighten. "So that means—"

"That means the killer could have ditched his clothes before calling nine-one-one. Or he could have worn cloth gloves—also easy to get rid of. We're not amateurs, Charlotte."

"Do you have *any* evidence that Thomas did this? Any at all?"

"I'm not a detective on the case. And even if I were, I probably wouldn't be allowed to tell you."

"They can't have much, or he'd be in custody."

Ben doesn't say anything to that, which means I'm probably right.

He glances over, and from his expression, I can tell he regrets this whole conversation. "Don't tell Dad I told you all of that. He wouldn't like it."

"Don't tell Dad I let Thomas carry me through the woods."

He scowls. But then he says, "Deal."

We fall into silence for the longest time.

"You're a good brother," I say eventually. "I'm sorry I scared you."

He reaches over and shakes my shoulder. "I'm glad you're okay."

"I'm just trying to give you a lot of practice for when you have three kids like Matt."

"Stop it. You're scaring me again."

I grin, glad the tension between us is dissipating. Ben always says he's more than happy to be an uncle forever, but he loves kids, and he's great with them. Danny will go home with anyone in a skirt, but Ben isn't like that. He gets enough attention thanks to his boy-next-door curly hair and brown eyes, and the badge and the uniform don't hurt, but Ben always says he's waiting for lightning to strike.

He made fun of my hormones at the funeral, but he's really the closet romantic.

"You know you'll meet the right girl, and you'll have three times as many."

He snorts. "I'm about to drive this car off the road."

"You don't want nine kids?" I tease.

"I'll just keep letting Matt have enough to share." He glances over at me. "Please promise me you're not going to pull a stunt like this again."

I sober. "I promise."

"Really, Char."

"Really. I promise. I won't go near him again."

"Dad won't send me next time."

"There won't *be* a next time."

We pass a sign for the hospital, and he flicks on his turn signal. "There better not be. I wasn't kidding about bolting your bedroom door shut."

"I wish people would stop treating me like it's nineteen-fifty."

"Maybe you could save that attitude for *after* I have to carry you into the hospital, ma'am."

"You mean you're not going to haul me in there in hand-cuffs?"

Ben pulls into a parking place reserved specifically for police officers. He gives me a grin and reaches out to chuck me on the chin. "I'll save that disgrace for next week."

CHAPTER ELEVEN
THOMAS

Four days have passed since I carried Charlotte through the woods.

Four days have passed since Stan and I had an epic argument about a murder I know nothing about, a murder he declared was *nothing like this one, Tom*.

Four days have passed since we formed an uneasy truce, and now we're living like roommates who don't have much to say to each other. The words *stir crazy* are taking on new meaning. I'm about ready to commit a crime just so I can look at four new walls.

I've pulled out my sketchbooks and my pencils for the first time since she died, but I stare at white paper and nothing happens. My thoughts won't settle enough for art. I stare at blank space, and my brain fills it with garish images. My mother in her bed. Bruises on her neck. Bulging eyes.

I could draw it, but it's bad enough seeing it in my head.

I wish I didn't remember her that way.

I try to think of her at other moments. Pushing my hair back from my forehead, telling me to get a haircut. Sitting in the kitchen in the early morning silence, nursing a cup of coffee while she read the paper. Dancing to terrible eighties music while she cooked Hamburger Helper.

Every image morphs into her final one.

I ended up putting my sketchbooks away.

At least in jail there would be someone to talk to. Without my phone, I don't have anyone's number—and I sure as hell never thought anyone back home would need Stan's. Stan told me not to post anything online, not even in a private message, because it could be used against me.

"Think about it, Tom," he said. "You make a joke or talk about anything nonserious, and it looks like you're not mourning your mother. You say something appropriate, showing how much you miss her? It's a calculated statement by someone capable of murder. Either way, you lose. I can't stop you from contacting your friends, but know that a prosecutor is going to interview anyone you talk to, and you can't control what they say."

It was enough to keep me off social media, but it's been weeks since she died, and it's either this or I go steal a car.

I log onto Facebook. I have to use Stan's desktop because my laptop is sitting in an evidence room somewhere. His computer isn't what you'd call state-of-the-art, and it takes a bit of time to load the webpage. I don't have many messages. I can't decide whether that's a surprise or not. I don't click on any of them, because I don't want anyone to see the little message confirming that I've read them.

Instead, I click on my notifications.

A lot of people have heard about Mom. A lot of people have posted on my wall. Even more people have tagged me in their own statuses. There are dozens of comments. I don't even *know* half of these people.

Some are sympathetic.

Some think I did it.

I always knew there was something sinister hiding under that perfect exterior.

Sinister? Perfect?

I frown and click the next one.

Have you ever seen the way Thomas Bellweather *watches people? Is anyone really surprised?*

Why the hell would someone tag me in that kind of status? I don't even *know* this girl, and she's going to talk about me watching people?

It takes every ounce of self-restraint I possess to keep from telling all of them to go straight to hell.

The next one punches me right in the gut.

Marie Bellweather was a beautiful, kind, and caring woman. She deserved a better son.

I jerk out of the chair so I don't throw the entire computer to the ground. The words are imprinted on the inside of my eyeballs.

She deserved a better son.

A better son. She deserved a better son.

I run my hands through my hair. My chest is caving in, and my eyes burn. The problem is that I agree. A better son would have been able to stop it.

For some reason, I thought I could somehow escape this mess and return to my old life.

I never considered that people from my old life would blame me just as much as the people here, who've never known me.

I think back to the funeral, how Mom's two friends couldn't get time off.

Was that it, or were they avoiding me?

I can't sit back down at the computer. I can't look at those words anymore. At the same time, I can't leave them on the screen, especially not for Stan to find.

I close the browser. Then I reopen it and delete the history. I don't know how savvy Stan is, but I don't need any questions.

Then I click the buttons to shut the damn thing down. The computer's fan slows and eventually stops.

The house falls into an absolute silence. For the time being, even the air conditioning isn't running. My breathing sounds loud and just a little nuts.

I'm walking before I know it. Stan never said I had to stay in the house.

I could cut through the woods and head east to get to the local grocery store, which is attached to a pretty basic strip mall. There's a Dunkin' Donuts, a bank, and a dry cleaner. Last time I headed that way, the grocery store manager chased me out of the store, and I'm not looking for a repeat performance.

I'm also doing my best to avoid Charlotte Rooker, because I think Stan will lock me up in a jail cell himself if he catches me with her again.

Guilt flicks me in the neck. I haven't asked how she's doing, how her leg injury turned out. Stan might not even know, but I can imagine how the conversation would go.

Hey, Stan, have you heard how Charlotte is doing?

Hey, Tom, hold still while I shoot you.

I have no idea what I'll find if I head west, but I'm not after anything in particular. Maybe I'll stumble onto a highway and an eighteen-wheeler will put me out of my misery.

Today's heat comes packed with a wallop of humidity. I'm wearing shorts and a T-shirt, but after three minutes in this weather, I feel like I swam a few laps in a pool and then got dressed without drying off. The trees offer some shade, but I might as well be walking in full-on sunlight.

Cars zoom along asphalt nearby, so I must be close to something. After a few more minutes of walking, I spot bricks. A building. Then a mostly empty parking lot. A few shrubs and flowers wilting in the heat.

A sign announces that I've arrived at the Garretts Mill Community Library.

Okay, seriously. I didn't expect to stumble into a rave, but surely fate could have offered up something a little more exciting than a *library*. They don't even serve food.

I sigh. Maybe I can get a card and some books to pass the time.

The air conditioning is such a relief that I want to hug the security posts just inside the front doors. This isn't a large library, but there's a small bank of computers off to the right, just past the circulation desk, and two older women are sitting across from each other, clacking at the keys. The center area sports four round tables, but only one is occupied. A young mother is reading to a young girl with pigtails who has absolutely no interest in being read to.

Bookshelves line all the walls of the room, with evenly spaced aisles leading to the exterior walls. Someone is shelving books off to the left, but I can only see the motion of the cart; the person is hidden by the stacks. The place smells like old paper and coffee and copy machine toner. I feel like I've stepped back in time about ten years.

The best part is that no one notices me. No one cares that I'm here. No one throws me out.

Maybe this place isn't so bad after all.

I walk up to the circulation desk. There's a little sign that says, "Ring bell for service."

There's no bell.

I stare at the sign for a moment too long. The heat has made my brain slow. *The sign says to ring a bell. There is no bell. Does not compute. Abort. Abort.*

A girl brushes past me and ducks beneath the counter to pop up again on the other side. She's blond and brown-eyed and a bit breathless. She's short and rail thin, with few curves to speak of. The only thing that keeps her from looking boyish is the waist-length hair and the fluorescent pink glasses. She'd be a piece of cake to draw, full of lines, with big round eyes like an anime character.

"Sorry," she says quietly. "It was slow so Carla went out to grab lunch."

I have no idea who Carla is. "There wasn't a bell," I say, like an idiot.

"Yeah, people complained about the noise so we took it away."

Yet they left the sign. Okay.

She smiles. "I know. The sign." She heaves a sigh and rolls her eyes, and then, I could swear she's batting her lashes at me. After my reception over the last two weeks, I've forgotten what it's like to have a girl flirt. Now I'm full of suspicion, and I'm going to look like a shady creeper.

"Trust me," she says, "I told them to get rid of it, but you have to file forms in triplicate to get anything done around here. Can you believe they said, 'How will people know they have to wait if there's no sign?'" She holds her arms out to indicate the space around her. "Like people wouldn't know they have to wait *if there's no one standing behind the counter.*"

She's animated and larger than life, and on someone so tiny, her attitude is almost comical. I smile before I can help it.

"So." She leans forward, folding her arms against the counter and giving herself the tiniest hint of a chest. "What can I do for you?"

I keep my voice low. "I think I need a library card."

She brightens, then pulls a clipboard out from under the counter. "You're going to have to give me your name and number first." She clears her throat and spins a pen between her fingers, and now she's *definitely* flirting. "For official purposes only."

I freeze. *My name.*

Of course she needs my name. What did I expect, that they'd just hand me a library card, like it's a grocery store membership or something?

Maybe I can give her a fake one. Is she going to ask for ID?

She's peering at me curiously now. The pen has gone still in her fingers. I've taken too long to answer.

I pull the hat lower on my forehead and look down at the form.

Name. Address. Phone number. Driver's license number.

This is never going to work. She's going to tell me to get out of here as soon as she hears my name.

"Wait a minute," she says slowly. "Wait. You're . . ."

"Forget it," I say bitterly. "I'll go."

She whistles softly through her teeth. "No wonder Charlotte sprained her ankle running after you."

There's not much that would keep me at this counter, but that does the trick. "You know Charlotte."

"Intimately." Then she makes a face. "I mean, not *intimately* intimately. We're not that close. But maybe if we're still single when we're thirty."

I can't decide if I like this girl or if she makes my head hurt. "She didn't break it, then?"

"Break what?"

"Her ankle."

"Oh! No. Char's family might want her to end up barefoot and pregnant, but she's tough as nails. It's a pretty bad sprain, so she's on crutches, but she got away with an ace bandage and a Velcro boot." She bats her eyes at me again. "Did you really carry her for five miles through the woods?"

I cough. "Ah . . . no. It wasn't anywhere near five—I'm sorry, who are you?"

She holds out a hand. "Nicole Kerrigan. Library page and best friend extraordinaire."

Her hand is tiny, and it's like shaking hands with a doll. "Thomas Bellweather." I hesitate. What do I say? Unemployed and friendless? I sigh. "Social pariah."

"Yeah, she said you weren't having any luck finding a job."

My eyebrows go up. Charlotte talked about me? "She did?"

"Yes. Is that why you're here? You should have told me you wanted an application."

I can't keep up with her. "Wait. An application? For what?"

She holds up her index finger, then slowly rotates it to point to her left. "Um. The job."

Right there on the counter, to the left of the sign about the bell, is a neon yellow piece of paper in an acrylic holder, declaring, "NOW HIRING. Technical Assistant. Part time. Flexible hours."

I frown.

Nicole ducks and pulls another clipboard out from under the counter. She slides it across to me. This one is an employment application. "Fill it out. Old lady Kemper hasn't been able to get anyone to apply for three weeks, and I think she's going to make me teach her to use a computer if we don't fill it soon."

I look at it, but I don't move.

"Please fill it out," she says in a low whisper. "The last time I tried to show her something, she thought she could speak into the mouse."

I pick up the pen, but still, I hesitate.

"What's the problem?" says Nicole. "Too good for the library?"

"No." Maybe.

I know beggars can't be choosers, but this doesn't seem like the kind of place where I can make enough money to eventually move out of Stan's place.

She shrugs and pulls the application back. "Suit yourself."

I slap my hand down on the clipboard and the sound rings throughout the library. "Stop. I'll fill it out." I start writing.

She watches me, and I sigh.

"This feels like a waste of time," I eventually say.

"Why?"

Maybe it's her talkative nature, but I find myself saying more to her than usual. I keep my eyes on the paper and try to keep any hint of self-pity out of my voice. It's more of a challenge than I expect it to be. "Because no one in this town is going to hire me."

"I find it hard to believe that any straight woman with eyes *wouldn't* hire you, but maybe that's just me."

That startles me into looking up. I'm not shy, but I've never met someone quite *this* forward.

Her expression is bold, and she's waiting for me to fire

back. I keep thinking of what Stan said, about how anything could be used against me. I don't know how to act, so I keep my mouth shut.

I glance around the library again. The mother with the little girl has poured some snacks onto the wooden table, and she's offering the kid a sippy cup. There's a huge sign over her head that says, KEEP OUR LIBRARY CLEAN: NO FOOD OR DRINK ALLOWED. Maybe she didn't see it. Or more likely, she doesn't give a crap.

The mother looks up and catches my eye. I quickly look back at the application before she can figure out who I am.

"Don't worry," Nicole says. "Molly didn't recognize you."

"Molly?"

"The lady with the kid."

Am I that obvious? "I've been locked in the house for days. They keep running my picture on the news. Everyone here seems to think I'm a murderer."

"I don't know about *everyone*, but Charlotte doesn't. She's my best friend. I trust her judgment."

This girl is a complete stranger, and she believes I'm innocent. Friends from back home are speculating that I did it all over Facebook. In a flash, I wonder if that will work against me. I imagine Ryan Jandy, a guy I worked with at Best Buy, sitting on the stand at a trial, telling them about how I always seemed like the type to keep a few dark secrets.

I bend over the application again, filling in data because it's easy and it keeps me from having to speak.

Nicole hasn't moved. I want to ask if she's memorizing my social security number.

"I like your handwriting," she says.

"I'll pass that on to my elementary school teachers."

"Did you do it?"

My hand goes still. I look up and meet her eyes. The question is asked just as equably as everything else she's said, but there's no doubt about what she means.

Nicole is tough as nails, too. She doesn't flinch, and she

doesn't look away. It's a real question, and she wants a real answer.

"I was asleep," I say. I keep my voice soft so it doesn't waver. "I found her. After."

Her expression softens. "How horrible."

"It still . . . it doesn't feel real yet. Sometimes it's like I'm still waiting to wake up."

Her lips part with a soft gasp, and in a flash, I can see her as a single thirty-five-year-old woman, writing letters to convicted felons because she finds their mug shots sexy. I'm not entirely convinced that she wants me to be innocent. Something tells me she's more of the rehabilitation type. She doesn't know me, but if she took the witness stand, she'd probably say that she always knew I had a dark side, but I knew how to look for the light.

I look back at the application and fill out the rest of the boxes, then slide it back to her. I have to clear my throat. "Do you know when I should hear something?"

"Give me a minute." She yanks the form off the clipboard and walks to a closed door behind her. She knocks, but doesn't wait for an answer. "Hey, Mrs. Kemper. There's a guy here who wants the computer job."

A woman's voice calls back, "Did he fill out an application?"

"Yup."

"When can he start?"

Nicole raises her eyebrows at me.

I raise mine back at her. "Now?"

"Now," she calls back.

"He's hired. Send him back."

CHAPTER TWELVE

CHARLOTTE

I'm sitting at the kitchen table slicing the ends off of green beans when my phone lights up with a text message from Nicole.

NK: Guess who's going to be working with me?!

Knowing Nicole, it could be anyone. The president of the United States. The garbage man whose pants fell down in front of her house because his belt snapped. Brad Pitt. The guy who loads groceries at Lauders. Anyone.

I slide my fingers across the face of the phone.

CR: I give up.

She sends back a photo. She's obviously taken it surreptitiously, but she's lucky enough to have one of those newer phones, so it's pretty clear. I recognize Mrs. Kemper, the older librarian, but it takes me a moment to recognize the guy standing beside her, holding a stack of books.

Thomas.

It's a good thing I've stopped slicing beans, because I'd probably cut a finger clean off.

I text back as fast as I can.

CR: No way. How?

NK: He walked in and filled out an application!

CR: And Mrs. K hired him? Does she know who he is?

NK: Yes! And I have no idea if she knows! OMG Char he is
so ducking hot. If your fam is going to keep you chained up
in the tower, can I have him?

A hand touches the back of my head. "How are my two
favorite girls doing?"

I jump and squeal and my phone goes flying. My father
gives me a puzzled glance, then crosses the kitchen to kiss my
mother. She's peeling potatoes, but she kisses him back with
gusto without losing her rhythm.

They make me blush, but they're so in love that it's charming, too.

And here I am thinking about my crush on an alleged
murderer.

My father stoops to get my phone, and I can see another
text live on the screen. "It's okay!" I cry. "I can get it!"

He gives me another funny look before scooping it off the
floor. "I don't need you falling out of the chair, Charlotte."
He holds the phone out without looking at it.

Maybe I can stop acting like a complete and total freak.

"Thanks," I say.

He taps my exposed toes. "How's the ankle?"

My foot is up on the opposite kitchen chair, my toes
painted fluorescent pink with yellow polka dots. My grandmother complained that the pink was too bright for digni-
fied young ladies, which made me add the polka dots. I'm
also wearing the shortest shorts I own, just to spite her.

She hmphed at me. I'm freezing in the air conditioning,
but she can suck it.

"The ankle is fine," I say. My phone keeps buzzing with
messages, but I don't want to look, just in case Nicole is
sending more pictures of Thomas.

I really, really, really *want* to look, hoping she *is* sending
more pictures.

"Have you been keeping your weight off it?"

I nod quickly.

He frowns. "Why do you seem so keyed up?"

"I'm not keyed up!"

Okay, maybe I'm a little keyed up.

"She's been sitting here all afternoon," says Mom. She glances over her shoulder. "Did something happen with one of your friends, sweetie?"

"Yes. Yes!" My brain finally kicks into gear. "Nicole. Work stuff. They're hiring someone to put the books on a new computer system, and they've hired some gross pasty nerd who keeps wanting to talk to her about his theories on *Game of Thrones*."

My father takes a handful of green beans and heads out of the kitchen, sufficiently bored by the conversation. "I'm going to get out of this uniform."

"Those aren't washed yet!" I call.

"If these kill me, I'm ahead of the game," he yells back.

I unlock my phone so hastily that I almost fling it across the floor again. Nicole has sent me nine more messages. Nine! Almost all of them are some version of my name.

NK: You know I'm just kidding, right?

NK: Char.

NK: Charlotte.

NK: Charrrrrrlllllllllooooootttttttteeee.

NK: I hope you haven't fallen out of your chair.

NK: No, seriously.

NK: Char. Answer me. Char. I was kidding about taking him.

NK: Are you mad at me? Do you think I'm serious?

NK: I'm going to call your house in a sec. Char.

I almost have a panic attack at that last line. My fingers trip over the letters from typing so quickly.

CR: NO. OMG DO NOT CALL THE HOUSE.

She responds immediately.

NK: Finally! What's going on?

CR: My dad walked in. I dropped the phone. Worried you were sending more pictures.

NK: Want me to?

CR: YES.

OMG, I so didn't just type that. If she sends me another picture of him, I will die. Right here in this chair.

A picture comes through almost immediately. He's wearing a T-shirt and that baseball cap, and he's carrying enough books to make his biceps flex.

I don't die. I bite at my lip and just keep staring.

She sends another text.

NK: I expected him to be scary. He's not. He's . . . I don't know.

I know exactly what she means. My fingers fly across the letters.

CR: Intense.

NK: Yes. Intense.

Mom glances over, so I cut a few green beans and try to look bored. Another text comes through, and I grab the phone.

NK: I can see why people think he did it. He makes you think, you know?

CR: Yeah, Nic, I do know.

She doesn't respond for a little while, and I go back to slicing. Five minutes later, another picture comes through. He's surrounded by stacks of books, and he's got his hat off. He's wiping his forehead on his arm and stretching at the same time. Biceps, check. Hint of stomach, check. He is so sexy. I wish I could blow these up and tape them to my bedroom ceiling.

I feel like a creeper.

I don't care.

Then another text.

NK: OMG HE CAUGHT ME

It's horrible but I burst out laughing.

Mom turns around. "Something's funny?"

"Nicole is being ridiculous."

Mom is used to that, so she turns back to the sink.

Another text comes through.

NK: Hey.

Hey?

Then another text.

NK: How intense am I being right now?

It's him. He has her phone.

I choke on air. I cannot breathe.

HE HAS HER PHONE. And he's reading her texts.

This is awful. I need to die.

Is he mad? Or is he flirting?

Another text.

NK: Nicole said you didn't break your ankle. I'm glad. I've been worried about you.

I still can't breathe. He's been worried about me?

"Almost done with those green beans?" Mom says.

"Just about." I haphazardly cut a few more, then check my phone again.

Another message.

NK: Should I give her back the phone? I'm texting over my head, but I think she's going to climb my body to get it back in a second.

I giggle and text back.

CR: Knowing Nicole, she'll really do that.

NK: Your friend isn't subtle. I got the memo.

Once again, I'm not sure how to take that. Playful? Or irritated?

I can't believe I'm exchanging text messages with him.

The next message tells me Nicole has her phone back.

NK: OMG. Char. He took the phone. He saw everything we said.

CR: Thanks. I connected the dots.

NK: I. Am. Mortified.

I am too. A little bit.

But I'm also a little excited.

And a little nervous. He's working with Nicole.

I don't know how to categorize all of my emotions.

Mom puts a glass bowl on the table, and I quickly scoop all the green beans into it. She brings me some onions to slice, and a piece of bread to put in my mouth so I won't cry.

When she turns her back again, I spare a glance at my phone.

NK: Holy crap, Char. He just asked if you ever come to the library.

Holy crap! My fingers almost won't work.

CR: What did you tell him?!

NK: I told him you were bringing me lunch tomorrow.

CR: NICOLE!

NK: You're welcome. Just make sure to bring me something good.

★　★　★

The next day, I have the hardest time getting ready. I want to look nice, but not *too* nice. Mom will never believe I'm bringing Nicole lunch if I overdo it. They haven't mentioned Thomas since the day I followed him through the woods, but I'm not in any hurry to relive the lectures.

I go with a casual sundress and leave my hair loose and air-dried. I can put on mascara and lip gloss in the car. The crutches make me look less sexy and more pathetic, but there's nothing I can do about that. At least it's not my driving foot.

As it turns out, I didn't even have to worry. Mom is meeting friends for lunch and shopping, so she's already gone. Dad is working. Grandma is knitting or crocheting or sitting around having judgmental thoughts. I have no idea. The food is packed into an insulated bag, and with a little maneuvering, I can manage the bag, my purse, and the crutches, too.

My grandmother's voice catches me. "Where are you going, Charlotte?"

She's sitting on the couch in the living room, nowhere near the front door. I'm not even sure how she knows I'm leaving.

"I'm meeting Nicole for lunch," I call back.

"Come in here. Let me see what you're wearing."

I heave a sigh. "I really need to get going."

"You can spare a moment for courtesy. You didn't even tell me you were leaving, dear."

I set everything down except the crutches, then hobble back toward the living room. I was right on my first guess: knitting needles fly between her fingers, and pale green yarn trails into a basket by her feet.

She gives me an up-and-down, and her lips flatten into a thin line.

"What are you making?" I ask, not because I care, but maybe it will distract her from my perfectly decent outfit.

"Your father told me one of the secretaries at the station is having a baby," she says, fanning the start of a blanket out along her lap. It's quite lovely, actually, alternating shades of green and yellow. I drop the crutches against the arm of the sofa and reach out to touch the yarn. It's soft and velvety, and something about it is familiar.

"That's beautiful," I say.

"Thank you. People don't make things themselves anymore. Blankets always come in handy with little ones."

I keep stroking it between my fingers. "This feels so familiar to me. I must have had a blanket like this."

"Of course you did." She gives me a look as if it should be obvious. "Yours was green and lavender, though. Your mother didn't want anything *pink*. God forbid we treat you like a young lady."

"Sometimes I wish you all would treat me *less* like a young lady."

She frowns, but instead of looking cross, she looks disappointed. "There's nothing wrong with being a young lady, Charlotte. I don't understand young women nowadays, so eager to dispose of anything feminine."

"I'm wearing a dress!"

She points a knitting needle at me. "That's not what I mean, and you know it."

Wow, for a second there, it seemed like we might get along. "Well, I hate to rush out the door, but I've got to meet Nicole for lunch, and then I'm going to shoot a few rounds at the range with Ben. If there's time, Matt said I could stop by, and we could work on takedown holds for self-defense while I'm injured."

She *hmphs* and looks back at her knitting.

My hand is still on the blanket, the softness of the yarn sliding under my fingers. For an instant, I feel guilty for what I said.

Then I think about the pursed lips and the constant stream of criticism that flows from her mouth, and I'm totally over it.

When I get to the library, I park under a tree, a halfhearted attempt to keep some of the oppressive heat out. Once there, I sit in the car. My thoughts argue with themselves.

My parents would kill me if they knew what I was doing.

No! It's fine! I'm just bringing Nicole lunch! I've done it a dozen times before.

Someone might see me with him. But probably not. Nicole said he was working in the back, so maybe no one knows he works here. It's not like the library is a hotbed of activity in the middle of the summertime. People come to the Eastern Shore for the beaches, not the reading.

I think of that last picture she sent me, the one where his arms are flexed and a bit of his stomach is exposed. I think of the feel of his body against me, first in the cemetery, and then later, in the woods.

I'm having a lot of feminine thoughts right now. Grandma would be so proud.

The memory of Ben's voice cuts through my thoughts.

You've got to watch out for yourself, Charlotte.

My hand freezes on the door handle. Maybe I'm being stupid. I close my eyes and take a deep breath.

A hand knocks on my window, and I jump a mile. I almost hit the horn.

Thomas stands there, looking down at me. He's dressed in a T-shirt and jeans, but there's no ball cap today. His hair is just this side of messy, and he looks rakish and unruly and immeasurably sexy.

Shut up, Ben.

Shut up, Brain.

"Do you need some help?" he calls.

I open the door. "I think I can manage."

"You don't want me to carry you again?"

His voice is teasing, but there's an edge to it. Almost a dare.

Yeah, I want to say. *Carry me again.*

I duck my head so he won't see the flare of heat on my

cheeks, then reach for the bag of food. "If you can carry this, I think I can get the rest."

He takes the bag. "What's in here?"

"Lunch."

"Oh. I thought she meant you were rolling through Mc-Donald's or something."

He sounds disappointed. I spent hours preparing something that would taste good, look amazing, and still not make him think I was trying to impress him, and he's disappointed that it's not frigging *McDonald's*?

I try to snatch the bag out of his hands, but I'm not on my crutches yet, and I almost fall out of the car. I get one strap in my grip and yank. "Fine. I'll go back out."

He holds fast, and my yank pulls him close to me. He's leaning over me, blocking the sun. "You don't need to go back out. Cold cuts are fine."

Cold cuts! I huff before I can stop it.

He smiles, and it's a miracle I don't melt right out of the car. "You look like you want to hit me."

"Maybe a little."

"I'm just yanking your chain. Nicole told me you like to cook. She promised me it would be the best food I've ever tasted."

Part of me wants to kill Nicole. Another part wishes I'd spent another hour searching Pinterest for recipes. "Well, I'm glad she kept your expectations low."

"I don't think I can repeat *exactly* what she said. But it involved the word *orgasmic*."

Oh my god. I will *kill* her.

I reach for my crutches to give my face a chance to cool. I'm regretting the sundress now, because I'm sure my entire chest is flushed. He watches me carefully lever myself out of the car, and his face loses its teasing look.

"Are you still in pain?" he asks.

"Nah. I don't even need these. I just use them for sympathy."

"It's working."

"I'm really okay. I can put a little weight on my ankle, but the doctor said it would heal more quickly if I don't. I'd rather be safe than sorry."

He walks beside me as I crutch-swing my way across the parking lot. "I've been wondering about you since Stan sent me to my room." His voice is rueful. "He wouldn't even let me ask how you were."

"My parents read me the riot act and told me I wasn't allowed to associate with you."

"Stan said the same thing to me."

I stop and look at him. "And yet here we are."

He looks down at me, and I could fall into his eyes. "I work here."

I half shrug. "I'm just meeting my best friend for lunch."

He smiles and starts walking again.

When I get through the door, Thomas keeps walking, but I stop short and look around. Carla, one of the librarians, is shelving on the other side of the library. There's a shady looking guy at one of the computers, but otherwise, the place is empty. Nicole rushes out from behind the counter and all but tackles me.

"You came!" she cries. "I was worried you'd chicken out!"

"Subtle," I say.

Nicole hustles us into the back room. "Carla said she'll watch the desk while we eat."

I was worried that Mrs. Kemper would be back here, but we have the room to ourselves. Nicole has already gotten sodas from the machine for us, and there's a roll of paper towels in the middle of a folding table.

Thomas takes my crutches and sets them against the wall, while I begin pulling food out of the bag.

My hand stops on the sandwiches. I know he was kidding about McDonald's, but all of a sudden I'm self-conscious. Maybe this was a bad idea. He might hate everything. He might be disappointed that I don't have a bucket of fried chicken and potato salad or whatever he was expecting.

"Come on," he says, that spark of challenge in his voice again. "The suspense is torture."

I slowly begin to lay them out on the table. I wrapped each sandwich in parchment paper, then sliced them in half, so they held together well.

His eyes are on me, not the food, and somehow I feel like I'm doing a striptease instead of unpacking lunch.

"I didn't know what you'd like," I say shyly, "so I made a selection. There's Green Goddess sandwiches, which are really just avocado, mozzarella cheese, onions, cucumber, and some spread. If you're more into red meat, I've got sliced steak with blue cheese and aioli."

"It sounds *amazing*," he says in an exaggerated voice. Then he stage whispers to Nicole, "I don't know what *aioli* is."

"Good," she says. "Then I can have them all."

I roll my eyes at her, but I can't look at Thomas because his teasing isn't helping my nerves. "I made plenty."

"Are you sure you didn't pick these up on the way here?" he says.

"Don't think I won't hit you." I pull a plastic container out of the bag next. "Fruit salad with honey glaze." Then a large plastic ziplock bag. "Potato chips."

He mock gasps. "Something store-bought?"

Now I do swat him on the top of his head. "Watch your mouth. I made these, too."

His eyebrows go up, and he loses the smile. "You made your own potato chips?"

"Mom doesn't like buying processed food if we can help it. We make almost everything."

"*Everything*? Like, the bread and the cheese and the . . ."

"Not the cheese." I giggle at his expression, then busy myself with pulling paper plates out of the side of the bag. "We don't have goats in the backyard or anything. But we make bread every weekend."

"Do you use electricity?" he says.

I can't tell if he's kidding or not, so I keep my eyes down, on the food. "Once you're used to it, it's not really a big deal. It's cheaper, too. I mean, I've got three brothers, and my grandmother lives with us. When you buy prepared stuff for a big family, it costs a fortune."

I put one of each sandwich on a plate, then a handful of potato chips, followed by a scoop of fruit salad. Then I slide it over to Thomas.

He looks surprised that I wasn't making the plate for myself. "I could have gotten my own."

I blush again. "Sorry. Force of habit."

Nicole is already tearing into a sandwich. Despite how skinny she is, she can put away a table full of food. "Char's family is super traditional. She'll probably clean up after you, too."

I frown, but she's right, so it's not like I can say anything to contradict her.

"Is that why you're so nice?" he says. "Good upbringing?"

Nice. It's such a bland word, and I can't tell if he's still trying to push my buttons. I keep my eyes on my plate and take a Green Goddess sandwich for myself. "I don't think I'm especially nice. I just think I'm myself."

"I have a lot of experience with different people," he says slowly. "Trust me. You're very nice."

I think about the conversation with my grandmother before leaving the house, and I wonder if she'd agree. I take a bite of my sandwich and the avocado practically melts on my tongue.

Nicole is making unabashed sounds of pleasure to my left. "Oh my god, Char, I swear I'm going to marry you one day, just so I can keep eating like this."

"You might have some competition," says Thomas.

My eyes flash to his, and I find him watching me. I don't know what to say to that, but I can't leave it hanging out there. "A marriage proposal, so soon?"

"I'm surprised too, but I've never had a girl cook for me before. Besides, I said *might*."

"Maybe you should feed him by hand," says Nicole. "Push him over the edge."

I almost choke on my food.

Carla sticks her head into the back room. When her eyes settle on Thomas, she scowls, but she doesn't say anything. "Nicole, can you come watch the desk for a few minutes? I need to run down to storage for some more end caps."

Nicole heaves a big sigh and heads for the front. She takes her plate with her. "Don't be naked when I get back," she calls.

"I can't decide if working with Nicole is better or worse than getting threatened with arrest at the supermarket," Thomas says.

"I'd tell you that you'll get used to her, but that might not be true."

"She cares about you a lot."

I look at him again. One of the steak sandwiches is in his hands, and he's eaten half of it, but I can't tell if he likes it or he's just choking it down for my benefit.

"We've been best friends forever," I say.

"She said. She also told me that she'd break my legs, stand on my chest, and shoot pepper spray directly into my face if I ever hurt you."

I smile. "I'd do the same for her."

"I believe it."

I wish I could stop blushing when he talks. This is the most relaxed I've seen him, and it's reassuring to know his personality isn't *always* intense. "You're the only one," I say. "To listen to everyone else in my family, I couldn't swing a flyswatter without a big, strong man to help direct my aim."

"Maybe they're trying to protect you so they can keep eating like this."

I smile. "It's no McDonald's."

"Now I feel bad for teasing you. I really would have been

fine with cold cuts." He leans closer, his voice getting softer. "I'm not sure I'm ready to agree with Nicole's . . . ah . . . word choice, though. The jury's still out on that."

It involved the word "orgasmic."

The air is warmer suddenly. I want to touch him, and it's all I can do to keep my hands to myself. I think of the way he carried me through the woods, the strength of his arms beneath my thighs. It's a miracle I don't leap across the table and tear his shirt off. I've never wanted to do that to a guy before—god knows I've never done it in actuality—but something about him makes me forget all sense of propriety.

His lips curl into a slow smile. "Penny for your thoughts."

"They're not decent."

I. Did not. Just say that.

His smile widens, and he looks genuinely amused. "Really. What if I offer you a dollar?"

I put my hands over my face. "Can we please just pretend this moment isn't happening?"

"Absolutely not."

"Shush, you. Eat your food."

Nicole cavorts back into the room, and her plate is completely empty. "Good!" she declares. "There's food left."

I could not be gladder that she has interrupted this moment.

"What were you guys talking about?"

Thomas's eyes meet mine. "Currency values," he says.

"Is that a euphemism?" she asks. "Like, are you hiding a roll of quarters in your pocket right now?"

"Nicole!" I can't look at Thomas now. I *cannot*. I take another bite of sandwich and act like my food is the most fascinating thing in the world.

"Please," he says, deadpan. "One roll of quarters? Give me some credit."

"A sleeve of Ritz crackers?" she suggests.

I cough and drop the sandwich. "Nicole. You are killing me."

She doesn't look a bit ashamed. She pushes her pink glasses higher up on her nose and blows a strand of blond hair out of her face. "I'm just trying to get you necessary information. It's what any good friend would do."

"I'm surprised there's not a camera in the men's room," says Thomas.

"Watch yourself." Nicole narrows her eyes and levels him with a potato chip. "There just might be."

"If there is," I say, reaching into the bag to pull out the dessert I packed. "Do *not* send me those pictures."

CHAPTER THIRTEEN
THOMAS

Loneliness is a funny disease. You don't realize how badly you're infected until someone gives you a shot of contentment—and then it wears off.

In other words, my lunch hour is too short. I feel like we've just sat down, but now it's time to clean up and walk Charlotte back to her car.

She swings along on her crutches and I carry the bag, just like before. Once we cross the threshold of the library, the heat smacks me in the face and reminds me how lucky I am to have found a job indoors.

Without Nicole, Charlotte is quiet again. Her friend is entertaining, but I like that Charlotte isn't afraid of the silence, that she can be quiet without being awkward.

Or maybe she's shy now that we're alone.

Once we reach her car, she digs for her keys.

"Here." I set down the bag. "Let me start it for you. It's going to be like a furnace in there."

"It's only been in the sun for an hour." But she hands me the keys, and I start the engine. She's right, it's only been an hour, but the car interior feels like someone's been running the heater the entire time.

Besides, this buys me a few minutes.

I flip a few dials until I get the air conditioning running, and then I step back out to close the door.

She's leaning against the back door, her crutches propped beside her. "Thank you."

"You're welcome."

We stand there for the longest moment. I must look like a freak, standing here staring down at her. She probably expected me to start her car and go back inside. Hell, the bag was empty. It's not like she needed me to walk her to her car.

Maybe I completely misread the whole not-awkward-silence thing.

I shuffle my feet and glance at the front door. "So . . ."

"So."

"Thank you for lunch."

"You already thanked me."

"It deserved extra."

She smiles, but doesn't say anything to that. Instead, she tilts her head and looks at me sideways.

"I don't understand that look," I say.

"I'm glad I got to see you like this," she says.

"Like what?"

"At ease."

At her words, I'm suddenly not. I stiffen and look away. "I feel like I'm hiding here."

"That's really not a bad thing."

"I don't like it."

"It's better than sitting in jail, waiting for a trial."

I snort. "Not much."

"What would you be doing if you were back home?"

My old life flashes before my eyes. Art. School. Work. "I have no idea."

She bites at her lip and studies me.

"What?" I say.

"You don't say much about yourself. People might be less suspicious if you weren't so determined to be a mystery."

The words hit me hard. "I'm not doing . . . *that.*"

She smiles. "We spent an hour together, and I still don't know anything about you. You sidestep anything personal.

For all I know, you go back to Stan's and stare at the walls until he gets home."

"You're not too far off the mark."

She raises her eyebrows, as if to say, *See?*

I glance around the parking lot, and even though it's not crowded, I move closer to her so I can speak low. "I can barely imagine what I'd be doing if I were back home. It feels . . . it feels like a different life now. A different person. I feel like my life has split into a third act, but I don't know my lines. I feel—" I scoff and look away. "I'm really helping the mystery, huh?"

"It's okay," she says. "It's okay. Keep talking."

I move closer, as if her presence is helping to keep me grounded. "I miss—" My voice catches, and I have to swallow. "I miss my mother. But I feel like I miss someone who never existed outside of Stan's house. Everyone hates me, but no one knows her." I wince, and the words claw their way out of my throat. "No one knew her. No one cares about her. No one cares about finding out who did this. They just care about how much they hate me."

I have to stop talking. I'm going to lose it right here in the parking lot.

Arms go around my neck, and I stiffen in surprise. She's hugging me. Charlotte is *hugging* me.

I can't remember the last time anyone hugged me.

Mom. On her wedding day. The memory hits me like a freight train.

Thank you for being here, Thomas. And for wearing a suit. You're such a good boy, humoring your mother.

I choke on a sob.

I was a terrible son, Mom.

"It's okay," Charlotte whispers.

"It's not." My voice breaks. My face presses against her shoulder.

She strokes my hair. It feels so good to be held that I don't want to let her go.

But I do. I have to. I draw back. My eyes ache, and I'm sure they're red. They feel damp.

This should be humiliating, but somehow it's not. Charlotte's eyes are full of sympathy, not pity.

"Hey!" Nicole calls from the main entrance to the library. "I know it's not Grand Central Station around here, but maybe making out in the middle of the parking lot isn't the greatest idea, huh?"

I snap back and swipe a hand across my eyes, glad my back is to her.

"It's okay," Charlotte whispers. "She can't tell."

"I didn't mean to lose it."

"She's going back inside." Charlotte's eyes return to mine. "If you were a girl, I'd tell you to go buy a pound of chocolate and a good book and get in a hot bath."

I try for a smile. "You mean I can't do that because I'm a guy?"

She smiles back, but it's a little hesitant. "Are you going to be okay?"

I feel too exposed now. I run a hand through my hair and nod. I feel like I'm in a dozen pieces. "Yeah. I'm good."

She frowns. "Is Stan going to be home when you get off work?"

"No, but it's okay. He's back on duty, so he's got the three to eleven shift." I try for another smile, and this one feels more genuine. "I can get back to staring at the walls."

She doesn't smile back. "I don't think you should be alone."

"I'm fine. Really." I'm even close to convincing myself.

She studies me for a moment. "Okay. If you're sure."

I nod.

She turns to open her car door, and the air conditioning is blasting. Cool air hits us both. She eases onto the seat and swings her legs in, then pulls her crutches across to lean against the passenger seat.

I hesitate before closing her in, but nothing I say is going to undo the last five minutes. I don't think I want it to.

Before I can think better of it, I slam the door. She shifts the car into gear.

I turn away.

I wish I'd said something more. I wish I'd *done* something more.

"Hey!"

I turn. Her window is down, and she looks at me, then back at the windshield. "You said Stan is working till eleven?"

"Yeah."

"I usually babysit on Friday nights, so my mom doesn't expect me to be home. You know. If you want company."

I don't know what to say.

She doesn't look away. "I really don't think you should be alone. I could come over. We could talk."

We could talk. From any other girl, that would be loaded with double meaning, but I think of the way Charlotte blushed at Nicole's teasing. There's no double meaning here. It's such an innocent offer, made more obvious by the fact that she doesn't even seem aware that it could be taken another way.

I should refuse. For exactly that reason.

I should refuse.

I think about loneliness. I think about her arms around my neck. I think about my mother and how isolated this quiet little town has made me feel. Sudden emotion almost chokes me again.

I should refuse.

"I'd like that," I say.

Charlotte knocks on my door at seven o'clock on the dot. She's wearing the same dress she wore to lunch, a hot pink sundress that stops halfway between her waist and her knees.

She's pinned her hair up, in some kind of clip that leaves curls spilling over the top of her head. The sun hasn't set yet, and the rays sliding between the trees stripe her hair with gold.

I have to remind myself that she's here out of sympathy, not for a booty call.

I have to remind myself to be a gentleman.

Either she's putting on a brave face or she's lost any trace of fear of me. Stan's house is somewhat remote, and there's no one to see her here or to notice the strange car in the driveway.

She doesn't look the least bit shy. In her hand is a plate of cookies.

I raise my eyebrows and take them from her. "Cookies? I thought girls only did that on TV. In the fifties."

"I always take cookies when I babysit."

"I can see I'm going to gain twenty pounds hanging around with you."

She smiles. "They're oatmeal raisin. Made with maple syrup and almond flour. Low sugar."

"I was kidding."

"Oh." She loses the smile. "Well. They are."

"Do you want to come in?"

"You don't want to sit on the porch this time?"

Now I lose the smile. She's referring to the afternoon when I carried her back to the house. When I spent the entire walk waiting for a bullet to get me in the back. Or the head. I can't tell if she's making a dig or if it's a genuine question.

"Your call," I say. "We can sit wherever."

She wets her lips and glances past me, into the dim foyer. "You're sure Stan won't be home for a while?"

"He's never come home early the whole time I've been living here." I shrug. "Which admittedly isn't very long. But still. He doesn't strike me as the type."

"Okay. I'll come in."

She steps cautiously into the house, glancing around like she's worried someone is going to jump out of the shadows.

"I'm the only one here," I whisper.

"I know. I'm being ridiculous. Half the time I wonder if my brothers are having me followed."

I stop short. "Is that a real possibility?"

She lifts one shoulder in a halfhearted shrug. "I don't think so. But Ben flipped out on me after I told him what happened in the woods."

"Where do they expect you to be babysitting? Will they drive by?"

"Nah. Other side of the county. I just have to remember to check in with my mom after the 'little boy' goes to sleep."

She's so guileless, and it's charming. There's also a part of me that feels like I'm corrupting her with half the comments I make. Like this one: "Does that mean you're putting me to bed sometime soon?"

She blushes and gives me a rueful look. "Don't make me regret coming here."

"I'll do my best."

Her crutches clack on the slate flooring, then go silent as she moves to the carpeting. She looks between the kitchen and the living room. "Now where?"

"Kitchen. Your cookies are going to be my dinner. There's iced tea, too."

"You didn't eat *dinner*?"

She's looking at me like I told her I haven't bathed today. "No," I say. "Stan was gone when I got home. Unlike you, I don't know how to cook much that doesn't come with directions on a box."

She immediately heads for the refrigerator. "What does he have? I can make you—"

"No." She is too much. I push the refrigerator door closed. "Sit. You don't need to cook for me twice in one day."

"But I could—"

"*Sit.*"

Charlotte tries to pull the door open again. "But—"

I put my hand beside hers and hold it closed. I lean in, until we could share breath. "Don't make me pick you up and put you in the chair."

Her eyes widen, and for a fraction of a second I think she's going to dare me to do it. This close, I can smell her shampoo or her lotion or something sweet that makes me want to get closer.

"Sit," I say again. "Stan would never believe I cooked something for myself, anyway."

"All right." She steps back and sits in the chair, but she doesn't look happy about it. She begins unwrapping the plate of cookies.

"Iced tea?" I offer.

She nods. "Please."

Then we're seated next to each other, a plate of untouched cookies and two sweating glasses between us.

All of a sudden, it's awkward again.

I realize that part of that is my fault. I look at the table and take a cookie. "I'll let you make dinner next time. I promise."

"Now you're just making fun of me."

A little. "Not at all."

"Don't you have any hobbies?"

"Of course."

She looks at me, waiting for me to elaborate, but I don't. Talking about anything creative leads to demands for some kind of demonstration. That always opens the door for rejection. Even if someone says they like your work, you get to know the difference between the genuine and the pandering.

Charlotte leaves me off-balance enough as it is. I don't have the courage to put my life's work in her hands.

I poke at the cookie, but I haven't taken a bite. "I didn't

mean to lose it this afternoon. I'm sorry I got . . . emotional."

Her brows draw together. "You don't have to apologize for that."

"I can go for a while without thinking about it. It's weird. Then something will trigger a memory, and . . ." My throat tightens, and I swallow. I don't want to lose it again. "I just can't."

"I remember when Ben came home from his first murder case. I don't think he slept for weeks. And that was a stranger. Someone he didn't know. It was just . . . too close to home."

"Ben." My mind seizes on the name. "Is that the case like . . . like my mom?"

"Yes, but no." Charlotte shakes her head. "I asked him about it. It wasn't like your mom at all. Apparently there were emails back and forth with a secret boyfriend, but they never figured out who he was. They had . . . you know . . ." Her cheeks actually turn pink and I can't believe she's glossing over the word *sex* in the middle of a conversation about murder. ". . . and then he killed her." She swallows. "I'm sorry—we don't have to talk about this—"

"No. No, I want to. It makes me feel like I'm *doing* something, instead of sitting around waiting for someone to arrest me. Stan said there were no other leads. None."

"I heard the same thing."

I break the cookie in half and shake my head. "I hate this. They're never going to figure it out, and I'm never going to get out of here. I'm going to spend my life followed by whispers in the grocery store."

"Don't say that."

"Why not? It's true, isn't it?"

She licks her lips. "You can't think of anything else that might help? A noise, a face, anything?"

I take a long breath and blow it out. "I wish. I wish I could. I think about that night, and all I see is *her*. It's on this nonstop reel in my mind. I walk down the hallway. I find her body." I have to press my fingertips against my eyelids, and not for the first time, I wish I could push the image right out of my mind. I finally let go and gesture at the walls. "This place is surrounded by woods. We hadn't seen rain in days. No tracks, nothing. You know how close we are to the road. He could have parked a car where you parked and gotten away without a problem."

"How did he get in?"

I hate this question. I can't look at her. The cookie has turned into a mess of crumbs on the table. I haven't eaten a bite of it. What she's asking is the most incriminating piece of evidence against me, and it's so damning. "I don't know. No sign of forced entry." I pause. "When the paramedics got here, they told the police I had to unlock the door to let them in."

Her eyebrows go up. "The door was locked after the guy was gone?"

I grit my teeth. "I don't remember. They said it was. They said they heard me throw the lock to open the door."

She falls silent for a while, and I wonder what she's thinking.

After a moment, she puts a hand over mine. "What are the first two acts?"

I look up. "What?"

"You said this afternoon that you felt like your life had split into a third act. What were the first two?"

I pull back, self-conscious. "That was stupid. I just meant before, with my mom. And before that. With my mom and my dad."

"Oh." She's quiet, and I can hear her thinking. "Are they divorced?"

"She left him. From what I remember, it was pretty sudden. We didn't hide, but it felt like hiding, if that makes any sense. She used to say he was bad news."

Charlotte studies me. "Did he abuse her?"

"No." I shake my head before I really think about it. Mom

never said he did, and until Charlotte asked the question, no one ever laid that option on the table. I realign some of my memories, trying to make her sudden departure seem like that of a battered woman. It doesn't *quite* fit—but it's not completely out in left field, either.

And Mom obviously isn't here to weigh in.

"Not that I know of," I finally say. "I never saw it. I always used to think he was into drugs or something illegal. She hid from him at first. I don't know all the details."

"Did you tell the police all of this?"

"Of course. But she stopped worrying about him years ago. She never mentioned him. When people asked about my father, she'd tell them he wasn't a part of our lives. I grew up like that, so I took it at face value. I actually thought he might be dead."

"But you don't know for sure. Is there any chance he contacted her?"

"The cops took her laptop and searched it. According to Stan they didn't find any contact with anyone that seemed threatening or even remotely concerning. Her cell phone records all trace to easily recognizable numbers. Me. Stan. Work. Her friends. Not a single unknown."

"Do you have her laptop?" Her eyes light with intrigue. "Would you recognize his name?"

"Sure, but I don't have it. The cops still do. And I told *them* his name, so . . ." I shrug. "I know they hate me, but I don't think they're entirely stupid."

"Did they go through her things?"

I snort. "She didn't have much. She hadn't even unpacked everything from the move yet. She said there'd be time for that after the honeymoon." My voice breaks, and I'm not ready for it.

Charlotte acts like it didn't happen, and I appreciate the chance to hold on to my dignity. She's like a dog with a bone, though; she won't let go of this line of questioning. "So your mom has things you haven't unpacked yet?"

"Yeah. But it's only three boxes. Just clothes and stuff from her bedroom back home."

"Did the cops go through those boxes?"

"I don't think so. I mean, why would they? I'm pretty sure they're still sealed. They're in the garage."

"Do *you* want to go through them?"

I hesitate. "Do I want to go through my mom's old clothes and sheets and pillows? I don't really see the point."

"Do you have any other ideas?"

I think about that for a minute, then look at her. I sweep the cookie crumbs into my hand. "Let me get some scissors."

CHAPTER FOURTEEN

CHARLOTTE

I'm not entirely sure what I thought would happen when we broke open the old boxes on the floor of Stan's garage. I suppose I imagined something right out of a mystery novel, like the boxes would explode with dust and we'd find a cryptic map that we'd follow to the murderer's lair. Or maybe there'd be a weapon tucked beneath the flap of one of the boxes.

Instead, it's just three ordinary cardboard boxes. No dust, nothing amiss at all. The garage isn't even creepy: Stan keeps it clean, and there are two single bulbs hanging from the ceiling, giving us just enough light to see what we're doing. The first box has a stack of sheets with four decorative pillows on top. The tape was holding it all inside, because the pillows almost fling themselves free when Thomas cuts the tape. We take everything out, but that's all there is.

To be thorough, I crush the pillows in my hands, just in case something has been hidden inside.

"Find anything, Nancy Drew?"

His words are teasing, but his eyes are serious, and there's a hollow undercurrent to his voice.

I remind myself that these things are familiar to him. They represent his mother.

I stop squeezing a pillow. "Are you okay?"

He nods. "They . . . they smell like her. It's . . ." His voice trails off.

"Do you want to stop?"

"No." He rips open the next box.

Clothes, and a lot of them, but it's all off-season fabric: corduroy slacks and heavy sweaters and turtlenecks and jeans. Winter clothes, packed away because she wouldn't need them for months yet.

"See?" he says. "Nothing."

"Let's check all the pockets."

"Are you kidding?"

My hands are already unfolding a down vest, but I stop and look at him. "No. We don't have to."

He's looking into the box with the clothes, sliding his fingers along the fabrics, and he doesn't answer. I wait, giving him time.

I'm a terrible person for thinking this, but I don't mind the view.

If he'd moved here a year ago, we'd be going to school together in a few weeks, and I try to imagine him fitting in at school. New kids are always hit or miss around here, thanks to how small the town is. They either leap into the fray with instant popularity, by virtue of personality or looks or athletic ability—or they fade into the woodwork for the time they're here, and they get the heck out of town as soon as they can.

Thomas would be part of the first group, I can already tell. If we'd met at school, I would have been too intimidated to talk to him.

I'm almost too intimidated to talk to him *now*, and we're completely alone.

He slides a sweater out of the box, then looks at me. His eyes are piercing, and just a bit bewildered. "Why do you want to do this?"

"It feels better than doing nothing."

He gives a laugh that doesn't sound like he is all that amused. "No, that's why *I'm* doing it. I'm trying to understand why *you're* doing it." He hesitates. "It's a Friday night. You could be out on a *real* date, for god's sake."

Is he calling this a date? "Clearly you haven't seen the pool of teen guys in Garretts Mill."

"You could be doing *anything*, Charlotte. Anything. But instead, you're sitting on a garage floor, sorting through clothes."

I don't know what to say to that. Since the vest is in my hands anyway, I check the pockets, then fold it and set it aside.

He follows my lead and sets the sweater to the side. He pulls out another. "Is this a rebellion thing?"

I raise my eyebrows at him and grab a pair of jeans. "A rebellion thing?"

He gives me a look like he knows I know what he means. "Yeah."

"You think I'm here just because my parents don't want me to be?"

"Are you?"

The jeans pockets have a receipt that obviously went through the washing machine, but I set it to the side anyway and add them to the pile of checked clothes. "You've got a cynical view of the world."

"I've learned to be cautious. Answer the question. Why are you here?"

I meet his eyes, and I can't say any of the words in my head.

I'm here because I've been attracted to you since the moment I saw you outside the church.

I'm here because you let your guard down around me sometimes, and I don't think you do that with anyone else.

I'm here because you make me feel like I have something to offer the world, instead of being someone who needs to be sheltered away.

And finally . . .

I'm here because I can't stop thinking about you, and I don't want to leave your presence until I've figured you out.

I've been staring at him too long, my hands still on the khaki slacks in front of me. He's waiting for an answer.

I blush and look away. My voice is hushed and shy, almost a mumble. "I'm here because I want to be. If you want me to leave, I can leave."

Then I busy myself with checking the pants pockets.

Thomas crawls across the floor to kneel in front of me. "Hey."

I look at him.

"I don't want you to leave," he says.

"Okay."

He lets out a long breath. "I don't know what's wrong with me. I almost can't believe you're here, and then I have to go act like you forced your way in." He shakes his head. "I always thought I could read people, and now I spend every day second-guessing myself."

"You don't have to *read* me," I say. "What you see is what you get."

That makes him smile, and he looks a little devious. "I'm beginning to realize that."

I smile back. "And it's funny?"

"It's funny because you should be spending your nights with some guy who thinks 'second base' means holding hands, who knows what *aioli* is, and would find some preppy job during the summer while working on his Harvard application essay."

"Ugh." I make a face. "You sound like my mother. I mean, like, word for word."

He smiles. "Instead, you're here with me."

"You're being a perfect gentleman."

"And you don't know how much effort that's taking."

The note in his voice makes my breath catch. My hands hesitate on the jacket pockets I'm checking, and I look up at him. His eyes are dark and intense, and for a moment I think of that instant in the kitchen.

Don't make me pick you up and put you in the chair.

I remember the strength in his arms when he carried me through the woods.

I want to feel his hands on me again. I'm flushed suddenly, thinking about it. It takes everything I have not to throw myself at him.

Like I'd have a clue what I was doing.

I thrust my hand into a jacket pocket, just for an excuse to do something, anything, that doesn't involve pushing him down on the floor and jumping on top of him. My hand closes around a folded piece of paper.

I yank it free and hold it up. He's moved closer somehow. Our breath sounds loud in the space between us.

His eyes don't even leave mine.

"Found something." I sound like I've been out running. My heart agrees.

He takes the paper. It's folded notebook paper, nothing special. It takes him a moment to look away from me, and when he does, I feel a release, like a spell has broken.

He unfolds it halfway, sees what it is, and lets it fall closed again. He drops it beside the receipt. "It's nothing." His tone has gone flat.

I pick it up. "What was it?"

"Just a sketch."

I start to unfold it, but his sudden mood shift warns me to wait. "Do you mind if I . . ."

He shrugs and grabs another pair of pants. "Go ahead."

The paper is smooth, only creased in half twice, like a note folded to fit in an envelope. When he said *a sketch*, I expected a goofy doodle, or a caricature of a teacher, or . . . anything, really. Anything except something that looks like it should be framed and hung on a wall. Or kept in a museum.

The drawing is done in pencil, and the artist has so much

talent that emotion almost pours off the page. The perspec-
tives are all perfect, the lines and shadows as clear as a photograph. A woman is sitting at a table, wearing a bathrobe
and looking out a window. There's a cup of coffee in front
of her. I don't know how I know it's coffee—but I do. Her
hair is piled high on her head in a messy bun. She's not
young, but there's a fullness to her mouth. A look of desperate longing in her eyes.

"She wants something," I say without thinking.

"Yeah," he says. "A cigarette."

I look at him.

"It's the day after she quit," he says.

"This is your mother?" I ask quietly.

"Yes."

"She's beautiful." I shouldn't be surprised. She had a beautiful son.

"She was. Yes." He takes the paper from me and folds it
back up.

"Did you draw the picture?"

He hesitates. "I wanted her to know what she looked like.
To remember that she made it through the first day, and
she'd never have to look that needy again."

I don't ask why he wouldn't have taken a picture. This is
better than a picture: this is her image in her son's eyes.

"She carried it with her," I say.

He shrugs. "Or she shoved it in this jacket and never
looked at it again. It doesn't matter."

I frown, unsure what to say.

He's an artist.

Don't you have any hobbies? Of course.

Why wouldn't he tell me? It's another piece of the mystery. I feel like I started with a twenty-four-piece puzzle box,
but inside is a five hundred-piece double-sided puzzle with
no straight edges.

He pulls another garment from the box and doesn't say

anything either. I follow his lead, grabbing another pair of jeans.

Nothing.

I want to ask him about art, about how long he's done it, whether he wants to study it in school, whether he wants to be an artist as a career. I've seen kids at school who enjoy drawing, but none of them were ever very good. The sketch of his mother—that took true talent.

The way he tossed the sketch down warns me to tread carefully.

We continue to work in silence.

Nothing.

Nothing.

Nothing.

"I can't do it anymore," he finally says. His voice is raw. We've made a small stack of receipts and scraps of nonsense.

"You want to stop?"

"No, not this." His eyes flick to the discarded drawing. "That. I sit down and try to draw, and I can't do it."

"Since she died?"

He nods. "I always used to have a drawing in my mind. Now, it's like I can't pick a pencil up without my hand wanting to draw her murder." He grimaces, then scrubs at his face with his hands, as if he needs to push away the image. "I didn't want to see it the first time."

I continue going through the clothes, because he hasn't stopped, and it feels easier to talk while we're doing something. "Maybe you should let yourself draw it."

"Yeah, right. Like it's some kind of mental block?"

"Maybe it is." I hesitate. "Maybe it'll help you remember something. Matt always tells me that when some insignificant detail about an investigation won't leave him alone, he knows it's his brain trying to tell him something. He's the most practical guy ever, but he takes that kind of thing really seriously."

Thomas doesn't say anything, so I keep sorting.

"I'll try it," he finally says.

"Now?"

He shakes his head. "No. I don't—I'm not ready. Not now. Not yet."

"Okay," I say softly.

He pulls the next item out of the box. At first glance, I thought it was a skirt, but when he pulls, it's actually a fabric shoulder bag, in a purple and blue paisley print, threaded with gold and silver.

"That's pretty," I say.

"I don't think I ever saw her use it. It's empty." He flings it on top of the pile of clothes we've already gone through, then thrusts his hand back in the box for another.

He frowns and fishes around, then rises to his knees to look in the box. "Holy shit."

"What?"

"This." He reaches down into the box and comes back up with a handful of envelopes. They've all been mailed to Marie Bellweather, with various dated postmarks. The handwriting is the same on all of them. The edges are worn where a letter has been pulled out and returned to the envelopes.

Thomas drops them on the floor between us.

Then he reaches back into the box and retrieves another handful.

And another.

When he's done, at least twenty-five envelopes are scattered on the floor.

We both stare at them for a moment.

"Is it weird," he says, "that I feel like I shouldn't be reading her mail?"

"No." I pause. "Do you want me to read one?"

"No. Not yet." He slides a letter out of an envelope. It's one page long, handwritten on white paper, the kind you'd pull out of a copy machine. The handwriting isn't neat, but it looks legible.

Thomas reads for a moment, not long enough to get

through the whole thing, before shoving it back into the envelope almost violently. His breathing has quickened. He pulls another one free and begins to read.

I pick up the one he discarded, easing the letter out of the envelope because I don't want to overstep my bounds.

The letter starts abruptly, without any introduction.

I wish I could talk to you. You don't know how much I wish I could see you.
I understand it, but this isn't fair.

Thomas tosses his letter at me. "Look at that one."
I put down the one I'm reading and pick up his.

You don't know how hard it is to know I could get in a car and come find you.
I won't. I made a promise, and I'll keep it.
But please write back to me.
Please.
I think about you all the time.
I need you.
Please.

I look at the date on the postmark. It's from eight years ago. I pick up another. It's from nine years ago. Another is almost ten years old.

"Do you recognize the handwriting?" I ask.
Thomas shakes his head.

"So you don't know if it's your father's?"
He laughs shortly, without any humor whatsoever. "My father left before I could read. I have no idea what his handwriting looks like."

"We should call the police."
He almost glares at me. "Why? To tell them we found a bunch of letters that are several years old? I bet that'll crack the case."

"These letters sound like they came from a stalker." I glare back at him. "They could investigate whoever sent them."

He picks up another envelope, and this time he looks at the return address. "Where the hell is Crisfield?"

"Maryland?"

He glances up. "Yeah. Do you know?"

"It's south of here. It's a small town. Right on the water."

He picks up another letter and taps it with his fingers. "I don't know what these mean."

I open another and read the first line.

I'm graduating from high school today.

Wait. What? I frown and look at Thomas. "These were written by a kid."

"What?"

"Well, a teenager. This says 'I'm graduating from high school today.'"

He moves over to kneel beside me, and we read it together.

I'm graduating from high school today. I sent you the announcement, but I don't know if you ever got it. I don't know if anyone is receiving these letters. They don't come back to me, so I guess there's some hope that you're out there reading this.

Then again, maybe this is sitting in the bottom of a dumpster.

Graduation is supposed to mean the end of one thing and the beginning of something else.

This is the end of my letters. I'm eighteen years old. I'm old enough to vote, I'm old enough to go to war. I'm a man, and I'm not going to cry for my mother to come back to me anymore.

I still love you. I still miss you.
I'm just not going to write to you anymore.

I don't know what to say.

Thomas takes the letter out of my hands. He's still staring at it. I'm not sure he's breathing. He's not making a sound.

I pick up the envelope. The postmark is from five years ago.

"He's twenty-three," I say. Ben's age.

"What?" Thomas croaks.

"Look at the postmark. He's twenty-three. If he was eighteen then."

He holds the letter out. "Read that again. Please. Read that again, and tell me it says what I think it's saying."

I don't need to read it again, but I take it from him. "You didn't know?"

His breathing is shaky now. "No."

"Is there any chance we're misunderstanding this?"

He doesn't move for a moment, then grabs another envelope in a flurry of activity. He pulls the letter free and reads it out loud. " 'I broke my leg today in football practice. It was my fault—I misread the call and I got tackled by the defensive lineman. I didn't think about you the way I did when I was young and I got hurt. I didn't think about you at all until the nurse in the ER said, 'Your mom will be here soon.' And then it hit me all at once how much I wished that was true."

Thomas looks at me. He takes a long, shuddering breath. "I don't think there's any way we're misunderstanding this." He flips over the envelope and looks at the return address again. "Can we go there? Can you drive me?"

"Now? I don't—"

"Please, Charlotte." I'm ready to refuse, but then his eyes meet mine, and I'm ready to drive him to California if he asks. "*Please.*"

"I'll drive you," I say. "But it's over an hour away, and I'd either have to leave you there or we'd have to turn right around and come back. If I don't show up on time, my father or my brothers *will* come looking for me."

I watch as he considers this information.

I bite at my lip. "I could tell them I have another sitting job tomorrow night. We could go then?"

He studies the envelope again. "Maybe that's better."

"I don't think this is the kind of thing you want to rush into," I say gently. "Maybe . . . maybe we *should* talk to the police—"

"No." He pulls the letter out of my hands like I'm going to call nine-one-one right this very second. "No." His breathing accelerates, and he sounds almost panicked. "You can't tell your family. Not yet. Please."

"Okay," I say quietly. "I won't."

"Please, Charlotte." He puts his hands on my arms and looks me straight in the eyes. "Please. I don't know what they'll do if they try to track him down. I know how they treated me, and I need—I need—"

"I won't," I assure him. "I won't tell them. I promise."

"And we can go?" he says. "Tomorrow night?"

I nod. My mom probably won't bat an eye. "We can go."

"Thank you," he says softly. "Thank you for doing this."

"A road trip to find a long lost brother? You don't need to thank me."

"A brother," he repeats. His voice is hushed, almost reverent. "I have a brother."

Then he picks up another letter. He reads it quickly.

"I don't understand," he says.

"What's it say?"

He shakes his head. "Not the letter. I don't understand . . . her."

"Your mother?"

"I don't understand why she kept this hidden."

"Maybe there are things about your mother you don't know."

He picks up the first letter, the one that sounded vaguely threatening out of context. "Maybe."

"Maybe there are things about your *brother* you don't know."

"We need to find out." I pause. "Tomorrow."

He nods. "Tomorrow."

CHAPTER FIFTEEN

THOMAS

After Charlotte goes home, I climb into bed, but I don't sleep at all.

My brain feels like someone has put a foot on the accelerator and won't let go. My thoughts keep spinning in so many directions.

My body eventually gives up on me. I fall asleep reading the letters to my mother. The letters from my brother. To *our* mother.

When I wake up, I read them again.

I have a brother.

I have a *brother.*

A brother.

I say the word in my head enough times that it starts to sound like a word I made up.

Brother brother brother brother brother.

I have a brother.

I also have fourteen hours to kill. It's three o'clock in the morning.

Brother!

The second time I wake, it's a more reasonable hour, and my thoughts are more orderly and less like the ravings of someone needing to be institutionalized. Sunlight streams through my windows, and Stan must be puttering around in the kitchen, because I hear dishes clinking together.

I slide the letters between my fingers again, reveling in the smoothness of the paper under my fingertips. My brother never mentions his name, and aside from the return address, there's no identifying information anywhere. Never the name of a school or a restaurant or anything.

Never any reference to the people he lives with or why he's there.

Maybe he's with my father.

The thought hits me like a bucket of cold water. I sit up in bed, my thoughts racing again.

I do the math quickly in my head. My father left when I was five years old. That's thirteen years ago. My brother—my brother!—would have been ten.

I rack my brain, trying to think. I remember my father. Not many memories but enough that I feel certain he lived with us. I remember being tucked into bed.

I don't remember a brother.

Why don't I remember a brother?

And wouldn't he mention a dad? His letters beg for the chance to see her. He didn't write often—or if he did, she didn't save them all—but he wrote often enough for me to get a sense of his longing. His loneliness. He missed her terribly, and even when he realized she wasn't going to let him back into her life, he wasn't a dick about it. He never says anything about a father, not about missing him, and not about Dad's presence in his life.

Wait. Maybe we don't have the same father.

That's another bucket of water.

I wish I had a cell phone. Only one other person knows about these letters, and I have no way to talk to her.

I imagine telling Stan.

I then imagine him handcuffing me to a radiator while the cops investigate those letters, track down my brother, and put him through what I went through.

No. No way.

But maybe I can get my hands on a phone.

I put all the letters together and slide them between my mattress and the box spring. It's not the best hiding place, but I don't plan to leave them there for long. I don't think Stan would search my room, but I don't *not* think Stan would search my room either. He's a cop. I'm still a murder suspect.

And I'm not an idiot.

They'll be safe enough while I get a cup of coffee.

Stan glances up when I come out of my room. He's by the stove, stirring eggs in a skillet. "You're up early," he says.

"I couldn't sleep."

"I heard you in there banging around."

That gets my attention. "Banging around?"

"Yeah." He pauses. "Nightmares?"

"I don't . . ." I frown. "I don't think so." The images I get during the daytime are bad enough. So far her murder hasn't haunted my sleep. Maybe I should be counting my blessings.

Then again, I could probably do that on one hand.

"Well, I looked in on you. Certainly seemed restless."

"You don't need to look in on me, Stan." Irritation leaks into my voice before I'm ready for it. I'm unsettled at the thought of Stan coming into my room when I'm asleep. I don't know why—it's not like I'm any less vulnerable when he's out in the hallway. Maybe it's a residual suspicion after Mom's death. Maybe it's the fact that he's a cop, and I'm hiding a pretty big secret.

He pushes the eggs around the pan. "I know I don't *need* to." He pauses. His voice hasn't changed, but I can tell he's picked up on my attitude. "You doing all right, Tom?"

I have a brother. It takes everything I have not to shout it at him. Throw furniture. Run out the door and track the guy down on foot. "I'm great."

He turns and looks at me. "Great?"

This conversation isn't going anywhere I want it to. "I need my phone back."

He shakes his head. "It's going to be a while. Just like your mother's car."

I don't know what they're still doing with her car. Investigating each individual fabric fiber? There was no evidence her car was ever touched.

I fidget for a moment, wondering how this next question is going to go over. Hating that I have to ask it. "Could I borrow yours?"

"Sure, the phone is right there."

Like I would do anything important on a cop's phone. "I meant your car."

"Why?"

"So I can go get a new phone."

"Why do you need a phone so badly all of a sudden?"

"It's not *all of a sudden.*"

I sound surly, but it matches my mood. He turns, looking startled at the attitude.

"I don't want to be grilled about it," I say. "If you don't want to let me borrow your car, fine. But I've been trapped here for weeks. The only place I can go is the library. I've already been thrown out of the grocery store, and the Dunkin' Donuts is practically a landing zone for cops. I'm stuck here all day long, and I have no one to talk to and nothing to do. If everyone in town hates me, *fine.* But I haven't done anything wrong. I'm not in jail yet, and I'm sick of being treated like I am."

Stan raises an eyebrow, then turns back to the stove and resumes stirring his eggs. He doesn't say a word.

After a long moment, I'm convinced he's not going to say anything.

"Whatever," I finally say. I don't wait for coffee. I just walk out the back door and drop into a chair on the porch.

I would have kept walking, but I'm still in the threadbare sweats and T-shirt that I wore to bed.

Even this early, the heat climbs on my back and wraps itself around my shoulders. I could swim through this humidity. The backyard smells like cut grass, and I wonder if Stan has already been out on his mower. It looks like it. Mom would be disappointed that I didn't offer to do it first.

I should be disappointed in myself, but I'm not. I can't shake this surly, trapped feeling. I have places I need to go and no way to get there. Stan can mow his own fucking lawn.

Crickets kick up a racket in the woods around the house. I expected Stan to come after me, but he doesn't. It takes a few minutes, but my anger begins to fade. Anger won't gain me anything.

My thoughts are still tangled up with the mystery of my brother. He played football—does that mean he's a jock? I'll throw a ball around for fun with anyone who asks, but I'm not big on organized sports. I barely know who played in the Super Bowl. Will we even get along?

He's well-spoken, too. Even in the earlier letters, when he was young, he sounds composed. A little desperate and emotional, but he was a kid. I think back to myself at ten, eleven, twelve, the years when Mom began to loosen up and give me a little freedom.

Mom.

If she had another son, why didn't she want to see him?

Why did she keep him a secret from me?

She read the letters. They were open before I read them and worn enough that I could tell they'd been read more than once.

When I hurt myself, she bandaged my scrapes or put ice on my bruises. She sang songs to me and hung my early artwork on the refrigerator. She took me for ice cream and left me alone when I needed solitude. She took her friends out to lunch when they were upset. She made soup for the elderly woman who lived downstairs from us. Mom was kind. She was good.

We didn't always get along, but she *loved* me. I know she did.

Why didn't she love him?

The back door opens, and Stan comes out on the porch. My eyes refuse to leave the tree line. I don't say anything to him.

He sits down at the table. "I'm not used to having a kid here, Tom."

I bristle at the word *kid,* but I don't want to pick a fight over semantics.

"I forgot that you're not a puppy," he adds.

I look at him, incredulous. "A *puppy?*"

"I didn't consider you being stuck here." He sounds abashed. "You don't say much. You walk to the library. I thought . . . it didn't occur to me."

Oh.

"You can't take the car," he says.

I scowl. Of course not.

"It's a police department vehicle," he continues. "That's just policy." He pauses. "If you want to go get a phone, I can drive you."

My eyes flick up. The offer makes me feel like I'm twelve, but Stan sounds genuinely contrite.

"Thanks," I say.

"We can go in an hour or so if that works for you. Give me a chance to get a shower."

"I'll be ready."

Stan takes less than an hour. He smells like aftershave, and I want to ask if he expects me to put out later, but I don't think that will go over well. The last time I rode in a car, it was a trip home from the police station, and it doesn't feel any less awkward now.

We drive in complete silence for a while. Stan wasn't kidding when he said he forgot that I wasn't a puppy. I'm tempted to hang my head out the window to see if he gets the point.

Eventually, he clears his throat. "Did you move your mother's things?"

My heart stutters, but I don't let it show. "No."

"It looked like someone cut her boxes open and then taped them back up."

"When?"

"I just noticed when I was pulling out of the garage."

I don't say anything. I don't know what to say. I want to lie, but I don't want to put him on the track of investigating something that will only lead back to me. I wasn't precise about re-taping the boxes, but they were just old boxes that I'd taken from Best Buy. It's not like Mom's packing tape was the first to ever touch the cardboard.

It never occurred to me that Stan would notice.

He glances my way. "Want to try a different answer?"

His voice is mild, and I can't tell if he's angry or not.

"I'm just looking for anything that could help," I finally say.

"What did you find?"

A brother. "A lot of old receipts and pocket lint."

For a while, I think he's going to accept that, but then he says, "You could have asked me to help you."

"I didn't want you to think I was crazy."

"You're not crazy, Tom." He pats me on the shoulder. "I want to know who did it, too."

The physical contact throws me. It's so . . . accepting. I almost spill everything, just to have someone to talk to.

Then my eyes fall on his radio, the strobe lights mounted on the dash of his unmarked car. I remember the way they dragged me out of the house to be interrogated. I remember the altercation at the funeral.

I keep my mouth shut.

We have to drive for a half hour, and when we get there, the mall is packed. I'd thought we would go to some stand-alone wireless store close to home, but Stan said this echoing marble-and-brick monstrosity was all we had locally. The whole place looks dated and depressed. The food court offers restaurants that no one has ever heard of, and my feet stick to the tile floor very slightly with each step.

I hate this place. I miss the city.

We're closer to Salisbury University here, so the shops are crowded with college kids looking to kill time for the weekend. The wireless store has a line of people waiting for a representative.

I sigh and put myself at the end of it.

Stan stands close to me. "I don't mean to pry, but . . . do you have money for this, Tom?"

"I don't need money. I was planning to wait until the sales guy was distracted, then run."

He gives me a look.

"I have money," I say, and I do. Not a lot, but I can afford a phone on what I'm making at the library.

"Are you sure? Because I can help you out if you need it."

I blink at him, surprised. "I'm all right."

He nods, then claps me on the shoulder again. "Good. Good for you." A pause. "I'm going to get a soda across the way while we're waiting. Do you want anything?"

"I'm good."

Then he's gone, and I'm left in this line of harried people who all look pissed off that we're here. At least we're far enough from Garretts Mill that no one seems to recognize me. I wore my ball cap just in case, but there are enough people here who are my age that I won't stand out. Somewhere on the other side of the store, a child is wailing. The woman behind me keeps making this *tsk*-ing huffing sound, as if that's going to make the store process things more quickly.

Some little girls dart between customers, playing a game that seems to be a combination of hide-and-seek and tag. Their mother is sitting on one of the few chairs in the store, breastfeeding a baby. There's a blanket over her shoulder, but it's pretty obvious. She calls out to the girls every now and again, asking them to settle down before their father gets here, but they obviously don't give a crap.

They begin weaving among the people in the line, sliding between people as if they don't have the slightest hesitation about getting up close and personal with strangers. *Tsk*-huff behind me does it louder. The man in front of me sighs and clears his throat significantly. I ignore them all and remind myself to always wear a condom.

"Lexi!" their mother calls. Her shirt is down, and she's glaring at them while trying to burp the baby at the same time. "Jenna!"

They giggle and hide behind me. They're whispering together, and when I shift to move so their mother can see them, they move with me, staying out of sight.

Now I want to *tsk*-huff myself.

Their mother is on her feet, the baby hanging over one arm, pudgy legs dangling. She storms over. "Jenna. Lexi. Get over here and sit down. Right now." She looks up at me. "I am so sor—"

She stops short. Her face kind of freezes.

She's recognized me. I can feel it in the air. I freeze, too. I don't know what to do. It's not like I can make myself look any *more* innocent. I'm just standing in line.

The woman snaps into motion. She reaches around me and grabs one of her daughters by the arm, trying to keep the baby out of my reach as if I've made a threatening move. I think she'd be grabbing both girls if she had a free hand.

"Stay away from them," she says.

"I didn't touch them," I snap back.

The other little girl is oblivious to her mother's panic. She giggles and ducks around me, pressing herself between me and the man in front of me.

"Lexi!" There's a note of panic in the woman's voice. The baby squeals and starts crying. "Lexi. Come here. Get away from him."

She finally gets a hand on her daughter and jerks her away from me.

Lexi starts crying.

We now have the attention of half the people in the store. The huffing woman has stopped.

I think someone on the other side of the store is taping this.

A man joins the mother. For a second, I don't recognize him. He's in jeans and a polo shirt, and he's just walked in from the mall, but he's sizing up the situation.

My brain snaps to attention. Charlotte's brother. *Matt.*

I can tell from his expression that he's recognized me on sight, too—not that I expected him to forget me. His voice is clipped and guarded, and he picks up the little girl who lingered behind me. "What's going on? What did you do to my kids?"

"I didn't do *anything*," I say tightly. "I'm waiting in line. Just like everyone else."

He glares at me for a long moment before looking at the other customers around me. They've all given me a wide berth.

"You shouldn't be here," he finally says.

"Who says? I'm not on house arrest. I'm not allowed to shop?"

He leans close and speaks low. "You're a suspect in an active murder investigation, in case you've forgotten."

I bristle. "Trust me. I haven't forgotten. Maybe you guys could do your job instead of hassling me."

"Does anyone know you've left town?"

Who does this guy think he is? I glare at him. "Go to hell. You're not my jailer."

One of the little girls whispers, "Mommy. He said 'hell.'"

The man moves closer. "You'll watch your language in front of the children."

"Fuck you." My head is buzzing, like that moment in the cemetery, when I hit Danny without meaning to. I lose awareness of the store, of the other customers, of the fact that we're in public.

Matt's eyes narrow. He's going to push me. I'm going to push back.

Then Stan appears beside him, and his tone is calm, very let's-all-get-along. "Hey. Matt, he's fine. He's with me."

Like popping a balloon, awareness snaps back into place. I hear the agitated murmurs behind me. The children who are still crying. The baby who is still wailing.

What the hell just happened?

Matt glances at Stan, then back at me. "He was causing a scene."

"Your *kids* were causing a scene," I snap.

Matt looks like he wishes he was armed. Or maybe he's wishing we were in a back alley so he could beat the shit out of me. Or the middle of a cemetery.

"Tom," says Stan. "Let's go."

"But I didn't even—"

"Let's go. Now."

I want to resist. I stood in this line, and I didn't do anything wrong. But I'm the center of attention, and none of it is good. You'd think some of these people would side with me, but they're all staring suspiciously.

"Fine," I say. "Whatever. *Fine.*" I move to follow him, but the mother is still staring at me, clutching her squalling baby like I'm going to snatch it out of her arms. Her expression is some combination of fearful and hateful.

"Better learn to control your kids," I snap. "I'd hate to see them get hurt by the likes of me."

Her eyes widen, and she pulls the baby closer.

Stan grabs my arm and jerks me toward the front of the store. "Are you crazy?" he growls under his breath. "Tom, you do not threaten a cop's kids. You don't threaten *anyone's* kids, but especially not—"

I jerk my arm away from his hand. "I didn't threaten his kids."

"What do you think that sounded like?"

"I don't care." I'm angry and irritated and ashamed that once again, I can't even get out of the house for a few hours without my life derailing. "He can go to hell. I didn't do anything."

"You can bet I'll get a call about this later."

"Sorry to ruin your evening."

"Damn, Tom." He slams through the doors to the mall, and we walk into a wall of humidity.

When he gets into the car, I can tell he's really pissed, because all his motions involve collisions. Slamming door. Jerking the seatbelt. Shoving the key into the ignition.

It feeds my own anger. "I don't know what you're pissed at me about. I didn't *do* anything."

"It sure didn't sound like you were being polite and deferential."

"It's not like *he* was!"

"He doesn't have to be. You're the one under a microscope. Don't you understand that?"

I clench my jaw and stare out the window. I hate this.

I hate it.

All my earlier excitement about my brother has fizzled and turned into nothing more than a few discarded streamers in the corner of my brain. This is what my life is like now. This and nothing else.

I almost want to confess to the crime just so I can get out from under that microscope.

Stan sighs. "I don't know what's up with you and the Rookers. I wish you could just stay away from them."

My head whips around. Does he know about Charlotte coming over last night? About her plans to pick me up this evening? Is that about to unravel, too? "What are you even talking about?"

"I'm talking about what just happened, Tom. What the hell do you think I'm talking about?"

My heart is stuttering and having trouble keeping up a steady rhythm. I cough. "What?"

"What, do you have a homing beacon for that family or something?"

Charlotte's brother. That's right.

She's going to hear about this.

Shit.

I wish I had a phone.

CHAPTER SIXTEEN

CHARLOTTE

"**A**nd then he threatened the kids." Alison is bouncing the baby in her lap while she picks at mashed potatoes. "You should have felt the atmosphere in the store. I told Matt they need to lock that boy up."

My heart feels like it's taken a direct injection of caffeine. I've been pushing food around my plate all evening, but I'm too keyed up to eat. I force enough food into my mouth so I don't have another episode, but I have to choke it down. Luckily Saturday night is family dinner night, and there are too many people at the table for my mother to notice my lack of appetite.

Especially with Matt and Alison's story about what happened at the mall.

I have to clear my throat, but my voice still comes out with a squeak. "Thomas threatened the kids?"

"He said I'm lucky they didn't get hurt."

Matt picks up a bottle of beer and takes a sip. "He didn't quite say that."

Alison puts a small bit of potato on her spoon and offers it to the baby. "Close enough. It was threatening. You know it was."

Matt spears some chicken with his fork. He grins at Ben across the table. "Yes, dear."

Alison rolls her eyes.

"Did he touch the kids?" says Danny. "I'll go pick him up right now."

My father points at him with his spoon. "You'll stay right there in your seat."

"Ben will go with me," says Danny. "Won't you, bro?"

Ben is actually in uniform, because he's working later tonight, but he grabs the creamed corn and scoops more onto his plate. "No way. Mom made pie. There'd need to be a felony involved for me to skip pie."

Matt's face turns serious. "There is a felony involved."

Ben puts his spoon down. He looks across at Matt. The table is suddenly quiet.

"No one is going to get anyone," says Dad. "Do you understand me?"

Matt and Ben are still looking at each other, having a conversation with their eyes.

I speak brother fluently, so I can read the looks.

Do you want me to go pick him up? I'm on the clock at seven.

Matt shakes his head, almost imperceptibly. *Not yet.*

"Are you feeling all right, Alison?" says my grandmother. "You've barely touched your dinner."

I quickly push more food around my plate before she looks at it. I'm wearing capri pants and a tank top tonight, and somehow that's escaped her notice.

Alison shakes her head. "I'm just not feeling very well tonight."

Matt puts a hand on her back and rubs. "Let me hold the baby."

Alison hands Madalyn over and glances at me. Her face *is* pale, now that I'm looking at her. "I should have booked you for babysitting tonight. I could use a twelve-hour nap."

"I'm already working," I say quickly.

"Your mom said." She grimaces. "Sure you don't want to take the girls with you, too?"

Is she serious? There's no *way* I can take the girls with me on this "job."

He threatened the children.

The thought hits my head like a two-by-four. I'm supposed to pick Thomas up at seven thirty, and this new fact is poking my sense of self-preservation with ominous warnings. *Be careful, Charlotte.*

I think about that drawing of his mother. The intricate detail, the shading around her eyes that spoke of desperation. She looked so tortured; the emotion almost fell off the page. Despite that, you could feel a grudging respect in the sketch. Thomas felt what she was going through, and he held her in high regard.

He loved her.

I can't see someone drawing that picture and later killing his mother.

Or maybe he loved her too much? I don't know.

I don't know how I can be with him and feel so certain that he's innocent—but when I'm anywhere else, doubts sneak into my brain and set up shop.

"I'll take the girls out for ice cream after the baby is asleep," says Matt. "You can lie down when we get home."

"Yay!" cries Jenna. "Ice cream!"

Matt points his fork at her. "If you finish all your dinner."

She promptly shovels a forkful of broccoli into her mouth.

"Excuse me," Alison says. She shoves away from the table and goes down the hallway.

"Poor thing," says my mother. "She doesn't look good at all. You could leave the girls here tonight, Matthew."

He grunts and takes another drink of beer. "She'll be all right."

"So sympathetic," I say.

"Did you not hear me offer to take the kids out so she could get some sleep?"

"Nothing is worse than being sick in the summertime," says Mom. "Do you think it's the flu?"

"Yeah," he says. "The flu that lasts nine months."

I gasp. "Matt!"

Mom has her hands over her mouth. "Oh! How wonderful!"

"Oh, Matthew," says my grandmother. "What a blessing."

Clearly all I need to do to win her over is have dozens of babies. While wearing floor-length dresses in muted colors and pinning my hair up.

My father comes around the table to give Matt a one-armed hug. He uses his other arm to grab a biscuit from the basket.

"Dude," says Danny. "Do you even know how to use a condom?"

"What's a condom?" says Lexi.

My mother smacks Danny on the back of the head. "Daniel. You watch your mouth."

"It's an apartment building," I say to Lexi. "You know, a condo. Like that place you stayed at the beach last summer."

Matt ruffles her hair. *Thank you*, he mouths to me.

"Seriously," says Ben. A sly grin is on his face. "I think we all deserve an answer to that question."

"Eh. Who needs them?" says Matt. He looks very pleased with himself.

"Alison is going to kill you for telling us without her here," I tell him.

"No, she won't." The baby starts to fuss, and he gives her his napkin so she can tear it apart. "She needs me to help chase all these kids."

Alison reappears through the doorway. She looks a bit green and leans against the molding. "I think I'm going to go sit in the living room if no one minds."

Mom rushes to give her a hug. "Oh, Alison. I'm so happy for you."

Alison looks startled, then bursts into tears. "I *knew* I was showing already. I haven't even lost all the weight from Madalyn."

"No, no!" my mother clucks, then ushers her out of the dining room.

My grandmother goes after them, but throws a pointed glance at me before crossing the threshold. "Charlotte, you can begin clearing."

Never mind the four able-bodied men at the table. I sigh.

"Why is Mommy crying?" whimpers Jenna. She sounds like she might start herself.

"She's okay," says Matt. "Finish your dinner." He looks across at Ben and says under his breath, "I'm about ready to move in with you. It's hormone central at my place."

" 'Yes, dear,' " Ben mocks.

Matt rolls his eyes. "Exactly."

"Maybe you'll get a boy this time," says my father.

"I think he deserves all the girls," I say.

"At least I've got brothers," says Matt.

Brothers. It brings my mind back to Thomas. I want to ask more questions, but there's no way to do that without rousing my brothers' suspicions. I know Danny would jump all over me if I so much as *mention* Thomas, and I don't need them even linking my name with his in their thoughts. I'm already on edge enough about tonight.

"I'd better start clearing," I say.

Matt pats Jenna on the back. "Help your aunt," he says.

She makes a face, and he gives her a poke. "Jenna. Don't be rude."

That pisses me off. Another girl relegated to dishes. "No," I say. "Let her play."

Jenna beams.

"If you have a brother," I tell her pointedly, "make sure he helps you with the dishes." Then I turn on my heel and carry the first set away from the table.

I hear Danny yell from behind me. "Hurry up, Char. We need to make room. I heard there's pie."

My irritation hasn't worn off by the time I get to Stan's—now Thomas's—house. Some of it is nerves, but it's easier to wrap fear in anger and go with that. I'm fifteen minutes late because I was the only one doing dishes. Everyone else was fawning over Alison. She totally deserves it, but that doesn't mean I deserve to do all the dishes for ten people by myself.

I barely register the empty driveway before I'm slamming my car door and stomping up the steps to knock.

Thomas opens the door, and his dark eyes register surprise. "Charlotte. I didn't think you were—"

"Here." I shove a saran-wrapped plate into his chest. "Did you really threaten my nieces?"

At least he has the grace to look ashamed. He takes the plate. "I know. I'm sorry. I didn't—it wasn't a threat. That's not how I meant it."

"Ben was ready to arrest you tonight."

A flicker of irritation crosses his features. "I'm surprised they waited that long."

"Alison was really upset."

"That's your brother's wife?"

"Yeah."

"She should have been watching her kids. They were all over the store. She's lucky someone else didn't threaten them."

"She's exhausted. She's pregnant and sick and she was trying to feed the baby. You couldn't give her a break?"

His eyebrows go up. "I was standing in line! How am I supposed to know all that?"

I huff and it takes everything I have to keep from stomping my foot. "Ugh. I am so sick of men."

He frowns and draws back. "Just who are you mad at here?"

"Everyone." I sigh and push hair back from my face. "Can I get out of the heat?"

He steps back and holds the door open, then follows me down the hallway while I head for the kitchen. Last night I was shy and nervous, but tonight irritation has crowded out all my anxiety. I can't wait to get driving so I can punch the accelerator and be in control of something.

"Is this a slice of pie?" he says, sounding amused.

I round on him. "Don't you dare make fun of me."

"I wasn't going to make fun of you." His mouth twitches. "Well. Maybe a little. I can't believe you're this angry at me and you still brought me dessert."

"Some days I'm so tired of being the 'little lady.' It's infuriating."

His face loses the smile. "I don't think of you that way."

"I know." I exhale, and it takes some of the fight out of me. "It's one of the things I like best about you."

He gets a fork from a drawer and sits down at the table. "I think your brothers underestimate you. You're one of the bravest people I know."

His words stop me short, and I stand there looking down at him. He unwraps the saran wrap slowly, careful to not disturb the crust. He looks good, a little more rugged than usual. I don't think he's shaved today, though he smells like he's taken a shower recently. I find myself wanting to pull closer to him.

In an instant, all of my irritation is gone. I almost forgot that I came over here for a reason, that I'm not supposed to just climb in his lap and make out with him.

My cheeks are on fire. "I'm not brave at all."

He gives me a dark smile. "You just brought pie to an alleged murderer." He kicks out the chair beside him. "Sit."

Don't make me pick you up and put you in the chair.

Breath catches in my throat. I ease into the chair.

"I've never had a strawberry pie," he says.

"I thought about bringing you pie from McDonald's."

He grins. "I'm never going to live that comment down. I can see it now." He pauses with his fork above the slice. "Do you want some of this?"

"No. I brought it for you."

He picks up a forkful, and I can't look away from the redness of the berries as they disappear into his mouth. I watched my brothers shovel pie into their faces for twenty minutes and wanted to kill them, but Thomas makes it look like the most sensual thing he's ever experienced.

"This is amazing," he says. "Did you make it?"

I nod. "Well. Mom made the crust."

"Are you still mad at all men?"

"All but one."

He smiles and meets my eyes. "Thank you for coming over." He hesitates. "After this afternoon . . . I actually thought you might not show up."

"Oh, no. We found those letters. I'm dying of curiosity. I'm all in now. You're lucky I'm not making you eat that pie in the car while I drive."

He loses the smile. "I don't think we should go."

I blink. "You what?"

"I don't think we should go." He pauses, and there's the slightest bit of tension around his eyes. "I would have called to tell you, but . . . I don't have a way to do that."

"You don't think we should go?" I all but slap the table. "Why not?"

He looks back at the pie and cuts another bite, but doesn't lift it to his mouth. He taps the fork against the plate, little clicks of steel on glass. His jaw is tight. "I don't want to get caught."

No wonder he's not champing at the bit to get out of here. I thought for sure I'd pull up in the driveway and he'd leap through the passenger side window and tell me to gun it.

"You don't have to stay in town," I tell him. "Even if you were out on bail, you wouldn't have to—"

"It's a perception thing," he said. "Stan told me that leaving town makes me look guilty."

"But we're not *leaving*, we're just . . . visiting."

"And how would I explain what we're doing there?" Some irritation finds its way into his voice. "Your brothers are looking for a reason to shoot me. I don't want to add kidnapping to the list of charges."

"Is it technically kidnapping if I'm driving?"

That makes him smile, but it's grim. "There are no other leads. I'm worried they're going to charge me just because there's no one else. Stan was telling me about a case in Baltimore that ended in a prison sentence based on the testimony of an eyewitness. That's *it*. No evidence or anything. One guy said he saw the other guy do it, and *bam*, thirty years in prison."

I frown. "We should tell the police about the letters." I hesitate. "Some of them are a little . . . intense."

Now his smile is genuine. "That's the same word you used to describe me."

"Exactly."

He considers that for a moment. "He was young. The letters aren't creepy. They're desperate. He wanted his mother." Thomas swallows, then shakes his head. "I wish I knew why."

I push the plate toward him. "Finish up. Let's go find out."

He takes a long breath and blows it out. "Charlotte . . ."

"Thomas."

His eyes settle on mine. "You're the only person who calls me by my full name." He finally eats that bite of pie. "I like that."

Part of me wants to say, screw the drive, let's stay here and get naked. It's so unlike me, but my body seems to have a mind of its own when I'm near him. A flush crawls up my neck to find my cheeks, but I manage to hold his eyes.

"We need to drive," I whisper.

"Why's that?" he whispers back.

Think of something. Anything. "Because we won't get caught. I'll drive the speed limit. No one in Crisfield knows you."

He doesn't answer. I can practically feel him deliberating.

"Isn't the curiosity killing you?" I say.

"*Yes.* You have no idea."

"Me, too!"

When he doesn't say anything, I jingle my keys in my

hand, taunting him. "If you don't want to go, I guess I'll just go on my own." It's not a complete bluff. I don't remember the exact address, but I know the street name, the town.

When he *still* doesn't say anything, I stand up. "All right, then. Enjoy the pie."

I'm halfway down the hall when his arm catches me around the waist. My breath stalls, and I all but collapse into him. My ankle gives a twinge. He holds me there just long enough to whisper in my ear. "You're dangerous."

I have to put a hand on the wall to stay upright when he lets me go.

"So you want to go?" I feel half-drunk. Or what I imagine I'd feel like if I'd ever had more than a taste of alcohol.

"I want to go. Stay right there. I need to get some things."

I'm breathless against the wall. It's going to be a miracle if I can keep the car straight on the road. "You . . . what?"

His voice is muffled when he calls back from his bedroom. "I need my sketchbook."

"Why?"

He reappears in front of me with a messenger bag slung over his shoulder. "Because I'm going to take your advice. I'm going to draw her."

CHAPTER SEVENTEEN
THOMAS

I'm glad Charlotte is driving. If we'd stayed in the house, there's a good chance I would have dragged her down the hall and coaxed her into my bed.

We only have an hour or so of sunlight left, but it's enough to see the sketch pad, to let the pencil drag my hand around the surface.

I've been staring at the white paper for a good five minutes. I haven't made a mark.

"You're killing me," she says. "You know that?"

I glance up at her. "Why?"

"*Why?*" She looks over and taps her fingers on the paper. "You're, like, this amazingly talented artist, and I have to watch the road."

I let the *amazing* comment go by without remark. I never know what to say to comments like that. Saying *thank you* feels arrogant. Drawing is as natural as breathing. How would she respond if I said, *You're amazing at respiration*?

Instead, I say, "I haven't drawn anything yet."

"I know. I'm just saying."

I make a face. "I don't know if anyone wants to see this."

She's quiet for a while. "Are you afraid to draw it?"

"Yes." I hesitate. "I got everything out last night, but I didn't want to do it."

This is true. I stared at this same blank piece of paper last night, and my eyes kept drifting to the pile of letters from my brother.

"Are you afraid to see it again?" she says softly.

"I see it again every time my brain settles and goes quiet," I say. "I don't need a drawing for that."

"Draw something else," Charlotte says.

I snap my fingers. "Quick, Thomas," I mock. "Draw me a pony. No. Wait. A unicorn. No, wait. A pony *riding* a unicorn."

She gives me a solid shove. "Shut your mouth. I mean, draw something *else*. Not your mother. Just make the pencil move."

I look at the paper. I think about the exercises I used to attempt, when I first began taking my art more seriously. A glass bottle. A woman's eye. Water pouring from a pitcher.

Every time my eyes blink, the image of my mother is superimposed over all of it.

"I can't do it," I whisper.

She's quiet again. We're on the highway finally, and the road hums beneath us.

"Draw your brother," she says.

Protests come up from my throat, but they don't make it to my lips. My hand is already moving on the paper. The pencil is forming a doorway. A bedroom doorway.

Well, right now it just looks like a door frame, but I add some shadow, then erase a bit, allowing for the glint of light on the doorknob. Short sloping lines begin the outline of a face: a man's jaw, his cheekbone, just the bare side of his mouth, enough to show he's not happy. I don't have his eyes yet, but they'll come.

I need a better eraser, but I can't take the time to dig around in my bag. Pink shreds of rubber appear all over the pad and I barely take the time to brush them from my drawing space. A hand appears along the edge of the door frame, four individual fingers, rough from work.

Back to his face. Shadow finds his jaw, tiny spots of darker stubble. He needs a shave. He's a little careless with his appearance, but his hair is cut short. He's lean, and fit, and the hand leads to an arm, and, above that, one broad shoulder. Erase, erase. He's wearing a T-shirt. I thought his eyes would be afraid, because his body is only half visible, implying that he's hiding. But there's no fear here.

He's determined.

Charlotte kills the engine.

I look up in surprise. We're parked on a narrow street, and the sun has fallen closer to the horizon, a bright beacon that burns my eyes.

"Wow," she says softly.

I want to flip the cover closed. It's ridiculous, but this feels too personal. I'm drawing straight from my imagination, from a deeply hidden place inside me, and having the image bared on the page is unnerving. "It's not done."

"I know. It's still . . . phenomenal." She hesitates.

"This is ridiculous." It takes everything I have not to rip the page up and crumple it in my fist. "I feel like I'm romanticizing the whole thing. Look at my big, defiant brother."

"Defiant," she agrees. "That's exactly what it feels like." She pauses. "What's he looking at?"

"I don't know." I give her half a smile, though my emotions are all over the place. "You stopped driving." I look around. We're parked on a residential street. The houses are small, not new, yet set a good distance apart, though none have driveways or garages. It feels like we've driven into a sitcom from the seventies.

"Is this it?" I say.

"Yes. The house is down the road a bit. I didn't want to park in front of it like a creepy stalker."

I give her a glance. "Now we just look like we're creepily stalking *this* house."

She shrugs and climbs out of the car. "Stay here, then. I'm going to check it out."

Like I'm going to let the girl limp her way down a strange street. I shove my sketchbook into my bag, throw the strap over my shoulder, and follow her onto the sidewalk.

The humidity is finally taking a break, and kids are at play in half the yards we pass. Gulls lazily sail through the air overhead. We must be close to the beach here. Sand appears to be mixed with the soil.

"Are you nervous?" she says.

"No." I watch two little girls run and shriek through a sprinkler in the next yard. "I'm not sure we'll find anything. The most recent letter was five years old."

She shrugs. "Danny still lives at home. Ben and Matt still come every Saturday for dinner. Small town living. You know."

"No," I say. "I don't know."

"Well," she says. "Maybe you'll get a chance to find out."

I've been watching the street numbers, and we're getting closer. They're descending, like a countdown. I calculate that we're four houses away, and I can see the frame of the house we're seeking, though large pine trees in the yard keep it mostly out of view. My heart trips and stumbles in my chest.

What if she's right? What if he's here?

What if she's wrong? What if he's not?

And then we're there, standing on the sidewalk, looking at a nice Cape Cod–style home, with white siding and a gray shingled roof. The house looks newer than those around it. The siding isn't quite as old, and the railing on the porch is made of vinyl instead of painted wood. A blue-and-black kid's bike rests against the side of the house, and a minivan is parked on the street.

My heart stutters again, before I remind myself that my brother is twenty-three, not six.

Nothing about this house looks like the brick wall I sketched, but I want to pull the drawing out of my bag to compare it.

I'm staring and I can't stop.

So much for not looking like a pair of stalkers.

"What do you want to do?" says Charlotte. "Should we just knock on the door?"

"And say what? That we found a bunch of letters, and we want to know if someone here wrote them?"

"Um. Yes?"

Well. I don't know if I can do that.

Something about all this feels wrong anyway. I can't put my finger on it, but my brother doesn't live here. He doesn't visit here.

At the house next door, a middle-aged man is dragging trash cans to the curb. He gives us an odd look. "You kids looking for someone?"

"Maybe," says Charlotte. She looks at me.

It's a prompt, but I don't know what to say. My brain is still taking in this small, white house. Did he use a fake address? Why?

Charlotte clears her throat. "His mother just passed away. We found some letters in her things, and they were sent from this address."

She's right. That was pretty simple. I've been spending too much time worried about every move I make.

The man sets the trash can against the curb. "Oh." His eyes soften. "I'm sorry, son."

I look between him and the house. "It doesn't look like a twenty-three-year-old guy lives here."

"No." He frowns. I don't blame him. I'm being abrupt. I didn't even thank him for his sympathy.

Then he says, "The Coopers moved in last year. One of those *We Buy Any Property* companies rehabbed the house after the Bellweathers died. But their grandson moved out a while ago."

The sentences come out of his mouth without any thought behind them, but they hit me like fists. *After the Bellweathers died. Their grandson. Their grandson moved out.*

Grandparents. He lived with grandparents.

I had grandparents!

My hand is gripping Charlotte's. I don't know if she grabbed mine or if I grabbed hers, but I'm going to fall over if she lets go.

"Do you know where their—where their grandson went?" I say.

He frowns, thinking. "He enlisted, if I remember correctly. Hurt his leg playing football, so he couldn't play college ball, but he passed the physical for the Navy. Or maybe the Marines?" He shakes his head. "It's been years. I just remember George talking about how they were worried he wouldn't pass the physical."

I swallow. "You wouldn't know where to find him, would you?"

He shakes his head and gives me a sad smile. "I'm afraid not."

Of course not.

Enlisted. This is a dead end. If he's in the military, he could be anywhere. He could be in a war zone, for god's sake.

He could be dead.

"It's okay," I say. My voice sounds hollow. "Thank you."

"Sure." He pauses. "Good luck."

A breeze rolls down the street, making the trees rustle. The man is halfway back up the driveway before I realize that I'm still just standing here, staring at the new house. This is a dead end. I knew it was. *I knew it.*

"Hey!" Charlotte calls.

The man turns.

"Their grandson," she says. "Do you know his name?"

He has to think for a minute, but then he nods. "Joe."

Joe. Like the newness of the house, it doesn't feel right.

"He's wrong," I mutter. "It's not *Joe.*"

Charlotte looks at me. "What?"

"I don't know." I shake my head a little. "It's not Joe."

She doesn't question me. She just turns back to the man. "Are you sure it's Joe?"

"Yes. Joe. Joe Bellweather." He turns back to the house.
I sigh.

But then he stops, turns, and snaps his fingers. "You know what? It wasn't Joe. John. I think it was John."

My heart bangs around. That's not it either, but it's closer.

"Jonathan!" he finally declares. "Jonathan Bellweather. That's it."

Jonathan. My brain clicks the names into place. That's it.

I have a brother.

And now I have his name.

Charlotte's driving again, and we're rolling through the middle of town. We've already passed the high school— closed for the summer—and now we're looking for places he might have hung out.

Well, I am. She's probably waiting for me to tell her what to do.

"What do you want me to do?" she finally asks quietly.

Exactly.

"I have no idea." I look at the shops lining the street. It's not like the gas station attendants or the workers behind the counter at KFC are coincidentally going to know him.

As we drive farther along, the storefronts begin to look older, more settled in the community. Brick facings abound, but an aged, weathered brick, nothing new or modern. This is an area where people used to shop, but now mostly avoid. An awning sags over a flower shop. Main Street Bank doesn't even have an ATM out front, but heavy bars block the windows. A tattoo parlor sports a pane of glass with long strips of duct tape hiding a crack. The next strip of shops offers a nail salon with a broken neon sign, two empty storefronts, and a bail bondsman. The light begins to fade, and shadows crawl along the sidewalk. My eyes fall on a crack in the pavement.

It's just a crack, but it looks familiar. This whole building seems familiar, like I've been down this street before.

I almost grab the steering wheel. "Charlotte. Stop. Stop the car."

She hits the brakes, and a car behind us lays on the horn. She winces and waves them by.

"Sorry," I say. "I just—that crack in the pavement—"

I'm about to sound insane. I shake my head. Then, without warning, I get out of the car.

"Hey!" she cries. "Thomas—"

"One second," I say. "I just need to check something." I walk to the edge of the building. The bricks are crumbling apart, barely held together by decades-old mortar.

Almost hesitantly, I place my hand against the corner of the building.

And that's it. I'm just standing here with my hand on some crumbling brick.

What was I expecting? A vision?

"Hey. Kid. You okay?"

A large black man has come out of the bail bonds shop. When I say *large*, I don't mean tall, either. His gut hangs over his waistband, and his jowls take up most of his neck. His arms are huge, though, and that's not just fat. He looks to be about forty or fifty years old, judging by the gray in his hair, but it doesn't make him look frail. In fact, just the opposite. This isn't a guy you want to screw with.

I shake my head. I don't know what I'm doing here. I don't know why I got out of the car.

He frowns. "You sick?"

"No." I cough. "I'm looking for my brother."

He looks up and down the street. "We haven't had any kids through here in a while. It's getting dark. Bedtime. Most kids are heading home." He says it like he has a few of his own.

I shake my head again. "Not a kid. He's older than me."

"What's his name?"

"Jonathan."

"I don't know any Jonathan. What's he look like?"

"I don't—" This is so frustrating. "I don't know."

"You don't know what your brother looks like?" He squints at me. "Are you on something?"

I feel like I need to be. "No. I'm—it's fine. I'm sorry I bothered you."

Back in the car, I have to run my hands through my hair. My breathing won't settle.

Charlotte eyes me with concern and doesn't pull away from the curb. "Are you okay?"

"I feel like I'm losing my mind."

"What just happened? Did you recognize that place?"

"Yes."

"You've been here before?"

I press a fist against my mouth. "No. I don't think so."

She bites her lip. "I don't understand."

"I don't know. Maybe it's something. Maybe it's nothing. I *remember* this place."

She glances at the building, then back at me. "Okay . . . ?"

I shake my head in frustration. "I have this memory—I don't know. Look." I flip through my sketchbook, to older drawings. I find one I did a year ago and show it to her.

"*Look*," I say again.

"I'm looking." But she doesn't sound like she's putting two and two together.

I point at the brick wall. "That's the *exact* wall I saw in my head. That's the exact sidewalk." My eyes fall on a line in the drawing. "Look!"

The penciled line in my drawn sidewalk corresponds almost exactly to the broken concrete of the actual sidewalk.

Charlotte frowns. "It looks like it. Couldn't it be coincidence?"

"No." I shake my head. "It's not coincidence. I saw exactly this place. I thought it was somewhere else, but . . . maybe it's here."

"Okay, so . . . you're psychic?"

"No. I don't know." I want to put my head in my hands. "I just know I've seen this place before."

"When you were a child?"

I think back to that memory of being with my father. Brick buildings just like these. A promise to get ice cream. I'd always assumed it was Baltimore with all the brownstones.

"Can we park?" I ask. "Can we walk around?"

"It's going to take over an hour to get back, so I'm already pushing it with my time limit." She looks around dubiously. "I don't exactly *want* to walk around here after dark, if you catch my drift."

Sometimes I forget she's so sheltered. This is nothing you wouldn't encounter in a city. This hasn't even hit my radar as a *bad area*. More economically depressed. We're only a few miles away from the wide-spaced houses and manicured lawns.

I glance at the clock. She's right about the time, though. We have maybe half an hour to spare before we *have* to leave, and that's if she slows to twenty miles per hour in front of Stan's driveway, and I leap out and roll.

"Maybe I could get another babysitting job later this week?" she suggests.

I give her a look. "You don't need to keep driving me down here."

She gives me a glance from under her lashes. "I don't mind the company."

Her expression makes me want to forget the brick wall and the sidewalk and drag her into the backseat.

"Drive," I say.

"Do you really want me to?"

"No," I whisper, and my voice is huskier than I'm ready for. I lean toward her. Inhale her breath.

And then her car door is yanked open, and someone drags her out of the vehicle.

CHAPTER EIGHTEEN
CHARLOTTE

I fight like hell.

A man has his arms wrapped around my midsection, trapping me against him. He's wrestling me away from the car. It's not the guy from the bail bond shop that Thomas was talking to, because I don't feel that kind of mass behind me. This man is lean and fit, and he's got me across the street before I realize what he's doing.

My instincts scream. He's going to get me in a car.

I fling my head back, *hard*. My head cracks and sends stars spinning through my vision, but the man yells. I get an arm free.

I owe Matt about a thousand free babysitting hours, because my body is responding automatically. I spin and thrust an elbow upward. I catch a jaw. My ankle screams as I pivot again, and then it gives out entirely.

He hits me between the shoulder blades and I go down.

An arm goes around my midsection again and I struggle, crying out.

"It's me," says Thomas. "It's me."

Then he shoves me through the door of the car, barely giving me enough time to move over before he climbs in with me and slams the door. He's in the driver's seat and I'm straddling the center console. His foot punches the accelerator. The car shoots forward. I nearly end up in the backseat.

He gets hold of my arm and helps me right myself. Parked

cars fly by the window, and he zooms through a yellow light just as it's turning red.

I can't get my head organized to yell at him.

"Holy shit," he says, breathless. "Are you okay?"

I don't know.

I honestly have no idea. My ankle is throbbing, and my elbow feels like I slammed it into a wall. I can't tell if I'm breathing or not.

"Hey." His voice is almost panicked. "Are you okay? Did he hurt you?"

I'm shaking. My brain suddenly decides to work, and everything snaps into focus. "Did you see him? Stop the car. We have to call nine-one-one."

"Do you really want me to?"

His voice is full of so many things. Worry, for me. He'll call an ambulance if I need one. But he's also warning me about what would happen if we called 911. There's no way we can report this. My family would find out. He'd end up in jail again.

Especially since he's driving right this second.

I swallow, hard, and glance at the speedometer. We're going sixty miles an hour through town. "Well, slow down at least."

He glances in the rear view mirror first, then eases his foot off the accelerator.

"Holy shit," he says again.

"See, and you wanted to walk around," I say weakly.

He's breathing heavily. "Charlotte. Are you okay? Did he hurt you?"

Did he? I don't think so. I'm shaking, though. Is this shock?

He glances over again. "How's your blood sugar? Do you have an epi-pen or something—?"

"That's for allergies." I take a long breath, hoping it'll help my brain stop spinning. I touch a hand to the back of my head. It hurts, but not too badly. "Just drive for a minute. I can't—this is—" My breath hitches as true pain starts to set in. "Just drive, okay?"

He drives. The inside of the car is so quiet that I hear crickets and tree frogs when we pass by stretches of woods.

After a few miles, he reaches out and puts his hand over mine. His hand is warm and secure, and it settles me. I twist my fingers through his, and he lets me.

"Seriously," he says. "I'll take my chances with the cops if you need an ambulance." He checks the mirrors again. "Or we can go straight to the hospital."

"No." I swallow. "Just drive."

He drives, but a few miles later, he kills the lights and pulls over on the shoulder.

I straighten in alarm. We're in one of the long stretches of farmland where there are miles between houses and no streetlights anywhere. "What's wrong?"

"It's okay." He gives my hand a squeeze. He hasn't let go since I grabbed him. "If I'm going to keep driving I need to adjust this seat. I'm not five-four."

I look out the window while he adjusts the seat and the mirrors. Darkness has fallen quickly, and it's like looking into an abyss.

I hit the button to lock the doors, just in case.

"Hey," he says softly. "Are you okay?"

I turn to find his eyes on me. His features are in shadow, but I can see his concern.

I shiver. "I don't know what just happened. Was that— was it a carjacking? I don't—"

"I don't know. Fuck, Charlotte. I don't know." He pauses, then shakes his head. "Something about that whole town bothers me."

He's not the only one. "Was he trying to get me into a car?"

"I don't know. He only got you into the middle of the street." Thomas pauses, and something like admiration creeps into his voice. "How did you know how to fight like that?"

"Matt." I choke on my breath. "God. Matt. Thank god for Matt." I want to call him right now and thank him, but I know I'll burst into tears the instant I hear his voice.

I glance back at Thomas, and my breathing settles. I should be frightened of sitting here in the darkness, but we're so far from anything that I actually feel more secure.

"Can we sit for a few minutes?" I say. "Please?"

"Sure," he says. "As long as you want." He rolls the windows down and turns off the car. All I can hear are the sounds of nighttime. It's so quiet that we'll hear anything long before it comes close to the vehicle.

I find his hand and thread my fingers between his again.

"Did you get a good look at him?" I finally say.

"Not a great look. He was Asian. Maybe thirty years old. He was wearing an apron." He says it like it's completely bizarre, and it *is*.

"An apron?"

"Yeah. Like he worked in a restaurant or something." He shudders. "I mean, who walks off the job and grabs someone out of a car? Maybe he's one of those creepy perverts who looks for opportunities to—"

"Stop." I squeeze my eyes shut, as if that will stop thoughts from racing through my head. "I hear enough from my brothers. I don't need to imagine more than what actually happened."

"Okay." A pause. "I'm sorry."

"Don't be sorry. Just . . . talk about something else."

He glances at me. "Do you need some food?"

Do I? I don't feel lightheaded. The back of my head hurts like crazy, and I'm going to want my crutches back tomorrow, but I don't think I'm low on blood sugar.

I shake my head, and my vision goes a little blurry. On second thought, maybe I have a concussion.

Without thinking about it, I lean over and rest my head on his shoulder. His arm is warm, and I can feel each breath as he inhales. Despite what just happened, I find myself re-membering the moment just before, when his breath mixed with mine.

"Anything else you're hiding?" he says to me.

I tilt my face up. "Hiding?"

"Amazing cook, badass fighter. What's next?"

"I can secretly fly."

His breath touches my hair. "I believe it."

Sparks flare in my brain, and this time it has nothing to do with the head injury. Being with him makes me brave.

"Were you going to kiss me?" I whisper. "Before?"

"Yes." He pauses, leaning closer, and a touch of wry humor enters his voice. "Were you going to let me?"

"Maybe."

He laughs softly. His hand traces the length of my forearm. Goosebumps spring up along my skin, and I shiver.

"Are you cold?" he says.

The sun has set, but it's still hot enough to cook an egg on the pavement. "Not cold." Warm, in fact, but it's the kind of warmth that begs for someone to share it. I wish I could shift closer to him.

Whoever put this center console here must have hated teenagers.

His fingers find my chin, and I inhale. His lips touch mine, and butterflies go wild in my abdomen. I have no experience with this, but he's gentle, and he's slow. When his mouth moves against mine, I respond in kind. One of his hands finds my waist, and there's a bit of skin bared between my shirt and my pants. His fingers find that spot and stroke, and I gasp into his mouth.

He pulls back, just an inch, maybe less. "Do you want me to stop?"

"I want you to keep going."

He smiles, but I can't take it. I press my mouth back to his. My hand reaches for his face, my fingers tangling in his hair.

His hand slides under my shirt, and the feel of his hand against the skin of my back sends a lick of fire up my spine. I want to pull him closer, and I shift in the seat, trying to draw him to me.

His tongue touches mine, and I break the kiss, startled. He tries to draw back, but I keep my hand on his face, holding him close.

"Sorry," he whispers.

I shake my head quickly. "Do it again."

He's more sure this time, and I'm all but panting into his mouth. My knees are on the seat and both his hands are on my waist, twin points of heat. The lower half of one hand is under the waistband of my capri pants, and I feel his finger slide along the lace hem of my panties.

I can't take it. I want to feel him everywhere. Without thought, I pull my shirt over my head.

"Charlotte." My name leaves his mouth in a rush of breath. "Charlotte. You don't have to—"

"Shut up," I whisper. "Don't stop kissing me."

He's a good listener.

His hands roam further now, sliding up my back, stroking my shoulders, tracing the edge of my bra. His thumbs slide up my abdomen to stop just at the base of my ribcage. He kisses my jaw, my neck, my shoulder. I press my face into the curve of his neck and inhale, brushing my lips against his skin.

Then his hand gets braver, as he strokes a thumb over my breast. I feel the touch all the way through my body. It lights a fire in my belly, and I climb over the console to straddle his lap. I'm pressed against him, and I can feel everything.

He hisses in a breath. "Charlotte," he whispers.

Light fills the car, and a horn blares. I jump a mile.

But then an eighteen-wheeler roars by, the force of its speed rocking the car.

Quiet overtakes us again.

I realize that I don't have a shirt on. That I'm straddling him. That I am feeling something I've only ever read about in health class and joked about with Nicole.

Heat flares on my cheeks. I press my face into his shoulder. "Oh my god."

Thomas keeps his hands on my waist. "Maybe we should slow down," he says carefully.

My voice is muffled as I speak into his shoulder. "All I can think about is a sleeve of Ritz crackers."

He bursts out laughing. "I guess I should be glad you're not thinking about a roll of quarters." He pauses, and I feel him move. That's both better and worse.

"Here," he says softly, and fabric brushes against my back. "Your shirt."

I draw back to look at him. Inexplicably, I want to cry. He must think I'm ridiculous.

His eyes are dark and intent on mine. He brushes a hand across my cheek, and I want to lean into him.

"You're beautiful," he says, reverence in his voice.

My breath catches.

His hand stops there on my face. "We don't have to do it all at once."

"I don't—I'm so stupid." I push my face into his shoulder again.

"You're not stupid."

"I am."

"I should have stopped you."

"You *tried*!"

He laughs again, more softly this time. "I didn't try very hard."

"I took advantage of you," I whisper.

He snorts with laughter and chokes on his breath. "You're hilarious. Seriously. Put your shirt on."

"Do I look terrible?"

"Charlotte. You kill me." He takes my shoulders and

pushes me back so he can look at me again. The heat in his eyes steals my nerves. "I'm a heartbeat away from telling you to take your pants off."

I blush again. The freakish assault on the street feels like it happened days ago.

He glances at the clock. "We need to drive."

I feel drunk on his presence. I pull the shirt over my head and gingerly climb back over the console. How did I do it so fluidly before? "I don't want to."

"I don't want to either." He leans down to kiss my temple. "But I think I'm going to find myself in need of a babysitter soon."

I'm twenty minutes late getting home. My phone hasn't rung, but I'm terrified to go through the door anyway, sure my parents are sitting up in the living room. I have no reason to think they would know about my adventure with Thomas, but guilt has a death grip on my chest all the same.

I'm still too keyed up. I can't go in there yet.

The man on the street still haunts me. The back of my head is still tender. Thomas said it was an Asian man in an apron—could that be more bizarre? Like he said, who walks off the job and grabs a girl out of a car?

Then again, I hear about enough freakish events from my brothers to fill a novel. Just because our town isn't a hotbed of crime doesn't mean we don't have some real freaks. Two weeks ago Danny came home disgusted because they caught a guy getting friendly with a dead deer on the side of the road.

I'm not a big fan of imagining someone like that getting his hands on me.

Maybe that's all it was, though. Just some freak acting on an impulse.

Acting on impulse. Kind of like the way I acted with Thomas.

I blush so fast and so hard that I need to slap my hands over my cheeks. Oh, this is no good. I need to put that out of my head to think about later.

In bed.

The blush is back. I can't *believe* the direction my thoughts have taken.

My phone chimes and I almost have a heart attack. I hope for a message from Thomas before reminding myself that's an impossibility.

I steel myself for a chastising message from my mother.

No. Thank god. Nicole.

NK: How was it?

CR: Amazing.

NK: Did you make him use a condom?

CR: OMG NICOLE WE DID NOT HAVE SEX

NK: Then what was so amazing?

I sigh and lean my head against the seat back.

CR: Everything else.

I've been sitting in the car too long. My parents probably know I'm out here. They probably know I was up to no good.

My heart is beating against my ribcage, looking for escape.

I need a story. I need a plan. Just in case.

Before I can think of one, the front door swings open, and Matt is standing there, illuminated by the light from the living room. I'm surprised he's here—it's after eleven, and he promised to take the girls for ice cream. He's got another beer in his hands, and he frowns at me. Any story I might have come up with dies in my throat.

He glances behind him, then closes the front door. "Are you okay?" he mouths.

Sheepishly, I nod, then climb out of the car.

He waits for me on the front steps. "Why were you sitting in the car?" he asks quietly. There's no suspicion in his voice—it's a genuine question.

At least I don't have to lie. "Texting Nicole. Why are you still here?"

He shrugs. "Mom offered to keep the girls overnight so Ali can get a good night's sleep. Dad just fell asleep on SportsCenter. I was getting ready to leave."

I stare up at him, his hair shining in the porch light. He's not the most handsome of my brothers, but he's the most honest and reliable. I feel bad for teasing him earlier—he's a great husband to Alison.

He's a great brother, too. If not for him, I never would have escaped the man in the street.

I throw my arms around his neck and hug him tight.

"Whoa." He rocks back a little before catching me and returning the hug. "What's this for?"

"For being a good brother." To my surprise, my voice is thick with tears. Too much emotion has filled the night. I press my face to his shoulder.

"Hey," he says. "Charlotte—what's wrong?"

"Nothing." But I don't let him go.

"You're not making a good case for *nothing*, you know." He keeps holding on, though.

After a moment, his voice is quieter. "Did something happen?"

Too much. But I can't say that. I shake my head.

"Do you want me to get Mom?"

I laugh a little, and draw back. There's a damp spot on his shoulder. "No. That's quite all right."

"Do you want me to go get you some chocolate ice cream?"

I mock gasp at him. "Mom would kill you, offering to get me something full of sugar."

He shrugs and gives me a quiet smile. "I know it would cheer Ali up."

"I'm okay. Just—it's been a long day."

He leans back against the porch railing. "Do you want to talk about it?"

The entire evening replays in my head. There is absolutely no way I can explain any of it—especially since I was supposed to be twenty minutes in the opposite direction, babysitting for a family from church.

I look away. "No." Then I glance back. "Thanks, though."

He offers a conspiratorial smile, then glances at the cast iron double rocker on the porch. "Do you want to sit and rock?"

I grin. "Okay."

When we're seated, he kicks at the floor boards, and we swing forcefully. He used to do this when I was little, and he had to babysit for all of us. Ben and Danny would try to kill each other in the front yard, and Matt would propel me back and forth on the rocker while he played some stupid hand-held video game.

Sometimes he wouldn't pay attention and I'd go flying, but for the most part, it's one of my favorite memories.

I study him. "I can't believe you're going to have another baby."

He takes another drink from his bottle. "I'm aiming for two more. Got to one-up Dad."

I snort with laughter. "Is Alison in on that plan?"

"Oh yeah. She'd have sixteen kids if I'd let her. Even when she's puking at three in the morning, she's telling me how she can't wait to meet the next one."

He feels the same way. I can hear it in his voice. That makes me smile.

He gives the swing another shove. We weigh a lot more than we once did, and the rocker shifts and scrapes against the porch floorboards.

"Do you ever worry about your job?" I ask him quietly. "Having all those kids?"

He studies his bottle for a good long while, and I don't

think he's going to answer me. It's not the kind of question I've ever asked Matt. He's not a talker, not about his feelings. He'll express emotion by talking about someone else.

"All the time," he finally says. "Sometimes I don't understand how life can be so thrilling and so terrifying, all at once." He glances at me. "Every baby is another one to worry about, you know?"

I nod.

He drains the bottle, then stops the rocker so he can set it on the floor. Once it's out of the way, he gives us another push. "It's like last week, when that kid was carrying you out of the woods. I've never shot someone, Char, but I knew what he'd done—and I thought he'd done something to you . . ."

He's talking about Thomas. I hold my breath.

His voice has grown too tight to continue. He has to take a breath. "And then to run into him today—to hear him talk to Ali—" He stops again and shakes his head. "I shouldn't have hit him the first time. I've never wanted to hurt someone the way I did that day. I've never done that before. I've never done *anything* like that before. It's just a job, you know? But with him—what he did to his own mother. . . . I don't know what it would take for someone to do that. I don't know if he's a psychopath or a schizophrenic or just a *bad kid*, but to strangle his own mother, and then to see him with you . . ." He lets out a long breath, then picks up his bottle again. "I'm about to need another one of these."

That guilt I felt in the car has tripled. Here he's unloading all this familial concern, and an hour ago I was making out with the very guy he's worried about. "Want me to get you another beer?" My voice is hollow, but I can't say anything else.

Matt smiles, but it's wan. "Nah. I've got to drive home." He shakes his head. "I shouldn't have hit that kid last week. I've never lost it like that. I'm lucky he didn't press charges."

I swallow.

Matt looks at me, and his voice is deadly serious. "But today—if he'd put his hands on Ali or the girls, I would have done it again."

Thomas wouldn't hurt them. I want to say it. The need to defend him is almost causing me physical pain. He's had numerous opportunities to hurt me, and he's never given me a moment's concern that he would.

I stare out at the darkened yard. I can't say a word.

Matt is looking at me. "What's wrong, Char?"

I shake my head. "Nothing."

"Secret boyfriend?"

I whip my head around so fast I almost fall off the rocker.

Matt's eyes go wide with surprise, but then he laughs. "Good for you, kid." He pauses, then loses the smile. "Unless he did something to you."

"No," I croak. I'm shaking my head so fast it might fall off. "He's very nice."

"Good." He musses my hair, which usually makes me nuts, but right this second, it barely registers. "I'm glad."

"You are?"

"Yeah. You deserve to have some fun. I don't know how you put up with Mom's meddling." He grimaces. "Or Grandma. God."

I let out a breath. "You mean they make you nuts, too?"

"Nah, I keep having babies so the oldest-son shrine in Mom's room is still intact." He gives me a nudge when he sees my scowl. "But I'm not an idiot. I hear the way they talk to you." He pauses. "I caught the little comment about the dinner dishes."

I don't know what to say. My emotions are all over the place, and this conversation isn't helping.

Matt thinks I have a secret boyfriend! He's right, but— OMG!

And he noticed that I was pissed about the dinner dishes?!

"I'm sorry," he says. "We should have helped you. You sprained your ankle last week, and we all just sat there."

I'm staring at him. "Who are you, and what have you done with my brother?"

"Ha ha. You're hilarious." He chucks me on the chin. "Just because someone tells you to do something, you don't have to listen. Say no. Ask for help."

"Yeah, okay, like you guys would—"

"I will." He puts out a hand. "Deal?"

I shake his hand before my brain catches up. "Deal? What's the deal?"

He smiles. "I'll help you with the dishes next time if you don't kill me for putting the girls to bed on the floor of your room."

"Matthew! They wake up at five in the morning!"

He mock flinches like I'm going to hit him. "They begged. They were so cute. They kept whispering that they were going to be like big girls now. I couldn't say no."

When he puts it like that, I can't even be mad. "You are such a softie."

"Shh," he says. "Let's keep that between you and me."

CHAPTER NINETEEN
CHARLOTTE

I dream of Thomas.

It's a good dream.

He's in bed with me, and I'm whispering at him to be quiet, that we'll wake the girls.

In response, he presses his lips to mine, a kiss to silence me. His body is heavy and warm against me, his hands sliding beneath my T-shirt to stroke across my abdomen. I'm wearing less than I was in the car, just an old shirt and some booty shorts, and he makes a low sound in his throat when he discovers I'm not wearing a bra.

"*Shh*," I whisper. Then his thumb brushes over my nipple, and I gasp and arch into him.

His mouth moves to my neck. He laughs, a low rumble against my skin. "*Shh* yourself."

He's going to wake the girls. I put my hand over his mouth.

He responds by sliding his hand along my thigh to skim beneath the edge of the shorts. I nearly cry out, but he's quick, and a hand goes over *my* mouth.

"Hush, Charlotte," he whispers. "We have to be quiet. We have an audience." Dark eyes twinkle in the night. I can't see anything but those eyes. They fill my vision. Everything else is sensation. He's on top of me now, pressing his body into mine. My shirt has vanished, and his has too, impossibly removed in this dream world. His hips thrust against mine until I'm making small gasps against his hand. My entire body is flushed, wanting him closer, wanting all of him.

He pushes my hair back from my face and kisses me again. He tastes like brown sugar and strawberries. My legs slide against his, and I wish the shorts would disappear like my shirt. I want to feel his hands everywhere. Heat pools in my belly.

His hand slides up my abdomen to cup my breast, then travels higher. He strokes a finger over my throat.

"What can I do to you?" he whispers.

"Anything," I breathe.

He laughs. His thumb brushes my jaw. Fingers trail through my hair, tracing a line down my shoulders. His legs nudge my own apart, and I almost cry out when I feel him more closely pressed against me.

"Hush," he says again. We're both slick with sweat. His mouth closes over mine, his hands holding my face, so gentle, so tender.

Then his hands travel lower. I don't know what to expect, but I'm almost moaning with the anticipation of it. His fingers move so slowly, trailing down over my chin, sliding along my neck. Then tightening.

Tightening.

His thumbs are over my trachea, putting just enough pressure there. I can't breathe. His body is still moving against mine, his lips kissing my eyelids. He must not realize. I struggle a little, grabbing his wrists.

He doesn't stop. His grip tightens. Too tight.

This is deliberate.

His eyes still twinkle. That's all I can see. Eyes. Darkness.

Fear floods my body, chasing all the heat away. I fight him, pulling at his arms now. I can't cry out. Air can't make it into my lungs.

I thrash against him, but he's too strong. His body pins mine. His hands grip harder.

"You said I could do anything," he whispers.

Stars float above my bed. Shooting stars. Fireworks. I wrench my head back and forth. His nails dig in. My skin tears. Now all I see is red. Blood. I can't feel my body. My arms flail.

Something sparks and crashes.

Someone screams.

And then I'm gasping. Choking. Someone is shaking me.

"Charlotte!" It's my mother. "Charlotte, wake up!"

I sit up in bed. She's sitting beside me, clutching my shoulders. The girls are crying.

Suddenly, I'm crying too. Huge, racking sobs. The nightmare won't let go of me. It hurts to breathe. It hurts to turn my head.

Mom puts a hand against my cheek. Why hasn't she turned on the light? I can barely see anything. "Charlotte. Charlotte. Did you check your levels before you went to bed?"

Nightmares are a symptom of insulin shock. I nod quickly and stutter through the tears. "Yes. Yes. I d-did. I'm fine." But I'm not fine. I'm shaking and I can't stop. "C-c-can't you turn on the light?"

"You broke the light. Girls, that's enough." She turns her head and calls out into the hall. "Phil? Phil, can you turn on the hall light?"

He doesn't. Danny's voice carries up from downstairs. "Dad, get down here. The front door is open. What the hell is going on?"

My heart stops. I reach up a hand to touch my neck, and it comes away wet.

Sweat. It has to be sweat. From the nightmare.

"I need a light," I say. My voice is thready with panic. "Turn on the light. Right now. Mom, turn on the light."

"Okay, Charlotte, just calm down." Her voice is the patient-yet-exasperated tone she usually saves for the girls when they're being ridiculous. "I'll turn on the hall light."

She leaves my side, and I want to pull her back. Instead, I grab for the girls and pull them into bed with me, hugging them to my chest and inhaling their little-girl sweetness.

The hall light flares. I wince and turn my head away.

"Char-char," whispers Lexi. "You bleeding."

Mom reappears in the doorway, and she gasps. Her hands go over her mouth. "Charlotte. Oh, Charlotte." She turns to yell down the stairs. "Phil, we need to call nine-one-one."

That mocking voice echoes in my head. *You said I could do anything.*

I gently disentangle myself from the girls. I move toward my closet mirror in a trance. Suddenly this feels like the dream, and everything before feels like reality.

Thank god the only light comes from the hall. That's bad enough. My hair is a wild mess of tangles. My face is white, like I've seen a ghost. Smudges of blood are everywhere: on my cheeks, on my shirt, on my thighs.

And on my neck are six long tears, like fingernails grabbed and pulled their way through the flesh.

Someone sobs.

It's me.

Danny appears in my doorway. He takes one look at me. "What the fuck."

The girls gasp. Mom hauls him out into the hallway, then rushes to my side. She wraps her arm around me. "Charlotte. What happened? Was someone in your room?"

I can't stop shaking. I collapse against her. My knees won't hold me, and she helps me to the carpet.

Dad replaces Danny in the doorway. "There's an ambulance coming," he says. His voice is fierce. "Did you see him, Charlotte? Did you get a look at him?"

I'm nodding. I'm crying. "I thought—I thought I was dreaming. I thought—"

Mom strokes my shoulder. "It's okay," she murmurs. "It's okay. Do you know who it was?"

I burst into a round of fresh sobs. "Yes. I do."

Dad kneels in front of me. He touches my shoulder, and he's so gentle that I throw myself into his arms. He'll keep me safe. I know he will.

"Who?" he says quietly.

"Thomas Bellweather."

CHAPTER TWENTY
THOMAS

Getting arrested in front of the church sucked.

Getting dragged out of bed, thrown up against the wall, and handcuffed, sucked *more*.

Two cops are interrogating me. I don't know either of them, but I've lost track of who I know and who I don't. They're not related to Charlotte and her brothers, and that's pretty much all I care about. I'm exhausted, and my head is pounding.

All I wore to bed were some threadbare sweatpants, so that's all I'm wearing now. Well, sweatpants and a pair of sneakers. The cops let me shove my feet into those. No socks, though.

The air conditioning is blasting, and I'm *freezing*.

A woman in a white jacket came earlier and scraped the junk out from under my fingernails. She had a police escort, but she treated me like a specimen. My fingernails weren't as clean as they could have been, what with the sketching in the car and the course of my day. I kept apologizing to her, as if acting like a gentleman would get me out of here.

She ignored me.

I was allowed a phone call, but the only person I could think to call was Stan. He didn't answer. I don't know anyone else. What am I going to do, call the library?

The cops keep shuffling me through different procedures. Mug shots. Fingerprinting.

Interrogation.

"What happened in the car?" asks Officer Franzen. He's tall and blond and practically sneering. He's probably an average guy in real life, but in here, he's been a real asshole. "She kept turning you down? Couldn't take it?"

"It was fine. We were fine. I told you that." I keep my eyes on the table. They haven't asked anything about our trip to Crisfield, and I'm not offering any information. I don't know what happened. Did Charlotte's family find out? Did she tell them? Were we followed?

I don't want to get her in more trouble if she hasn't volunteered where we were.

"But you wanted to go back for more, is that it?"

I raise my eyes enough to glare at him. "I don't know what you're talking about."

The other guy, an older man with graying hair and darker skin, named Officer Danesh, frowns at me. He's sitting more casually, tapping a pen on a notepad. "You understand you're being charged with burglary with intent to commit a crime of violence, don't you, Thomas?"

"She let me drive her car. I didn't break into it."

"No one is saying you broke into her car." He pauses. "We're talking about her house."

"What about her house?"

"You broke into her house, asshole," says Franzen. He looks like he might flip the table, just for effect.

"I've never been to her house," I snap.

Officer Danesh won't stop tapping that pen. "Then where were you tonight?"

"Sleeping! You found me in bed!"

"Uh huh." A mark on the notepad that I'd swear was a doodle. "I think it's time for you to be honest with us, kid."

"I am being honest!" I want to pound my hands on the table, but I'm handcuffed, and the little chain rattles every time I move. It's humiliating and terrifying at the same time.

I grit my teeth. "I'm so damn sick of you people hassling me."

A knock strikes the door, and another cop sticks his head in. "Danesh. The DA called. They're changing the charges."

Danesh steps out. Franzen whistles through his teeth. "I'm guessing attempted murder."

Blood freezes in my chest. Attempted murder?

"Is she hurt?" I whisper. "What happened?"

"Save it, kid. Probably the same thing you did to your mother."

I jerk hard against the handcuffs and try to go after him. The restraints do their job—but he falls back anyway. His ass hits the ground, and he's got a hand over his face. I see blood.

I freeze. I didn't touch him. I swear I didn't touch him.

"You little shit!" he yells. "You little—"

The door opens. "Franzen. Get out here."

My eyes are wide. It's like with Danny. I lost a moment of time somehow.

Franzen finds his feet and storms through the door. I'm left alone. Boo hoo.

Blood was on his face. Had I gotten close enough to hit him? I don't think so. Nothing on *me* hurts. Idiot probably poked himself in the nose while he was trying to get away from the local killer.

Danesh comes back in, and he's alone. I watch him as he sits. This time, the notepad is dropped on the table, with the pen on top of it.

"The District Attorney has adjusted the charges," he says. "Burglary with intent to murder. It's a felony." He pauses. "Officer Franzen is trying to add assault on a police officer."

Of course he will. I slouch back in my chair and glower. "Fuck him."

Danesh ignores me. "You'll be held until your bail hearing, which will probably be this afternoon. If you're denied bail or if you can't post the funds, you'll be taken to the county detention center to await trial. Do you have any questions?"

The words are dropped so simply, like he's reading me a shopping list, not telling me that I'll be in a cage for who knows how long. A vise grip encircles my chest and somehow squeezes the anger right out of me. Fear slides into place.

"Is she okay?" I say softly.

His mouth is a line, and he doesn't say anything for a moment.

I stare at him beseechingly until he sighs. His voice is very low and quiet. "Physically, she'll be fine."

Charlotte. What happened? My eyes fill, and I try not to blink so tears won't fall. When I speak, my voice sounds husky. "Do I need a lawyer?"

He hesitates. "Yeah, kid. You need a lawyer."

Sunlight finds the small window at the back of the cell. I hear the rumble of people arriving for work, people departing, normal daily activities.

Back here, I'm alone.

For a while, I thought about Stan, hoping he'd come to see me, to have a few words about how we're going to handle everything this time.

Stan doesn't appear.

When the sunlight fills the window completely, a thin black man in a uniform comes to the cell door with a tray.

"Breakfast," he says dispassionately.

He sets it on the floor and slides it toward me, then slams the gate, all in one fluid motion.

I glance at it. A biscuit, a sausage patty, and a short yellow cylinder that might be eggs, plus a bottle of water.

Fifty bucks says they deconstructed a McDonald's breakfast sandwich to bring me this food.

"Hey!" I yell.

"Bail hearing is at noon," he yells back. "Eat up."

Bail hearing. At least I won't have to wait all afternoon. "Hey!" I yell again. "Hey! I'm supposed to get a lawyer! What's going—?"

"You'll get a lawyer." The officer stops at the edge of the cell. "He'll be here in half an hour."

My lawyer is hung over. Actually, he might still be drunk. I can smell whiskey on his breath, and he desperately needs to wash his face. He introduces himself as William Shevalevsky. He's fifty if he's a day, and he's sporting a comb-over that's not fooling anyone.

Still, he's my key to finding out what's going on.

"What's happening?" I demand, when we're moved into a little room with a tiny table and two metal stools attached to the floor. My hands are chained to my stool, like I'm the Texas Tower Sniper and not some kid who's had some really shitty nights lately. "I didn't do anything. Don't they need some proof? Why have I been arrested?"

He clears his throat and actually has to check a folder. He burps. Definitely whiskey. "Ah. Um. Attempted murder. Burglary. Have you thought about how you want to plead?"

"I didn't try to kill anyone. Charlotte and I went to Crisfield last night. She dropped me off. I didn't hurt her. I didn't put my hands on her."

He has to check the folder *again.* "It says here that you broke into the home of Charlotte Rooker. Attempted to kill her through manual strangulation." William looks at me as though I've just sat down in front of him. "Where's your shirt?"

"What did you just say?" I almost come out of my chair. "What happened to Charlotte?"

"I just told you. Your shirt?"

"They arrested me at two in the morning. I wasn't wearing one. What happened to—?"

"You'll need one for the hearing."

"Would you shut the fuck up about a shirt? *What happened to Charlotte?*"

He looks pissed. "I'll ask you to watch your language, young man. I'm here to help you. How would you like to plead?"

"Not guilty! What the hell do you think it's going to be?"

He purses his lips, shoves the folder in his briefcase, and stands.

"Wait a minute!" I cry. "I need to know what's going on!"

"You tried to kill someone. You got caught. Now you'll be charged, and you'll either get bail, or you won't. I'll see you in court."

The cops give me a shirt. It's bright yellow, and it says CCDOC on the back. I have no idea what the CC stands for, but the DOC is plain as day. Department of Corrections. This is a jail shirt.

This will totally help me seem innocent in front of the judge.

Garretts Mill doesn't have many criminals, so I'm taken to the county courthouse alone. It's a forty-minute drive from the middle of nowhere to the middle of somewhere else. When I get there, however, I have to wait. I'm put in a tiny holding cell that has a bench on one wall, and that's it. There's barely enough space to turn around. I've seen a few of the other guys they've shuffled past my cell, and I'm glad to have the space to myself.

For the hearing, I don't get to stand with my lawyer—if I can even call him that. I stand with a uniformed officer, and William speaks for me.

I don't recognize anyone in the courtroom. Stan isn't here. Neither is anyone from Charlotte's family. Some people look vaguely familiar, but maybe I saw them at the funeral.

Or at the wedding.

The weight of the past few weeks falls onto my shoulders

like someone dropped it from an airplane. I want to collapse under the strain of it all.

Charlotte.

What happened last night? Is she okay?

The judge is a slender Asian woman with bright red lipstick. She listens to the prosecutor explain that I allegedly killed my mother three weeks ago, and due to a lack of evidence, I was allowed to remain free. The prosecutor is slick, polished. His suit is pressed and looks expensive. If he weren't talking about me personally, I'd believe him. He goes on to explain that I've been secretly seeing Charlotte Rooker, and after she rejected me sexually, I snuck into her room and attempted to strangle her.

I'm choking, gasping, unable to form words.

Finally, I do. "None of that happened!" I yell. "I didn't touch Charlotte!"

The judge looks at me. "You'll be quiet or I'll have the bailiff escort you from the room. This is not a trial. This is a bail hearing. Am I clear?"

I clamp my mouth shut. My breathing is so loud and fast that I'm worried I'm going to hyperventilate.

William is glaring at me from across the courtroom. "Shut up," he mouths.

I glare back.

"How does your client plead?" she asks William.

He checks his folder *again*. "Not guilty, your honor."

She bangs her gavel. "Bail is set at one million dollars. Next case."

Thank god the bailiff takes me by the arm. I almost collapse. *One million dollars.* I don't have that. Stan doesn't have that—if he would have paid bail in the first place.

I'm going to prison.

I'm going to prison.

The room spins. I don't register the double doors. I don't register the tiny holding cell—more of a closet—where they leave me, awaiting transport to the correctional facility.

I'm going to prison. Fear constricts my chest. I can't go to prison. This isn't supposed to happen. This is too fast. I didn't do anything. They can't send me to prison without proof, right? Without evidence?

I remember Stan's story about the kid who was convicted based on nothing more than a witness testimony.

Everyone in town hates me. They probably wouldn't even require a witness.

I'm going to be sick. I shouldn't have eaten breakfast. I should have left that stupid egg on the tray. I clutch my arms to my stomach.

Charlotte. Charlotte, what happened?

Not for the first time, I wish I had a phone. I wish I could talk to her.

I wish I knew if she was okay.

I rub my hands over my face.

Metal grates against metal as the locks to the door are thrown. I choke down a sob. This is it. They're going to take me to prison.

An officer holds the door open. "Thomas Bellweather?"

"Yeah?" I croak.

"You've made bail. Follow me."

I what?

I *what*?

I stumble to my feet and follow him. Did Stan do this? I'm going to owe him a million dollars. I'm going to mow his lawn every day. I'll clean his kitchen floor with my tongue. I'll never say anything nasty to him again. Ever.

But Stan isn't in the waiting room. There's a long counter with cashiers behind barred windows and three rows of plastic chairs. A few cops are around, a few men and women of varying ages, and one guy in the corner in a wheelchair.

I don't recognize anyone.

My heart hasn't stopped thundering in my chest. I look around a second time. One of the cops peels himself away from the wall and approaches. He's not in a uniform like the rest of them, but he's obviously in law enforcement because he's armed and he's wearing a vest with BEA in gold letters across the left breast. He's young, with short dark hair and dark, appraising eyes. He looks familiar, but I can't place him.

He watches me like a cop, that's for sure. "Ready to go?" he says.

I blink. Is this part of the procedure? There have been too many shocks in the last fifteen minutes. "Where?" I say dumbly.

"Home."

"You're taking me to Stan's?"

He smiles, like he's genuinely amused. "You poor, confused kid." His eyes flick to the cop who brought me out here. "Thanks, Jerry. I'll see you later this week, I'm sure."

The cop snorts. "Always a pleasure, JB."

JB. The first name to come to mind is Justin Bieber. The only thing worse would be if those initials were reversed. I feel giddy. Crazy. I almost burst out laughing. I gulp on air instead.

I'm losing my mind.

JB's eyes lock on mine. "What's so funny?" he says.

Wait. Did I laugh? What's happening here?

He claps me on the shoulder. "Come on. We need to get you something better than this getup."

I swallow, but he's walking, and I'm left with no choice but to follow.

The sunlight hits me in the face, blinding me. A microphone appears in front of me.

"Thomas Bellweather," a reporter is saying. "Why did you kill your mother?"

Another microphone. "Did Charlotte Rooker know the truth? Did you try to shut her up?"

Another shout. "Are you into erotic asphyxiation? Were you romantically obsessed with your mother?"

Oh my god.

Suddenly they're in front of me. I can't see JB. All I see are microphones. All I hear are shouts.

I'm gasping for air. My head is buzzing.

A hand grabs my arm. "Easy, Tommy. Take it easy." It's him. "No comment," he says strongly to the crowd. He propels me through the crowd, much like Stan did once. JB is more sure than Stan was, like he plays this role all the time.

I expect a police car like Stan's, but JB has a massive blue SUV. Steel grating separates the front from the back like a cop car, however. I can see it through the window. I expect him to put me in the back, but instead, he opens the front door.

I stare into the cab like I've never seen a car before. For an instant, I consider that I don't know this guy, and I don't know if I should be getting in a car with him.

He gives me a little push. "Get in."

All of a sudden, it's like the choice is taken from me. Reporters have followed us, but I launch myself into the passenger seat, and JB slams the door. The car is hot, but after my hours in air conditioning, it's the best feeling in the world.

A moment later, he climbs into the cab and starts the engine. I expect him to flip a few dials to get the air conditioning running, but he doesn't. Instead, he says, "Let me know when you've warmed up. I'm dying in this heat. People think the desert is bad, but it's nothing like this humidity."

I stare at him.

He glances at me, then at the rear view. "Jesus. I wish it were legal to run over the press." He slowly presses on the accelerator, probably giving them room to get out of the way.

When he turns onto the main road, he makes a right, instead of a left, which would lead to Stan's. I haven't stopped staring at him. I feel like I'm missing something big, but my brain can't find the right combination to unlock the mystery.

He glances at me again. "You all right? We'll get some lunch, but I can't take you somewhere looking like that. I'll loan you some things."

My mouth is dry. I have to lick my lips, but my voice still comes out with a rasp. "Who are you?"

He smiles, looking amused again. "You haven't figured it out yet? Honestly, I'm a little disappointed."

I haven't figured it out . . . ? My thoughts spin.

Easy, Tommy. Easy.

Only my mother ever called me Tommy.

My breath catches.

"If you're going to throw up, I'll pull over."

"JB," I whisper.

"Yeah."

"Jonathan Bellweather."

"At your service." He gives me another glance. "I wasn't kidding about pulling over. Can you hold it together?"

"Yeah. Yes." I lick my lips again. "What are you—how are you—what—" I reel my thoughts in so I can get one clear sentence out. "What are you doing here?"

"You're in a world of trouble, little brother." He looks over again. "I'm here to help you."

CHAPTER TWENTY-ONE

THOMAS

My brother isn't much of a talker. I'm sitting in the front seat, trying to figure out when my life went flying off the rails, and he's singing along with a country-western song on the radio while we fly down the highway.

Three hundred questions crowd my brain, but all I can think to say is, "Did you really pay them a million dollars?"

"Wrote them a check. We'll be long gone before they cash it."

I turn wide eyes his way, and he laughs under his breath. "You're too much."

"Seriously."

"*Seriously*, I gave them a bail bond. Normally, you have to have ten percent to get one of those, but I know a guy."

Either lack of sleep has stolen my senses, or this conversation is going over my head. "Ten percent? What?"

He glances over. "If you need to bail someone out of jail, you have two options. You can pay everything up front, at court. The bad guy gets to go free, until he's required to show up for court. If he shows up, the person who paid bail gets their money back. But if you don't have that much money—like a million dollars—you go to a bail bondsman, and you give them ten percent or so, and they provide a bail bond for the whole thing. If you show up for court, great. They get their money back and everyone is happy. If you don't show up, the bail bondsman is allowed to come after you and drag you back."

"So you paid a hundred thousand dollars?" My brain is still reeling.

"No." He flicks the dials to turn on the air conditioning. "Sorry, I can't take it anymore."

"I'm fine."

"Good."

I study him, trying to remember if my sketch in the car with Charlotte came close to what he really looks like. Do we look alike? I can't tell. Now that he's driving, he's wearing sunglasses that hide his eyes. He's not a big guy, but he's bigger than I am—he looks like he lifts weights on a regular basis. His biceps strain the sleeve of his T-shirt, leading to clear definition along his forearm. I guess that would make sense, if he was in the military and he's now in law enforcement.

"So . . ." I turn his explanation over in my head. "You know a bail bondsman?"

"I *am* a bail bondsman."

I blink. "I thought you were a cop or something."

His nostrils flare, and he glares at me like I just suggested he should be responsible for cleaning toilets at the bus station. "No, I'm not a cop. What the hell would give you that idea?"

He looks like he expects an answer, and I'm not sure what to say. My eyes flick to the weapon holstered at his waist. "Um. The gun. The vest."

He glances down. "BEA. Bail Enforcement Agent." He grins, and any irritation leaves his voice. "The gun is for skips. They don't exactly leap in the car when I show up."

I need a glossary for this conversation. "What's a skip?"

"Someone who didn't want to stick around for court. Clarence mostly handles the paperwork side nowadays, and I chase down the idiots who don't stick around." He lifts a hand to acknowledge someone who changes lanes to let him pass.

He's driving really fast, but he's not aggressive about it. In fact, people seem to get out of his way when he approaches. Maybe seeing an SUV doing ninety miles per hour in the rear view mirror provides a lot of incentive. Wherever we're going, we'll get there in record time. I clear my throat. "Clarence?"

"You met him last night. Big guy on Main Street."

I met him. Big guy on Main Street.

"In Crisfield?" I whisper.

"Yep."

"At the bail bonds place."

"Yep."

My head hurts. "But I told him I was looking for you! He said he'd never heard of you!"

"He didn't know who you were. You told him you were looking for your brother, but that you didn't know what he looked like. He thought you were coming to settle the score for someone I'd picked up." He gives me a quick once-over. "Honestly, I don't know why he was worried."

He's insulting me? He's fucking *insulting* me right now?

He gives my shoulder a little shove. "Lighten up. I'm yanking your chain."

I take a long breath and blow it out. "I can't lighten up. I don't understand anything that's going on." I look at him again, thinking of everything that happened last night. "Were you there? When I was looking for you?"

"No. He called me. Why?"

I think of the Asian guy who grabbed Charlotte. Today has been bizarre, but there's no way to fit that puzzle piece in. Maybe it was an anomaly, like I said to her last night. The rest of today, though . . . I shake my head. "I don't know. I don't know what happened. I know I didn't attack Charlotte. We were—we were okay."

"First girlfriend?"

"She's not—"

"Come on." He gives me a withering glance.

I swallow and shake my head again. The yellow CCDOC shirt catches the sunlight, providing a glaring reminder—literally—that my life has gone to hell overnight. "She was my friend. She was the only one who believed me." To my shame, my eyes go hot, and it takes everything I have to keep emotion out of my voice. "I didn't hurt her. I wouldn't."

He sighs. "Of course she believed you." His tone is resigned. "You wanted her to."

He flicks the turn signal to exit the highway. We're nearing Crisfield—and it took twenty minutes less than when Charlotte and I made the exact same drive.

"Do you believe me?" I ask quietly.

"About Charlotte? Sure. She wouldn't be the first girl to change her story after letting regret settle in."

"They said someone tried to strangle her."

"That does complicate things." His voice doesn't make it sound complicated at all.

I keep staring at him. He keeps staring at the road.

"What about Mom?" I finally ask.

His voice is flat. "What about her?"

I don't know what to make of that. He must know she's dead. What did he say when I climbed into the car? *You're in a world of trouble, little brother.*

My voice comes out hushed and gravelly. "Do you think I killed her?"

He shakes his head, but not like he's answering me. More like he's upset about something. "She should have told you."

"Who?"

"Your mother. She should have told you what could happen." He turns at the first light, which isn't close to the bail bonds shop, but isn't far either.

Your mother. Not *our* mother. "What could happen? What are you talking about?"

Another turn, this time into a parking lot. We're in front of a squat brick apartment building. The architecture is old-fashioned, making it look like it should be doing double duty as a retirement home. JB swings his SUV into a parking place and kills the engine.

He slides his sunglasses into a spot on the dash and doesn't look at me. "Come inside. You can clean up. I'll get you some clothes."

"I still don't understand what you're talking about. What could happen?"

He keeps his eyes on the dashboard. "I'm talking about you, Tommy. She knew what you were, and she knew what could happen."

I want my brain to reject all these statements, but it's accepting all of it. He's not lying to me, and it doesn't feel like he's misleading me. "What am I?"

He sighs and taps his fingers against the dashboard. "Come in. Clean up. I'll—"

"Tell me!"

He looks at me, and his dark eyes are intense. "You asked me if I thought you did it."

I nod. "Yeah."

"I don't need to *think* you killed her." He pushes open his door, but his eyes don't leave mine. "I know you did."

Then he's gone, out of the car, slamming the door behind him.

My breathing is loud in the empty cab. *I know you did.*

I can't move. I sit there, watching as he goes around the front of the car. My pulse roars in my ears.

An image springs to mind, completely unbidden. My mother in that darkened bed, fingers wrapped around her neck, choking the life right out of her. The hands are mine. I can actually feel her windpipe collapsing.

I'm going to throw up. My thoughts seem completely detached from my body. Time has frozen, or maybe I have.

I know you did.

He opens my door, and I launch myself at him. It's not like Danny or the cop in the interrogation room. I *want* to get my hands on him. I want to punch him in his lying face.

He dodges my hit easily, then my next one, but he doesn't strike back. "Chill out, Tommy."

I hate that he calls me that. "I didn't touch her," I'm saying. I sound like I'm choking. "I would never—I would never—"

"Come inside."

"Fuck you." I take another swing at him.

He's quick. He sidesteps, leaving me to follow again. "I'm trying to help you."

"By telling me I killed my mother?" Tears. My voice is thick with tears. I can feel them on my face now. The day has been too long, and I can't trust anyone. I don't know what made me get into the car with him. "I didn't do it," I say. "Take me back. Take me back to prison."

"You don't want to go to prison."

"I don't want to be here with you." He's not moving, so I shove him in the chest, hard. "*Take me back.*"

He sighs and falls back. "If you'd stop chasing me around the parking lot, I could explain—"

I swing a fist. I want to hit him so hard that it breaks every bone in my hand.

I don't get the chance. He catches my forearm and spins me. My chest hits the pavement, and the only reason my face doesn't smash into asphalt is because he's got an arm around my neck. I must have hit my knees at some point, because it feels like I've torn right through my sweatpants.

I was wrong earlier. *This* is humiliating.

He does nothing more than pin me there for the longest moment. Proving a point? Being an asshole? I don't know.

I do know this hurts. The pain chases away some of my anger.

"I get it," I say, my voice grating. It's hard to breathe with my neck twisted this way. "You're stronger than me. Let me go."

"I really am trying to help you," he says.

"What's wrong?" I wheeze. "Can't take a punch?"

"You're funny. Are you going to behave yourself if I let you up?"

I have to squeeze my eyes shut. My brain keeps supplying images of my mother's body, but now, instead of seeing her corpse, she's alive, choking, fighting for breath. I see hands wrapped around her neck. Fingers smudged with charcoal.

"I want to curl up in a hole and die."

"No, you don't." He lets go of my neck. Pressure eases from my lower back, and I realize he was kneeling on me to pin me there.

I press my forehead to the pavement. We're in the middle of the parking lot, but I don't care. The world is spinning, and there's a good chance I might throw up.

I don't know what's happening to me. "I didn't do it. I loved her. I didn't do it."

"It's okay. You'll be okay."

"None of this is okay."

My brother blows a long breath through his teeth. "Some of it is. Seriously, Tommy, you're going to have to get off the ground, or my neighbors are going to think I brought a tweaker home."

I shift until I get my feet underneath me. I don't want to move, but my muscles respond when I force them. My sweatpants are torn, and my knees sting something fierce. I can't look at him, so I busy myself brushing grit from my clothes. Once my body is in motion, I convince my brain to move forward, too.

I can't talk about my mother again. I need to set that aside for a minute.

I can't stand here in silence, either.

"Can you speak English for five minutes?" I say bitterly. "What the hell is a tweaker?"

"A meth addict."

Nice. I scowl.

He gives me a look up and down. I still can't meet his eyes, but I can feel the air shift as he loses the mockery. "Come inside. You can get cleaned up. We can talk. Okay?"

I don't need to think you killed her. I know you did.

I force my eyes to lift. "I don't think I want to talk to you."

"That's not true."

"What are you, a mind reader now?"

He smiles. "Sort of."

"Sort of." I scowl. "What does that mean?"

"It means sort of." He turns away and pulls keys out of his pocket. He starts walking, not even looking back.

"That's it?" I call after him.

"That's it." He keeps walking. When he gets to the door, he punches a code, and a buzzer sounds, releasing the lock.

"What if I don't want to follow you?" I yell.

He stands there holding the door. "You do."

He's right. I do.

My brother's clothes are too big for me, but nothing about them announces that I'm a criminal, so they're a big step up from the fluorescent shirt the cops gave me. He gave me jeans and a T-shirt, and I could use a belt, but otherwise, I'm dressed and I'm free—for the time being—and that's a lot better than the direction I thought my day was headed in.

He's got a nice apartment—nicer than I expected. Third floor, with a balcony off the main room. The bathroom is huge, and his towels are thick and plush. The mirror is large enough to give me a good look at the bruises forming on my knees around the abrasions. I look like a toddler who hasn't learned to run yet.

When I come out of the bathroom, I don't see him, so I take a moment to look around. Two bedrooms are on either side of the bathroom, one of which is set up as an office. He didn't make his bed this morning, but there aren't any clothes lying around. I spy an expensive looking laptop on his desk. Two tall safes stand along the wall behind the desk, and my eyes stop there for a moment. Does he keep a lot of cash here or something?

A big screen television is mounted on one wall of the living room, over the top of what looks like a gas fireplace. His couch is a large, beige L-shaped sectional, and his dining room table is a solid slab of stone mounted on a wrought iron base.

He's not a slob, but the place looks lived-in.

"I ordered a pizza," he calls from near the living room. Must be the kitchen—it's the only room I can't see from here.

"Thanks," I say.

"You want to come sit down and talk, or are you going to keep hiding in the bathroom?"

I ease my way out of the shadowed hallway and find him sitting in the one chair of the stone table that was hidden from view.

"I wasn't hiding."

He gives me a look that tells me he thinks I'm full of shit. "You want a soda?"

"Okay."

He uncurls from the chair and goes to the refrigerator. He's lost the gun and the vest, but he's no less intimidating.

I still can't quite believe that this man is my brother. My brain keeps thinking that he's just some guy who knows a little bit about me.

When he comes back to the table, I haven't left the corner of the hallway, but he sets the soda in front of the seat opposite him, then drops back into his chair.

I clear my throat. "How do you know about me, when I don't know anything about you?"

"Because I remember when you were born." He pauses, and his eyes narrow just a little. "You must know something about me. You came looking for me."

I swallow. "I found your letters." Now I pause, considering what he just said. "You remember when I was born?"

"Yeah. I knew you for one year before she ran." He traces a line in the stone surface of the table. "She kept my letters?"

"Yeah." The apartment is so quiet in between our words. "She ran?"

"You know she ran."

He's right. I do know she ran. But she ran when I was *five*, not when I was a baby. I shake my head, trying to make the timeline work in my head. "This doesn't make any sense. I remember her leaving Dad—" I stop short and look at him. "Do we have the same father?"

He nods.

"Is he—is he still alive?"

"Yes." He grimaces. "Probably. It's been a few years. I haven't seen him since I enlisted."

"So you *did* join the military!"

"Yes." His dark eyes flick to the soda. "You going to sit down and drink that?"

I slide into the chair, but I don't touch the soda. We're on eye level now, and neither of us looks away.

"How'd you know about the army?" he asks. "I stopped writing to your mom before that."

"I went to the old address. Talked to a neighbor."

"You detective, you." He rubs a hand over the back of his head. "Those letters probably sounded nuts. I was an . . . an *emotional* kid. Needy. I can't believe she kept them."

"Yeah, well, I can't believe she never told me about them." I pause, considering how he'd said *your mother* again. "Wait. We do have the same mother, right?"

His expression goes still. "You think I'd write those letters to someone else?"

"No! I just—I'm trying to understand."

"You're asking the wrong questions. This really has nothing to do with your mother."

I frown. "Why do you keep saying that?"

He raises his eyebrows, looking for clarification.

"*Your* mother."

He leans in against the table. "It's been too long. She doesn't feel like my mother anymore, Tommy." He shakes his head, and he seems almost wistful. "I thought I'd feel something at the funeral, but it was like a stranger."

I almost fall out of my chair. "You were at the funeral!"

He gives me a look. "You saw me."

I rack my brain. There have been so many new faces over the last month, but my time at the funeral was short lived. I remember the car ride with Stan. The stifling heat. The cops in dress uniforms standing in clusters. Charlotte.

And then I remember: the guy in the parking lot on the cell phone.

"That was you," I whisper.

"That was me." He comes halfway out of his chair to grab the soda I haven't touched, and he takes a long sip. "For a minute, I thought you knew. You looked right at me. Then the cutie with the curls walked over, and I knew I couldn't compete with that."

"Charlotte." My brain is still spinning. "I hit her brother. Danny. The cop. You saw me get arrested."

"Yeah. That." His eyes sharpen. "We need to talk about that. Why the hell did you let that cop take you out of there?"

"Why did I let the *policeman* that I'd just *hit* take me out of there?"

"Yes."

"Um. Because I was in handcuffs?"

"Wrong answer."

A buzzer rings, and he stands to go to the door. He pushes a button, then stays by the door to wait for the pizza guy to climb the stairs. He turns to look at me. "You could have changed the trajectory of that whole interaction. Don't you know that?"

I scowl. "It was a shitty day. I didn't want to be there. I know I should have gotten myself together—"

"That's not what I mean. How the hell could your mother have let you get this far without telling you . . . *anything*?"

"I don't know what you're talking about."

"I'm telling you that you could have convinced that cop to *bawk* like a chicken if you wanted to. You could have told him to pull out his gun and shoot himself. You could have done *anything* besides letting him handcuff you and put your ass in a patrol car."

"How?"

A knock sounds at the door, and JB—Jonathan? I still don't know what to call him—swings it wide. A delivery guy stands there with two pizza boxes.

"That'll be twenty-six fifty," he says apathetically.

My brother pulls cash from his pocket and holds it out. When the guy reaches for it, JB doesn't let go.

"Why don't you come in and have some with us," he says. I frown.

The pizza guy snorts. "Yeah, whatever."

"I'm serious. Summer day? You probably haven't even gotten a break yet, I'd bet."

What is he *doing*?

The delivery boy takes his red and blue cap off and pushes damp hair back off his forehead. "I'll get in a load of trouble."

"Nah. Just have a slice and go. They won't even notice. I used to deliver pizzas, and it's not like they've got a GPS in your hat. You can always say that a customer hassled you over toppings or something. You look like you're starving."

A short laugh. "I am pretty hungry."

JB stands back and holds an arm out. "Then come on in. My brother and I are just hanging out."

I stand up. I don't know what this is—but I don't like it.

The pizzas slide onto the table, and I step back until I hit the wall.

JB gives me a look. "Stop being weird."

He wants *me* to stop being weird. Hilarious. Or it would be if this weren't all so unsettling. I swallow hard.

The delivery guy gives me an odd look and holds out a hand. "Hey, man. I'm Liam. Thanks for sharing lunch."

I glance at his hand, then back at his face. He's my age, maybe a little older. Reddish blond hair, skinny build. Jeans that are tighter than I'd ever wear, but hey, I was wearing a prison shirt two hours ago, so I'm not in a place to judge.

"Don't worry about him," says JB. "He just got out of jail."

Liam blinks. "No shit?"

"No shit," I croak. My throat feels dry.

JB goes into the kitchen and returns with plates. They make a grinding noise as they slide across the slate surface of the table. "Yeah," he says. He throws two slices of pizza on a plate and pushes it in front of Liam. "Tommy and I were just catching up."

"Nice," says Liam. He picks up the pizza and takes a bite. "My brother and I don't get along at all."

Why am I the only one finding this whole scenario bizarre? Who invites a pizza guy inside? In the middle of a conversation?

I don't move from the wall.

"What was jail like?" Liam asks.

"Empty," I said. It's the first word to come to mind.

His brow furrows, and I add, "Small town. I was the only one in the cell."

"Poor guy," says JB. He takes a bite. "All by himself."

Liam clears his throat. His eyes look concerned. "Must have been lonely."

"I guess."

"Scary?"

This guy doesn't even know me. I glance at JB, but he's

eating pizza like this is the most normal thing in the world.
"Kind of."

"Why don't you welcome him back to the land of the
free?" says JB.

My head whips around. "What?"

Liam blushes. "I don't think so."

"Go ahead," says my brother. "Give him a hug. He *really*
needs one."

"What are you doing?" I hiss, like Liam isn't sitting right
there, rising from a chair not five feet away from me.

"Proving a point."

"What point?" I take a step back, sliding along the wall toward the corner. "That you set up some guy to trick me?"

Liam has come around the table, but he stops and frowns.
"I'm not tricking you." He glances back at his pizza and
blushes again. "Maybe I'm getting mixed signals here."

"Yes," I say. "You are."

"It's okay," says my brother. "He's just playing hard to get.
He wants you to come after him."

Liam takes a step forward. His eyes are a very dark blue,
close and intent on mine. For some reason I expect him to
look dreamy, disoriented, but he doesn't. He looks perfectly
lucid.

That makes it more creepy.

"Stop it." I take another step back.

"It's okay," Liam says softly. "I get it. No one needs to
know."

"You get what?" He takes another step, so I fall back again,
but I hit the corner.

"Are you really running from a hug?" says JB.

Liam smiles and glances at him. It's a conspiratorial look.
When his eyes return to mine, they're almost mocking.
"Yeah. Seriously."

"I'm not running from a hug," I say. "Tell me what the
fuck is going on."

Liam gets closer, and now his expression is vaguely teasing. "You're even cuter when you're angry."

His hands find my waist, and I inhale sharply, sucking myself back against the wall. He's slight, and I'm not afraid of him—I'm more afraid of this *feeling* about him, like someone else is pulling the strings.

In a way, that makes it both less and more uncomfortable.

"You're so tense," Liam whispers. He shifts closer.

I glance at my brother, who isn't even watching us, he's eating pizza and looking at his phone. "Did you slip him something?"

"No." He sounds offended.

Liam breathes against my neck. He smells like sweat and sunlight and pizza sauce. His hands haven't moved, but if I took a deep breath, our chests would touch. I've never been this close to another guy.

"Are you making him do this somehow?" I ask.

"Yes."

"Well, *stop.*"

JB's voice is amused. "Don't you want to see how far he'll go?"

Liam whispers against my neck. "How far do you *want* to go?"

His hands begin to shift, and I grab his wrists, squeezing until he freezes. I hear his indrawn breath of pain.

"Stop it," I say.

"Tom." For the first time, my brother's tone isn't amused. "Don't hurt him."

"Then get him off me."

JB puts his pizza down. "Liam. I think he's had enough."

The delivery boy takes a step back. He looks flushed. Confused. Longing. "Sorry," he says. "I'm not usually that forward."

My heart is pounding. I can't make sense of anything. I look at JB. "Did you slip *me* something?"

"No. Jesus, Tommy. You didn't even drink the soda. Sit down." He pulls another twenty out of his pocket and hands it to Liam. "Get out of here, kid. Take another slice of pizza if you're still hungry."

I rub my hands over my face. I wonder if this is how people feel when they try drugs for the first time.

The door slams, and I jerk my hands down.

Liam is gone. JB is putting a slice of pizza on a plate and sliding it toward me. "Eat. You'll feel better."

"You did that."

"Yes."

"How?"

"He was attracted to you. I just gave him a push."

I swallow. "How?"

"Easy. I'm an empath."

I feel like I'm free falling. My head is buzzing. "You're an empath."

"Yeah." He smiles and picks up his soda, then tips it toward me. "Just like you."

CHAPTER TWENTY-TWO

CHARLOTTE

By late afternoon, I'm home and in bed. I've been surrounded by my family since two o'clock in the morning, but that wasn't a bad thing. I felt safe. Protected. No one could get to me.

Now, I'm home, and I'm alone. I'm in bed, but I'm not sure I want to be here. I'm exhausted, but I can't close my eyes without thinking of Thomas looming over me. The memories are tangled in my brain: the reverence in his voice when he called me brave, superimposed by the dark, intense eyes that bored into mine while his hands wrapped around my throat.

It takes hours—and some drugs—for sleep to find me.

One moment, I'm curled up under my quilt, watching the afternoon sun trace shadows on my wall, and the next, I'm dreaming.

I'm not in my bed this time.

I'm in Lilly Mauta's.

I've never been to her house, and it's been years since she died, but the proof is everywhere. The block letters that spell out *LILLY* over her bed. The used pairs of well-worn ballet pointe shoes tacked along the walls. Stuffed animals line the top of her bookcase, abandoned relics of childhood but not yet thrown away.

I'm sitting cross-legged on her bed with an older model laptop in my lap. Chipped red nail polish decorates my dusky nails.

These aren't my hands. These are Lilly's.
I'm not just in her room. I'm in her body.
She's—we're—typing an email.

**I can't wait to meet you. I've been dreaming of your words,
imagining the sound of your voice. I might force you to read
some of your emails out loud, just so I can see if the voice
in my head is anything like the real thing.**

She's swooning a little bit when she presses SEND. I feel
her chest rise and fall with a happy sigh.

Almost immediately, her inbox lights with a new message.
We click to read it.

**I'll read you every word.
Only a few hours. Can you wait a few hours?
I'm not sure I can.**

Her—our—heartbeat accelerates, and she quickly types
back.

You have to wait. My housemates won't be gone for hours.

Housemates. My brain spins, trying to remember Lilly
sharing a house with someone else. She was an only child.
Wouldn't she say "parents" or "family"? I don't call Danny
my housemate.

Regardless, he writes back just as quickly.

I feel like you're hiding something from me.

She *is* hiding something, but I'm not sure what. All I can
feel is her panic about being found out. Our hands freeze
over the keyboard. Then we type back.

**I've never met someone on the Internet before. Too much
pressure for our first real date. I want it to be just us.**

Stupid. She's fifteen years old—she has to be, because that's how old she was when she died. Doesn't she read the news? I want to smack her. Especially since I know how this ends.

Unfortunately, I'm just along for the ride. I can't even force her eyes to flick up, to read the name of the sender.

The bedroom door opens, and we slam the laptop lid closed. It's Lilly's mother—I recognize her from ballet class. The last time I saw her was the funeral. Her face was lined and sad, no light at all.

This is a different woman. Her smile brightens the room. Dark, shiny hair makes her look younger than she is. "Lilly-bear, it's almost time for dinner. Are you done with your homework?"

We smile back at her. "Almost, Mom."

"We need to eat quickly so your father and I can get on the road." Her smile wavers. "Are you sure you're not anxious about spending the night by yourself?"

We shake our head. "Nope. I'm going to make popcorn and watch a Channing Tatum movie."

"My little girl, spending the night with a hot guy," she teases. "Maybe I should stay home and keep you out of trouble."

We roll our eyes. "Don't be ridiculous, Mom. What's the worst that could happen?"

Famous last words. This would be a cliché if it weren't so sad.

When Mom is gone, we open the laptop again. Another message is waiting.

Just you and me. I like the sound of that.

Lilly likes the sound of that, too. Her heart flutters. I wonder if she's seen a picture of this guy. I wonder if she knows anything about him.

The dream shifts, and we're standing in front of a dressing

table with a large mirror. Lilly has put on a slinky green dress that I just *know* has come out of her mom's closet. It might as well be a nightgown. Or a slip. My grandmother would have a heart attack.

We're penciling Lilly's eyes with dark eyeliner, followed by gold shadow. Red lipstick makes her lips pop. The innocent girl from ballet class is gone, replaced by a stunning young woman. The right bouncer would let her into a nightclub, no problem.

She chooses a diamond pendant from the dressing table, and as I catch sight of the array of jewelry, I realize she's in her mother's room. The necklace adds another year to her age. The diamond sparks with inner fire as it shifts in the light. Obviously real. Obviously expensive.

She stands back from the dressing table, lifts her cell phone, and takes a selfie.

She examines it for a moment, scowls, and deletes it.

Six more pictures before she's satisfied. I can't disagree: it's a good one. Her lips are slightly parted, her eyes wide, like she's just been surprised. She held the phone above her head, so you can see the shadow between her breasts, and the flare of the dress is just a bit blurred. The diamond at her neck sparkles.

She starts a text.

LM: Ready and waiting.

Then she sends the picture.

A text comes back in seconds.

AS: I almost drove off the road.

AS. I don't know anyone with those initials. I wish she'd look at the top of the screen. I wish I could see his name.

Then I realize it doesn't matter. Whatever name he gave her has to be a fake. I've already discussed this case with Ben. They found her emails. They would have searched her phone.

She writes back.

LM: Send me a picture.

I don't think he will, but to my surprise, a photo appears. Obviously a photo taken while driving, because we don't get his whole face. It's pitch black outside, but the flash lights him up like a Christmas tree. A gray Henley. The edge of a jacket zipper is visible. He needs a shave, because stubble lines his jaw.

My stomach clenches. I don't know any fifteen-year-olds with that much facial hair, and I've grown up with three older brothers. Not to mention, he's driving. He'd have to be almost seventeen to be driving without supervision.

Seventeen and fifteen isn't *that* big a gap. Senior-sophomore romance?

But she said *housemates*. Why would she say housemates to someone who would also presumably live with parents?

I'm not an idiot. I'm rationalizing, but I already know this guy isn't in high school.

The highest the photo captures is just the side of his eye. The flare makes his skin look stark white in places, but in the sides of the photo, he looks less Caucasian. Maybe Hispanic. Maybe Indian, like Lilly herself.

The dream shifts again, and someone is knocking on the door. Lilly is standing in her foyer—in her *parents'* foyer—with a pounding heart. She wants to open the door so badly, but common sense is sending up a hardcore warning.

Don't do it, I think. I beg. I plead.

I can't affect the past, and I certainly can't affect this dream. She opens the door.

And I wake up.

Metal clicks near my head. The noise is so out of place in my bedroom, and the spinning anxiety from the dream still clouds my consciousness. I fling myself upright before I'm fully awake.

My grandmother is sitting in my bedroom armchair, hands flying as she works on the baby blanket.

As much as she annoys me, I'm glad I'm not waking up alone.

My phone is blinking with a text message, so I press a button to wake the screen. For a fractured instant, I'm worried that something from Thomas will be sitting there, taunting me, but it's not. There's a message from Nicole.

NK: Can't believe it. Be over as soon as I get off work. LMK if you need anything. XOXOXO

My grandmother's knitting needles continue clicking. "Thanks for sitting with me," I say. My voice sounds rough.

She doesn't break the rhythm. "You don't need to thank me for that, dear."

I touch my neck, hoping for a moment that the time with Thomas had all been a dream, just like the time I spent in Lilly's body.

My neck aches as my fingers find the scratches that the nurses at the hospital cleaned and bandaged. My arms are still sore from struggling against him.

That wasn't a dream.

I feel so weak. So stupid. They all warned me. My grandmother shouldn't be kind—she should be doing her usual pursed-lips-berate-Charlotte-for-living routine. Right now I actually *deserve* it.

In my sleep, I was judging Lilly. Now that I'm awake, I realize I was no different. Thomas wasn't a stranger from the Internet. He was worse. He was a real boy, and his crimes were splashed across the front page last week.

Tears burn my eyes, and I try to sniff them back. "How could I be so stupid?"

"Mistakes are a part of life, Charlotte. You should count your blessings that this one didn't come with a higher cost."

The words are harsh, but her voice isn't. It might be the

first time I've heard my grandmother speak to me with something close to kindness.

"Does everyone hate me?" I whisper.

Her hands go still, and she looks at me. "Hate you? You dear child, we love you."

I can't remember my grandmother *ever* saying she loved me. Fresh emotion wells in my chest, and I burst into tears.

True to form, she doesn't comfort me. She resumes her knitting. "I can see how it would be exciting, spending time with a dangerous young man. You girls today can't seem to separate your fact from your fiction. Life is not a movie."

Her practicality causes my tears to dry up. "That wasn't it."

"Isn't it?"

"No. He was different. I thought he was different."

She sighs. "Of course you did."

"I don't understand it. He never hurt me. He never treated me badly. He had plenty of opportunities to hurt me, but he didn't." The corner of my sheet makes a good make-shift handkerchief. I wish I could stop crying.

"He had plenty of opportunities to hurt his mother, too, I'd bet. We can't understand the motivations of people who are emotionally disturbed."

I think about that pencil drawing of Thomas's mother. He loved her. Respected her. There was no rage there. No anger. Had something changed? Had he given me clues that I blindly ignored?

He'd been unable to draw her after the murder. Was he afraid he'd give himself away?

My grandmother lifts her eyes to meet mine. "Your father and your brothers warned you to keep your distance from that one. You should have listened."

"I know, I know. All the men in the family know what's best for poor, defenseless Charlotte."

"Obviously."

Obviously. I flop back against my pillow.

Lilly thought she had everything under control, and look what that got her.

Have I been just as stupid?

Knuckles rap on my doorframe, and I look up to find Ben there in the doorway. He must have just gotten off work because he's still in uniform. He glances at Grandma, then back at me. "I thought maybe I could take the next shift."

I want to launch myself at him and scream, *YES, BEN. SAVE ME FROM THIS TORTURE.*

Instead, I'm more subtle. I clutch my hands together in prayer and mouth it.

My grandmother stashes her knitting in her bag. "I'm not blind, Charlotte."

"Sorry," I say, but I'm not really sorry. She's leaving, and Ben is coming in, and that's all that really matters.

He sits on the bed, and I scoot over, giving him room. He takes the invitation and sits up against the headboard beside me.

After a moment, he puts out his hand, and I hold it.

"You look like you've been crying," he says quietly.

"Grandma said she loved me."

"And you cried? I'm surprised you didn't faint from shock."

I bump him with my shoulder.

Then emotion overtakes me, and I'm crying again. I lean against his shoulder, and he puts an arm around me. I can't believe he didn't take time to change out of his uniform.

"Why didn't I listen to you?" Tears burn my eyes, and I try to sniff them back. "How could I be so stupid?"

"You're not stupid." He pulls my hands down and brushes the tears away. "You're not stupid at all."

"You're only saying that because you're still feeling sorry for me. Trust me, tomorrow you'll be thinking I'm stupid. I got the memo from Grandma, loud and clear."

"Nah. I'll leave that to her and Danny."

I smile through my tears. "I can't even be mad at him. You know I'm screwed up when I'm not mad at Danny."

His bedroom door must be open, because he yells down the hall, "I love you too, Char."

I laugh under my breath and swipe my eyes. Danny carried me downstairs last night. He rode in the ambulance with me. He held my hand at the hospital and told the doctor that I needed to be attended by a female physician.

When Dad demanded answers for everything I'd done with Thomas, Danny told him to back off and give me some space to breathe.

I was glad for that. I wasn't ready to tell anyone about the trip to Crisfield, so they don't know anything about Thomas's brother. I'm already in enough trouble. I don't need them knowing I was halfway across the county.

And it's not like we found anything.

In the hospital, when I could finally speak without crying, I thanked Danny for being so kind.

He leaned down close to me and said, "If I stop holding your hand, I'm going to go shoot that motherfucker in the head."

And for the first time, I'd appreciated his white-hot temper, because I understood that it underscored a deep protectiveness for his family.

Ben swipes more tears off my cheeks. "Matt is fit to be tied. He says you told him you were seeing someone. He thinks he should have paid closer attention to what you were saying. He wished he'd stayed the night."

"I wish I hadn't lied to him."

"He thinks he should have figured it out."

"I think *I* should have figured it out." Again, I wrack my brain, trying to think of some sign I missed, some obvious comment or action that should have told me I'd find Thomas in my bed in the middle of the night, trying to strangle me. The whole thing seemed like such a dream. Even now, all I remember are his eyes, boring into mine, and the feel of his hips grinding into me.

I flush, remembering it. Up until the end, I wasn't even fighting him.

I can't reconcile it with the boy who was scared to draw a picture of his mother.

"You didn't need to figure it out, Char." Ben's expression is serious. "It was already figured out."

"No, Ben. It wasn't."

"I can't believe you're still defending him!" Ben shifts to face me, and he seizes my shoulders to give me a little shake. "Do you understand that he tried to kill you? He could have killed the girls! They were right here, Charlotte! What if he had strangled them first? What if—"

"Stop it!" Emotion chokes me, and I almost can't speak for the images his words are putting in my brain. "Stop it, Ben."

Danny appears in the doorway. "Dude. She's been through enough. Leave her alone."

"She's still defending him."

"I'm not," I cry. "I'm not defending him. I just . . . I can't wrap my brain around it."

"You shouldn't be able to wrap your brain around it," says Danny. "You think I want to wrap my brain around why he slugged me at the funeral? No. I just put his ass where it belongs."

Ben snorts. "Too bad we can't force him to stay there."

Danny meets his eyes, and Ben nods.

"What?" I demand. "You guys always think you're being sneaky, but I'm not stupid."

"Oh really?" says Ben.

I hit him in the shoulder, too hard to be sisterly. "You don't think I feel bad enough?"

"You don't think I want to lock you in here so he can't get to you again?"

"Why do you need to lock me anywhere? Isn't he in jail?"

They exchange glances again.

"*What?*"

Danny clears his throat. "I'm assuming that mofo isn't in jail anymore."

All of my bravado evaporates in a heartbeat. I touch a hand to my neck, feeling the bandages there. "He's free?"

"He made bail," says Ben.

I glance between them. "Stan bailed him out?"

"No. A bail bondsman." He pauses. "Dad talked to Stan. He's in rough shape. He feels guilty for sticking up for the kid. He feels partially responsible for this happening to you. He wouldn't have bailed him out."

"So you don't know where Thomas is?"

"No," says Ben. "He could be anywhere."

"Doing anything," says Danny.

"So you see," Ben says, sitting back up against the head-board. "We're not leaving you alone for a minute."

CHAPTER TWENTY-THREE
THOMAS

JB is driving again. He got a call on his cell phone and said we had to go. He won't tell me where we're headed, but when I refused to go, he threatened to invite more people over to his apartment to see how I liked that.

I got in his car in a real hurry.

He's singing along with the radio again, sunglasses in place.

I fidget because I'm not sure what else to do. I can't get comfortable. I don't know him at all—but where else would I go? What else would I do?

Stan probably wouldn't throw his door open wide and welcome me in with a hug. Part of me wants to call him, if for no other reason than to get access to my things.

I clear my throat and look at JB. If I sit here in silence too much longer, my brain is going to revisit his comment about knowing that I killed my mother. I can't process that right now. Everything else, as weird as it is, seems safer.

"You've got questions," he says. "Ask them."

I wonder if I'm that transparent or if he can feel it somehow. "Doesn't that ever make you feel . . . wrong?"

He keeps his eyes on the road. "What?"

"The pizza guy. Compelling someone to do something like . . . *that*."

"Like what?"

I flush. Two days ago, I was laughing at Charlotte because

she couldn't say the word *sex*, and now I'm feeling just as shy. "Forcing someone to do something sexual."

"Sexual? Did something happen that I couldn't see?"

I refuse to let myself back down. "I know you know what I mean."

"I needed to do something extreme so you'd get the point. That said, I can't compel someone to do something they don't genuinely want to do. There has to be something to work with." He glances over. "Like believing me. You're not there yet. I can't *make you* believe me."

I swallow. "So it works on me, too? Even though I'm . . . what you are?"

"An empath." He emphasizes the word like I need help pronouncing it. "It's even easier with you. You're completely unguarded. You amplify every emotion around you without realizing it, but you're not doing anything to protect yourself." He pauses, his jaw set. "Honestly, you're lucky someone else didn't find you first."

I roll that around in my head for a moment. "So there are more like you?" I pause. "Like us?"

"Yes." He glances over. "And we're not all good."

I think about that one memory I can't ever seem to let go of. Dad in the street, the man looming over me. The promise to get ice cream. "And Dad was like this too?"

"Yep." JB finally looks away from the road and studies me over the rim of his sunglasses. "Haven't you ever had problems at hospitals and funerals?"

"I've never been in the hospital." I swallow. "And I've only ever been to one funeral."

"Yeah, and look at what happened."

I study him, not tracking. "What happened?"

"If you hadn't been thrown in a patrol car, you would have been in a real mess. Couldn't you feel how you were drawing them all to you?"

I try to remember the morning of the funeral. I *was* a real mess that morning. I couldn't tie my tie. I remember wanting to rage at them all for treating Mom's death like an excuse for a party. Even the memory has me clenching my fists.

JB *tsks* under his breath. "You remember."

"Stop it."

"I can't," he says equably.

"I still don't know what that has to do with anything."

"Oh, so pretty girls walk up and try to comfort you at the drop of a hat?" He whistles through his teeth. "Wow, Tommy, you are one lucky guy. Teach me your secrets, little brother."

I glare at him. "So you're saying she only came over because I *wanted* her to?"

"Yes. But she was a little curious, too. You were mad at everyone else, so they were mad at you." He reaches out to tap my forehead. "*That's* what I mean about amplifying everyone around you."

"And I'm supposed to be able to avoid this somehow?"

"Yes. You need to figure out how to build a wall around that mind of yours. Right now, you're like a feeding trough for all the weaker-minded."

I purse my lips and look out the window. *Build a wall.* How do you put a wall around your thoughts? One part of my mind feels like I've been left behind, like I never learned to recognize my numbers and colors, but I've just been dropped in a paint-by-numbers class.

Another part of me wants to roll my eyes at this whole thing. I just met this guy.

I look back at him, feeling my eyes narrow. I don't even have proof he's my real brother.

"February thirteenth," he says.

I jump. "What?"

He glances over. "Your birthday. February thirteenth?"

"Oooh, did you just pull that out of the air?" I say sourly. "That's on my driver's license, and probably my court records."

He smiles, a little. "Your mom was so disappointed that you couldn't wait one more day. She'd bought this ridiculous newborn cupid outfit. She dressed you in it anyway. Dad said it made you look a little creepy. Who puts wings on a kid who can't hold his head up?"

I stop breathing. I've heard this story. Mom used to shake me good-naturedly every February. "You couldn't hold out one more day, could you, Tommy?"

And I've seen my newborn picture. Mom used to keep it on the bookcase. Big red velvet diaper, a plush bow-and-arrow, and bizarre sparkly wings. I do look creepy. I used to turn it around when friends came over.

Right now it's taped inside a box in Stan's garage.

Breath finally whispers into my lungs. "How—how did you know what I was thinking about?"

"You don't need to be psychic to feel the skepticism in this car, Tommy."

I'm stuck on another part of what he said. "Mom used to say we had to hide from Dad. What did he do to her?"

"He didn't do anything to her."

I swing my head around to look at JB. He's watching the road, but his forearms are tense. If I'm supposed to be able to figure out his emotional state, I've got nothing.

Then again, he's the only person—literally the *only person*—who might be able to unravel the mysteries about my mother and father and what happened to her.

Without wanting them, images of her death flock to my mind. Like before, they're not just images of what I found afterward.

They're rapid-fire images of the act. She's fighting. Trying to draw breath to scream. Her neck is rubbed raw from her struggles.

She's screaming my name.

I clamp my hands over my ears, like it's happening here in the car. It doesn't help.

"Stop it!" I cry. "Stop it!"

The images come faster, until it's a filmstrip on a reel, flickering with light and terror and death.

"Tommy." His voice is whisper soft. His hands close around my wrists. "Tommy. Look at me."

The car is on the shoulder. We rock with the force of passing vehicles. I'm practically whimpering.

The images, the sounds—they've stopped. The car is quiet, aside from my panicked breathing.

Any mockery and good humor is gone from my brother's face. "You all right?"

I jerk my hands free from his and slam my fists into his chest. "Why would you do that? What the fuck is wrong with you?" I'm crying and I don't care. "I don't want to see it? Okay? *I don't want to see it.*"

"I didn't make you see it," he says softly.

"You did!"

"I didn't. Tommy, I didn't."

Just this once, Tommy.

I press my fists to my eyes. My shoulders are shaking. "Stop calling me that."

He inhales like he's going to say something, but he must think better of it, because he shifts back into his seat and lets the breath out. After a moment, he puts the car back into gear and we merge into traffic.

I can't look at him. I wish I'd jumped out of the car when we were stopped.

"You're different than I thought you'd be," he finally says. His voice is gravelly.

I don't know what to say to that.

He's quiet for a few miles. The radio is silent now. I wrap my arms around myself and stare out the window. I watch concrete barriers fly past. Trees. Clouds. Anything but him.

But while we're cruising along in the silence, I realize that I *am* aware of him, beyond just the fact that we're sitting in the car together. It's like a tiny hum in the back of my head, so quiet that I wouldn't notice it unless we were in almost complete silence, like this.

My hands lose the death grip on my biceps as I try to identify that feeling, but it's like a tiny metal ball that's been dropped on a hardwood floor. It rolls fast and it's hard to catch.

"Relax," he says.

My eyes flick his way. I'm still not entirely sure I want to talk to him again.

But that's all he says. *Relax*. The word itself has power. I'm taking a deep breath, and my shoulders relax before I'm aware of it.

"Stop," I say. "Stop making me do things."

"I'm not," he says. His voice is quieter now. Repentant? "I'm just trying to put you more at ease."

"I think you screwed your chances when you tried to tell me I killed my mother." My cheeks still feel damp.

He doesn't say anything for a long moment, but then he takes off his sunglasses and runs a hand through his hair. "Tommy, I—" He stops and winces. "Tom. Others are drawn to our ability. Our minds are drawn to strong emotion. We thrive on it. Feed on it, in a way. Left unchecked, empaths can find themselves seeking more powerful emotions. Catching someone's eye turns to true attraction. Attraction turns to infatuation, which turns to romance, and maybe even love." He snaps his fingers. "It can be quick. The course of a month. A week. A day."

I don't say anything. My eyes fix on the windshield and refuse to look away.

But I'm listening.

He must know it, because he keeps talking.

"We can get ourselves in trouble. Sometimes we end up chasing the emotions without considering the people behind them. Imagine your friend, Liam."

My voice is tight. "He wasn't my friend."

"He could have been. He could have been a lot more.

And I'd bet, if you'd let him keep going, that you would have woken up tomorrow morning and he would have been hopelessly devoted to you."

I think about Liam's hand on my waist, how he would have gone a lot further if I'd let him. "But I'm not gay."

"It doesn't matter. It's all about the power of his mind and the depths to which you'll let *him* feel. It's possible to lose yourself in someone else's feelings." He pauses. "The way you kept provoking the police . . . I thought you were riding the energy of it. I thought you were cocky. I thought you knew."

"I don't understand any of this."

He's quiet for another long minute. "Sometimes, when we feel strongly about something, we instinctively push harder, trying to take the emotion to the next level. We look for the next limit, especially if feelings are changing. It can be unconscious. What we are—it's a double-edged sword. Amazing power, but in the wrong moment, we can actually love someone to death."

His voice is careful now. My fingers are clenched on the seat cushion. In a way, I don't want him to keep talking—but I do. Sweat collects on my temples.

"Your mother had a new husband," he says quietly.

"Stop."

"She loved you, but that love was turning away."

"It was okay." My voice is shaking. I don't want the vision of her death to come back. "I was okay."

"There's usually a triggering event for that kind of power. For me, it happened in Afghanistan. I saw a guy step on an IED. He was blown apart."

"Jesus." I'm horrified. He is too. Maybe he's feeding me the emotion or maybe I'm feeling it, but a sickening coil has gripped my chest.

JB shakes his head. "I knew what I was, but I couldn't wall my mind up against that kind of onslaught."

I don't want to imagine it. "Nothing happened to me." I swallow. "I didn't have a triggering event."

"New home, new stepfather . . ." He shrugs.

"It was okay," I say again. "Stan . . . I liked Stan."

"This has nothing to do with *liking* anyone, little brother. You loved your mother, and you still—"

"Shut up." My heart punches me in the ribs, over and over again. "Do you hear me? Shut up."

"It's the pursuit of the emotion that matters."

My voice is a whisper. "Stop talking."

"You're hearing me. I know you're hearing me. What spurred it? Did you and your mother have a fight?"

My throat is closing up. "I don't remember. She was asleep."

"You remember, Tommy."

I squirm in my seat. My head is buzzing. "Stop calling me that!"

"She should have told you," he says quietly. "You could have protected yourself. You could have seen the signs."

"Stop." I'm practically wheezing. "Please. Stop."

"Did you have a fight? Fighting can bring on aggression, which can bring on fear, which can turn to—"

"I didn't kill my mother!" I shout at him.

He winces. "I think you don't know your strength." He glances at me again. "And I think your brain built a wall to protect you from it. That's why the truth keeps breaking through. Those visions? They're *yours*."

"You don't know any of this! This is all *fake*. This is all a *joke*."

"It's not," he says. "You want proof?"

"Yes." I suck in a breath like I've been drowning. "No."

He pulls the car over to the side of the road. At some point, we've found our way into the city. My brain is so scattered I don't know if he's brought me to Baltimore or Washington, D.C.

Once the car is in park, he looks at me hard. "Proof: Look at what you did to your cute little girlfriend last night."

I stare at him.

"I heard the charges," he says.

"I didn't do any of that. I didn't break into her house."

"I'd bet you've done a lot of things you don't remember doing."

I think of waking in the middle of the night. Walking down the hallway. Finding her body.

I think about the deadbolt, the lack of clues.

I swallow.

"Think about it," he says. "Really think about it."

I didn't hurt my mother. I didn't hurt Charlotte.

But I think about our relationship so far, the way we've come together over the last few weeks. Every time we're close, I feel as though I can't get enough of her. It takes all of my self-control to keep from pressing down on the accelerator until we're going a hundred miles per hour, leaving clothes in our wake.

Innocent little Charlotte, climbing in my lap in the car, jerking the shirt over her head.

Sweet Charlotte, watching my lips or tracking my movements.

Her indrawn breath when I said, *Don't make me pick you up and put you in the chair.* The excitement that coursed through me when I thought about doing it anyway.

"I was a gentleman," I whisper.

"I know," he says. "And I think that was the whole problem."

And with that, my brother gets out of the car, slamming the door behind him.

CHAPTER TWENTY-FOUR

THOMAS

I follow him. What else am I going to do, sit in the car?

We're in a gritty part of the city. This has to be Washington, D.C. I don't know every back corner of Baltimore, of course, but this doesn't have the feel of my home city. The architecture is vaguely different, maybe. No putrid stench from the harbor here.

There are plenty of disgusting odors to make up for it. JB is walking down an alley lined with dumpsters, and I hustle to catch up to him. Rotting food makes my stomach turn, mixing with a burned grease odor that tells me we're near several less-than-healthy restaurants. A rat skitters behind a box when we approach. Two men, one black and one white, are having a conversation up ahead, and they stop talking and glare at us. The white guy takes a long draw from a cigarette. His eyes track us suspiciously.

Again, I'm reminded of the disparity between me and Charlotte being mirrored here in reverse. JB is confident, no sign of hesitation. For the most part, I grew up in Baltimore City and I have no qualms about walking the streets, but there are still areas where I won't go.

This alley feels like an area where I shouldn't go. I don't like the way they're watching us. A promise of violence hangs in the air.

"What are we doing?" I ask under my breath.

"Show and tell."

"What?"

"What do you feel?"

"I feel . . ." I swallow. "I feel like we shouldn't be here."

"Why?"

He sounds like a teacher. I don't mind. I feel like I need one. "Because they don't want us here."

"You're right. Do you think they'll hurt us?"

"I have no idea."

He gives me a look. "Yes, you do. Pay attention."

The white guy takes another draw from his cigarette, then leans close to the other man to say something. The black guy nods and ducks back through a door.

I'm paying attention to the remaining man, trying to sort through what I'm feeling. He's middle-aged with graying hair, but he's built like a hard life got him here. Tattoos crawl down one arm. Lines surround his mouth as he inhales the smoke from his cigarette. His eyes flick to me, and then to my brother. They stay on JB—probably smart. I'm not the threat here.

As we approach, he stubs out his cigarette on the wall. I let my eyes unfocus and try to force my mind to . . . do something. I'm not entirely sure what. This is like playing one of those cheap kids' games, with the plastic maze and the tiny ball. As soon as I lock on something, it slips out of the space.

Then, almost by accident, I get the little ball into the slot. Suspicion, check. Fear, check.

Deception. Check.

"Hey," says JB. "I'm looking for Mark Duplessy."

The man flicks the stubbed cigarette at JB's feet. "I don't know him."

He's lying. I feel it so strongly, as if the lie lodges in my brain and leaves a residue there. My heartbeat skyrockets and I want to shake JB's arm.

I don't. He knows it, too. I have no doubt.

JB says, "Maybe we can try again. I'm looking for Mark Duplessy."

"Look, asshole, I said I don't know him."

Do you think they'll hurt us? Pay attention.

No. This man won't hurt us. If anything, he's going to run. If I could take his pulse, it would beat mine in a race. He's feeling a little confident, though, like he has an ace up his sleeve.

JB reaches into his jacket pocket and pulls out a folded piece of paper. I can't tell what it is from here, but it looks like a mug shot with a bunch of other text on the page.

He doesn't look away from the man. "Funny. You look just like him."

The air shifts. The man bolts. He shoves the door open so quickly that it bounces back against the frame before JB follows.

"Come on, Tommy!" he shouts.

I only knew it a moment before he ran, but I knew it. I *knew* it.

I'm giddy, but I follow. Down a few concrete steps, and then through another door. We burst into a dank restaurant kitchen.

And we're immediately surrounded.

We skid to a stop. All the breath leaves my lungs in a rush. Four men and two women block our path. The man we saw earlier has a gun, and it's pointed right at JB. The tension in this room is so strong I'm worried it's going to rattle me apart. A fryer sizzles somewhere to our left, and the heat down here is enough to knock me out.

Mark Duplessy is beyond the group, near another doorway. "Fuck you, assholes," he says. Then he shoves through the swinging door with bravado.

The man with the gun shakes it, gesturing toward the back. "Y'all better get out the way you came."

I would feel so much better about this whole interaction

if this guy didn't have a gun pointed at us. He's confident. Protective, but not angry. Definitely not afraid.

"I can't leave," says JB. "I have a court order to reclaim Mark Duplessy. So if you'll just step aside——"

The man cocks the hammer. "Get out."

JB grabs his wrist and throws a punch. His movement is so fast, I lose track of it. The gun skitters to the floor, and the man goes down. I feel like I missed a moment of time again. I need a replay button.

"Don't just stand there!" JB shouts at me. "Go after Duplessy!"

I run for the swinging door before I can rethink this. Maybe he's making me do it somehow. I push through, and I'm standing in a small restaurant. Small tables, torn vinyl seats. A few people are eating, and they look up in surprise as I burst out of the door. No one here is a threat to us. There's no sign of Duplessy.

Then a woman at one of the tables points to the door. "He ran out."

Her companion shushes her, but that's all I need to hear.

Do I go after him? Do I wait for JB? I can't catch my breath. I don't know what I'm doing.

If I find this guy, what am I supposed to do? JB is armed. I'm not.

Then JB is through the swinging door. Swearing erupts behind him.

He's rushed, but not bothered. "Kid, you're supposed to be chasing him."

"I didn't—what happ—?"

"Come on." He pushes through the front door into the sunlight.

I'm only a second behind him, but he's running down the sidewalk before I even get there. I have no idea how he spotted his mark, because the streets are crowded with pedestrians, but there, a good twenty feet ahead of him, runs the man we're chasing.

"Holy shit," I say.

Then the restaurant door is flung wide, and the man with the gun is coming after me.

I run like hell.

This is totally not how I expected my afternoon to go. I really didn't think my day could get more surreal.

My brother is fast as shit. I'm not slow, but I feel like it. I'm guessing he does this a lot. Adrenaline pushes me faster. I keep waiting for shots to explode behind me, but they don't. It doesn't feel like anyone is chasing me.

I chance a glance back, and I'm right. The man from the restaurant didn't pursue me.

Horns blare from the road. Mark Duplessy is bolting into traffic, narrowly avoiding getting hit by a city bus. Then he heads down another alley and disappears from sight.

JB is equally fearless. He cuts a similar path through traffic and doesn't hesitate as cars miss him.

I'm not that badass—or that insane. I wait for a gap and run after them.

This alley is deserted, a dark tunnel of heat between two buildings, but I hear a shout farther down. I run to catch up. I turn a corner just in time to see JB slam the man against a wall. He's got one of Mark's arms twisted up and behind his back, but the other man is taller and he struggles. Maybe something has shifted in me, but emotions come to me in waves now.

The most powerful ones can't be ignored. Fury. Fear. Anger. Others have less of an impact: Resignation. Regret.

"Get my gun," says JB. His voice is tight and thready.

My eyes widen. "Me?"

"No, him. I want him to get my gun." He shoves the man against the wall again before he can get leverage. "Come on, Tommy."

I stop hesitating, and I put my hand on the butt of the gun and pull it out of the holster.

Until this moment, I've never held a firearm. It's heavier

than I expected, a solid weight of metal in my hand. My index finger hovers near the trigger, but now that it's against my palm, I'm almost afraid to have it in my grip. It's not like holding a knife or a hammer. This thing is specifically designed to kill people. In a weird way, I suddenly feel more powerful.

I'm not sure this is a good feeling.

"Shoot him," says JB.

The fear in the alley triples. I'm not sure if it's Mark's or it's mine. I almost drop the gun. "What?"

"Shoot him."

Mark redoubles his struggles. "Fuck you! You fucking dirty bastard! You—"

"Shut up." JB does something that makes him grunt in pain.

Something flickers in me. My finger shifts before I can stop it. The surprise has worn off, and the only fear left is in the man pinned against the wall.

JB was right. There's power in the emotion. I want more of it.

I don't even know this guy. I don't want to hurt him. But this fear . . . I wish I knew how to cock the hammer of the gun, because I think the sound would do interesting things.

This is heady. I'm scaring myself.

"In the head or in the leg?" I hear myself saying. My voice is even. Confident. Unafraid.

Fear explodes like starbursts behind my eyes. Mark tries to throw JB off. The man starts screaming. Crying for help.

Metal rattles. JB has handcuffs, and he's slapping them against Mark's wrists efficiently. "Shut up," he says again, exasperated. "No one is going to shoot you." He pulls on Mark's arm and drags him away from the wall.

Then he puts out a hand to me. "Give it back."

My breathing feels too quick, but I'm so charged I think I could run a marathon right now. "What just happened?"

"We'll talk about it in the car. Give it back, so we can get this guy out of here."

"I'm going to report you assholes," Mark says. "I'm going to get your license pulled—"

"Yeah, yeah." JB gives him a shove. "Tom. The gun."

I move to hold it out to him, and he quickly grabs my wrist and turns my hand away. His expression is aggrieved. "Without pointing it at me."

"Sorry." My mouth is dry, but I swallow. I release the gun into his hand, and he shoves it back into the holster, then pulls on Mark's arm again.

"Don't you have to read him his rights?" I say, once we're walking.

"I'm not a cop."

"No," snaps Mark. "You're a dirty fucking bounty hunter—"

"Shut up," JB says again. "Before I change my mind about shooting you."

By the time we're in the car, my heart rate has found a normal rhythm. Mark has kept up a litany of profanity the whole way back to the vehicle. I was worried about walking in front of the restaurant again, but JB assures me that no one will bother us.

"How do you know?" I asked.

"Some people will help a skip get away, but they won't risk themselves to stop you once you've caught him."

And he's right. No one comes out of the restaurant. People on the street treat JB like he's a cop. No one stops him. No one questions him.

In the car, Mark spits at us through the grilled partition and bangs his head on the metal, making it rattle. I'm glad for the barrier. No mental powers are needed to understand his mind-set right now.

This is going to be irritating as all get-out for the drive home.

"Check this out," JB says, as we pull onto the highway. He presses a button on his center console, and a layer of glass rises between the front seats and the back. We can still hear Mark and his invectives, but they're muffled.

"Handy," I say, impressed.

"You have no idea. Best money I've ever put into this thing." He puts out a hand and smacks me on the shoulder. "You did good, kid. I wasn't sure how you'd handle it."

I glance at him, and then back at the road. For the first time in a long, long while, I feel a glow of belonging. "I'm glad you didn't tell me what we were doing."

"I didn't want to leave you alone, but I wasn't sure you'd come if I told you we were picking up a drug dealer."

Wow. I let that go. "So you're allowed to just . . . do that? Arrest people?"

"If they skip bail? Sure." He hits the turn signal to merge into traffic. "When we post bail, they sign a contract, waiving their rights if they decide not to show up for court. We can arrest them, we can cross state lines, we can break into their house if we think it's warranted . . . you name it."

"And that's all legal?"

"Yep." He glances over. "You signed the same thing. You should learn to read, little brother. Better not think about running."

I snort, but his words inspire just a tiny inkling of fear. "I don't have anywhere to go."

"Neither did this guy, but he found people to take him in."

"How'd you find him?"

JB looks at me over his sunglasses. "I am very, very good at finding people."

I hesitate.

"Ask your question," he says.

"Stop that. Why did you tell me to shoot him?"

He looks over again. "What scares you more? That I told you to do it, or that you thought about it?"

I look back out at the road. Cars still give way around us, and this time, I wonder if this is another extension of his empathic abilities. "Both," I say.

"I knew you wouldn't shoot him. I wouldn't have let you take the gun."

"How?" I demand. "How did you know?"

"Because you weren't in the right mental state. You had no stake in killing him." He pauses, then gives me a smile. "Scaring him, though . . ."

I keep my eyes on the road, warring with my own morality. "I didn't like it."

"Liar."

"It feels wrong. Playing with someone's emotions. It feels wrong."

"Is eating wrong? Having sex? Sleeping? It's part of your makeup, Tommy. It's not wrong. You didn't hurt him."

"I think we're splitting hairs a little too finely." I glance at him. "Is that why you do this? Do you get off on the fear?"

"I don't play with them like that. If I got off on fear, I wouldn't pick this occupation. I only did *that* to show you what I meant."

"Effective."

"I know." He pauses. "Nothing is ever one hundred percent, though. I want to make sure you understand that. People have free will. They can surprise you."

"So I could have shot that guy."

"Probably not."

I glance in the backseat, where Mark Duplessy has finally given up; he's staring out the window with gritted teeth. I can still feel the remnants of his fear coursing through me. "But I could have. Just like what you think I did to my mother. Or to Charlotte. Is that another point you're trying to make?"

"Just like that, Tommy." He pats my shoulder again, but this time it's more sympathetic. "Just like that."

CHAPTER TWENTY-FIVE
CHARLOTTE

That night, I dream of Lilly again.

As much as I wish this dream would start where the last left off, it doesn't. It starts at the beginning. We revisit the emails, her mother's intrusion, the playing dress-up in front of her mother's mirror.

In a way, that's a good thing. It allows me to watch for clues.

In another way, I know this is ridiculous. This is a dream. I wasn't there. I didn't see this. This is my subconscious feeding me someone else's imaginary memories.

But because it's a dream, I'm along for the ride.

His initials stick in my head. *AS*. I don't know what they stand for, and it's got to be arbitrary. I don't know anyone with those initials.

The selfie he sends her . . . What kind of car is it? What's he wearing? What's in the background?

I can't tell. She only looks at it for a moment, and I can't tell. The background is too dark, and I don't know enough about cars to pick one out from the seatbelt mounting.

So far, I'm a pretty crappy dream detective.

When he knocks on the door, I'm worried I'll be knocked out of the dream again, but this time I'm with Lilly as she throws it wide, smiling shyly at her visitor.

Through the whole dream, I've had this feeling of anticipation, that she'd open the door and I'd have this huge *Aha!*

moment, that I'd wake up from this dream and be able to solve the crime.

But no. I have no idea who this guy is.

He's not quite as old as I'd feared. I'd thought she would be opening the door to some thirty-five-year-old skeeze in a polyester suit. This guy is college age, with dark, softly curling hair, and warm brown eyes. Too old for Lilly, but maybe he gets a pass if she lied about her age. As I'd guessed, he's not white: he's Hispanic, or maybe Middle Eastern.

His eyes light up when he sees her. "Wow," he says, laughing under his breath. "I thought maybe you'd sent me a fake picture."

She blushes, pleased. "Thanks." We look up at him through her lashes. "You too."

He hesitates, then holds out a hand. "It's nice to meet you in person, Lilly."

She smiles and we shake his hand. "It's nice to meet you, too, Alex."

Alex! We have a first name. His palm is warm and dry. I'm screaming at her to shove him out the door, but at the same time, I'm not getting a creeper vibe off him. Going off first impressions, it's hard to believe this guy would strangle her.

Then again, look at my first impressions of Thomas.

When she goes to pull away, he doesn't let go of her hand. We hold our breath, but he leans in conspiratorially, his voice gently teasing. "I don't think you've been honest with me."

She pouts. "What makes you think that?"

STOP FRIGGING POUTING, I want to yell.

His smile widens. "This place has mom-and-dad written all over it. You didn't have to lie to me. I've only lived on campus for the last year. You think I'm going to bolt if I know you live at home?"

Campus. Good. He's probably twenty-two. Or younger.

Lilly's response is smooth as butter. We look away shyly. "Usually when I tell guys I still live at home, they don't even write back. It's so obvious what they're after."

He gives her another up-and-down. "Their loss."

We blush hotly.

"Do you want to go out?" he says. "Or did you want to stay here?"

Her heart trips and stumbles at the suggestion. It would be safer to go out, but she doesn't want to risk being seen with him.

"We can stay here," she says softly. "Would you like something to drink?"

"Sure," he says. "You have any beer, or would your parents freak?"

She almost falters, but I can hear in his voice that it's an innocent question. He's a college student and thinks she is, too. "Sure," she says. "They're cool. They won't care."

Inside, her heart is thumping along. Her parents will care. She's figuring out how to cover for missing bottles later. But she fishes two bottles out of the refrigerator and finds a bottle-opener without too much trouble.

He asks if she wants to watch a movie or if she'd rather talk. She decides on a movie, and they sit on the couch and look at each other shyly.

Honestly, as far as first-dates-ending-with-murder go, this is starting off pretty boring.

Then the front door opens and closes. Lilly—we—jump a mile.

"It's all right," says Alex. "He's a friend."

I wake up to a hand on my arm and a man leaning over me in the darkness.

I don't think. I react. My hand flies out, and I hear a startled cry.

He jerks back. "Holy cow, Charlotte! It's just me!"

Matt. I tell my heart to turn off the alarm.

"Sorry," I whisper. "I didn't know you were here."

"Now I'm sorry I taught you to go for the eyes."

"Are you okay?"

"Yeah." His voice is husky. "Yeah." When my eyes adjust to the darkness, I can see him rub at his eyes. He shakes his head. "No. I'm lying. I'm not okay."

I sit up in bed. "What's wrong?"

He gives a startled laugh. "What's wrong? That kid practically killed you in front of my daughters, and you want to know *what's wrong?*"

My brain is finally starting to work. I swallow. "I am so sorry, Matt. I can't tell you how sorry I am."

He runs his hands through his hair. "The worst part is that I can't even be pissed off at you because you got hurt in the middle of it."

"I know. I'm sorry."

He takes a long breath, then sits down on the edge of my bed. I can barely make out his expression in the darkness, but his unhappiness practically fills the room. "How could you listen to me last night and not say anything?"

I reach out until I find his hand. "I didn't mean to put them in danger, Matt."

"I know you didn't. I don't want you to put yourself in danger either, Char."

"I know." I crawl across the bed to hug him. At first, his body is stiff, and that, more than anything, is a sign of how pissed he is. But then he yields, and he sighs and hugs me back.

I feel leather crossing his shoulders, and I draw back. "Are you wearing a gun?"

"I'd rather be safe than sorry. He got in here once."

Matt isn't the type to overreact. His voice is like steel.

I sit against him and wonder if my brothers are right to be so worried. Would Thomas break in here again? I still can't wrap my head around him doing it the first time. It feels like a dream, like it's no different from my brain's impressions of Lilly's murder.

"Were you having a nightmare?" Matt says quietly.

"No."

"You cried out."

I look up at him. "I did?"

He nods. "You said, 'No.'"

"I was dreaming of Lilly."

"Lilly who?"

"Lilly Mauta. The girl who died."

"Years ago? Your school classmate?"

Of course he wouldn't remember it as clearly as Ben did. I shake my head. "I knew her from ballet."

"Oh. I remember. Ben was a wreck."

"Yeah."

He's quiet for a little while. My eyes begin to drift closed when he says, "I wonder if Ben is thinking about that one, too." He pauses. "He said he couldn't go through this again." Then he grimaces. "Don't you dare tell him I said that."

"You guys try to hide it, but I know you're human."

He gives me a hug. "Mom wouldn't go to bed until I told her I'd stay up with you."

"I'm sure Alison appreciates that, being home with the little girls and all."

"She was having some friends over for a girl's night. It worked out."

"And I'm guessing you wouldn't have left her alone with Thomas roaming the streets . . . ?"

He rests his chin on my head. "You'd be correct."

I drift again, leaning against him, feeling his heartbeat. "Do you believe in dreams?" I say slowly.

He doesn't answer for a while. "I believe our subconscious has the ability to tell us things, if that's what you mean."

"I think so."

He runs a hand over my hair. His voice is gentle. "Are you remembering something from last night?"

I shake my head. "From Lilly's house."

He frowns. "Were you there?"

"No. Only in my dream."

Again, he's silent for a while. I wonder if he's dozing the way I am. I like this quiet period in between words. It makes this space feel safe.

"Maybe you're dreaming of Lilly because your subconscious is trying to tell you something about yourself. She was attacked by a boyfriend, too."

"He wasn't her boyfriend. She'd just met him over the Internet."

"You dreamed that?"

I shake my head. "Ben told me." I pause. "And yes, I dreamed it. His name was Alex."

"Hmm." That's Matt's word for when he wants to sound supportive but he doesn't know what to say. I actually think he's half asleep.

"There was another guy there," I say. "Do you know if Ben knows that?"

"Do I know if Ben knows there was another guy in your dream?" He sounds sleep-confused.

"No, in Lilly's house."

"Charlotte. Kiddo." He's fully awake now. "It was a dream."

I inhale to protest, but anything I say is going to sound ludicrous.

He's right, of course. It was just a dream. I can't see the past. I wasn't there. I've never even seen Lilly's bedroom.

He yawns, then pats my shoulder. "You should get back to sleep. I'm sorry I woke you."

"It's okay," I whisper. I lie down. He sprawls in my armchair again.

But I can't sleep. I keep replaying the scene in my head. The nice college boy—and his friend.

"Char," Matt says. "I didn't mean to discount what you were saying. Maybe your brain is really trying to tell you something."

I roll up on one shoulder and look at him in the darkness. "You think my dream means something?"

"Do I think you're having a psychic connection with a girl who died years ago? No."

I sigh.

Then he says, "But dreams always mean something to the dreamer. It's just a matter of figuring out what."

CHAPTER TWENTY-SIX
THOMAS

I have a restless night. I'm not one to be up before sunrise, but this morning I was relieved to see the sun, because it meant a reasonable time to get out of bed. JB has a futon in his office, but he offered to let me have his bedroom. I wasn't going to accept, but he insisted. I don't think he wanted me going through his things.

Check that. I *know* he didn't want me going through his things.

I keep replaying the events of the day. The trip to pick up the fugitive—the *skip,* as JB had called him. His explanations of what we can do.

His insistence that I had something to do with my mother's death and Charlotte's attack.

I can wrap my head around the rest of this, but that's the hardest thing. After the visions in the car, I'm careful not to let my mind drift to thoughts of my mother. I don't want to relive that again.

Charlotte had told me to sketch her, and I hadn't been able to do it. Was that part of my mind protecting itself? Would I have drawn my own hands?

I creep out of JB's bedroom, not wanting to risk disturbing him, but to my surprise, he's already up and showered and dressed.

In half a second, I go from worrying I'm up too early to panicking about being up too late.

"You're fine," he says. He's sitting at the kitchen table, drinking a cup of coffee while scrolling through Buzzfeed. "Do you drink coffee? I made a whole pot."

"Um." I run a hand through my hair. I'm not what you'd call a morning person. Today, especially, I feel like I've been hit by a truck. "Yeah."

"Cream in the fridge. Sugar by the pot. I set out a mug."

"Thanks." I shuffle into the kitchen.

"Did you sleep okay?" he calls after me.

"I feel like crap." I find the mug and the coffee and dump more sugar than is good for me into it. "Stan told me I was having nightmares the other day. Maybe they're keeping me awake or something."

"We don't dream."

I stop stirring the coffee and turn around to look at him. "What?"

"We don't dream. Ever." He glances at me over the computer screen. "Our brains don't work like that."

I don't know why this one silly minor detail is throwing me, but it is.

"Think about it," says JB. "Have you ever remembered a dream?"

No. I haven't. I wonder if this is the kind of thing I should have noticed, or if it's something I *wouldn't* notice, because it never happened.

I bring the coffee back to the table and sit across from him. "Weird."

"Not weird. Probably a . . . a protective thing. Think about it. We could dream that we're being hurt and start projecting fear or aggression."

"Huh." I take a sip of coffee.

He goes back to looking at his laptop. I study him. At first, I wasn't too sure about him, but he's all right. He's not deliberately cruel. He stopped me before I could hurt the pizza guy. He only gave me a glimpse of my abilities with Mark Duplessy—and I sense that could have gone a lot further than it did. Despite the fast action chase from yesterday afternoon, he takes his job very seriously. He was up late last night organizing leads and making phone calls. He seems honest, and direct, and while not exactly patient, he could be putting me through hell. And he's not.

I like him.

He clicks on something on his laptop, then strikes a few keys. "I like you too, kid."

"Stop it."

He smiles. "Did you have anything you wanted to do today?"

"Let me check. Nope. Schedule is wide open."

He looks at me over the computer screen. "Do you want to go get your stuff?"

I set my coffee mug down. "You mean from Stan's?"

"Yeah."

I look down into my coffee and wonder how that would go over. I had a key to Stan's house, but I didn't have it on me when they arrested me, so I don't have it with me now. Stan didn't come see me in jail, and he didn't answer when I called him. If we showed up at his house, I have no idea how he'd react.

I can practically guarantee he wouldn't be happy.

I try to imagine what he'd make of JB, and I come up with nothing positive.

"I don't know if that's a good idea," I say.

"You don't have anything you want?"

"Yes. Lots of things."

"Well. Let's go."

I wince. "I don't think that's the greatest idea. I don't want to get into it with Stan."

"He won't get into it with you."

"How do you . . ." JB is smiling thinly. "Oh." I hesitate. "I'm still not sure how I feel about this whole making-people-do-what-you-want thing."

"It's not quite that easy," he says. "Look at Mark Duplessy. Like I told you before, they don't exactly jump in my car."

"And you couldn't have made him?"

"Nope." He closes the laptop. "I probably could have gotten him to go for my gun and shoot me with it." He studies me. "Even without knowing what you are, I'd bet you've used this for your own purposes before."

"No. Never."

He looks at me sideways. "You're not even thinking about it." His eyes narrow, just a bit. "I'd bet you got away with all kinds of things in school."

I stop with my coffee mug halfway to my mouth. I remember all the teachers who let me coast by with minor infractions. I remember breaking that stupid television at Best Buy, how another guy had gotten fired, but my error had barely been acknowledged.

"Why couldn't I get myself out of jail?"

"Too afraid, and they weren't predisposed to let you out." He leans back in his chair. "Yelling at the judge probably didn't help your case. If you'd been trying, I bet you could have pulled some sympathy and gotten the whole thing thrown out."

"Wow," I whisper. I almost want to go back through the previous day again with this insight.

Almost.

Then reality comes crashing back down. "Charlotte," I whisper. "She must hate me."

"Want to go see her too?"

I do. Desperately. I want to see if she's okay. I want to apologize. "There's a court order saying I can't see her. Her brothers would shoot me on sight."

"That court order means *you* can't go near *her*. Not the other way around."

"She doesn't want to see me."

He half shrugs. "You might be surprised."

I hate that he's inspiring my curiosity. Again, I'd kill for a phone. Then again, I'm not allowed to text her either.

Then I remember Nicole.

I look at my brother. "Maybe we could stop by the library. Her best friend works there. I could find out how she is."

"See? Look at that. Your schedule is filling up already."

We're on the highway, beating down the path back to Garretts Mill. I've grown more comfortable in his car, in his presence, and for the first time, I don't feel like anxiety is going to tear me apart.

"Will you tell me about Dad?" I ask him, out of the blue.

He doesn't say anything for a moment. He must have mile high walls, because sometimes it's very difficult to pull emotions out of his head. "What do you want to know?"

"Anything?"

His eyes flick toward me. "I didn't live with him once I turned ten or so, and even before that, it was off and on. I grew up with our grandparents. I didn't see him often." A pause. "I haven't seen him since before I enlisted."

"Why?"

He hesitates. "Remember when I told you that there are people like us who don't use these abilities for good reasons?" When I nod, he says, "Dad is one of those. He's very powerful. He can control other empaths. When I was young, I couldn't fight it. When I grew strong enough to resist, I didn't want to have anything to do with him."

Walls or not, he doesn't like this line of conversation. It practically radiates from him. "Why?"

"Because he'd use me to do things." His hands are tight on the steering wheel. "Not good things."

I'm horrified at his choice of words, and I'm sure he can feel that. "Like . . . what?"

"He made me stay with him." He glances over at me. "When I was young. He made me hate her." He pauses. "It wasn't just you, Tommy. She wanted to take me, too. I fought her like hell. Ran away from her and right back to him."

Our mother. I don't know what to say. My voice is husky. "I'm sorry."

"She came back for me. Spent a year with him trying to get to me, but my grandparents—our grandparents—were under his spell, too. They helped him keep me away from her. You would have been four or five." He pauses. "He eventually let her see me, but he'd make me think she was there to hurt me. I wouldn't let her get near me." He hesitates. "I was already so screwed up. I tried to hurt her. He'd taught me well."

I swallow. "How?"

He glances at me. "I convinced her I was going to kill you. I couldn't help it. He was in my head, and everything he wanted me to feel, I'd feel. He taught me with violence and threats, so I'd retaliate against her the same way." There's so much regret in the car, I almost can't breathe through it. The most heartbreaking part of his story is that he blames himself for all of it. I can feel that. "Eventually, she ran again. That time, it was for good."

"How did he make you do all of this?"

He takes a long breath and blows it through his teeth. "You name it, Tommy. If I fought him, he'd do something worse. When I was thirteen, I had a crush on this girl named Annabel. Dad caught us in the backyard, and he inspired so much lust in her that I couldn't get her off of me without hurting her. And I did hurt her. I had to. It was either that or—" He breaks off, his breathing fast. "He'd do this shit for *fun*, Tom. He's a sick fuck, and I'm glad to be rid of him."

Now I understand the note in his voice when he warned me away from Liam. *Don't hurt him.* "How did you get away from him?"

He glanced over. "I joined the army."

So that's why he enlisted.

"I was good at football," he said. "When you can sense where the other players are going to be—it gives you an advantage. But my knee couldn't take it. I had to have surgery when I was sixteen, and it never came back all the way. I almost didn't pass the physical to get into the army, but I gave the doctor a little nudge."

"Wow." I look at him. "I'm sorry. I never knew."

"I know." He glances over. "I know. I'm sorry too."

"You don't have to be sorry," I say.

He reaches out and ruffles my hair, then turns it into a good-natured shove. "Thanks, Tommy. You're a good little brother."

"Nah," I say. "You're probably just making me act that way."

I was secretly hoping that Stan would be working and he would have accidentally dropped his keys in the driveway.

Unfortunately, he's home, and he comes out the side door when we pull up the driveway. He's wearing khaki shorts and a polo shirt. At first, he looks confused at the unfamiliar vehicle, but then we pass below the trees lining the driveway, and he can see me and JB. His mouth settles into a line, and his eyes are hard.

"Yeah, so I'll wait here," says JB.

My head whips around. "What?"

"I'm kidding. He's a cop, right?"

"Homicide detective."

"Well, that's kind of hilarious." He says it like it's not hilarious at all. He kills the ignition. "I hate cops."

"You do?"

"Yes. It's one of the few things I have in common with Dad."

"Why?"

"Because they're a pain in the ass. You'll see. Come on."

Stan folds his arms across his chest and looks at both of us, but he only addresses me. "Tom. What are you doing here?"

I stop halfway across the driveway. Even under the shade of the oak trees, it has to be in the high nineties. We're both sweating just from the effort it took to get out of the car.

Stan's face is closed down. Suspicious. Angry. I didn't expect him to welcome me with open arms, but I wasn't ready for hostility. "I wanted to come pick up some of my things."

"Who's your friend?"

I glance at JB, unsure how to explain his presence. *This is my brother* probably wouldn't go over too well.

But JB holds out a hand to Stan. "JB Augury. I'm a friend of Tom's. I'm letting him crash with me for a while."

"A friend." Stan shakes his hand, but something about it seems like a challenge.

"Yep." JB gives me a nudge. "Go get your stuff."

Stan lets go of his hand. "No. I'll get it." He glances at me, and I'm ready for him to say something openly aggressive, but he doesn't. "Wait here," he bites out. Then he turns and goes into the house.

Once he's gone, JB says, "Want to put money on how much stuff the cops have already taken for evidence?"

I've been wondering about the last name JB gave him, but that throws me. "What?"

He glances at me. "You thought you could be arrested and charged with attempted murder, but the cops wouldn't search your stuff?"

Fury grabs me, searing in its potency. "There's no *evidence*. I don't care what you said. I didn't hurt Charlotte." I swallow. "I didn't—" I can't finish this sentence. After the episode in the car, I'm scared to even think of my mother.

"Okay, Tommy." His voice is even, placating. "Hold it together. I didn't realize this would come as a surprise."

"Well, it does." Then I turn to look at him fully. "What if they found your letters?"

He shrugs. "If they found them, they found them. I'm not worried about someone reading a bunch of letters I wrote when I was a kid."

"You're not?" I look between him and the door. "But you just called me a friend—"

"I'm trying to spare you an hour of questions. He's already suspicious. We don't need the cops thinking you've been hiding a brother on top of everything else." He rolls his eyes. "Honestly, I don't need the hassle."

I wonder if Charlotte has already told them. She couldn't possibly, if Stan isn't drawing a connection right now.

I wonder why she'd cover for me.

I study my brother. "You think they'd question you, too?"

"I know they would."

"Is that why you gave him a fake last name?"

"You think I made that up on the fly?" He laughs under his breath. "It's our grandmother's maiden name. I enlisted under it. It's on my driver's license."

Stan returns with a worn plastic bin stacked with clothes. My messenger bag is thrown on top. He thrusts it at me unceremoniously. "I'll box up the rest of your things this weekend. You can call me, and I'll tell you when you can pick them up."

This is it. My entire life reduced to a box. My mother's husband, one of the few people in this town who'd bothered to show kindness to me, reduced to another cop who hates me. I take it from him, surprised at the sudden emotion that snakes around my throat to pull tight.

"Thanks." I turn away.

He catches my arm. "Tom."

I stop, but I don't turn back to face him. "What?"

"Are you okay?"

Stan always surprises me. I look at him. "Yeah. I'm okay."

He glances at JB. "How long have you known your . . . friend?"

"Not long. He's all right." I begin to move away.

He lets me go, but he watches me. "Tom."

I shove my box into the backseat, then turn to look at him. "What?"

Uncertainty almost shimmers in the air between us. "You can call me if you're in trouble. You know that, right?"

JB climbs into the car and slams the door. My nerves are shot: the sound makes me jump.

I look back at Stan. "I tried that once. You didn't answer."

His face falls, and I can feel his shame. It's amazing how emotion seems to have taken on a crystal clarity now that I'm aware of it.

I pull open the passenger door.

Stan doesn't move, but he wants to stop me. "Tom."

"I'll call you next weekend." I climb into the cab.

"I had hoped everyone was wrong about you."

I can't look at him. "They are wrong."

Then I slam the door in his face.

JB doesn't even ask if I'm okay. He can probably figure out my mental state better than I can. He just drives.

We're a few miles down the road before I let out a breath. "That was both better and worse than I thought it would be."

"He's worried about you. He doesn't trust me." JB shrugs. "Kind of touching, really. You and he get along?"

"Yeah. Sort of. He said I was like a puppy."

JB gives a quick burst of laughter. "A puppy?"

"Yeah. He said he wasn't sure how to have a teenager in the house."

"I can see that. He seemed kind of stiff." He pauses. "Did your mom love him?"

"Yeah. She did." I think of the excitement in her voice when she told me Stan had proposed. "He loved her, too."

"Good," says JB. "She deserved that much."

And then, before I can say anything more, he reaches out and turns up the radio until it's too loud for conversation.

For some reason, I thought JB would have a hard time getting Nicole out of the library. I wait in the parking lot by his car, because I'm worried she'll panic at the sight of me.

He's inside for less than ten seconds before she comes flying out the sliding doors. When she sees me, she storms across the parking lot.

I'm glad I'm starting to be more in tune with people's emotional state, because I have a little warning before she takes a swing at me.

"Nicole!" I push her arm away, and she uses the other one. Thank god she's so tiny. It's like being attacked by a vicious kitten. "Stop it!"

"I told you I'd kick your ass if you hurt Charlotte." She tries to smack me, and I throw an arm up. "I can't believe I defended you. I can't believe I *covered* for you."

"Want me to take her down?" says JB. I've been so distracted trying to defend myself that I didn't even see him come out of the library.

I'm beginning to know when he's kidding, but he's so deadpan that she whirls around. "Ooh, you can try. I'll kick your ass, too."

He glances at me, eyebrows raised, wondering if she's for real.

"Nicole," I say. "I just came to see if she's okay."

"No, she's not okay." Nicole's chest is heaving, and she glares between us. "You need to get the hell out of here before I call the cops. She can't sleep, thanks to you. She's scared to be alone. Are you a psychopath? What the hell are you even doing here?" Suddenly, her face goes pale, and she takes a step backward, glancing between me and JB, who's leaning against the car behind me now. A lick of fear threads through the air. "You leave me alone, Thomas Bellweather, and you, too, creepy other guy. Do you understand me? If you put so much as a *hand* on me—"

"Nicole." I'm torn between laughing at her and crying at how serious she is. "I'm not going to hurt you. I'm not going to touch you." I put my hands up in surrender. "I just wanted to see if Charlotte was okay. Is she hurt?"

"Yeah. Okay. Like I'm falling for this." She turns and puts up a hand. "You get out of here. I'm calling the police."

"Nicole!"

She gives me the finger and keeps walking.

Shit. *Shit.*

JB calls after her. "Don't you want to hear what he has to say?"

Her steps slow, and she hesitates, but then keeps walking.

"He didn't want to hurt her," JB says. "You know that. You can feel it. Don't you think *Charlotte* would want to know what he has to say?"

Nicole stops. Her chest is heaving, but she's stopped.

"Holy crap," I whisper.

"No one is going to hurt you," JB says. "You wouldn't be out here if you thought you were truly in danger."

She turns around and walks back to me. Her arms lift, and I'm ready for her to try to deck me again, but instead, she throws her arms around my neck.

"I knew there had to be some mistake," she breathes. "I knew you were too hot to be a killer."

My brain can't handle the one-eighty. I look at JB helplessly.

He's looking at his phone, not even paying attention now. "You're welcome," he says.

I put my hands on Nicole's arms and gently push her back. "Is Charlotte okay?"

Nicole nods. "A little banged up, but she's okay." She pauses. "She's very confused. She doesn't understand."

I let out a breath. "I barely understand it myself."

Her eyes narrow, just a little. Questioning. "Did you break into her room?"

"I—don't know. Something is happening to me. I'm losing time or something. I don't—I don't remember doing it."

She frowns.

"Careful," says JB. I have his attention now.

I run my hands back through my hair. I sound insane. I'll drive her away again. "Please. Nicole. Please just tell her I never meant to hurt her."

Her expression sobers. She nods. "I will."

"Tell her . . . I'm sorry." I pause, surprised by the sudden well of emotion. My voice turns husky. "Tell her that her kindness meant everything to me. I would never . . . knowingly hurt her."

Nicole studies me. "Is that all?"

I hesitate, then nod. "That's all."

"You . . . don't want to see her?"

I put my hands to my face and rub at my eyes. "I do." I give a choked laugh. "I want to see her so badly."

Nicole throws her arms around my neck again. She kisses me on the cheek. "I'll tell her." Then she starts jogging back toward the library. "I need to get back to work!" Then she stops. "Wait. How can she get in touch with you?"

I frown. I never thought I'd be so desperate for a cell phone.

"Here." JB hands me a small card. At first I thought it was a business card, but it's more like an index card. All he's written is a number.

I hold it out to Nicole. "Here."

She hugs it to her chest. "I can't wait to tell her." Then she dashes back through the entrance.

"What the hell just happened?" I ask.

JB sounds bemused. "She's something."

"Tell me about it. Now what?"

"Now we wait."

CHAPTER TWENTY-SEVEN
CHARLOTTE

I'm in Lilly's head again. We're watching a rom-com with Alex. His arm is across our shoulders, but otherwise, it's the most boring first date I've ever been on.

Except for the other person in the room.

I haven't really seen him. I can't force Lilly to look at him, and once Alex told her that there was nothing to worry about, she hasn't so much as glanced in his direction. He hasn't said a word. He's just *there*.

It's weird. Creepy. Unsettling.

She's completely relaxed, like random strangers come into her house all the time. When Alex begins to play with her hair, we gaze up at him and smile.

At first, I didn't mind going through the motions with her.

Now, I'm waiting for the other shoe to drop. It's terrifying.

I don't want to live through this with her. When Thomas was on top of me, choking me, it was terrifying enough. I don't want to go through Lilly's murder. I wish I could claw my way out of her body. I wish I could get her to wake up and pay attention to what's going on.

I can't. I'm stuck.

The scene shifts. We're in Lilly's room. On her bed. Her dress has been pushed up our body, and Alex's hands are everywhere. Stroking, caressing, sliding between her legs. Inside, I'm scrambling away, covering my eyes.

But she's not fighting him. She's enjoying herself. She's happy to be here. If not for the fact that she's fifteen, I'd be giving her a high five and telling her to enjoy herself and practice safe sex.

She moans. I really don't want to be a part of this.

Alex laughs under his breath. "Don't forget. We've got an audience."

Lilly sucks in a breath and turns her head.

For the first time, I catch a glimpse of the stranger. He's handsome. Young. I've never seen him before.

He puts a finger to his lips. "Shh. This will all be over soon."

I sit upright in bed. Afternoon sunlight arcs across my wall, and for the first time in days, I'm alone in my bedroom.

We've got an audience.

That sticks in my head. I don't know why, but it does.

"Charlotte!" My mother is calling from downstairs. "Dinner is ready!"

I rub my eyes. There's an imprint in my cheek, and I look down at my mattress. I fell asleep on my book.

I guess I didn't get much sleep last night.

"Coming!" I yell back. "I need a few minutes."

My hair is a wreck. Curls everywhere. I pull it all up into a high ponytail and wash my face, then brush my teeth.

We've got an audience. The words won't get out of my head.

I prick my finger with a lancet and squeeze a drop of blood onto a test strip, letting my brain work while I wait for the meter to spit out a number.

Those four words are killing me. They're hopping up and down in my brain, begging for me to figure them out. I'm missing some key connection, I'm sure of it.

"Charlotte!" my mother calls again. "Are you all right?"

"Just checking my sugar!" I call back, because I know she'll leave me alone if that's the answer.

I stare at myself in the mirror. I still have Band-Aids on my neck, and they're beginning to look a little ratty. I carefully peel them off. The marks on my neck have scabbed over.

We've got an audience.

Lilly saw him. I saw him too, but his image is frozen somewhere in my awareness, just beyond my reach. I can't force him back into view.

"We've got an audience," I whisper.

Then I have it. The answer comes to me so quickly that I almost knock the meter in the toilet.

Thomas said it. Two nights ago. I thought he meant the girls.

Did he mean he wasn't alone? Did my subconscious recognize someone else in the room with us?

Is that why I'm dreaming about Lilly? Is this my brain's way of showing me a connection?

Who's the guy in my dream? Who am I missing in this equation? Was it the same stranger in Lilly's bedroom, or is it someone else entirely?

What did Ben say about Lilly's murder? They had a suspect, but they couldn't bring it together.

We interviewed one guy from the local community college whose name matched the emails, but he didn't even know her, and we couldn't trace the email account as belonging to him.

Was he really innocent, or had he been there and just couldn't remember?

And what would cause that? Rohypnol? If a girl could be conscious yet not remember a rape, could a guy be drugged and coerced into murdering someone? I don't *think* so. But maybe there's another drug?

Too many questions. I can't draw enough connections.

Ben must be here, because I hear his voice when I go down the stairs. Danny's working tonight, so I know he won't be at the table. I hear an unfamiliar voice and hesitate before rounding the corner, but Ben catches me standing at the bottom of the stairs.

"Who's here?" I mouth to him. I'm only wearing a tank top and yoga pants.

"It's all right," he mouths back, then tilts his head to encourage me to come the rest of the way into the dining room.

I come around the corner and stop short.

Stan is sitting at the table next to my father. He stops talking and stands up when he sees me.

He clears his throat. "Charlotte."

It shouldn't, but this feels terribly awkward. He's not Thomas's father, and I'm not Thomas's girlfriend.

Somehow, it feels just the same.

"I'm so sorry this happened to you," he says, and I can tell that he is. He looks so remorseful, you'd think he had something to do with it.

"I'm okay," I say softly.

"I never thought the boy had it in him."

I wet my lips and glance at my father. "I didn't either."

My mother comes to the doorway, a casserole dish balanced between oven mitts. "There you are," she says. "Would you mind getting the side dishes?"

I go for the green beans and the mashed potatoes, bringing them out to set on trivets at the table.

"Your ankle isn't giving you much trouble then?" says Stan when I make a trip back for the water pitcher.

I make sure to fill my grandmother's glass first, because I'll hear about it later if I don't. "It's okay if I take it easy."

"Are you absolutely sure he didn't have anything to do with that?" Stan's eyes narrow. "There's no sense in protecting him now."

"No. He didn't have anything to do with it. I was stupid."

No one at the table disagrees with me. Well, then.

I sigh and sink into my seat at the table.

"We've been worried he might make another attempt," my father says.

"He didn't give me any indication of that this morning," said Stan. Then he looks somewhat abashed. "On second thought, maybe I'm not the best judge of character. I think I gave him a lot more passes than I should have, what with him being her son and all."

"You saw him?" I say.

Ben's eyes lock on mine with laser-intense focus. I ignore him.

"Yes," Stan says. "He came for his things. Showed up with a guy named JB Augury. Said he was crashing with him."

JB Augury. The name means nothing to me. I frown. "Who is he?"

"I don't know." Stan shovels mashed potatoes onto his plate. "I was kind of hoping Tom might have mentioned him to you."

"No. Never."

"I snooped on Tom's Facebook page, but he doesn't have any friends by that name."

I know for a fact that Thomas didn't have any friends in town at all, so I can understand why Stan would sound concerned. Despite what happened, I'm concerned, too. As terrifying as the assault was, I still can't shake the feeling that I'm missing something. That we're *all* missing something. "Thomas said he was staying with this JB guy?"

"What difference does it make to you?" says Ben.

There's no gentleness in his voice. Just metal barbs.

I look back at my plate. "I'm just curious."

"I didn't get a good feeling about the whole thing," Stan says. "I would have felt better if he hadn't made bail."

"So would we," my father says.

"Was this JB guy the one to post bail?" I ask.

"I don't know," says Stan. "It was through a bondsman."

I don't know what to say to that. Could this be someone Thomas knew from Baltimore? I fall silent for a while, half-listening as the table talk shifts to more innocuous subjects.

We have an audience.

Was Thomas alone that night? Or did he have someone with him? I turn that theory over in my head and examine it from multiple angles.

"How did he get in?" I ask.

The table falls silent, and everyone looks at me. They were in the middle of a conversation about baseball.

Ben looks like he wants to kick me under the table. "Let it go, Charlotte."

"What, because I'm a girl I can't try to figure it out, too?"

"There's nothing to figure out," Ben snaps.

"Charlotte," my grandmother chides. "We have company."

Like I'm the one snapping at people. "I'm just saying . . . how did he get in? The door's not broken."

My dad's expression is a cross between exasperated and concerned. "He didn't break the door." He pauses. "We don't know how he got in."

Something else occurs to me. "How did he know where I live?"

Mom gives me a look. "What's with the questions?"

Ben throws his fork down so hard that it rattles against his plate. "I don't know what he did to her, but she's still defending him," he says hotly. "Let it go, Charlotte."

"I'm not a child!" I snap at him. "I wish you'd stop worrying about me and start looking at this analytically. You're supposed to be a cop, not me."

My mother points at the stairs. "Go," she says. Her eyes are hard, and she's using her I'm-your-mother-don't-screw-with-me voice. "Upstairs. Now."

Ben and I both shut up and look at her.

"Which one of us?" Ben says. He might be grown up and live on his own, but he still knows the voice well.

"Charlotte," she says. "Go upstairs."

"Fine." I throw my napkin at the table and storm toward the stairs.

I wish this meant I'd get a free pass from clearing the table, but I'd bet good money I'll be allowed back down in time for that.

"Take your plate with you!" Mom yells.

Ah, yes. Always protecting the blessed blood sugar. I don't want to push her more than I already have, so I return, grab my plate, and head back for the stairs.

Ben glares at me the whole time.

I know they love me. I know they're looking out for me. But it's like their worry won't let them look past the facts. The details. There's more at work here than just a crazy guy breaking into a girl's house to rape her. They have to see that.

A tiny, niggling voice in the back of my head warns me that I'm still romanticizing him.

I tell that voice to stick it.

JB Augury. I wish I knew the name. It means nothing. I find it hard to believe that Thomas would find a guy to open up his home to him so quickly. Everyone around here hates him or is afraid of him.

I replay our trip to Crisfield. He'd been sketching in the car. He drew a picture of his brother. We walked through the neighborhood and met his brother's neighbor. We stumbled over names.

Jonathan Bellweather.

JB.

I almost fall off the bed. Did he find his brother? When? Only a few hours passed between the time I dropped him off at Stan's house and the time Thomas attacked me in my bedroom. Had he found his brother in those hours and decided to attack me? That seems like a pretty narrow window, to meet someone and commit a crime together.

My parents keep the desktop computer downstairs, next to the kitchen. Originally, it was to keep an eye on the kids and what they were doing online, but now it's just there because that's where we've gotten used to it. There's no way I can stroll down there and start researching.

Could I text Nicole? I look at the clock. She'll be eating dinner, and her mom would have a stroke if she started texting at the table—if Nicole has her phone with her at all. I've got to wait. I slide my phone back into my pocket.

Hmm.

Danny. He has a computer. And he's at work.

I sneak down the hallway to his room and ease around the creaky spot in the floor. I tiptoe across Danny's floor and ease myself onto his bed. His laptop is *right there*. My heart bounces around in my chest, but I keep my movement stealthy.

I fire up Google. First, I search for "Jonathan Bellweather." I get a ton of hits—it's not that unusual a name. I narrow it to "Jonathan Bellweather, Crisfield, Maryland." Now I get a lot of hits about high school football. Google offers images, so I click on the link. They're all school football game shots from six or seven years ago, interspersed with a dozen random people, half of which are women. None of this is helpful.

I try a search for "JB Augury."

The first link is for American Bail Bonds in Crisfield.

I frown. We were parked in front of a bail bonds place when the Asian guy dragged me out of the car. Coincidence? I click on the link.

My cell phone buzzes. I'm so on edge that I almost drop the laptop.

Nicole.

NK: You will not believe who I saw today.

CR: I give up.

NK: Thomas!

I choke on air. My fingers won't type fast enough.

CR: You did?

NK: Yes! I tried to punch him in the balls for your benefit, but then he started apologizing. He feels terrible about what happened. He seemed very upset. He wants to talk to you.

I stare at her message. I almost can't believe this is happening.

CR: Was he with somebody?

NK: Yes. I didn't recognize him. He gave me a number where you could reach Thomas.

I don't want the number. I don't want it. I don't. I'm full of crap.

CR: Give it to me.

She does. I save it in my phone and look back at the computer.

It's an "About Us" page. No pictures, unfortunately, but each person has a bio. I skip past Clarence Brown and Martin Creighton, and stop on JB Augury.

JB Augury is a licensed Bail Enforcement Agent. He has been with Crisfield Bail Bonds for two years. JB spent several years serving our country with the U.S. Army, until an old knee injury earned him a trip home. JB specializes in apprehending citizens who do not fulfill their contractual obligation to appear in court.

I remember what the neighbor said about a knee injury. It's him. It has to be him.

How did Thomas find him?

Then I scroll a little further. There are three images at the bottom of the screen. One is a large black man—the guy we saw on the street. One is a middle-aged white guy with a comb-over.

And the third, the youngest guy of the three, makes me give a little yip of surprise. My subconscious fires up.

Shh. This will all be over soon.

It's him. The guy from my dream.

Not Alex. The other one.

The one no one knew was there.

CHAPTER TWENTY-EIGHT

THOMAS

I fall asleep on my sketchbook.

It's one of the few things I was able to get from Stan. My sketchbook, my pencils, and my clothes. He didn't even pack up my toothbrush.

He really wasn't kidding about forgetting I'm not a puppy.

I wake up to JB leaning over me. He's close, almost close enough to share breath, and I jerk back in surprise.

He glances at me. "You're really talented. I had no idea."

Then I follow his original gaze. He wasn't leaning down over *me*, he's leaning over my sketchbook.

I shift up on one elbow and look down at my drawing. Warmth floods my cheeks. It's the sketch I started in the car with Charlotte. Of him. I hadn't intended to keep working on it, but last night I flipped to the page, and I couldn't help but fix the angle of his shoulder. That turned into more shading around the door. The addition of a bed, only the corner visible.

It had been like regaining the use of a broken limb.

Now, with JB staring down at the sketch of himself, I want to slam the cover closed—but that would be more obvious than the heat on my face.

Who the hell am I kidding? He knows exactly what I'm feeling.

"Did you do this last night?" he says.

"No." I shake my head. "Well, not all of it. I started it in the car with Charlotte."

"So this is where you funnel your ability." His eyes flick up to find mine. "No wonder you're not the hot mess I was expecting."

Before I can ask what that means, he reaches out. "May I?"

I shift so I'm sitting upright, leaving him room to sit on the side of the bed. He drops to sit beside me, then slowly flips through the book.

"Some of those are old," I say, by way of explanation. Mom used to tell me she loved them all, but I can see the difference between my early drawings and what I can put on paper now. My lines are cleaner, my dimensions and proportions more accurate. Sometimes I want to rip my early sketches out of the book because I find them so appalling.

I leave them because I like some record of how far I've come.

"Do you draw these from sight?" he asks. "Or from what you see in your head?"

I feel heat on my cheeks. "Both. But mostly from my head."

"Dad is an artist, too."

"He is?" I'm intrigued in spite of myself. After what JB told me about the man, I'm not sure I want to find anything in common between us.

But JB nods. "Not like you, though. Holy crap, kid, these are amazing."

"Thank you."

He looks up at me. "Do you ever feel like you have to get the image out of your head and onto the paper? Like you can't contain it all?"

My eyes widen. "Yes. Exactly that."

He looks back at the sketchbook again. "That's what he used to tell me. I never knew if what he would draw was something he'd done, or something he wanted to do."

Nothing about that sentence sounds positive. I think about

how Charlotte kept telling me to draw my mother's murder, and I wonder if I would have found a clue there.

I wonder, again, if I would have drawn my own hands committing the crime.

I hesitate.

JB glances at me. "It bothers you, me looking at these."

"No."

"Come on."

I frown. "It doesn't bother me, exactly." I think about that for a moment. "I don't mind you looking. But some of them are embarrassing."

"None of these are embarrassing." He turns the page and stops on a drawing of Mom. She's in the kitchen, mid-sashay as she makes dinner, dancing around the kitchen with the radio on. I remember being proud of it when I drew it—I captured motion in the sway of her skirt and the lift of one foot. She looks young and happy and full of life.

"You loved her so much," JB says. His voice is rough. Uncertain.

"I did," I agree. I bite the inside of my cheek. I did love her. I still love her.

Which is why my brain still won't accept that I've killed her. I don't care what proof he shows me.

I can believe the empath stuff.

It's the murder I'm having a hard time with.

He slams the sketchbook closed, and I jump. His eyes flick up. "I'm sorry." He pulls his phone out of his pocket. "Your girlfriend called while I was in the shower. Didn't leave a message, but she sent this text."

I look at his phone.

CR: I'm trying to reach Thomas Bellweather. Is this the right number?

I respond without thinking about it.

JBA: Hi. It's me.

She doesn't respond. I wait a full minute.
Nothing.
I add another line.

JBA: Please. Charlotte. Please. Talk to me.

Nothing.

JBA: I would never hurt you.

Nothing.

JBA: You have to know that. I would never hurt you.

Nothing.
Then his phone buzzes. She's calling.
I'm so excited that I almost fling the phone at my brother.
"Chill out and answer it," he says.
I slide my finger over the screen. "Hello? Hello." I sound deranged.
Her voice is a whisper. "I have to be careful. I don't want my mother to hear me."
"I understand." I pause. "Are you okay?"
"No. Confused."
I let a moment pass. "Okay."
"You found your brother?"
My eyes flick up to JB. "How did you know that?"
She laughs a little, but it's a bitter sound. "No one thinks Charlotte can figure things out on her own."
"I don't think that. You know I don't think that."
"I've had an armed guard since Saturday night."
I imagine her brothers standing outside her room, alternating shifts. "Seriously?"
"Yes. Seriously." Her voice gets softer, if that's possible. "So you found him, and you're living with him?"
She sounds disapproving. "I had nowhere else to go."
"But you don't know him."
"I don't know *anyone*, Charlotte! Would you rather I sleep in the street?"

She's quiet for a moment. For a long moment. "Did you break into my house and try to strangle me?"

I put my hand over my eyes and let out a breath. "I don't know. I don't remember doing it. I swear to you. I don't remember it." I'm not making any sense. "Something has happened to me, Charlotte."

"Something has happened to me, too."

My hand falls to my lap. "Are you all right?"

"I think so." She pauses. "I need to see you."

My heart thumps hard. "Yes. Name the place."

"I need to see you alone. Your brother can't come."

I frown. "Okay."

"If he wants to come, I don't want to be there. Do you understand?"

JB is standing right in front of me. He can obviously hear her. He looks just as puzzled as I am, and he gives a little shrug.

"Sure," I say. "I can come alone."

"Promise me," she said. "Promise me you'll come alone."

JB pulls his keys out of his pocket and holds them out. "You can take the car," he says.

Charlotte's gasp is a whisper of breath in my ear. "Is that him? Your brother?"

"Yeah. This is his phone. He said I could take his car. Where do you want to meet?"

"By the creek."

My eyebrows go way up. "The creek? I might need you to be more specific."

"The creek. Behind the cemetery. Where we met. Sort of." She pauses, then sounds sheepish. "I think my parents will let me out of the house if I tell them I'm volunteering at the church. And the creek can't be seen from any of the buildings."

"Okay." I hesitate. "You're being a little weird, Charlotte. Are you all right?"

"This whole situation is weird." Some rustling, like she's moving around on her bed. Suddenly, her voice is very muffled. "Can you meet me at noon?"

I raise my eyebrows at JB. He shrugs assent.

"Sure," I say.

CHAPTER TWENTY-NINE
CHARLOTTE

In my dream, I was mentally throttling Lilly, telling her she was an idiot for meeting a guy without telling anyone about it. How could she be so stupid?

Now I'm being just as dumb.

Well, that's not entirely true. I told Nicole. She's the only one I *could* tell.

And I have a plan. I'm prepared. I know what I'm doing. Sort of.

When I get to the church, I park in the side lot, under a tree, where my car won't be easily noticed. The place is mostly deserted, which isn't too uncommon for a Monday afternoon. I told Mom I'd be helping to set up for the newly organized mother's group this afternoon, and I'd be helping to take care of the little ones while the moms drink coffee and eat cookies or whatever they do.

I have no idea, because I made the whole thing up.

My pulse is racing, and I can't get it to slow down.

I've never put much stock in dreams. They're like reading a story with no plot.

I *do* agree with Matt, though. These dreams may just be my subconscious trying to tell me something.

But if that's true, it means Thomas's brother was in my room that night.

What does that all mean? Has Thomas been working with

his brother all along? Am I a stupid fool for sitting here right now?

Or is Thomas somehow being manipulated by his brother? How would that work if they've just met?

I've been trying to run it all through my head, and none of it makes any sense. If he knew he had a brother, why would he go through the whole charade of finding the letters? It was *my* idea to even go through her things—he couldn't have set that up on the fly, right?

Wait. It was my idea, wasn't it?

This is making me crazy.

I need to talk to him. I can't tell my parents or my brothers any of this. Every word I mention about Thomas gets sidelined as some type of infatuation.

I am so sick of being *handled*. Of being treated like someone who can't think for herself.

I fish out my phone and send a text to Nicole.

CR: I'm here. Text me every 15 minutes. If I don't respond, I want you to call 911.

NK: Seriously?

CR: Yes. Seriously. Set your phone timer.

NK: Maybe this isn't a good idea. I can come meet you.

CR: No. I need someone to be able to call for the cavalry if this goes south.

NK: Then maybe I should text you every five minutes.

I think about that for a moment, and another text comes in.

NK: It would take less than 15 minutes for him to strangle you.

CR: Thanks for the positive thinking.

NK: You're the one keeping me on standby to call 911.

CR: Good point. 5 minutes.

NK: On it.

I keep my phone in my hand and climb out of the car.

I head toward the cemetery. The humidity hangs thick as soup, and I can feel my curls frizzing almost immediately. I feel very exposed walking across the open land. Today I'm more sensibly dressed for this kind of adventure. No dress and heeled sandals like the day of the funeral. Short shorts— to irritate Grandma—and a tank top.

And tennis shoes. In case I have to run.

If I can run. My ankle gives small twinges when I walk, but nothing painful.

Positive thinking.

We haven't had rain since Thomas and I were last out here, so the grass is dry and crunchy. Heavy clouds loom overhead, warning of bad weather to come. Wind rustles through the trees, and I wonder if this is all some kind of sign that we're coming full circle.

I try not to think about the fact that I almost died the last time I was here.

My phone vibrates.

NK: First check in.

CR: All good. He's not here yet.

I keep my back to the water, because that's the only direction he *won't* be coming from. I have to keep reminding myself that I'm not a lamb waiting for slaughter. I'm prepared to talk to him, and I'm prepared to defend myself.

By the time he shows up, I'm ready for him to come charging through the trees.

Instead, he's walking, pretty sedately. For some reason, I expected him to look cocky. Arrogant, like he's just pulled one over on the whole town, and I'm the moron who keeps showing up for more.

He doesn't. He looks tired and drawn and anxious. He stops once he sees me.

Something falls in his face, and he looks at the ground before looking back at me. "You're afraid of me," he says.

"Not afraid," I say, but it's a lie. My mouth is dry, and my hands are itching for a weapon.

"You are." He swallows. "Charlotte, I'm so sorry. If you don't believe anything else about me, please know that. I don't want to hurt you. I never wanted to hurt you."

My eyes scan the area around him. "You came alone?"

"Yes. Of course."

"Where's your brother?"

He frowns at me like I'm nuts. "I don't know. He said he was going to grab a coffee and he'd be back in the parking lot in twenty minutes."

"Okay." My heart is still pounding, and I wish it would dial down the panic. "Okay."

He glances around, taking in the landscape, and I realize he's looking for my brothers. We're both totally on edge, neither fully trusting the other.

He clears his throat. "Did you want to talk to me?"

"Yes." But that's all I can say.

He cocks an eyebrow at me. "Can I come closer, or do you want to yell everything back and forth?"

It takes me two tries to speak. I'm about to stake my life on a theory about a dream. "You can come closer."

He crosses the ground in a few strides, and it's all I can do to remain still. I feel like a gazelle on the Savannah, forcing herself to remain in one place while the lion descends.

My phone buzzes in my hand, and I jump and give a little *yip*.

It's so sudden that Thomas jumps, too.

I hold up my phone. "Nicole," I say by way of explanation. I don't even read her message, I just reply with *All OK*. I think about telling him that I'll be texting her every few minutes, but I don't want him to know the plan, just in case he tries to keep it up after killing me.

Ugh. I need to stop it.

"I was only kind of kidding," Thomas says softly. "I can wait across the way. I don't want to make you uncomfortable."

I look into his eyes, and the emotion there is enough to halt my breath. He's genuine.

"Do you remember breaking into my house?" I ask him.

There's a little flinching around his eyes. "No."

"Do you remember climbing on top of me? Making out?"

He shakes his head.

"I saw you."

Thomas studies me. "I don't know how to explain that."

"I don't think you were alone."

His eyes widen. "What?"

I force my voice to remain even. "I don't think you were alone. That night. I think your brother was there."

"Wait—what? You know my brother?"

"No." I shake my head quickly. "I haven't met him, but I looked him up online. I saw his picture. And I've seen him before. I've been dreaming about him since the night you . . ." I stop and swallow. "Since the night you broke in."

He takes a deep breath and blows it out. A line has appeared on his forehead. "I didn't meet him until *after* I was arrested. He bailed me out."

"Why?"

That line on his forehead deepens. "What?"

"*Why*?" I demand. "He doesn't know you. Why did he bail you out? Why did he know you were there?"

"I—I don't know, Charlotte. He said he was there to help me, which is more than I can say for pretty much anyone else in my life right now."

I put my hands up in surrender. "I'm just asking you to think about this. Why did he know you were there?"

"You want me to think about why my brother showed up to get me out of jail because you had a *dream*?" His tone implies that the only thing he's thinking about is checking me into an insane asylum.

"Yes," I say simply. "I think it's my subconscious trying to tell me something."

Thomas gives a tight sigh. "God, Charlotte, I don't know

what I expected from this meeting, but this isn't it. JB hasn't done anything illegal since I've met him. I don't even remember breaking into your house, so how the hell would I remember whether he was there?"

I want to hit him. "I know I sound crazy. I just need you to think about it! I don't know if he's drugging you or what, but I think he was there, and I think he made you do it somehow."

Thomas goes still. "What did you just say?"

"I think he made you do it. Could he have slipped you something?" I put a finger to my lips, thinking of the night he attacked me. "What about the night I dropped you off? Did you eat anything at home? Could he have drugged—?"

"He didn't drug me," Thomas says. His voice is hollow.

I study him. His expression is on the edge of panicked.

"There's something," I say. "What are you thinking about?"

"I don't know." He shakes his head, then presses his hands to his eyes. "I don't know."

"Talk to me." He's scaring me and not in the way I'd worried about when I got here.

"I can't, Charlotte. I barely understand it myself, and now—" He breaks off and looks at me. "I need to go. I don't understand any of this anymore."

"Stop. Wait. Please."

"No. I can't." He starts walking. "I'm not supposed to be near you. I shouldn't have come."

"Thomas—"

My phone buzzes. Damn it. I stop to respond to Nicole. *Still fine.*

Thomas is striding across the open ground, heading back toward the church. I jog to catch up with him before he makes it to the trees.

"Please," he says. "Please leave me alone."

"Just stop. Tell me where you're going. Tell me what's going on."

Thomas whirls on me and grabs my shoulders. It startles a gasp out of me, but that's all he does. "You think my brother was in your bedroom that night."

"Yes," I whisper. "I do."

"But you didn't see him."

I shake my head. "I'm not sure. I don't understand it. I keep *dreaming* about him. And then when I saw his picture . . ." I let my voice trail off.

"You saw his picture?"

I nod. "I looked him up when I heard who bailed you out. I couldn't figure anything out. Why you'd hurt me. It didn't make sense." I pause. "Once the initial panic wore off, I realized that it seemed completely out of character."

He frowns and his hands go gentle on my shoulders. "Once again, you're the only person who believes the best of me." He snorts. "Most people would be sending me for a psych consult."

"Maybe we can do that next." I hesitate. "Talk to me. Tell me what you know."

He grimaces, then his eyes lock on mine. "He told me we can do things with our minds. That we can force people to do what we want."

I wet my lips. "And you believed him?"

He turns away. "This sounds crazy. I can't do this, Charlotte. It sounds crazy in my own head."

I go after him and catch his arm. "No. Wait. Stop. Talk to me."

He stops and turns and looks down at me. His eyes are so troubled, like the day we met.

"I think you're the one with the power," he whispers.

His voice is intense, and it takes me a moment to find my own. "Me?"

"You." He puts his hands on either side of my face. His palms are warm and secure, and any fear I may have felt earlier has completely melted away. "You can make me do whatever you want." He closes his eyes. "I never meant to hurt you. If he made me do it . . ."

"How?" I whisper, matching his tone.

"I don't know enough about it yet." He shakes his head, and I'm surprised to see his eyes are rimmed with red, like he's a heartbeat away from crying. "He's my brother. He's all I have left. I want to trust him."

I think about my own brothers, their own reactions to Thomas. They've been overbearing and a pain in the butt, but they were just looking out for me. I love them, and I trust them, too. I can understand why Thomas wants to trust his brother.

"He's been good to me," he says. "He hasn't given me any indication he's misleading me."

I hold his gaze. "I'm accusing someone based on a dream. I could be wrong."

He grits his teeth and shakes his head a bit. "It's what you said. About forcing someone to do something. He *can* do that. I just can't wrap my head around *why*. Why bail me out of jail? Why give me a place to crash?" He pauses, and his thumb strokes over my cheek. "Why force me to hurt you?"

"Maybe we're missing something. Something big." I put my hands over his. "How is he doing this?"

"Like this." His hands wrap around my throat.

And then he begins to squeeze.

I've been ready for it since I got here, but I almost miss the attack. He had me fooled. He cuts off my air supply almost instantly. I fight like hell, clawing at his hands, before all of Matt's self-defense training kicks in. I drop my chin and seize his wrists, pulling myself closer.

Then I kick him right in the crotch, as hard as I can.

He yells and lets me go. I bolt.

Thank god for the tennis shoes. I'm tearing through the trees, praying for the open air of the field beside the cemetery. My ankle screams at me, and I ignore it. I'm trying to get my hand into my purse, but I'm more focused on running. It doesn't sound like he's following me. I chance a look over my shoulder.

Then I slam into someone. Hard. My ankle gives and I hit the ground, rolling with the force of our momentum.

I'm fighting before we stop rolling. Matt always gives the chilling warning that I can apologize later if I'm wrong, but I can't apologize if I'm dead. One hand is still stupidly tangled in my purse strap, but the other goes for his eyes.

He's quick and he's strong and he pins me before I can do more damage than that. I'm face down in the tangled brambles, one hand trapped underneath me, in my purse, the other pinned by his hand.

This sucks.

He's not even out of breath. "I don't think we've officially met."

I strain against him, but he's too heavy, too strong. "You're Thomas's brother. You're Jonathan. JB. Whatever."

"Yes. And you're going to be a problem."

"My family knows I'm here," I say. "You won't get away with this."

"I don't need to get away with anything," he says.

I wiggle my fingers in my bag. The zipper scrapes at my wrist, but I ignore the pain.

"What are you going for?" he says. "A phone? Pepper spray? Go ahead. Won't matter."

My hand goes still. Footsteps crunch through the underbrush nearby, and I hear Thomas's fractured breathing. "You caught her," he says. He sounds uncertain.

"I caught her," says JB.

"Why are you doing this?" I cry. "I didn't do anything to you."

"I need him," JB says. "This has nothing to do with you."

"You need him for what?" I demand. I feel an urgency to keep him talking, because if we're talking, I'm not dying.

"You don't have to be afraid of me," JB says. "I'm not going to harm you."

"Yeah, this seems like it's going to end really well for me." I struggle against him. "Thomas, I don't know what he's doing to you, but you need to snap out of it."

"He's not doing anything to me," Thomas says. "He told me what *you're* doing."

JB leans down and whispers, like we're sharing a secret. "He can't snap out of it. No matter what you say. I'm too strong, and he's too weak."

"Thomas," I cry. "Thomas, listen to me."

JB sighs. "He won't listen to you. You were setting him up again. You were luring him out here so your brothers could shoot him. Guess how easy it was to make him believe *that.*"

Very easy, I can imagine. I don't even need to think about how my brothers have treated him over the last few weeks. "I wasn't! Thomas, listen to me! If my brothers were here, they'd be *shooting your brother right now.*"

"Go ahead," whispers JB. "The more you say, the more he'll think it's a well-laid trap."

"Fuck you."

"Aw, the little church mouse has some spit and fire after all? It's a shame I need him to kill you. I would have loved to try some of those desserts you kept bringing him."

I freeze. Was he following us? The whole time? I wish I could reevaluate every moment I've spent with Thomas.

I shift my hand again. One more inch. That's all I need.

I hear the smile in JB's voice. "I hope you do have some pepper spray. Piss him off and it'll be even easier to make him retaliate. Hell, we could probably even claim self-defense. *You* asked *him* to meet you."

Crap. I need to think. "Why?" I say quickly. "Why do you need him to kill me?"

"Because it'll destroy something inside him," says JB.

"Every death he causes will reinforce the belief that he can't do anything to stop it."

"Why? Why are you doing this to him?"

"Because," he says, and for the first time I hear true pain leak into his voice. "I can't keep letting my father do it to me."

Then he rolls off of me, and I'm free. My hand locks on heavy plastic inside my purse. *Finally.*

"Shoot her," JB says. "She's got something in her bag, Thomas. She's going to hurt you. Shoot her."

I roll over, and only have a heartbeat of time. Thomas is pointing a gun at me. His eyes are lucid, just like Alex's from the dream. He's cognizant of what he's doing—he just believes he's doing the right thing.

I don't know how JB is doing this, but I know he's pulling the strings somehow.

Thomas doesn't want to shoot me. Uncertainty flares in his eyes, and the gun wavers.

"Shoot her, Tommy." Beside me, JB's voice is even. Steady.

Thomas cocks the hammer.

I yank my hand out of my bag, drawing my own gun.

I'm too late. Thomas pulls the trigger.

CHAPTER THIRTY

THOMAS

JB goes down.

I kind of expected something more spectacular, for him to go flying back and land in the dirt. He's wearing his vest, so I know I didn't kill him. It must absorb some of the shock, but not all of it, because he kind of crumples.

His arms are wrapped around his midsection and he's making little choking sounds. I can feel his pain like a pulsing, living thing in the air, raining down on me.

Good.

I almost couldn't do it. Even now, it's like looking at the past fifteen minutes from the other side of a waterfall. I can barely remember why we came here. The force of his will is fighting mine already, trying to regain control of this encounter.

I have to think of Mom. I know what he did now.

I know what I did.

Charlotte is gasping, one leg cocked, her gun still pointed at me.

I put my hands up, real quick. "Don't shoot. Please, Charlotte. Don't shoot me."

Her gun is steady, and she sidesteps away from JB with a limp. "Put your gun down."

"I won't hurt you. I swear I won't hurt you. I had to make him believe I was still working with him. I need to make you understand. What you said—about someone controlling me—I put it together—"

"I told you to put the gun down!"

"I will. Okay? I will." I very slowly lower my hand with the weapon, but I don't want to give it up completely. I don't know how quickly my brother will recover. Once he can start talking, we might be screwed. I pull out my waistband and start to slide the gun there.

"Don't put it down your pants!" she yells at me. "Are you stupid?"

"Yes," gasps JB. "He's stupid. Shoot him, Charlotte. He just tried to kill you." Another gasping breath. "You're lucky I came back early. I caught him trying to strangle you."

"Shut up," I tell him.

"Think of how violated you felt," JB says to her. "When he broke into your room. In front of those little girls."

"Stop it." I look at Charlotte. "I never meant to hurt you. You know I never meant to hurt you."

Charlotte's gun hand is shaking.

JB takes a moment to catch his breath. "Didn't you think, just for a moment, that he might have finished with you and moved on to them?"

"Shut up!" I yell at him. I point the gun at him. "Just shut up!"

"You won't shoot me," he says. He's got his hands underneath him now, but he winces when he looks at me. "You're my little brother. I'm all you have left."

The strength in his words is almost overpowering. I almost lay down the gun. It took every ounce of strength in me to shoot him the first time. I don't know if I'm going to be able to do it again.

I banish the self-doubt from my mind. If he suspects it, he's going to exploit it.

Hell, he's probably exploiting it now.

"Roger that," says JB.

"Fuck you."

"What is this?" whispers Charlotte. "How is he doing this?"

"Your emotions," I say. "He can manipulate your emotions." I pause. "He forced me to attack you."

"You liked it," says JB. "You *loved* it."

I want to kick him in the face. "Shut the fuck up."

"She's not even the first one, Tommy."

I freeze. The horror of that implication is almost enough to make me lose my focus.

He laughs, but it's a bit choking. "Ah, kid, you make it too easy." He looks between me and Charlotte, then gingerly gets to his feet. "Both of you do, really. Neither of you wants to kill me. You might as well put the guns down."

A siren splits the air somewhere close. A few more kick up alongside it. Cops. For the first time, relief swarms through me.

JB raises his eyebrows. "You think the cops will help you? The kid who strangled his mother, then tried to rape and murder his girlfriend? The kid who's standing here with a gun right this second?" He pauses. "You don't think they'll believe me when I say I wrestled you off her and got shot while she was trying to shoot *you*?"

"They'll never believe that," says Charlotte.

"They will," I say resignedly. "They'll believe every word. I've seen him in action."

"I'll tell them the truth," she says.

JB laughs at her. The sirens grow closer. "What, that I mentally compelled Thomas to hurt you? Okay, let me know how that goes over. Maybe you'll be able to convince them I got the Chinese carry-out guy to attack you, too."

"That was you, too?" I demand.

"I wanted to see how you'd handle it."

My hand shakes on the gun. I want to shoot him so badly, but I can't pull the trigger. I'm almost breathless with wanting to harm him.

His eyes flick to me. "Fight it all you want, kid. I've been fighting it all my life, and he still gets me to do what he wants. We're family."

Our father. I wish I'd paid more attention in the car. I remember JB's tension, his anger. I just never realized how deeply it ran. "You've never been my family."

"Oh no?" For the first time, his expression shows true fury. It bleeds into the air around us. "You don't think there's a small part of you that *likes* this? I know you feel it, Tommy. I know you do."

"You don't know anything." His power is pulling triggers in my mind, though. I think of the man in the alley, the addictive feel of his fear.

Sirens squawk closer, and I know our time is limited.

"I do know, Tommy." JB pauses, and I can feel the truth in his words. "I just can't do it anymore. Don't you understand that? He tried to make me kill her. I just couldn't do it. I couldn't kill her."

"But you could make me do it," I bite out.

"It was so easy the first time. I knew I finally had a way out."

"You won't get away with this," Charlotte says. "I'll tell them everything. I'll make them believe me."

"You're sweet." JB takes a step closer to her, and she sucks in a breath and steps back, gun still level at his chest. "Put it away," he says. "You're not a killer."

"I will shoot you," she says. "Back off."

"No you won't." He steps closer. "You're sweet, and kind, and full of all the good things that people like Tommy and I are missing. You're good, Charlotte."

She begins to lower the gun.

"Don't do it," I say.

JB takes another step, and his voice goes soft. He's right in front of her, and she's not making a move to either defend herself or flee. "You wouldn't hurt a fly. I can feel it."

She lowers the gun further.

Then, she lifts her gun hand and swings hard. She clocks

him right in the side of the face. I hear the crack of metal against bone.

He goes down. The gunshot wasn't spectacular, but *this* is.

"Feel that," she says.

"Holy shit!" I say.

She swings her gun around to point it at me, but her breathing is rapid and panicked now. "Are you on my side or not, Thomas?"

"On your side," I say. My brother is down in the grass, so I set my weapon on the ground. "Always on your side."

With that, she starts crying, and she throws herself into my arms.

And that's exactly how the cops find us.

CHAPTER THIRTY-ONE
CHARLOTTE

Three weeks later

I'm sitting on the front porch with Nicole. She's sipping iced tea. We're speaking very quietly because I don't want my mother to hear us.

I've told Nicole everything. The real truth, not the truth Thomas and I manufactured for the cops.

"So," she whispers. "That JB guy is locked up?"

"For now. I actually thought he was going to get the charges dropped, but Stan found his letters, and some of them were pretty creepy. The DA says that points to motive for wanting to kill his mother."

"And he was the guy who tried to strangle you?"

I push off against the porch swing. I had worried it would be difficult to convince the police of that one, but we told them that Thomas had *followed* JB to my house, and my skin got under his fingernails when he was trying to wrestle his brother off me. He never said anything about it because his brother was trying to blackmail him for his mother's murder.

Thomas had worried JB would be able to convince the authorities of his innocence, but listening to Thomas explain things, I almost believed him myself.

"More or less," I say.

"What about you and Tom?"

"I don't know."

"You don't *know*?" she squeals. "How can you not *know*?"

I watch the ice swirl in my glass. "It's complicated." I hesitate. "We need some time. He needs to figure out who he is."

"Is that your idea or his?"

I frown. "His." And it was. When the dust settled and I tried to talk to him, he said he needed time. I asked if that really meant we were over, and he smiled and brushed a kiss against my cheek and said, "No way. I can never go back to McDonald's food *now*."

But I haven't heard from him since then.

"So what are you going to do now?" Nicole says.

"I'm going to spend time with my family. Thomas says that JB hated cops because it's hard to break through their natural suspicion. I'm not a police officer, but I know how they think. It's in my blood. I wonder if my own suspicion helped keep me safe, too."

"You're going to spend time with family?" she squeaks. "When the hottest guy to set foot in this town is still mooning over you somewhere?"

"Yep," I say. "I'm right here. He knows where to find me."

CHAPTER THIRTY-TWO
THOMAS

Stan and I are sitting across the dinner table. We're not talking, but Stan is never much of a talker.

He let me move back in after JB was arrested.

He also apologized for abandoning me at the police station after what happened with Charlotte. He felt bad about that— I could feel the shame pouring off him. He stood in front of me and offered his hand, then said, "Marie wouldn't be proud of me, Tom. I'm sorry for the way I treated you. You'll always have a place to stay with me."

I shook his hand and moved back in.

Like always, I had nowhere else to go.

But, no. There's no animosity there. Stan is good. He's kind. He's not afraid of me. And JB is locked up, so I'm safe.

I could do worse.

Tonight, though, Stan is fidgety. He runs a hand over his head.

"What's up?" I say.

"I'm having a crisis of conscience," he says.

I frown. I can sense he's feeling conflicted, but I don't have a clue about why. "I'm not sure what that means."

"It means I got a check from the life insurance company." He pauses and looks at me. "From your mom. You know. Surviving spouse."

I stare at him, not sure where this is going. "Okay."

"I don't want the money, Tom. I think it should go to you."

He's such a good, honest man. Sometimes I wonder how I could have ever suspected him. "I don't want to take your money, Stan."

"It's not my money."

"It's not mine, either. It was hers." I think about Mom. We never talked much about money, but I know she loved Stan.

He hesitates. "Well, not really. I mean, that's not how life insurance works. It was the insurance company's money."

I look at my food. It doesn't seem right to take the money from him. He supported me when I had nothing. He's supporting me now.

But money could help me get back on my feet.

Now I understand his crisis of conscience.

I take a bite of food and look at him sideways. "We could split it," I offer.

"Done," he says. He puts out a hand. We shake on it.

With that settled, the unease is gone from the room. I drop back into my chair.

"How much is it, anyway?" I say.

He shrugs like it's nothing. "Fifty thousand dollars."

I choke and need a gulp of water to get my food down.

Stan can still surprise me.

I lie in bed and think of Charlotte. She's the strongest girl I know. I wish I had a video of the way she knocked my brother on his ass.

I want to call her, so badly, but I'm not ready.

I'm scared of what I can do. I'm scared of what I *did*. I know JB lied to me about why I hurt my mother and Charlotte, but he didn't lie about all of it.

I must drift to sleep, because I open my eyes, and it's just after two o'clock in the morning. I lie in the quiet darkness for a long while before I hear the tapping.

It's my window.

I jerk out of bed. A letter is taped to my windowpane. I

stare out into the yard, which is lit by a security lamp, but there's no one there.

My heart flutters and I think of Charlotte. I pull the letter inside.

It's not from Charlotte.

If you thought a jail cell would hold me, you were sadly mistaken.
Truce?

CHAPTER THIRTY-THREE

CHARLOTTE

I'm on a grocery store mission again, this time for coconut flour. Of course it's on the top shelf, pushed back, and I can't reach. I stretch as tall as I can, until I'm practically climbing the shelves, but my fingertips barely graze the packaging.

"As much as I appreciate the view, I feel like I should offer to help you."

I yip and spin, yanking my shirt down to cover my stomach. Thomas stands behind me, his dark eyes amused. He must not feel the need to hide anymore, because his ball cap is missing.

We haven't seen each other in over a month, and I thought my feelings for him had finally cooled. I was sure I'd eventually see him around town, and I'd be able to give him a disinterested glance while saying, "Don't I know you from somewhere?"

Instead, I throw my arms around his neck. "I've missed you so much."

I reconsider my actions a heartbeat later, worried he's going to jerk away in surprise or shove me away. Just because *my* feelings haven't cooled doesn't mean his haven't.

But he hugs me back. "I've missed you, too," he says quietly.

I revel in it for a moment, but then I draw back and smack him on the shoulder. "Then why haven't you called?"

He inhales, but then shakes his head. "I should have. It's been a long few weeks." He hesitates. "It took me a while to figure out how to deal with everything."

"And how's that going?"

A grimace. "It's . . . going."

We stand there and study each other for a moment, and I realize that him showing up at the grocery store isn't the same as him calling. Maybe he didn't intend to run into me at all.

Throwing my arms around him was probably completely inappropriate. I might not have his gift of reading emotion, but I'm not an idiot.

I take a step back and glance up at the shelf. "I was just getting coconut flour. Mom and I were in the middle of muffins. I should get back."

He steps closer to me, which makes my breath catch. But then he reaches over my head and grabs one of the packages that had eluded my grasp.

He holds it out. "Just one?"

I nod, dumbly, and take it. "Thanks."

"Sure." He doesn't move.

Eventually, one of us has to. I turn away from him, hoping he'll call me back.

Hoping. Hoping. Hoping.

He doesn't.

I'm about to put the flour on the conveyer belt at the register when he appears by my side again. "Charlotte."

I look up at him expectantly.

"Do you know what panko bread crumbs are?" he says. "That's what Stan sent me to get, but they're not with the bread, so . . ."

I sigh. "Sure. Come on."

We find them in silence, and then he follows me back to the register.

I don't know what to make of this whole interaction. My

thoughts are scattered across a spectrum from attraction to irritation.

We both pay, and then we're out in the sunlight.

He points left. "I'm over there."

I'm to the right. Of course.

"So," I say.

"I'll see you around," he says.

So that's that. I start walking.

He follows me.

Halfway across the parking lot, I stop and face him by the shopping cart corral. "Stop. I can't do this. I'm sure it's difficult, and I realize I'm being an insensitive bitch, but I can't read minds, so I don't know—"

He kisses me.

It's a good kiss. Movie-worthy. When his hand comes around my back, I actually drop the bag of flour.

When he draws back, I breathe up at him. "You really did miss me."

He smiles. "Oh, yes." His eyes spark with wicked amusement. "Want me to show you again?"

I might not survive it. "Then why—?"

"Because I'm afraid of what I can do." He pauses, losing the smile. "And JB isn't in custody anymore. I'm afraid of what he can do, even more."

"I'm not afraid of you." I pause, putting steel in my voice. "Or him."

"That makes one of us." His brows knit together. "You're not worried about him coming after you?"

"Not at all. I think he's a coward. Why do you think he made you do his dirty work?"

The way Thomas's face shifts tells me he's never considered this. I put a hand against his cheek. "Are you worried he'll come after *you*?"

He looks away. "A little. He asked for a truce, and he hasn't bothered me, but I don't trust him."

"He asked for a truce?"

Thomas nods and pulls a folded note out of his pocket. I quickly scan the two lines. "When did he leave this?"

"Two weeks ago."

I knew JB had been released because my brothers were keeping tabs on him, but I didn't realize he'd reached out to Thomas. "Have you heard from him since then?"

Thomas shakes his head.

"If you do, we'll deal with him then."

Thomas smiles. "I know you won't have any trouble."

I make a muscle and blow on my biceps. "You can just hide behind me."

He laughs. "Maybe you can show me some of your moves."

"Name the place and time, and I'm there."

He loses the smile. "Tomorrow night?"

My heart stutters, but somehow I manage to speak clearly. "What's in it for me?"

"Maybe I can show you some of *my* moves." Then he leans in to kiss me again.

I don't know if it's his ability or my own intuition, but this time his kiss fills me with warmth, lighting me from inside, and leaving me with no doubt about how he feels.